T0065295

While investigating that phenomenon in the sky Art is tipped off about the harrowing situation and conditions in which many undocumented girls and women from Sub-Saharan Africa find themselves after giving up the known for the unknown, in their quest for a supposed better life overseas; where the streets are believed to be paved with gold; and the ploys employed by dangerous well-organised criminal gangs to effect People Smuggling and Human Trafficking. He is also informed about the intimidation tactics; psychological and physical; which the gangs employ. Following that tip-off Art embarks upon a mission: to unravel the complex network of the gangs' numerous illicit activities.

THE
STATUETTE

BRIGITTE EAGLE

authorHOUSE®

AuthorHouse™ UK
1663 Liberty Drive
Bloomington, IN 47403 USA
www.authorhouse.co.uk
Phone: 0800.197.4150

Published by AuthorHouse 08/20/2015

ISBN: 978-1-5049-4200-3 (sc)
ISBN: 978-1-5049-4199-0 (hc)
ISBN: 978-1-5049-4201-0 (e)

Print information available on the last page.

CONTENTS

CHAPTER 1

Friday the thirteenth dawned like any other day in that memorable month of August. The fact that it was Friday the thirteenth had no bearing whatsoever on the events that were about to unfold — at least not in anyone's mind in this country — because in Spain, Tuesday the thirteenth is the date that gives people the gooseflesh; this is the day you should neither set sail nor get hitched.

Anyway, Madrid, like the rest of Spain, was in the grip of an unmerciful heat wave. Soaring temperatures in the high 30s and mid 40s had been reigning over the nation for weeks on end. According to the weather forecast there was no likelihood of things letting up soon.

'Tomorrow, nothing's going to be different as far as temperatures go,' Mr Menudo the weatherman had declared the previous evening in his usual rambling manner. 'I wish I could conjure up rain like witch doctors are claimed to do in parts of Africa,' he added, with a smile that came out like a wince.

Although the latter was meant as a joke, it fell flat on its face because Mr Menudo always managed to make everything that tumbled out of his mouth sound like a sermon. His serious countenance and his general demeanour guaranteed that. His turnout did not help matters much: his appearance usually gave the impression that he had just rolled out of bed. Apart from attracting jokes from viewers about his wardrobe, he was also the butt of unkind jests in talk shows for his inaccurate weather forecasts. Unfortunately, being the constant bearer of bad news about the weather that summer did not do much to improve his reputation.

The weather had become a very popular conversation topic — even among complete strangers — at bus stops, bars and supermarkets; you name it. Debates raged as to whether mankind was getting its just deserts for years and years of abuse inflicted upon the environment. The expressions "global warming" and "global warning" had become omnipresent features in many of those debates. On-screen or off-screen, one thing was clear: everyone was desperate for rain. Even a drizzle would have been most welcome.

Therefore, when the heavens roared at 3 p.m. and the hitherto bright summer sky grew darker than a starless winter night many people looked skywards relieved and thankful, believing that at long last their wishes were about to come true. Then their eyes popped. Mouths agape they gawked at the strange phenomenon in the sky.

Almost immediately though, the sky became as bright as ever. Although what transpired in that brief interval would be reported differently by eyewitnesses later, right then they were all displaying the same symptom: speechlessness.

That strange phenomenon happened so fast that even though it was observed by many, it was never recorded except in people's minds. The vast majority of people could not reach for a camera of any sort. And, inexplicably enough, the handful who managed to react fast enough would later discover, to their utmost consternation and frustration, that all they got for their efforts was just a streak of light.

The fact that the true version of what happened in the sky was never documented graphically made people push their imaginations to the limit when it came to narrating what they claimed to have seen. It is said that an idle mind is the devil's playground or workshop — depending on his mood — and it could not have been truer on that occasion. It was August and most people were on holiday so they had more than enough time on their hands. Consequently, imaginations simply went haywire.

Many people swore they saw a great ball of fire that split into three smaller ones, each letting out a deafening thunderous clap and lightning as it disappeared in a different direction. Some people reported seeing a strange, unearthly form hurling the ball of fire, while others affirmed that it was hurled by a human form. Among all the versions of the phenomenon tendered, those just described were the most moderate so one could imagine the rest. Soon afterwards, what transpired in that short interval was dubbed the "paranormal phenomenon".

In the days following the phenomenon, the constant chatter about the weather was relegated to the background. The incident provided good fodder for all sorts of media, from the serious to the absurd. It was discussed everywhere: reality shows, talk shows, debate programmes and whatnot. Some found it particularly amusing because as a rule in Spain, the news in the summer months is dull. Not much happens in this time of the year, not even on the political scene since politicians are usually in recess. Thus, the story managed to grab people's attention and to entertain a good number of them for a good while.

'Entertaining!' was how some people, particularly those in the world of entertainment, described the ongoing fuss about what really happened in the sky at 3 p.m. on Friday, 13 August 2004. Few people considered the incident as anything but entertaining — not even after three local papers reported that exactly when people were observing the paranormal phenomenon a thunderbolt had struck a target in each of the localities, provoking a serious fire.

'So what, after all thunderbolts do provoke fires, don't they?' the sceptics argued, stoking up the excitement and causing the debate to rage on.

Admittedly, fires were not unusual when thunderbolts struck, especially given the prevailing atmospheric conditions then. What with so many months of no rain. Indeed, at that point in time in Western Europe, Spain was the country suffering the severest drought in recent history. Be that as it may, those tendering that argument were probably unaware of the nature of the fires and the magnitude of the destruction the fires left in their trails or they were simply ignoring both.

Two days later, curious details about the fires were compiled from each locality. They were published and presented in special packs dubbed "Sunday Special" by the local papers. One of the most mind-boggling aspects of the matter was that each fire was completely out by the time the fire-fighters arrived. That did not mean that their arrival took ages. It was just that one minute there was what some eyewitnesses described as a towering inferno and the next minute there was nothing, absolutely nothing but blackness and smoke. The fire-fighters attested to that being true. They affirmed that on arrival they only doused each location with jets of water as a precautionary measure. The head of one of the teams described it as the strangest experience in his long professional life.

Following those newspaper stories in which important facts were revealed, the whole incident became more than a mere source of amusement to some. Subsequently, this group continued poring over the publications and mulling over the mysteries surrounding the fires. The most important revelations were:

One of the fires was in Madrid, in an artist's studio. The studio was razed and the artist's entire body of work and part of his collection perished. Despite the destruction, a bronze sculpture in the studio was unaffected by the fire — it was as clean as a whistle, as though it had been placed there afterwards.

The second fire was at the same artist's mansion, which was about fifty kilometres north of Madrid. A whole wing of the sumptuous mansion was razed to the ground and although the artist was in that very wing at the time the thunderbolt struck and set off the blaze, he did not suffer even a burn. He was found lying sprawled in one of his gardens — he was presumably flung there by the impact of the thunderbolt. According to the publication, in comparison with the destruction that the thunderbolt and the resulting blaze left in their wake, the fact that he only lost his right eye and got the right side of his hair bleached silvery white was tantamount to a miracle. He walked away relatively unscathed.

In a third case, which occurred in a town about eighteen kilometres south of Madrid, the story did not have such a miraculous ending: It ended in a fatality. The victim was an African businessman in his early 30s. He was struck in his flat, which also got razed. It was reported that his body did not suffer any burns.

Since two of the locations involved the same individual, many people began wondering if there was any relationship between him and the deceased victim or if their locations had been chosen at random by the thunderbolt. Trying to connect those dots became the latest excitement. A lot of theories sprang up. All of a sudden, everyone became an expert on the paranormal or thunderbolts or even adverse weather conditions.

To understand why the incident in the sky took on a very new angle for many people after they read those newspaper articles, one must understand that although Spain is a nation which officially professes the Roman

Catholic faith, a great majority of the people are superstitious. Lots of people believe in the occult, the paranormal and stuff like that though only a few openly admit it. People from all walks of life would stealthily creep in and out of psychics' homes. The golden rule is: never get caught! Funnily enough, almost everyone knows of someone who has been to a highly gifted psychic and obtained incredibly accurate readings but of course, no one has ever visited any. Such stories are never first-person experiences — they are usually those of friends or friends' friends. Generally, anything connected with the paranormal sells and any business associated with the unknown, the supernatural and all that is huge business in Spain. As a result, charlatans often have a field day ripping off the gullible.

Such beliefs notwithstanding, people still have faith in the mediating powers of the heavenly dwellers, such as saints and angels, when miracles are needed. People call upon them and light candle after candle to them when in need. Believers also wear small scapulars, medalets, medals or medallions bearing representations of the Virgin Mary or one or more saints around their necks for protection. This could sound a bit odd to non-Spaniards but, the dividing line between religion and superstition is often blurred here.

Considering this background of superstition, the incident in the sky was indeed a big deal to many. To others though, it remained just what they deemed it from the very start: nothing more than a diversion. Consequently, such people gradually went back to their normal lives, to their daily activities and to their main preoccupation: how to cope with the heat. For them, the weather simply sprang back to the foreground.

One person, though he was not Spanish, was absolutely convinced that everything about those fires was unusual. He believed that there was more to the whole episode than met the eye and that the incidents in the three different localities were strongly linked. That person was Art O'Connor-O'Carroll, an Irish freelance journalist in his mid 40s.

Before that Friday's happening for three nights running, Art had been jolted awake at exactly the same time — 3 a.m. — after having the same dream. It always began with the same voice whispering with urgency, 'Look at the sky!'
Each time he did, he noticed that the sky was rough and awfully dark.

'I can't see anything beyond the darkness,' he said.

'Look harder; look beyond the surface. Remember, things aren't always what they appear to be,' he heard.

The sequence was always the same. Art decided to start a dream journal in case the recurrent dream was pointing somewhere. He had just concluded recording it in a diary when the Madrid sky darkened at 3 p.m.

Art had a nose for the paranormal. According to him, some people dabbled into the occult as a mere curiosity but for him it was a conviction. He lived it — he breathed it, dreamt it and practised it. He wore an amulet around his neck, the origin of which he had never revealed as that would make it lose its potent magical powers, or so he believed. He never took it off and he would not let anyone touch it.

Art had come to Spain at age eighteen to study Spanish history and after obtaining that degree he studied journalism. Thereafter, the years rolled by and he never returned home except for visits. He was fondly referred to as *'El Irlandés'* — The Irishman — by his Spanish friends, especially by the senior citizens whose company he cherished because he believed they were a fountain of knowledge as far as oral history went. He spent a good part of his free time with them going over the Spanish Civil War days — his pet subject.

He could be terribly disorganised, careless and lost in thought. For instance, although he lived on the seventh floor of a block of flats, there were numerous occasions when he got off the lift on the wrong floor and tried to insert his key into a neighbour's lock. At first, his neighbours found the routine utterly exasperating and annoying, particularly very late at night. With time, however, they came to realise that he meant no harm, that he was simply in his own world — a very absent-minded one! So when they heard his keys rattling as he tried futilely to insert one of them in their lock they simply called out,

'Go upstairs, *Señor* Art!' or 'Go downstairs, *Señor* Art!'

'I'm sorry!' he would call out in bemusement or amusement, depending on his mood or his state of mind or soberness, as he retraced his steps.

His apparent state of constant haze notwithstanding, as a professional no details, no matter how minute, escaped him. Generally, he left no stone unturned when chasing a story. He was pretty inquisitive by nature too, a quality which made him quite thorough in his investigations, apart from getting him into trouble occasionally. His extremely curious nature made him dabble into all sorts of practices. As he was wont to say, 'How can you judge what you don't know?' He believed that practically every sensation was best described through experience — 'even death,' he often added with a wink and a broad smile. He was a very affable type and could spend ages talking about nothing and yet his listeners would believe that he was talking about something important. He saw himself as a free spirit who lived life on his own terms.

Physically, he could not be described as plain. His curly blond hair and rosy cheeks gave his face a cherub-like appearance, particularly with his long-lashed clear blue eyes that lit up mischievously when he flashed one of his quick smiles. If he ever bothered to take the minimum care of himself he could have been considered as being strikingly handsome. Nonetheless, it was not the case because he did not really care. His otherwise-athletic build; square shoulders and his six-foot-one height; conveyed signs of a life of indulgence and a sedentary existence. His slight paunch was a clear reflection of a lifestyle of very little physical exercise. He would often joke though, that his well-developed biceps more than compensated for that minor defect. According to him, his biceps were well-developed because he was a champion in his own sport, weightlifting — "weightlifting" being the action of lifting his beer mug from the bar counter to his lips and down again. He often ended that joke by flexing his arms to show off his virtually non-existent biceps and roaring with infectious laughter. In a nutshell, although the qualities of an undeniably handsome man lurked beneath his ungroomed appearance, he did nothing to highlight them.

Apart from contributing articles to and filing reports for magazines that dealt with the occult, esotericism and whatnot, he also earned a living giving private English classes. He loved people as much as communicating so for him, teaching was not at all like work. In fact, he described himself as highly privileged because he earned a living doing the things that gave him the most pleasure. He rated his job situation as exceptional: he got paid for practising his hobbies. Among other things, he was writing a book about the Spanish Civil War. He believed that though many books had already been written on the subject his was "the book". If there was anything he did have a good quantity of, it was vanity. However, he dished it out in such tiny doses that to the listener, it was never offensive.

Anyway, since the paranormal attracted him like iron filings to a magnet he immediately linked his recurrent dream to the event in the sky and vowed that he would not rest until he got to the bottom of the ongoing story. First of all though, he needed to establish the link that each fire had with the others — he needed to connect those dots. He decided to visit the sites where the incidents took place. What better way could there be of initiating his quest?

CHAPTER 2

The first place he visited was the premises housing the studio of the artist Santiago Pereira, popularly known as Santi. It was located in an upscale neighbourhood in the north of Madrid, in a housing estate with high-rise buildings of identical design set on a rambling acutely uneven terrain. The levels were artfully interconnected with steps, ramps and tree-lined cobbled pathways. Vast gardens, perfectly manicured lawns and hedges as well as trees and flowering shrubs lay between the buildings. The vegetation all over the property was so lush that it brought Paradise to mind.

Going there by car would have made his journey less tedious. However, a conservationist to the core, he avoided the use of private transport in the city. Actually, he owned no car despite the inconveniences of standing outside — often under extreme weather conditions like scorching sun, gusts of wind or freezing temperatures — waiting for public transport. Even with the frequently jam-packed buses and tube trains, he was convinced that no sacrifice was too great to save the environment from its slow death.

On getting off the bus he panted and puffed his way up endless steps to get to his destination which was slap-bang in the middle of the housing estate. Luckily, despite the long distance he had covered and the unbearably hot weather he was not at all sweaty when he arrived because the sprinklers were on full blast everywhere, producing a cooling effect all around, apart from serving their original purpose.

When he came face-to-face with the artist's secretary he did not need to introduce himself; she recognised him immediately. She was a regular reader of one of the magazines dealing with the paranormal to which he contributed articles. She was thrilled to see him in person. After introducing herself as Charo she laughingly confessed that her teenage daughter was stuck on him. He laughed too. She was a very friendly funny chatty and chubby middle-aged woman with a cheery smile and large sparkling beautiful dark eyes. He found her ways endearing.

They engaged in chit-chat for a bit before he told her why he was there. She became slightly guarded and when he sought her permission to take a look at the razed studio she got even more cautious. Nevertheless, he soon won her over by assuring her that nothing he saw then would be published until he had obtained the green light from her boss to visit the studio. Thus reassured, she smilingly offered to accompany him; it was her break anyway.

After locking the door leading into the reception area she led him round the building and up a flight of steps towards the wing housing the studio. That was when he learnt that in addition to owning the burnt-out art studio Santi also ran a language school in the same location. Art was surprised to discover that even though the sections housing the language school were not physically detached from the art studio, they were perfectly intact. As he and Charo went along she engaged him in conversation related to the paranormal — it was as though she could not stop talking about the subject. Her passion for it was so contagious that for a while he was swept along by her enthusiasm. However, he had to control himself; he reminded himself that he was there for one reason. Gradually, he steered the conversation to it.

Despite the flicker of disappointment that flashed across her face initially, she soon warmed up to the subject: the studio incident.

'Does your being here mean that you believe that the incident has some supernatural overtones?' she asked him.

'I can't reach that conclusion without a thorough investigation and that's why I'm here. I won't go away with a conclusive opinion either since I'm yet to visit the other locations,' he replied with a smile, after shrugging. Then he asked her,

'Did you see the bronze sculpture before it became so popular?'

'It's curious that everyone is asking about it,' she remarked.

'What do you mean by that?' he asked, showing surprise.

Screwing up her brow as though in thought, she finally shrugged before replying hesitantly,

'This morning, I was paid a visit by two African males who claimed to be journalists. They were interested in seeing the statuette mentioned in the newspapers.'

'African journalists?' he asked, showing great interest.

'Yes. They identified themselves, showing me their credentials. Curiously enough, they used the word 'statuette', not 'sculpture' as it had been referred to in the papers.'

'Yes, that's curious. And what did you tell them?'

'Nothing; I couldn't help them because the statuette is no longer here. But, even if it were here I wouldn't have shown it to them.'

'Why?'

'There was something about them that made me uneasy.'

'Really; what was it?'

Charo was silent for a while. She seemed to be giving his question serious consideration. Then she shook her head.

'I wish I could tell you but sincerely I just can't describe it.'

'That's okay,' he smiled reassuringly. 'Anyway, where is it?'

'Where is what?'

'The statuette,' he smiled.

'Ah, the statuette, of course!' she exclaimed. 'How silly of me,' she smiled embarrassingly, tapping herself on the head. Then she replied, 'It's at Santi's.'

'I see. Did these journalists leave any contact address?'

'No. They left as soon as I told them the statuette was no longer here.'

After saying that she nodded towards a makeshift screen, stating that they had arrived at their destination. At first sight there was not much to be seen — the screen had been put up to shield the gaping black void which was all that was left of the room that used to be there. Looking over the screen, all he could see were carbonised objects; it was as if the place had been bombed out.

Art wondered how a statuette could have stood intact in all that chaos and how it had remained spotless, as had been reported in the newspaper articles. He heard Charo say in an awestruck tone,

'Almost incredible that anything could have survived in there, right?'

'You read my thoughts,' he stated, turning to face her.

'You should have seen it,' she intoned, her face reflecting her wonder.

'Oh! So you saw it?'

'I did. It was right there, on that furniture — on that spot that's not as sooty as the rest. Can you see it?' She was on tiptoe, craning her head forward over the screen. 'As you can see,' she continued, 'the furniture's intact too. Isn't that just incredible?'

'Amazing,' he whispered, awed.

'Beyond amazing, it's mystical. Want to see more of the studio?'

'What else is there to be seen?'

'The studio's more than just this room.'

'Is that right? Sure, why not?' he uttered, excitedly.

She led him towards the back of the building and when she opened the back door into the place he discovered that the studio was made up of four rooms. That fact raised his astonishment to another level. If there were so many rooms how come just the one with the statuette got so totally destroyed? One of the rooms held the artist's own work. Though he did not have time to study it closely, the bit he saw was not to his taste.

'What's your impression?' Charo asked, studying his face smilingly.

'Different strokes for different folks,' he replied, noncommittally.

'I think so too,' she laughed.

They moved on to another room that held all sorts of bronze and clay figures as well as several masks. Some of the masks gave him gooseflesh. Charo explained that most of the collection was African and that her boss had regular suppliers who he referred to as his art dealers. Art was surprised at the huge amount of assorted artefacts left lying around inside the room. Although the collection looked like an assortment of junk, some of the pieces appeared to be genuine. He was still musing about the entire jumble when she announced that her break was over and that they could continue the tour on some other day hopefully with her boss's say-so.

Despite being disappointed by her announcement, as there was one room he had not seen, he did not want to abuse her generosity. He smiled gratefully and gracefully stated,

'Thanks immensely. Shall I invite you to a quick coffee?'

'No, thanks — an autograph for my daughter will do,' she smiled back.

'I have a better idea,' he said, reaching for his backpack.

He got out the latest issue of the magazine they had discussed earlier — it was not at the newsstands yet. He autographed it and handed it to her. Her large eyes grew to twice their original size as her reaction went from absolute incredulity to excitement. At first she could hardly find the words to thank him. When she finally did the words came tumbling out almost unintelligibly. He smilingly brushed her thanks aside telling her that he owed her more gratitude.

Before they parted company he asked if he could talk to the teachers at the language school. She replied that the evening was a better time since only a couple of them were around then. Telling him where to find them anyway, she hurriedly bade him goodbye and rushed off; the phone in the reception was ringing incessantly.

Art was able to locate three teachers. Understandably, at first they were pretty reluctant to air their opinions. When he guaranteed them that nothing they said would be published, they did not mince words as they expressed their views about their boss. Though he talked to each teacher separately, they all coincided on one viewpoint: their employer's fantasy often ran too wild — he had a tendency to exaggerate greatly. What they were trying to say was that he told lots of lies. The excessive fantasy bit is just a euphemistic way people have of stating that simple fact in this part of the world.

The frankest of them all was Jerry, a young English teacher. He gave a hilarious account of some of his boss's eccentricities. He could hardly hold back his laughter as he stated that he knew that his boss was really losing his marbles the instant he told him that he often got artistic inspirations in his dreams from Pablo Picasso.

'No other than Picasso; can you imagine that?' Jerry roared with laughter. He then went on to imitate his boss's way of talking. He took him off well and Art found the performance absolutely side-splitting.

'Seriously Art, you should talk to him. He really is something!' Jerry managed to say before he began laughing so hard that he could hardly continue speaking.

Art also spoke to Jean Pierre, a French teacher, who confessed that when he joined the staff three years earlier he initially did not know what to believe when his boss started telling him stories. With time, however, he learnt to take most of the stories with a pinch of salt. Thenceforth, he would often act like he was listening with interest when actually, he was thinking about other things while his boss rambled on. He admitted though that he occasionally found the stories entertaining. Laughing, he said that his boss once claimed to have received the stigmata after a vision he had during Holy Week when he was thirteen. He had even shown him the scars on his palms. Lowering his voice, he confided to Art that for all he knew, those scars could have been painted by his boss.

'He also claims to be able to heal through the laying on of hands. Can you beat that?' he asked with a smile, shaking his head. On that note, their interview came to an end.

Art then went on to interview a German teacher called Anja. After the ice had been broken and they had been chatting for a while, she asked him if he had seen her boss's collection of sculptures. Art said no. Of course, he could not let on that the secretary had given him a brief tour.

'Oh! You really should,' she laughed.

'Why is the collection so funny?' he smiled.

Still laughing, she told him that she would rather he saw it himself: it was something that should be experienced first-hand. He laughed. Thereafter, he steered the conversation to the object of his visit.

'Did you see the bronze statuette that's making news?'

'Who didn't see it? He showed it off, claiming it was special.'

'Did you notice anything special about it?'

'Not just that statuette — everything about Santi's collection is special. He sells every new acquisition of his as unique. I'd got so tired of hearing that worn-out old phrase that I didn't pay much attention to the statuette. You know, sometimes he gets really tiresome. Anyhow, I've learnt to smile through it all and get on with my stuff.'

'This one did turn out to be special though,' he joked.

'Indeed, it did,' she laughed along with him. 'He must be enjoying the publicity this whole thing's generating.'

'Do you really think so?'

'Think? I'm totally convinced; Santi loves the limelight. That's my boss for you.'

When Art left the language school he went in search of Santi's neighbours. He wanted to view Santi from another angle. Most of the neighbours he interviewed referred to Santi as a different breed of cat; some even felt he was way-out weird. What many found really odd and disgusting about Santi was his dumpster-diving habit. Santi claimed that the things he retrieved from the garbage bins were of artistic value. Since the neighbourhood was select it stood to reason that that practice was noticed and frowned upon by all and sundry. The neighbours complained that he usually recycled those objects one way or another as part of his so-called artistic expression and then pestered them, mainly those with kids in his language school, inviting them over to his studio to admire his "marvellous" works of art.

One woman with an affected way of speaking described that experience as torture.

'As you can imagine, good breeding compels most of us to ooh and aah over those monstrosities he calls art,' she concluded with a toffee-nosed air.

Another woman jeeringly referred to him as "the modern day Picasso", rolling her eyes as she said so, before adding that she was not sorry that his works were gone.

'At least for a good while, we'll be spared the ordeal of acting like we admire his so-called masterpieces,' she sneered, smirking.

Art smiled inwardly, wondering what her reaction would be if he told her that a good number of them had survived the fire.

At a stage during the interviews he was tempted to conclude that the fire had been provoked just to get rid of those works of art since he was yet to find anyone who said anything positive about them. Actually, he pitied Santi slightly; so far, everyone he asked about him had bashed him left, right and centre.

Roughly three hours after he began his interviews he paused to analyse his progress. His first observation was that though he had gathered lots of interesting information about the personality of that enigmatic figure from those he had interviewed, none of them had given him any important information directly related to his investigation. Nevertheless, he was not overly disappointed since his findings during his tour of the studio had made his visit worth his every while. Discovering first-hand that the studio was made up of several rooms and that the other rooms were all intact and seeing the state in which the room that housed the statuette had been left by the fire were experiences he would not have given up for anything in the world. After taking stock of his achievements he was considering calling it a day when he sighted another resident. He decided that if she agreed to an interview that would be it for the day.

Approaching her proved to be a mighty blessing. Although at first her view was somewhat similar to the rest — she could not stomach Santi's idea of art either — she surprisingly offered him something which the rest had not. According to her, at about 3 o'clock in the morning on the eve of the paranormal phenomenon, her five-year-old son whose bedroom lay right above the art studio had burst into the master bedroom jolting her and her husband awake. He had been trembling terribly with fear so they tried their best to calm him down. Eventually, he managed to tell them that he had heard drumbeats and footsteps in the artist's studio.

'Drumbeats?' they had asked in unison, listening intently.

'Yes, drumbeats,' he had replied as he started shivering anew.

When they told him that they could not hear anything he said that the sounds had stopped hence he had been able to run out of his room; adding that he could not move at all while they were going on. Since he would usually seek any excuse to sneak into their bed they had made room for him. They had treated the incident as nothing but a nightmare, even though he swore that the sound had woken him up.

Come morning, he had not mentioned the incident and she and her husband decided not to either since the boy was acting perfectly normal. By the end of the morning they had tossed it behind them. Nevertheless, the fire outbreak brought it back to their minds. They wondered if their son had not been dreaming after all and if what had happened that night could have been related to arson.

'You know, this so-called artist is so weird. I won't be surprised if someone finally succumbed to the temptation to burn down his studio.'

'Do you think people could be that radical?' Art asked.

'If you lived close to that man, you could be tempted to do anything,' she bridled.

The smile on her face was totally gone, fully replaced by a scowl. Cuddling her poodle, she declared that it was time for her to run along since she had oodles of things to do.

Thoroughly stunned by her information and her scathing remark, Art stood on the same spot gaping at her receding figure till she went round a corner and out of sight. The latter part of the interview was weird and the part that referred to the drumbeats was remarkable. The child had likened the beats to those in the film *The Lion King*, meaning that they were African drums. Furthermore, before dozing off he had told his parents that the footsteps were actually dance-steps. While she had laughed off that bit as part of her child's fantastic imagination, Art believed otherwise.

After mulling over the interview he began leafing through his notepad, putting together all he had been told about Santi. His impression was that no one seemed to understand him, maybe due to his eccentricities. It was clear that he found it difficult to separate fantasy from reality, which was perhaps what everyone liked the least about him. Some of his neighbours had described him as 'having birdies in his head', meaning that he was full of fantasies. He seemed to provoke amusement or irritation in most of them but not hatred and certainly not indifference. Before snapping shut his notepad Art concluded aloud, 'The man is a dreamer who often spices up his stories. He's either a true eccentric or a make-believe one.'

Just as Art was considering heading home he sighted an African cleaning lady. She was close to the language school, hovering uncertainly. Something about her behaviour prompted him that she knew things about the matter under investigation so he approached her. She started acting as if she was terribly busy — too busy to talk. But he was convinced that it was just a show. He sensed that she was extremely scared and not as busy as she was trying to appear. After several attempts to get her to talk to him failed, he decided to let her be. Precisely then something utterly unexpected happened.

'Things aren't always what they appear to be,' she mumbled.

'What?'

'Things aren't always what they appear to be.'

He froze. He had heard that before. Indeed, it was part of the message in his recurring dream and the voice was exactly the same.

He was still analysing those facts when she said,

'To get real answers, you must scratch beyond the surface.'

That too was part of his dream. He was stunned.

'Answers to what?' he asked, rushing after her.

'To get to the bottom of this whole thing, take nothing at its face value,' she whispered, looking around furtively and quickening her pace.

'Please stop speaking in riddles, tell me what you know.'

'I know nothing. Sorry, got to go.'

He was wondering if he should press her for straight answers when she stunned him yet again.

'Follow the trail of the fires,' she whispered softly.

'What's that?'

'Follow the trail of the fires,' she repeated, without looking at him.

'Yeah, I heard it, but I don't get it.'

'Think about it,' she whispered, looking around.

'Could you at least point me in some direction?' he implored.

'There are certain things you must find out by yourself.'

She quickened her pace even more and he increased his to try to keep up with her.

'Can't talk now; please let me be,' she pleaded, her eyes darting around.

'It'll take just a sec,' he tried to persuade her.

'No, no, I can't. Anyhow, thanks for finally seeing me.'

'Thanks for finally seeing you? What's that supposed to mean?'

'Most people don't see me,' she stated sadly.

'Can we talk about that?'

He was hoping that if she agreed to that proposal he could, along the line, steer the conversation to his reason for being there.

'I'm afraid we can't; I've got to go,' she insisted.

Although he was disappointed, he did not want to offend her — he had a gut feeling that she was going to be of immense help to him. So he let her be. However, that was only after hastily scribbling the address where she could find him if she changed her mind, on a piece of paper. She looked around cautiously before practically snatching it from him without as much as a glance in his direction. Then she was gone in a blink. He shook his head, wondering if she was really that fast or if his eyes had played a trick on him.

After her flash exit he continued thinking about her. Apart from being truly intrigued by her and by her weird behaviour, he was further intrigued by her thanking him for finally seeing her. Eventually, he concluded that the only logical explanation for that could be found in the prevailing attitude all around. Many of the denizens of that housing estate were full of airs and graces and it would not be surprising if they simply looked through her, treating her as if she was invisible. Perhaps in their eyes, she was nothing but a cleaning woman.

'But, why the word 'finally'?' he wondered aloud.

'It could've been a slip of tongue, what with her agitated state,' he analysed slowly.

That encounter would not leave his mind because of that gut feeling he had about her, the feeling that experience had taught him never to ignore. His inability to interview her became the only smear on what would have been an impeccable day as far as his journalistic quest went. His earlier feeling of satisfaction became clouded by that single fact. It would hang over him like a shroud for the rest of the day.

CHAPTER 3

It was the day after those interviews and Art was taking it easy in his pet haunt, a tavern. He was singing with great zeal. His left fist and those of a dozen or so senior citizens — his "*camaradas*" — in the room were raised in the air. The *camaradas* were singing too. Their eyes, like his, were gleaming with emotion. They were singing a verse from a Spanish Civil War tune "*Jarama Valley*", penned by Alex McDade, a Welsh volunteer who fought with the XV International Brigade in that war. The tune had been sung by the men of the International Brigade and by the rest of the men who had fought on the Republican side. It was one of Art's favourite songs. His *camaradas* loved it too. Although they did not sing it with the same clarity as he did, each time they chose to sing it in English, they did so with similar fervour.

History has it that following his unsuccessful attempt to capture Madrid General Francisco Franco ordered that the road that linked the city to the rest of the Republican Spain should be cut to isolate Madrid from Valencia which had become the Republican capital. His men crossed the Jarama River on 11 February 1937 and on 12 February, on what became known as Suicide Hill, the Republicans suffered heavy casualties and were forced to retreat to the next ridge. Franco's Nationalists advanced up Suicide Hill where they were routed by Republican machine-gun fire. What went into record as the most ferocious and the bloodiest battle of the Spanish Civil War ensued. That battle is believed to have been decisive in the defence of the Madrid–Valencia Road. About 20,000 men died in ten days and though two-thirds of them were Republicans, the Republicans stopped the advance thus thwarting the Nationalists' objective.

The senior citizens Art hung out with in the tavern on most Tuesday and Thursday evenings were veterans of that bitter war and survivors of the oppressive days of the post-war dictatorship. They had been part of the resistance which included artists, the literati and the intelligentsia. When the dictator General Franco was in power that tavern had often doubled as a clandestine meeting place for the resistance. That explained why they still frequented the place — out of habit and to relive those days. The men often talked about their experiences, the underground movements and the frequent close shaves they had. They also related sad stories of comrades who had been caught and tortured and of those who never made it back to the fold to tell their stories. Teary-eyed, with voices shaking with emotion, they regularly drank to the memory of those fallen comrades and to the survival of the hard-earned Spanish democracy.

At other times though, the roles were reversed: they became the willing listeners whom Art regaled with stories about that same Civil War. Although they were veterans of it, he had such a special gift when it came to storytelling that he always managed to hold them glued to their seats, occasionally teary-eyed as distant memories came rushing back. He also loved talking about the present, analysing the political situation in Spain and in the world as a whole or simply going over current affairs, with them.

That joint was Art's favourite haunt because apart from enjoying his *camaradas'* tales of the acts of bravery that had taken place there, he also relished the great times he shared with them.

The place used to be a traditional tavern and it still conserved most of its original features. It was located in the city centre, in an area that had become quite "in" as far as nightlife went. It had two floors — the upper one was at street level and the other was in the basement. The space on both floors was defined by fully exposed load-bearing walls and arches. That layout and the lighting gave the place, particularly the lower level, an aura of mystery and cosiness. The walls were covered with intricately patterned tiles. Copper pots and pans, as well as canvas oil paintings of bullfighters adorned the walls. The general decor was old-time.

On the day in question there was a slight variation in the *camaradas'* long-standing solemn rite, at least for Art, because as the emotive singing was coming to an end he caught sight of a pretty ebony-skinned woman in her mid 30s standing at the top of the stairs. She had been listening to the emotion-filled voices and taking in the scene below. As soon as he spotted her he headed for the foot of the stairs, from where he smilingly beckoned to her.

She was the cleaning lady he had stumbled across close to the artist's studio, the previous day. Although he had told her where to find him if she changed her mind, he had not really expected her to seek him out — not so soon anyway. Actually, that morning on awaking he had made up his mind to visit her the next day. So he was pleasantly surprised that she had sought him out instead.

Wondering why she had suddenly changed her mind, he broadened his smile and rushed up the stairs to meet her midway. He greeted her and told her to watch her steps. In broken Spanish, she thanked him and apologised for appearing without notice. He told her not to worry, that there was no way she could have notified him anyway. Unlike most people he owned no mobile phone and though he had a home phone, he was seldom there to answer it. Tracking him by phone required an excellent knowledge of his routines.

'We can speak English if you'll feel more comfortable,' he smiled, leading the way to a table in a corner, far removed from the staircase.

'Oh! Yes please. Thanks,' she said, sighing with relief before adding, 'I'm Regina.'

'Art. I'm pleased to meet you, Regina.'

'Art? Art as in 'fine art'?' she asked with a smile.

'No, Art as in 'outstanding warrior or champion'. It's an Irish name, the equivalent of 'Arthur',' he explained with pride, sticking out his chest.

'Interesting,' she said, letting out tiny laughter at his performance. 'Nice place,' she observed, looking round nervously as she eased herself into the chair he had indicated.

'Yeah, it has loads of history too,' he stated.

'Mm, I can imagine,' she mumbled, still looking around.

'See that wall over there? It's false. It's actually a door that leads into a back alley. It served as a quick-getaway route for the resistance in the dictatorial days of General Franco. During most of his tyrannical rule it was considered highly illegal for more than two people to get together in public places. The punishment was severe since breaking that law was tantamount to committing treason. Regardless, an arm of the resistance maintained those meetings and came up with lots of strategic moves to loosen his iron grip right here.'

She was quite impressed by the brief history lesson and her face momentarily reflected her admiration as her eyes continued roving the place. Observing her, he continued wondering why she was there. He could read the signs of fatigue and worry that were boldly written on her face. She was terribly ill-at-ease and jumpy too. As he was busy analysing her, she was busy studying the decor with great interest — or so it seemed. Then he remembered his manners.

'Something to drink?' he smiled.

'A Coke, please,' she replied eagerly.

'A Coke?' he asked, mildly bemused.

He had got so used to hanging around the beer-quaffing and wine-downing crowd that he had almost forgotten the existence of other types of beverages, especially the soft ones. That realisation made him smile to himself.

'Yes — if they serve it here, that is,' she replied hurriedly with a tired smile, thinking that that was the issue.

'Ah! Sure, I'll get it. Would you like anything else?'

'No thanks. That'll do,' she replied, flashing him another tired smile.

She was looking so frail that despite her negative answer he felt a strong urge to coax her into having a bite. However, he did not want her to get the impression that he was being patronising so he checked himself and walked away to get her drink.

'Cold enough?' he asked, after she had taken her first sip — it was more like a gulp.

'Yes, thanks,' she smiled as she daintily dabbed at her lips with a paper napkin.

He took a generous sip out of his beer mug and waited patiently for her to speak. Wondering how long it would be before she volunteered info, he let his mind wander. It raced back to part of his personal story.

His passion and fascination for Spain and everything related to it went back to his childhood days. His bedroom had been a mini museum full of miniatures of all kinds, from soldiers to bullfighters, and his walls had been covered with colourful posters of Spain. That passion made him choose to study Spanish history, which was how he landed in Spain. At university he was once required to write a paper and he chose the Spanish Civil War, *The Battle of Jarama* to be specific. Call that choice a coincidence, call it a design, call it whatever but, it opened the door to a new facet of his life and provided explanations to many hitherto unanswered questions about it.

Being a stickler for details, after making that choice he decided not only to visit the place where the battle took place but also to camp out there for a whole weekend. It had been spring and the weather was splendid, so why not? Single-minded and thorough, as he usually was when working, he chose to carry out his research alone to avoid distractions.

It was during that life-changing weekend that he had had his first past-life regression. It happened on the first night. He described the experience as overwhelming, hair-raising and eerie. Through that regression he discovered that he had been with one of the British battalions sent by General Miaja to the *Jarama Valley* to block the advance of the 40,000 men sent by General Franco. In other words, he was one of those brave ones who fought that ferocious battle in the valley of river Jarama in February 1937, which was why he referred to his veteran friends as *camaradas*.

Every detail of that battle had been re-enacted for him. He had heard the brutal artillery barrage and every sound that was uttered — the voices of fear, desperation, frustration and anger and the cries of wounded and dying young men calling out in pain, some calling for their mothers, as many of them were quite young. He also heard the fierce cursing and swearing all around during those endless days and nights of ferocious battle.

He even relived the sensation of the bitter winter cold biting into his bones. He actually felt the initial burning sensation he perceived when he was hit in the chest by a bullet. He recalled how that burning sensation turned into excruciating pain. Since proper medical assistance was virtually non-existent he felt life slowly draining out of him under the helpless teary gaze of his friends and comrades.

On awaking from that trance-like state he realised that the birthmark on his chest was actually the point of entry of the killer bullet. It was his "scar" from that war.

Although the flashback brought him lots of painful "memories", it also helped him sort out many issues in his life including certain nightmares he had been having since he was a child and some dreams which until then he had simply regarded as strange. Additionally, it gave him answers to certain flashes he often got: flashes similar to the ones one gets when trying to recall a dream or a blurred past incident. Apart from making him understand many things about his present life that trance also gave him fleeting glimpses into his future.

He occasionally went back to the site of that fierce battle to be on his own and to meditate. Sometimes, his going there was to pursue a hobby he took up after that first visit. It was: hunting for memorabilia — bullet shells and other objects like buttons and medals — related to the war. His fervour for that hobby became such that eventually, he bought a metal-detecting gadget for it. Though those items were relics of magnificent quality and incredible monetary value, he collected them for their sentimental importance rather than their economic value. His amazing collection was proudly displayed in his home.

'I knew this was going to happen,' Regina uttered quite unexpectedly, startling him.

'That what was going to happen?' he asked, after assimilating what she had said.

'Everything,' she replied, shuddering. 'I knew that the African bronze sculpture was going to cause great problems. This is just the beginning.'

'What African bronze sculpture?' he inquired, eagerly.

'Don't act like you don't know what I mean,' she replied, with a smile.

Something about that smile made him feel uneasy. He shuddered. Then he heard himself stating in a trembling voice,

'Honestly, I don't know what African sculpture you're referring to.'

'I mean the bronze sculpture that's been all over the news. The statuette or however it's being referred to,' she explained, looking around.

She had been looking around since the very first time he saw her. He wondered why. He toyed with the idea of asking her if everything was okay but he did not want to pry. Besides, he did not want to lose that great opportunity that she had just sprung on him.

'Is that statuette African? And how is it responsible for everything?' he asked her.

He felt like letting out the *Aha* sound. By now he was sitting bolt upright — his eyes had grown to about three times their size and his mouth was wide open as he eagerly awaited her reply. Meanwhile, his mind was racing, trying to connect the dots. He remembered his immediate sensation and then his suspicion after reading the very first article in the newspaper about the incident, particularly the part that affirmed that a bronze sculpture was the only object that had remained intact in the studio. Since then there had been no doubt in his mind that that piece of sculpture was an important piece in a huge puzzle. What he did not know then was that it was African. Not even Charo had referred to it as such. Suddenly, the word "African" seemed to be everywhere. He recalled Charo's information regarding the two African journalists who had inquired about the 'bronze statuette' and Santi's neighbours' son mention African drumbeats. Also, the only fatal victim in the three fires was African. Since he was attracted to the paranormal like a bee to honey, he needed no further evidence to assert that he was definitely onto something.

Wow! This is too much, he said to himself, shaking his head in wonder.

'Yes, it's an African statuette,' her voice reached him, jolting him out of his reflections. 'To be more precise, it's Nigerian.'

'What does this African statuette have to do with this whole thing?'

'Everything, Art; everything,' she stated sombrely.

'So ...?' he prompted, barely hiding his impatience.

'So ... what?' she asked, slightly confused.

'How is it related to last Friday's incident?'

She told him that Santi loved collecting works of art and that he had been doing some art deals with a couple of Nigerian young men whom she knew. Actually, it was through one of them that she had obtained her cleaning job with Santi. She stressed that though she was not trying to say that Santi and the young men had been engaged in any shady deals, she could not categorically state that all the artefacts had come through the right channels either. She confided that although in the course of her working there she had seen all sorts of pieces of art, as soon as that statuette had appeared she knew that it was a piece of bad news and she refused to go close to it despite Santi's insistence.

When Art asked her why she had refused, she replied that it reminded her of a piece with macabre stories surrounding it. He asked her how macabre, and she replied that it left a trail of blood behind it. Hence when Santi proudly held it towards her asking her to hold it for a close observation, she recoiled from it. Ignoring her reaction, Santi stated that he had learnt from the art dealers that it was from an important national shrine and that it had tons of history behind it. At that point he cracked what she deemed a bad joke: that the proof of its authenticity lay in the fact that it still bore traces of blood from human sacrifice. She paused and looked around before telling Art that even though it was no secret that Santi often told tales, on that occasion she took him seriously regarding the authenticity of the piece. However, while she had no doubt about its authenticity, she did about its provenance.

She explained that first of all, in Nigeria there are no such things as national shrines. Secondly, in the region where it originated, it was not unusual for families to own shrines, no matter how tiny, in honour of ancestral spirits and deities to whom they regularly poured libations and often made animal sacrifices. That fact made the matter even more worrying because no family would willingly part with such pieces that represented their ancestors and their preferred gods. In other words, that piece must have been stolen so devastating consequences were bound to follow, which was exactly why she never wanted anything to do with it. But, she knew that trying to explain that to Santi was out of the question since apart from being terribly intransigent by nature, he would surely have laughed in her face.

'What do you mean by devastating consequences?' Art asked.

After studying his face as if trying to ascertain if she could trust him she replied,

'Like what's just happened.'

'Are you talking about what happened last Friday? How's that possible?'

'All I can tell you for now is: this whole business bears the signature of *Shango*.'

'Who's *Shango*?' he asked, expectantly.

'*Shango*'s the god of thunder and lightning. Art, most of the stuff people claimed to have seen in the sky is true. And, it isn't over yet.'

'What?' he uttered. 'Tell me Regina, why would a god want to be involved in this whole story — in what happened in the sky and all that?'

'It's because this god has certainly been called upon to intervene.'

'To intervene; by whom?' he asked, excitedly.

'It's most likely by the family that the statuette was stolen from. There are waters into which people should never wade. Why do you think I recoiled from it?'

'Waters into which people should never wade?' he asked, confused.

'I'm speaking figuratively, Art.'

'Ah, of course; excuse me,' he smiled, blushing. 'Regina, this is all so new to me and so exciting. That's precisely why I want as much information as you can offer.'

She was beginning to look really uncomfortable, as if she would rather drop the topic. Though he noticed her discomfort he was so excited by the revelation that he could not stop himself so he went on to ask if she could shed more light on the intervention bit.

'Some other day, if you don't mind,' she replied, looking around.

'Yeah, sure,' he agreed with a nod, concealing his disappointment.

Even though he wanted to gather as much information as possible within the least possible time, he did not want to put her off by applying unnecessary pressure on her. There was no doubt in his mind that she was a goldmine of valuable information.

Since she had made it clear that she would rather they suspended that line of the interview for the time being, he decided to try another angle.

'You said you had no doubt about the authenticity of the statuette.'

'Yes,' she nodded.

'If you don't mind me asking, how come you know so much about such matters?'

'That's because I was a curator in a museum,' she replied sadly.

'You're a curator?' he asked in wide-eyed surprise.

'Don't I look like one?' she asked, sounding humorous for once.

'Yeah, I guess you do,' he smiled, jokingly pretending to study her face.

Then he got serious, preparing to ask his next question. Although he knew that it could bother her, he just had to get it off his chest. He tried to make it as inoffensive as he could manage by choosing his words carefully.

'Excuse my indiscretion but, given your education why are you scrubbing floors?'

Her face clouded over. She bowed her head and would not meet his gaze; she seemed to be fighting back tears. Then suddenly, she looked at him and inquired,

'Which do you prefer, the abridged version of the story or the full one?'

'The latter,' he replied, leaning forward expectantly.

'I'll give you the former, it's simpler. I came in search of a better life."

'And, have you found it?"

'Does it look or seem like I have?' she laughed sadly.

'Ironical, isn't it?'

'That's an understatement,' she smiled wistfully and said, 'Well, it could be worse.'

'Worse?' he asked, his eyes widening. Deep down, he wondered: *What could be worse than an art connoisseur scrubbing floors?*

'Being forced into prostitution would definitely be far worse. Anyway, crawling home with my tail between my legs isn't a valid option,' she stated vehemently.

At that point everything changed: he saw her in a different light. He thoroughly admired her courage and her knowledge, not to mention the dignified way she carried herself despite her circumstances. She was frail-looking, soft-spoken and gentle but at the same time he could sense her hidden strength. She was such an enigmatic lady and the longer he sat there talking to her, the more he wanted to find out everything about her. All of a sudden, he realised that he was taken with her and with her gentle ways. He was still musing when her voice reached him from what seemed like miles away.

He almost fell off his chair — a consequence of the unexpectedness of her voice and of the contents of the information it conveyed.

'Did anyone tell you about the mysterious glow of light that emanated from the artist's studio before the incident?' she asked, almost casually.

'A mysterious glow of light?' he inquired.

'Yes. I heard about it from one of the live-in cleaning ladies.'

'That sounds spooky!'

She added that the woman claimed that the glow had appeared for three consecutive nights, at exactly the same time — 3 a.m. The night preceding the paranormal phenomenon was the last of the three sightings.

'Wow!' he let out.

Then there was a lull in their conversation during which she looked over her shoulder several times. Finally, she announced that it was getting late so she had to go since it was a long way to her dormitory town. She explained that she usually left home at 5.30 a.m. therefore she loved to be in bed early. He was disappointed because there were still so many things he wanted to know from her and about her. He asked her when he could go over to her place of work to talk to her.

'I work in so many places,' she replied.

'Oh! I see,' he said, fully understanding why she looked so tired.

'Well, if you're thinking of coming to where we first met, it's unsafe.'

'What's unsafe about it?' he asked, rising; she was already standing.

'Things could get uglier,' she replied.

'What makes you think so?'

'Sheer instinct,' she stated hurriedly.

'Instinct or insight?' he smiled.

She shrugged, gave him a tense smile and started walking towards the stairs. He quickened his pace to catch up with her.

While accompanying her to the bus stop he thanked her profusely for making out time to come to see him, despite her crowded schedule. He smilingly added that he thoroughly enjoyed talking to her since she was an invaluable source of information.

Thereafter he asked her the one question that he had been asking himself from the very moment he saw her standing on the stairway of the tavern: Why had she taken great pains to locate him? She replied that right then, they needed each other. Though he tried to coax clues out of her, she refused to help him unravel that puzzle. She simply smiled and told him that with time he would understand.

Before her bus arrived, he managed to extract a promise from her to meet him a couple of days later for another interview. As she was about to get onto the bus he asked,

'Regina, could you arrange an interview for me with Santi's art dealers?'

'Practically impossible,' she replied.

'Why is it so?'

'Remember the guy who got struck dead by lightning?'

'Yes?' he replied, expectantly.

'That's one of them.'

'What?'

'Uh-huh. See what I mean?' she murmured.

He shuddered, braced himself and asked, 'What about the other one?'

30

'That's a long story.'

'Could we start it on Thursday?'

'We'll see. But remember, things aren't always what they appear to be.'

As he was assimilating her advice the bus started pulling away and she called out,

'Follow the trail of the fires!"

He was still glued to the same spot scratching his head when something came to his mind: his hunch that all the three fires were related when he first read about them.

'I knew it, I knew it!' he let out, punching the air, totally oblivious to the fact that he was attracting curious gazes.

CHAPTER 4

'**F**ollow the trail of the fires!' kept going round and round in his head. He could not get Regina's advice or prompt out of his mind. The fact that it was her second time of saying it before departing made it even more difficult for him to do so. He could not keep still. He was dying to get answers to the scores of questions he had for her.

Two hours after turning in for the night he was still unable to fall asleep. He tried every trick in the book to court sleep — even counting sheep, silly as he had always considered the practice. However, nothing worked. Eventually, sick of tossing and turning in bed, he decided to go for a long walk, hoping to get worn out.

Shortly after he hit the street he was swallowed up in the teeming metropolis. It seemed as if everyone was out there — not too surprising considering the sweltering August weather. Even as late as it was the thermometers were showing readings above 36ºC. He did not try to fight his way through the milling crowd; he simply let himself be swept along. After all, he was headed nowhere in particular. The atmosphere was contagious and he began feeling pretty bubbly as he got swept along by the human tide. It was one of the things that he really loved about Madrid — the night was always so alive, mainly in summer.

'African sculpture, African journalists, African drumbeats and dance steps and an African mortal victim,' he kept repeating the words as he wandered around the vibrant city.

He was lost in thoughts, considering how to get to the bottom of the whole puzzle. Though Regina had asked him to follow the trail of the fires he was not too sure about how to do so effectively to obtain answers.

Goodness! If only I could fast-forward time! he lamented inwardly, with a tinge of impatience. He was desperately looking forward to Thursday and to obtaining answers to his questions.

He was drifting along the wide pavement of a popular boulevard when he decided that it was time for a drink; he was feeling dehydrated. He began wriggling his way out of the middle of the crowd in order to squeeze into any of the narrow cobbled streets on either flank of the boulevard. Those streets were lined with bars, cafes, cafe bars, pubs and whatnot. They were the choice haunts of fun seekers year-round.

Gradually, he made it to one end of the crowd. Greatly relieved, he was turning into one of the winding streets when a young black man bumped into him; actually, it was more like he barged into him. The contact produced an explosive impact on his shoulder — it felt like being brutally tackled in a contact ball game. The man simply strutted on, without as much as a backward glance, as if nothing had happened. Though Art cursed, he did not go after the receding ramrod-straight figure since he assumed that the incident had been nothing but an accident. He felt, however, that the man should have apologised. Feeling pretty ruffled and slightly out of breath, he told himself that he more than needed a drink.

The street he squeezed into was bristling with pub crawlers. He stepped into a jazz bar and immediately released a sigh of pleasure and approval because the joint was cool, literally and figuratively. It was in full swing. He noticed that those present were mainly foreigners — tourists and expats. Most of them had their eyes glued to the stage where a group of foreign jazz artists was performing. He headed straight for the bar as the tables were all taken. Spotting a free barstool, he manoeuvred his way past those standing around and chatting away. He had barely perched on it when he ordered his drink. After taking his first sip of the chilled beer — exactly what he needed — he smacked his lips. He then took a cursory look around and nodded in approval. He loved the decor and the music was excellent. Most importantly, the space was smoke-free. He was feeling absolutely comfortable and at home. He then turned his full attention to the stage.

He was having so much fun that he totally lost track of time. When he realised that it was 5 a.m., he knew it was time to go. Calling for the bill, he reached for his wallet and felt the presence of a piece of paper in his pocket. He found that rather odd because his trousers were fresh from the laundry. Squinting at the paper, he made out a hastily scrawled message in reddish-brown ink.

'Back off, gringo!' it read.

He blinked and read it again. His eyes almost popped out of their sockets. He could not fathom out how the paper had got there, nor could he make much sense of the message.

As he was trying to figure out both puzzles he had the strong sensation that he was being observed. He raised his head and let his eyes roam the room. He soon sighted someone glowering at him: a young man standing close to the entrance. Art thought he recognised the hostile stranger but he could not place him right away. Just as he decided to approach him to find out if they had met before, the man made a slashing gesture across his throat with his index finger and swung around to leave. Seeing his back brought back the full memory of their encounter to Art.

'Ah, yes!' he exclaimed as realisation hit him.

That was the man who had bumped into him so viciously in the street earlier on. Although he had not seen his face then, he was absolutely sure that the young man who had just glowered at him was the very same person — there was no way he could mistake his strut. He would have shrugged off his being there as a coincidence if the man had not made the throat-slashing gesture. He shuddered.

Before spotting the man Art had been about to pay his bill, however, when he noticed that the stranger was leaving he shoved his wallet at the barman, saying that he would be right back. He heard the barman calling out something as he rushed towards the entrance but he was too focused on trying not to push and shove past those standing around to hear him. Despite his rush, by the time Art got to the door the stranger was gone.

Dashing outside, all he could see were pub crawlers, most of them looking wasted and oblivious to the world around them as they crawled home. Running his fingers through his hair, he stood outside for a moment, trying to figure out what was happening. He looked at the scrawled message once again to see if it could give him some sort of clue. He was bristling. Slow to anger by nature, one of the few things that could get his goat was being called an Englishman. But being called a gringo? That was the height of provocation. He read the message a couple of times.

'Ignorant idiot!' he cursed under his breath.

All the fun he had been having had just been put to a very rude end. He simply wanted to rush straight home.

Still bristling, he returned to the bar. He could clearly read the incredulity on the barman's face when he appeared. Apparently the barman had not been expecting him to return. He noticed that his wallet was lying on the bar countertop — the barman had not touched it. He had either been too suspicious or too cautious to do so. Both reasons would be in order and not at all surprising since in this day and age of IEDs and dirty bombs, anyone could drop off whatever, wherever.

It was only then that the enormity of Art's action hit him. What if the barman had decided to go after him aggressively or worse still, what if he had called the cops? He was grateful that neither scenario had occurred.

He paid for his drinks and apologised to the baffled barman for the way he had rushed off, giving him some explanation which he himself could barely remember after leaving there — he was that embarrassed and confused. He made a hasty exit, his face totally flushed. He needed not have worried though since the scene that he had just played the protagonist in had gone mostly unnoticed by those in the still-crowded bar.

'Back off, gringo!' he said half aloud as he stepped onto the street.

He stood on the same spot for a while, thinking. He could not imagine why that advice should be directed at him. He was very concerned but at the same time, curious. He wondered if whoever slipped that message into his pocket had taken him for someone else.

Still unable to find answers to those puzzles, he began his homeward journey. But, he soon came to a halt. The full impact of the message had struck home. He had been dwelling on whether the message was actually meant for him and on how it had made its way into his pocket rather than on its true meaning.

'Back off!' he repeated several times. 'What an idiot!' he muttered, tapping himself on the head repeatedly as he began pacing.

'Of course it's all related!' he uttered, coming to an abrupt halt.

He asked himself how he could have failed to figure out the connection earlier. Equally, he could not understand how what to him was just a paranormal phenomenon could make anybody feel so uneasy. Regina flashed through his mind. He started thinking about her evasiveness the very first time he approached her, her furtive glances then and when she dropped by at the tavern and her general behaviour. He wondered if she was being threatened or harassed. Instantly, her advice,

'Follow the trail of the fires!' echoed in his ears.

He heard it distinctly. In fact, it was as if she was standing right there beside him. That riddle was getting clearer. Though he had yet to figure out how the fires were related he believed that he was not far from the truth. Smilingly congratulating himself, he drifted homewards in a haze, oblivious of his surroundings — a result of the number of cold beers he had downed and of his new feeling of exhilaration.

On getting home he rushed over to his desk and made some bubble diagrams, mapping out his next course of action.

Satisfied with his progress, he decided to turn in again, for the second time that night. When he began undressing he discovered that his shirt sleeve had a cut in it, a neat slash made with a very sharp object. He inspected it for a while before the full meaning sank in. He was shaken, but only momentarily. If Art was characterised by any traits, they were his bravery and stubbornness while on the job, often to a point of foolhardiness. He tossed the shirt aside.

Before taking off his trousers he dug his hands into the pockets, as usual, to empty them out. He got out the hastily scrawled note and inspected it, asking himself if it could be some dirty joke. He then tossed it into the pedal bin in his bathroom.

But, what if it isn't a joke? After asking himself that question he fished the note out instantaneously and placed it in his medicine cabinet.

The actions of bending down and stretching out his arm to retrieve the note set his shoulder afire, anew. He inspected it and discovered that apart from the redness all around it, there seemed to be no further damage from the jostling the stranger had given him. At least, it did not seem to have been dislocated by the impact.

As he opened his medicine cabinet again and reached for his packet of painkillers, it dawned on him that that shoulder was the right one and that the note had been in the right pocket of his trousers. That immediately answered his question as to how and when the note got there. Obviously, the guy slipped it in when he collided with him.

'Could the slash in my shirt sleeve have been made at the same time the note was being slid into my pocket? Or could it have been before or after?' he wondered aloud as he took a painkiller and absent-mindedly went through his toilette routine. His head was full of the night's happenings.

It had been an intense night with all kinds of new emotions, experiences and discoveries. Still lost in thoughts, he headed for bed taking his notepad with him. His latest findings made him amend his bubble diagrams slightly. He then added some annotations and switched off his bedside lamp.

'Follow the trail of the fires,' he intoned before drifting off to sleep.

He was so excited and somewhat worried about the latest developments that he had a fitful sleep. Consequently, he got up much earlier than he had planned to. Paradoxically enough, although he had had practically no sleep he was bubbling with energy from the instant he stepped into his slippers.

The first thing he did was make himself very strong coffee; it was going to be a long day. While enjoying the first cup, the only cup he usually took his time over, he went over the bubble diagrams and the annotations he had made before dozing off. Thereafter, he had a swift shave and a rushed shower and then raced out. He was headed for the train station, on his way to try to connect another dot in that huge puzzle: *Follow the trail of the fires!*

His destination was the second site of those fires — the place where the fire had claimed a life. It was a dormitory town, 18 kilometres southeast of Madrid, with a population of about 206,000 of which 11 per cent were immigrants, mainly from Africa and Eastern Europe.

The station was a twenty-three- minute walk from his home and even though going by bus would have been faster and more comfortable, he chose to walk. He reckoned that that would be an excellent way to be alone to do some serious thinking.

He had barely stepped out of his building, however, when he sensed that he had company. Uneasy at first, he soon shook off that feeling. He was determined not to let any intimidation tactics stop him from reaching his goal. His resolve notwithstanding, he kept reminding himself of the need to remain prudent and extremely alert.

When he finally made it to the station he was greatly relieved. He almost whooped with joy when he walked through the sliding doors into the air-conditioned space. He was sweating profusely due to the mixture of the broiling temperature and the stress he had undergone, trying to play detective, all the way there. Actually, he had chosen a longer route to see if he could identify the person shadowing him but, his effort had been in vain.

The air-conditioned commuter train pulled out of the station right on schedule. Art spent the first few minutes studying the faces of his fellow passengers. Although they were of different shapes, sizes and colours, they had something in common: signs of fatigue. The signs were of varying degrees but they were there. The previous night had been mercilessly sweltering so it was not surprising that everyone was looking so exhausted.

Generally, in Spain, it is not unusual to see people wearing such tired looks in summer — they hardly spend enough time sleeping at night. And the summer nightlife is so enchanting that it is almost impossible to break away from its grip — it is sheer magic and excitement. Many people feel that it is too good to be wasted sleeping. They prefer to spend the night hours socialising and having fun.

Traditionally, this insufficient night-time sleep was amply made up for with a siesta. The unlimited afternoon slumber not only made up for the previous night's little or no sleep but also charged people's batteries in readiness for the night ahead — and so went the cycle. The fact that August used to be observed as a holiday month nationwide made it easy to preserve that very popular siesta tradition.

However, such treasured customs are now being threatened with extinction; only an extremely lucky few could afford to keep up either. The imminent extinction of these much cherished traditions is a consequence of the new working timetable imposed by multinationals and the increasingly domineering national companies. Is it a fair price to pay for modernisation, economic development and advancement — professional as well as personal? This debate has been raging in recent years, especially when the summer months are approaching and it will surely continue.

After taking in his immediate surroundings Art began gazing through the window at the scorched landscape. No trace of green was in sight as the train rolled on. The effect of the severe drought, not unrelated with global warming, was evident. He wondered how long the earth would be able to put up with all the abuses it had been suffering. He felt somewhat sad because he was convinced that even though so much was being said about the deplorable state of the planet earth, little was being done to remedy its condition and save it from withering away.

The effect of the previous night's too-little sleep soon became too much to fight off and he was lulled to sleep by the motion of the train and the agreeable temperature. At a stage he felt the train pulling away from a station and he sprang up, startling an elderly man dozing peacefully by his side. Apologising to him, he frantically looked through the window at the black-and-white signpost indicating the station they were leaving behind. On discovering that it was not his station he sank into his seat awash with relief.

His relief was short-lived though. Just as he settled back into his seat he saw a back he thought he recognised. No sooner had he caught sight of it than it disappeared into the toilet down the aisle. He told himself that he was either getting paranoid or indeed, he was being tailed. If the latter was the case then more than one person was following the trail of the fires. He nervously wondered why.

Shortly afterwards, he was jolted by a deep male voice harshly barking out what sounded like an order in a foreign language. He discovered that it belonged to an African young man. He was in the company of four garishly made-up gawky young girls. One of them was visibly cowering — she was the one who had just been growled at. Art was wondering what the relationship among them all could be when the man caught his inquiring gaze and glowered at him. The look was so piercing that if those eyes were daggers, he would have dropped dead instantaneously. They seemed to be saying, *Mind your own blinking business or else.* The mood Art was in was not exactly that for engaging in a "let's see who blinks first" contest so he turned his gaze to the window and the near wilderness out there. From that instant what had hitherto been a stress-free journey became everything but that, what with the back he thought he recognised and then this bully.

He was literally sitting on the edge of his seat when after a relative eternity the train pulled into his station. He was not sure if he should be relieved or if he should be worried since he did not know what awaited him outside. Gathering his stuff he got off, looking around tensely, very much on the alert.

As soon as his feet touched the platform he winced — the weather was baking hot, even though it was only 11 a.m. The pleasant temperature he had been enjoying in the train made the heat seem more intense too. Bracing himself for the terribly hot day ahead, he got his baseball cap out of his backpack, placed it on his head and put on his sunglasses. Looking over his shoulder, he set out uncertainly on his quest to find the residence of the only mortal victim of the fires.

He stopped twice to ask for directions, seizing the opportunity to check if he could spot the individual he had seen on the train, knowing fully well that since the town had a high number of sub-Saharan Africans, spotting him would be highly improbable. In addition, he had a very vague idea of who he was keeping a lookout for especially since he had seen his face only briefly the previous night.

When he ultimately got to his destination — a five storey building in a middle class neighbourhood — the first person he came across was the cleaning lady. She was leaning on her mop stick, chattering away with a couple of women at the entrance lobby. She was a sturdily built woman, seemingly in her late 50s, with a high-pitched voice — one of those voices that could be heard miles away, long before the owner is seen. Her bulging darting black eyes gave the impression that they missed nothing.

The sight of her brought a smile of amusement to Art's face. She looked every bit like *Doña* Pepa, his unbearably nosy elderly neighbour. Although she was a younger version of *Doña* Pepa, the resemblance was uncanny. She even had buck teeth like *Doña* Pepa and she had the same way of sticking them out when listening attentively, as though they were an additional auditory aid. She also had similar mannerisms. He soon discovered that most importantly, they shared the same hobby: an ultra-high interest in other people's affairs.

She seemed quite pleased to see him and, taking his smile of amusement for a friendly hello smile, she gave him a toothy grin. After she and her friends had exchanged greetings with him, she got rid of them with alacrity — she wanted to have this stranger all to herself. Since they were dying to find out more about the foreign-looking stranger, they looked extremely disappointed as they made their reluctant departure.

He chuckled. *Certainly, they'll swoop on her right after my departure, to make her share her scoop,* he thought.

Once they were alone it took no time for him to discover that part of the reason she seemed so welcoming was that any excuse was good enough for her to break the monotony of the dreary task of cleaning and, what excuse could be better than tongue-wagging. Chatting with a stranger would provide her with something new to twitter about later, rather than going over the same worn-out local gossip. So, why pass up that opportunity, especially since the stranger was good-looking and charming? Such opportunities did not pop up everyday.

She introduced herself as Catalina and he remarked that it was a beautiful name. Her grin broadened — she felt absolutely flattered. She seemed unable to take her eyes off him as he introduced himself in return. In addition to being curious about him she liked him too. That was no surprise since Art had a way with people, particularly women. He was every inch a gentleman. She warmed up to him even more when she discovered his reason for being there. The incident was still the buzz in the locality as a whole — in fact, that was what she had been discussing with her friends when he arrived.

Meeting her turned out to be an immense blessing since she knew so much about it. Through her he learnt that the young man's landlord lived on the fifth floor of the same building — an invaluable piece of information. Black eyes twinkling and buck teeth bared in a delightful grin, she offered to act as his escort promising to introduce him to some of the neighbours who she swore were sources of juicy information.

Before he could assimilate that most-unexpected boon she snapped off her gloves, ripped off her apron, patted her shiny shoulder-length jet-black curly hair into place and virtually ordered him to follow her. Everything happened so fast that he was caught flat-footed. He watched in bemusement as she stumped towards the lift.

'Come on, let's go!' she called out excitedly, beckoning to him.

Slowly, he snapped himself out of his brief haze-like state and, smiling confusedly, he practically broke into a run to catch up with her.

CHAPTER 5

Since it was August many people were home on holiday, including the residents that Catalina took Art in search of. The fact that she was with him made matters very easy; seeing a familiar face not only made them throw their doors wide open, but it also made them open up to him. He discovered that to them she was not just a familiar face — she was someone with whom they had extraordinary relations.

Could it be because she's a good source of juicy gossip, apart from her evident sociable nature? he mused with a secret smile while she went fluttering all over the place.

There were four flats on each floor and his first interview was on the deceased young man's floor with the next door neighbours, a middle-aged couple. Shivering, the wife said in a near whisper that she frequently heard the tinkling of a bell in his flat late at night and that it was usually followed by what sounded like chanting or incantations. Lowering her voice further, she added that on the night before the fire she had been awoken by what sounded like drumbeats, but that the sound had been momentary. Asking herself what time it was, she checked her timepiece and wondered if her neighbour had gone crazy.

Art asked her what time it was and she replied, 'About 3 a.m.'

That information stunned him since it reminded him of what the last woman he interviewed in the language school premises told him about her son's experience — the time was the same and 3 a.m. had also featured in his conversation with Regina. After a brief pause to digest what he had just heard he asked her if she remembered anything else about that night and she shook her head uncertainly. She looked uneasy — she seemed to be holding back something. Suddenly she began trembling violently and her husband put his arms protectively around her.

At that point Art sensed that the interview was over. Although curiosity was gnawing away at him and he was dying to ask her more questions, he decided to respect her feelings. Wondering what could have frightened her so much and what she could be holding back, he thanked the couple and stood up. He was truly perplexed. Still hoping that she would decide to share more information, he walked slowly towards the door. However, he was not called back. Then he walked through it.

'Know what? She says she's been hearing strange things in the man's flat and catching whiffs of his fragrance in the hallway,' Catalina whispered, right outside the door.

'Sounds in his flat and whiffs of his fragrance?' Art whispered, amazed.

'Yes. But, she drinks a lot so nobody really believes her.'

'What if she's right? She looked genuinely affected.'

'Affected? She's just cuckoo. She claims to have special powers.'

'She could too. Why not?' he stated, wishing he could talk to her again.

'Come on, let's go. What she has is a crazy mind and lots of imagination.'

'Curious,' he mumbled, doubling his steps to catch up with her.

His bafflement was deepening. Despite Catalina's scepticism, he believed that the tormented woman knew far more than she had been willing to divulge. He wondered if he could have done anything to get her or her husband to be more forthcoming.

Their next destination was the flat above the young man's. The owner, a retired widower, claimed that what he had heard the night before the fire was not a product of any weird dream because he had been fully awake. It had been a terribly hot night so he found it impossible to get any sleep. He had been considering taking a cold shower when he heard drumbeats. Since he was used to his downstairs neighbour and his guests sometimes partying till the wee hours of the morning, he did not make much of the beats. It struck him as odd though that instead of playing music like they usually did they had resorted to playing the drums. But the thumps stopped instantly. Only then did he realise that there was no partying noise in the flat downstairs nor was there any sound for that matter. He confessed that since the beats had been so short-lived, if the young man's next-door neighbours had not mentioned them the next day he probably would have questioned the accuracy of what he had heard.

After they had seen everyone available Catalina led him to the flat where the victim's landlord Aurelio lived with his wife Guadalupe. They were an elderly couple. The door was answered by Guadalupe and after Catalina explained why she was there with Art, Guadalupe called out to her husband. He seemed slightly reluctant at first but his wife was clearly interested in the interview and she urged him to participate. It was glaringly obvious that she loved gossip and she was dying to indulge. In fact, she was Catalina's good friend.

She led them into the living room and told them to feel absolutely at home. She then offered them coffee and cupcakes. Art opted for coffee. He was getting drowsy, for obvious reasons. Aurelio was a soft-spoken gentleman, the direct opposite of his wife who never stopped twittering and interrupting. While his wife was getting coffee ready, he informed Art that two days earlier they had been paid a visit by two young men who claimed to be African journalists. However, they did not say what country they were from. After some chit-chat, they had asked if they could take a look at the deceased's flat.

Art inquired if he had granted the request and as Aurelio began replying Guadalupe walked in bearing a laden tray.

'No way,' she butted in. 'Those people weren't journalists. I don't know who they were, but I'm convinced they were nothing of the sort.'

'How do you know that?' Art asked, smilingly.

'Call it instinct, call it whatever, but I just know!' she emphasised.

'So, they didn't go in then?'

'Of course not!' she snapped.

'We're still talking to our insurance company. Later, we'll consider handing the keys over to whomever they recommend,' Aurelio stated, levelly.

He then mentioned that the previous day, three gentlemen who claimed to be from the Nigerian embassy had come by, asserting that they needed to take stock of the man's personal belongings since they were planning to repatriate his body and his property.

Guadalupe interjected that she was sure that the very same people who had come earlier on were the ones who returned, camouflaged as embassy officials, bringing a conniver along with them. Art asked her how she could be so certain and she stated,

'Although those people all look alike, I'm sure of what I'm saying.'

'Mm, I absolutely agree with you, they all do look alike,' Catalina chimed in.

'What people?' Art asked, seriously lost.

'Those people; you know what I mean,' whispered Guadalupe, conspiratorially.

It took him a good while to realise that she was trying not to say "black people". The cliché in this part of the world is that it is difficult to tell black people apart.

Ignoring the point she was trying to make, he asked her why she was so convinced that it was the same people trying to get into the flat. She replied that it was a hunch, adding that judging from their insistence, she was sure that there was something in there that they were interested in. He found the information interesting. He recalled Charo telling him that she had been visited by two men who had claimed to be journalists from Africa. He wondered if they were the same people. If so, were they genuine or were they impostors after something, like Guadalupe had just asserted?

Assuming that she's not being paranoid, what could they be interested in? he was musing when her voice reached him.

'We know you're an authentic journalist so we'd let you see the flat before you leave, if you so desire,' she declared, beaming.

'Really?' he asked with enthusiasm.

'Would that be legal?' Aurelio asked her.

'As long as no one gets to hear about it, I don't see any problem there,' she replied, looking at Catalina.

Definitely, it was a subtle message to her to keep her trap sealed.

'Oh, of course; don't worry about me,' she squeaked, looking away.

Clearly, she caught the message. Whether or not she would abide by her hypothetical promise would be another story.

Guadalupe then turned her attention to Art. Looking directly at him, she inquired if he promised not to let it be known that they let him in.

'You have my word!' he stated earnestly.

'Good!' she uttered with satisfaction.

'But ...' Aurelio tried to interject.

'No buts, Aurelio. We're taking this genuine journalist there to find out what those impostors are after,' she declared.

Art was amused. The men's supposed intent on getting into the flat had aroused her curiosity to such an extent that any excuse was enough for her to go there to snoop around. His arrival was just perfect. Later, if need be, she could always explain off her being there by saying that she had simply been honouring an investigative journalist's request and nothing more. He gave her a knowing smile and she beamed with satisfaction.

After her rather unexpected vote of confidence, though the true reason was not altruistic, he chose to grab that opportunity to avoid any likely change of heart.

'Would you mind us visiting the flat now? We can continue the interview there or come back here to do so later if you prefer,' he addressed her and her husband.

'Oh, yes, yes,' she replied enthusiastically, getting to her feet.

'I'll get the keys,' her husband stated with resignation.

By the time he emerged the two women were in the hallway, itching to get going.

On the way to the victim's flat the couple explained to him that the fire-fighters had had to break down the old door for rapid access, so they had had to have it replaced. Therefore, even if the young man had given a spare set of his keys to someone — something they suspected he had done since his mailbox had been cleared about twice since the incident — that person would not be able to gain access to his flat. That probably explained why those men had come to ask them for the keys. They declared that they would hand over a copy of the new keys only to the victim's legal representatives and only if their insurance company said so. But such parties would have to present credentials substantiating those links.

The two women made the sign of the cross as Aurelio was turning the key in the lock and, as soon as the door stood open they practically pushed past him and rushed in — that was how impatient they were to get in to snoop around. Conversely, Aurelio was dragging his feet, not too surprising since he had practically been dragged along. After asking Art to get in before him, he looked over his shoulder before entering and shutting the door slowly. Even after stepping in he seemed reluctant to go any further; he stood in the hall, looking around uncertainly. Then he bowed his head, apparently in sorrow. He would later explain his every action as being induced by fear — totally paralysing fear.

The two women were already in the living room when Art walked in. They were chattering away excitedly. They soon wandered off; an action which he appreciated because it meant that he could make his observations and assessment in peace. He stood in the middle of the living room, looking at the smoke-blackened walls. The smell of smoke was everywhere. Apart from the smoke aspect, the extravagantly furnished living room seemed to be intact. Guadalupe called out to him and following her voice, he walked into a room with a gaping hole in the wall. The room was burnt-out. She said that it was the master bedroom, the room where the young man was when he was struck dead. Nothing in there was intact. Everything was burnt down, completely charred.

Looking around, he could not understand how the man's body could have been intact, as had been reported in the local paper. He asked Guadalupe if that was true and she said that although neither she nor her husband saw the body, they learnt from reliable sources that that was the case. Those sources were from the circle of the fire-fighters and from someone who worked in the morgue. Though Art had always affirmed that anything was possible as far as the paranormal went, looking around that room he got so mystified.

The next room was full of crates of artwork of all kinds: paintings, carvings and sculpture. There were also boxes overflowing with handbags, shoes, belts, watches, clothes, jewellery and perfumes. They were all brand new — every one of them still had its price tag firmly in place. Even though the assortment was vast, the one thing they all had in common was that they were very expensive brands, brands that were out of the average man's reach. Yet for some reason, which not even Art's fertile imagination could figure out, there were stacks of them lying around.

This room is a diamond mine, he thought. Right away, it dawned on him that he was not the only one who was awestruck — the eyes of everyone around him had grown to twice their size. What a puzzling discovery!

When he finally found his voice he asked the couple how they got to know the deceased. They replied that he had been introduced to them by a friend of their youngest son. That friend had introduced him as a business man, an importer/exporter. However, they never asked what he imported or exported. They had not pried since their son's friend was like a son to them. The victim had been their tenant for slightly over a year and he had been very respectful and correct all through. He had paid his rent and bills promptly, an ideal tenant. They had fond memories of him.

Earlier on though, some wagging tongues had informed Art that the incident had dealt them a terrible financial blow; it had made them lose a good source of steady income. According to those "bad tongues", the rent they had been receiving from the deceased had been double what they would ever get for that flat. Actually, some inferred that the loss of that high rent, rather than any affection they might have had for him as a person, was the real reason why they were so emotionally affected by his dramatic end. Regardless, unless they were really good actors Art's impression was that they were not faking their grief.

The party had moved away from the "diamond mine" and they were standing outside the room next to it. The door was closed. Art reached for the knob and turned it slowly, but nothing happened. He tried harder, but still nothing.

'That's strange,' observed Aurelio. 'The door has no lock.'

He then joined in the effort. After a number of yanks and shoves the door sprang open as if it had been pulled from the inside, sending both of them flying and landing on either side of it. Stunned, they both got shakily to their feet before the unbelieving gazes of the dazed women.

The room was in complete darkness because the Venetian blind was all the way down. Art noticed the light switch by the door — it was phosphorescent. As he flipped it he felt a strange sensation start from his unsteady hand and go up his arm. Simultaneously, he heard a sizzling sound and the switch lit up in a glow. Subsequently, it blew up with a popping sound. They all started. Then there was absolute darkness and heavy silence. Heart pounding, he dug into his backpack and got out the ever-present torch. The powerful beam revealed a scene that held them all spellbound; nobody could venture in. Everything they took in was from the door and that was more than enough for them. The scene, or maybe what it represented, left every one of them speechless. Their faces gave the impression that they were afraid to breathe, that they were holding their breath. Not even the chitty-chatty Guadalupe or her friend Catalina was able to wag her tongue.

The room looked like a shrine. It contained the most unexpected paraphernalia related to the occult. The scene at the end of it, directly in front of them, was what shocked them the most. It was a sort of altar, draped with red damask. There was a display of strange scary wood carvings, plus pieces of ornaments made of bronze, as well as a tiny ornamental bell made of some precious metal on the altar. A huge mirror covered the wall behind it and, there were weird amulets hanging on either side of it.

The bell reminded Art of the different declarations about the tinkling of a bell late at night. He shifted his gaze to the floor. He beheld a white circle, described by a substance that looked like salt. Within the circle, there were more bronze figures; they were coated with what looked like caked blood. He noticed traces of soft down feathers on some of the figures. An ornamental earthenware pot containing a dark liquid, from which withering palm fronds were hanging out, stood in the centre of the circle. A horned skull and some bones were lying in front of the pot. The quality of the light available rendered the scene even more sinister.

He could feel his hair stand on end. As much as he would have loved to hotfoot it out of there, he could not because apart from the fact that his natural curiosity coupled with his professional inquisitiveness would not let him, his feet were glued to the spot. His eyes, like those of his companions, were glued to the scene. There was absolute stillness.

Heart pounding away, he eventually managed to reach for the potent amulet around his neck, which he never took off. Still speechless, he held onto it for reassurance and for protection. Almost immediately, Aurelio and Guadalupe reacted.

'Jesus!' they exclaimed in unison.

That seemed to break the spell they had all been under.

'Let's get out of here!' Catalina shrieked, scuttling away.

In the midst of the entire din, Art remained motionless and speechless. When he finally found his voice, he croakily asked Aurelio if he could take pictures of the scene. Since he got no answer, he looked around and realised that he was alone. The rest of the party had disappeared. Shrugging, he decided to go ahead and take some shots anyway.

But, as he was about to do so with trembling hands the torchlight began dimming, until he could barely see beyond his nose. He could not believe what was happening since the batteries in the torch were brand new. Imploring the torch not to fail him, he tapped its bottom repeatedly, but that action proved of no avail. The torch simply went dead. He was just about to rummage in his backpack for spare batteries when he heard something that sounded like a short thunderclap. His heart skipped a beat and he felt blood rush to his head. His head and heart started pounding away crazily. He got dizzy. Unknown to him, the flat had become shrouded in total darkness following the explosion sound.

Miles away, he heard some commotion. Slowly, it registered in his befuddled mind that the racket was being created by his companions. They were scrambling for the main door, desperate to leave. He hazily wondered where they had been hiding and if Aurelio, who had so graciously allowed everyone in before him, was being equally gracious then. Despite himself, he smiled. That smile made him know that he was regaining his wits.

He noticed that he was trembling uncontrollably. His hair was on end again. He felt that someone was standing behind him, breathing down his neck — literally. Regardless of the summer heat he was shivering violently, his teeth clattering. His nose twitched. There was a fragrance in the air: male cologne. He was engulfed in it. He made an attempt to reach for his amulet but he could not move.

'Not everything has a logical explanation,' a male voice stated.

What? He wanted to ask, but his voice failed him.

Though he was trembling seriously, he tried to control his panic. He reminded himself that he was alone, so nobody else could be speaking.

'No, you're not,' the voice stated.

I must be going mad, he thought.

'No. But you will if you don't leave now!' whoever thundered.

All panicky, Art started fighting to free himself from the grip of paralysis. Eventually, it left him and he frantically reached for his amulet and stumbled out of there on wobbly legs, blindly bumping into objects along the way. He heard a staccato of outlandish laughter behind him, but he could not look backwards.

When he finally made it to the main door he could barely sustain himself on his feet as he stumbled through it. He found his companions winded and huddled together in the hall outside the door, trying to regain the use of their legs. Despite not faring much better himself, the sight they presented really amused him.

Catalina looked the most whacked. Her buck teeth were sticking out more than ever as she went on struggling to regain her breath. Her huge dark eyes were wide open like a pair of headlights and she kept dimming them every now and then as she continued fighting for breath. She was really a comic sight.

At intervals between heavy breathing Aurelio let out,

'See what you've got us into? Are you happy now?'

He was addressing Guadalupe, who was too winded to care about his reproach. Funnily enough, she was leaning against him and their chests were rising and falling at a uniform rhythm. Watching them, Art kept telling himself that the scene was beyond surreal. Fortunately, he was too breathless to burst into laughter.

Needless to say, the tour was over. As they staggered back to the couple's flat nobody uttered a sound. However, as soon as they got in and locked the door, they all let out a huge, synchronised sigh of relief.

'Remember, we have a deal,' Guadalupe spluttered, facing him.

Thereafter, they all regained their power of speech. Though their appreciation of what they had perceived visually in the flat varied for obvious reasons, they all attested to having felt a very strong presence there, a truly intimidating one.

'Did you catch a whiff of his fragrance?' the couple asked in unison.

'Did you say a whiff? I'd say: it's stifling!' Catalina gasped, before adding, 'Oh, my God, so she isn't so crazy after all!'

That was in reference to the neighbour whose claim to that effect she had scoffed at, earlier.

Actually, that same claim had been repeated by a couple of neighbours who Art interviewed after that poor distraught woman. One of them had declared that when all the residents were back from their holiday, she would suggest that a priest or a psychic should be called in if the creepy occurrences in the common spaces like the hallways did not cease.

Art was particularly affected by his experience outside the shrine-like room since he relived what happened to him during his past-life regression: that state of total paralysis during which he had perceived everything going on around him but had been absolutely incapable of directing any of it. It had been the eeriest of sensations. The impact was such that he had not made full recovery when he eventually departed.

On the train, he analysed the information he had gathered from the neighbours. Despite their slightly differing opinions about the victim, they held a roughly uniform view regarding the fire: It was the oddest fire they had ever seen or heard of not only because it did not extend beyond that one room but also because it had just enough time to gut the room and then go out before the arrival of the firemen. Those facts were sources of awe and mystery to them. There was still so much fear about the incident: Most of those he interviewed lowered their voices when describing it, as if they were afraid of being overheard by some secret listener.

He gathered that the young man was a mysterious figure, nothing short of an enigma. He simply appeared and disappeared. He was always travelling too. They claimed that when he was not away on a trip, he usually got home late. According to them, he often entertained his friends and they played loud music, dancing and singing aloud until the wee hours of the morning. But since those entertainments were usually at weekends, the neighbours did their best to overlook the nuisance that such rowdy behaviour constituted. They averred that he had an elevated lifestyle — he was always expensively and excellently dressed and he wore very expensive colognes which he applied generously. At the end of the day, each of the neighbours admitted that he was quite cordial and courteous, the fact that he never mixed up with them notwithstanding.

When the train got to his destination, Art was still slightly at a loss because despite everything he had learnt about the man's supposed oddities and ways, the link between his fire and the other fires remained indistinct. He was sure of something though: each room in the man's flat — the blown-out master bedroom, the diamond mine and the shrine — held a mystery. Reflectively, he resolved that although he had yet to uncover those mysteries he certainly would, somehow. Heaving a sigh, he stood up and alighted.

CHAPTER 6

Art was still slightly dazed the following morning — the impact of his experience in that flat was too strong to be just shrugged off. The hang-up calls he received several times during the night did not ease matters. The persistent interruptions got so annoying that finally, he was forced to take the phone off the hook. However, by then it was too late since he could no longer go back to sleep. Eventually, he got up and tried to get some work done.

Though he could not accomplish much due to his inability to concentrate, he did manage to put some of the notes he made during that visit in order. The visit was extremely useful because through it he discovered all that was hitherto unknown, never photographed nor published about the incident. He also detected the contradictions and inaccuracies contained in the articles published about it.

After arranging the notes he revised his questions for Regina. He had such a burning desire to ask her so many questions related to the weird things he had seen in the victim's flat that he could hardly wait to see her. Nevertheless, time seemed to have come to a halt. He was desperate to make headway in his investigation.

In the end, tired of waiting for the appointed time to arrive and frustrated about not being productive enough, he went for a walk to clear his head. He almost wore himself out. Time seemed to stand still; no matter how much he walked he still seemed to have so much of it left. When he could no longer walk, he dragged himself over to his favourite haunt, their meeting venue.

While there he engaged in the usual debates about this and that with his *camaradas* and as always, they accompanied their debates with *tapas* and red wine or beer. This time around, however, he engaged in those recreational pursuits with less enthusiasm than usual. His eyes were glued to the clock on the wall.

At length, the appointed hour came. But it went by without any sign of her. He became more restless as minutes ticked by. Minutes soon became hours and there he was, hoping that she would appear. Even after it became obvious that given how far away she lived and how late it had got her showing up was most unlikely, he chose to hang around though his friends were gone. He continued quaffing beer while trying to keep his mind engaged by browsing through his notes until the joint was about to close. Then very reluctantly, he got up and left.

He had been looking forward to that meeting so much that it really crushed him that she did not appear. Since he did not feel like going home just then, he took to roaming the streets. Soon afterwards that now-familiar feeling of being followed returned. At first he tried to wave it aside, telling himself that he had probably had too much beer and could be imagining things. He also wondered if the conspiracy theory he had formulated around the investigation could be taking its toll on him. Much as he tried to disregard that feeling of being followed, it increased by the second. His discomfort soon got to such a level that he decided to stumble home. It was quite late anyway.

He had barely staggered into his flat when his doorbell rang, almost making him jump out of his skin, what with his street ordeal. Wondering who the visitor could be, he looked at his wall clock. Its dial indicated that it was nine o'clock. Only then did he realise that it was not working. Shaking his head, he fished out his pocket watch.

'It's awfully late; who could be out there?' he muttered, since it was past 3 a.m.

'Who's there?' he growled.

'Open, it's us,' a female voice he recognised called out.

Oh, no! he groaned inwardly.

The voice belonged to his elderly neighbour *Doña* Pepa, the most gossipy of his neighbours — a true nightmare — though in his characteristic carefree liberal ways he always managed to overlook her and her non-stop wagging tongue as well as her long nose. He usually viewed her with amusement and very often with pity. He reckoned that she was a victim of idleness and boredom.

Peeking through his peephole he made out the faces of three more of his elderly neighbours, besides *Doña* Pepa's. Although they all shared the same pastime of snooping around none of them could outdo her; she was in a class of her own.

The full committee's here, he moaned to himself.

Even though what he could see was a distorted image of their faces — the product of most peepholes — he did notice that that natural distortion notwithstanding, they were indeed wearing grim expressions.

'What do they want that can't wait till morning?' he groaned aloud, flinging his door open and giving them a questioning look.

'Good evening, *Señor* Art,' they chorused.

'I'd say 'Good morning',' he replied, uncharacteristically gruff.

'Have you seen this?' *Don* Paco, the eldest person in the pack asked.

He wondered if the man had chosen to ignore his insinuation regarding the time or if he had not heard it. He became rather ruffled. On flinging the door open he had expected either an explanation or an apology or even both, for their intrusion at that ungodly hour, but definitely not that question.

'Seen what?' he asked, his tone reflecting irritation.

Before their startling knock he had been wallowing in disappointment apart from feeling pretty shaken due to the scare he received in the street. Hence standing there before them, he was getting more miffed by the second by their intrusion and the last thing on his mind was a game of twenty questions. He was going to tell them just that when he noticed that the four pairs of eyes were looking downwards. Following their gaze, what he saw almost made him pass out.

Apart from being absent-minded by nature, he had been so preoccupied with the issue of Regina not showing up, not to mention the quantity of beer in his system, that on getting home he did not notice that his jet-black Bombay cat Ebony was lying in his doorway in a pool of blood. He had simply stepped over it. Inconceivable though this might sound to most people, one simply needs to know him to believe how easily he could step over whatever and keep going, as long as he did not trip over it or it did not trip him over. That was how distracted he often got.

'Who did this?' he raged, scanning their faces through bloodshot eyes.

He was rocking slightly, forwards and backwards, close to tears. They would not meet his gaze as they huddled together like frightened children. His immediate suspicion rested heavily on any one of his neighbours, including those four.

Most Spaniards have this thing about black cats. They believe that black cats bring bad luck and negativity, especially when they cross your path. It is not unusual to see people stop dead in their tracks and wait stoically for a black cat to walk by before continuing on their way. They believe that by letting a black cat cross their path they are bound to experience a period of misfortune.

Thus none of his neighbours ever found Ebony's presence in the building amusing. They always stayed out of her way. For her and for them, it was a constant cat-and-humans game which they did not find the least bit funny. Conversely, Ebony relished it because she was very playful. That got them even madder. With Ebony's sweet face, Art never understood how anyone could imagine that she could be a bringer of ill luck. Gazing at the four seemingly concerned faces before him, he was convinced that on discovering her lifeless body they had had some celebration.

'We don't know, we found her that's all,' they finally chorused, in answer to the question he had almost forgotten he asked.

'How come nobody knows anything?' he asked, barely stopping himself from adding, *as nosy as you all are?*

'Look closely,' *Doña* Pepa whispered, pointing at the body.

He went down on his knees and picked up Ebony's stiff, lifeless body. Stuck into her rounded head, right between her large round wide-set copper eyes, was a dagger. It looked like an antiquity; the design on its protruding hilt was quite ornamental. Her hitherto gleaming black satin-textured coat was blood-soaked. Regardless, he hugged her close.

'How could anyone have done this?' he asked, in a near sob.

Something caught his attention. It was a blood-soaked piece of paper pinned to her head with the dagger. He did not have to remove it to be able to read the crisp message:

'Back off!'

He was jolted. He became almost sober instantaneously as reality grabbed and shook him. He nearly dropped the body. He realised that the message could not have been written by any of his neighbours since they had no knowledge of English. So that barbaric act could not have been committed by any of them. Apart from the language detail, he had a vague feeling that that message was not exactly unfamiliar. However, he could not determine why. His mind, still slightly befuddled, simply refused to cooperate.

What's going on here? he wondered as he started trembling visibly.

'Are you okay?' *Doña* Pepa asked.

'Barely,' Art mumbled, rising shakily to his feet.

'Any idea of who might've done it?' *Don* Paco asked.

'If you don't mind, I have to go,' he whispered.

'Pity, isn't it?' *Don* Paco's wife mumbled as Art shut his door.

Once inside he let his tears flow freely. Ebony had been his faithful companion for nine years. He continued staring at her heavy blood-soaked lifeless body, which he was still cradling. Her lifeless copper eyes were staring into his blue ones. His whole body was wracked with sobs. Though he could not figure out how anyone could be savage enough to inflict such harm on an innocent harmless pet, he was fully convinced that their reason was not unrelated to his investigation. He was feeling terribly guilty for having brought such an undeserved brutal end upon her.

Ebony had been a typical Bombay cat: outgoing, friendly and playful. He often put her on a leash on Sunday afternoons and walked her in *El Retiro*, Madrid's most popular park. She had seemed to look forward to that activity. She was sociable and entertaining and through her Art made acquaintances in the park. Children loved romping with her on the grass. She was so agile and bouncy that apart from keeping him and everyone amused with her acrobatics, she often wore him out. Indeed, she used to be his main source of exercise, other than his mug-lifting. Naturally, those who found her and her antics so amusing were mainly foreigners.

He kept reminiscing about her and thinking about how to handle the situation till the crack of dawn when he finally placed her body on a blanket on the floor to take pictures of it. The latter act was because he had decided that first and foremost, he should file a police report before pursuing any other course of action. Avoiding any contact with the hilt of the dagger, so as not to contaminate any fingerprints it might bear, he underwent the painful chore of taking a number of shots of her stiff body.

Though the tone of the message attached to her head was a main source of worry to him, his paramount concern was the fact that anyone could hate him so much as to brutally execute a poor innocent cat. Until then he had believed himself to be an easy-going guy who never got in anyone's way. Hence in spite of being sure that the police would ask if he knew of anyone who, for whatever reason, might have harmed his cat just to get at him, he could not think of an answer.

He soon got so drowsy that despite his worries he caught himself nodding off a couple of times. Finally, he crawled into bed. He knew that he should take a shower, it had been a long day and an even longer night but, he just did not care. He was feeling out of sorts, apart from dozy. He did manage though, to rip off his blood-soaked shirt and trousers.

As he was drifting off the full meaning of the scrawled message sank in. Asking himself why it did not occur to him earlier, he sprang out of bed.

'Of course it's all related!' he exclaimed, standing before Ebony's body.

His fatigue simply vanished. He grabbed his camera and, still avoiding contact with the dagger, he took several close-up shots. He discovered that the hilt bore a symbol and some strange inscriptions. He realised that as well as being ornamental, the dagger could be ceremonial. His heart started pumping away — his earlier suspicion that he was onto something important was getting stronger. He switched on his very old computer which usually needed a whole decade to warm up and while it was taking its time to awaken, he made himself a mug of very strong black coffee. He needed to be super alert.

Soon afterwards, steaming mug of syrup-thick black coffee in hand, he plunked down in a chair in front of his PC. After enlarging the pictures as much as possible he printed three copies of each. Thereafter, he was about to run a search on Google to see what information he could find in relation to that symbol when it occurred to him that he had a faster and extremely reliable source nearby. His very good friend Diego worked in the Special Crimes Unit of the police force. Ignoring what time it was, he dialled Diego's number. He was just too fazed to care about conventions.

The phone rang for an eternity before Diego finally answered it.

'Who's this?' he growled sleepily.

'Hey, buddy, Art here.'

'Dude, do you realise what time it is?'

'So sorry, but this is an emergency,' he explained.

'Killed anyone?' Diego asked, sounding more awake.

'What a question, buddy. Of course I didn't!'

'What a relief! Where are you?'

'I'm at home.'

'Good; that's where you're safest. I'll call you later in the day.'

'Safest? Not too sure about that,' he replied, his voice rising slightly.

'Meaning what?' Diego asked, sounding fully awake.

After Art replied that he would rather they discussed it in person and straightaway, Diego explained that he had just got home and stumbled into bed after a special operation.

'Believe me. If it wasn't absolutely important, I wouldn't call you up,' Art insisted.

'Come on, is it really that bad?'

'It's far worse than whatever you're thinking.'

'Okay, okay. Just say where.'

Though Art could be really persuasive and hardly ever took no for an answer, on that occasion his success in making Diego change his mind was a mixture of those qualities and the fact that Diego detected an uncharacteristic note of urgency and desperation in his friend's voice.

After replacing the phone Art rushed into the shower to get rid of the blood covering most of his trunk and neck. Next, he hopped into a fresh pair of trousers and threw on a shirt. Then grabbing the pictures, he stuffed them into an envelope and dashed out. He was in the lift when he realised that he did not lock his door. Cursing, he ran back and did so.

When he stepped onto the street he was hit in the face by a blast of hot air. Even though it was just dawn there was every indication that it was going to be a pretty nasty day, heat-wise. He cursed in irritation. He often missed the mild Irish summer. It was still early for public transport to start running and, with no cab within sight, he set out in a near run to the venue of the meeting, a 24/7 convenience store which was about a twenty minute brisk walk away.

By the time he got there he was puffing and panting and practically drenched with sweat. He stumbled towards the dining section and collapsed into a chair to regain his breath and cool off. Luckily, since it was so early most of the patrons were either nursing their first coffee of the day and struggling to come fully awake or had yet to go to bed after a night out on the town and were trying their best to fight off sleep. Consequently, nobody paid the least attention to him or to his ghastly appearance.

Regaining enough breath to speak, he ordered some coffee and he was still waiting to be served when Diego arrived.

'Oh, man, you look like shi—' Diego began, on seeing him.

'Please don't go on,' he interjected wearily. 'Thanks for the compliment, anyway.'

'Any time; what are friends for?' Diego joked, despite his own weary look.

'Coffee?' Art asked, in a bid to turn the attention away from his scruffy appearance.

'No thanks; I'd like to return to bed as soon as we're through. It's been an effing long night and the day's not going to be any better.'

'Yeah, you mentioned that. I appreciate your being here.'

'It's okay. Seriously, you do look like something the cat brought home.'

'Please don't talk about cats,' he moaned.

'I shouldn't. Oh, boy! You've got problems with cats too?'

Art could not reply to that, he had a lump in his throat. He was fiddling with his coffee cup and staring right into it.

'Talking about cats how's Ebony doing? I haven't seen her in ages.'

'There,' he croaked, tossing the envelope with the pictures on the table.

'What's this?' Diego asked in surprise.

'Check it out,' Art replied, still staring into his cup.

Giving his friend a questioning look, Diego picked up the envelope. The first picture was one of those showing a full view of Ebony's head.

'What's this; some sort of macabre photo trick?'

'You know I'm not into trick photography.'

'Then is this really what I think it is?'

Art nodded sadly, close to tears once again.

'Who did this?' Diego inquired, still flipping through the pictures.

'That's why I'm here, to see if you can help me answer that question.'

'Damn!' he mouthed every now and then as he continued flipping through them.

Suddenly, the flicking sound stopped and Art looked up from his coffee cup. He noticed that Diego had placed the pictures on the table and was squinting at one of them with great interest. It was one of those showing the hilt of the dagger.

'Does it look familiar?' he asked, expectantly.

'Just a sec, not sure,' Diego replied, scratching his head.

'There are some close-ups of it,' Art stated in excitement. 'Give me a sec and I'll show you a couple,' he added.

He picked up the rest of the pictures from the table and began zipping through them while Diego continued studying the one in his hands with knitted brows. Soon, he held out one of the close-ups of the hilt. Diego looked at it and sat bolt upright.

'I'm almost certain that I've seen it before,' he stated grimly. 'Looks very much like the one that was found stuck in an African sex-worker's body weeks ago.'

'Stuck in an African sex-worker's body?'

'Uh-huh. It's almost identical. I'll run a check though and call you.'

'Can it be today, please?'

'I'll do all I can. By the way, what's going on?'

'The truth is, I don't know. I can only speculate.'

'What's your speculation?'

Art launched into his story at the end of which Diego sighed heavily before exclaiming, 'That's really weird!'

'Yeah, and it's getting more so by the second.'

'Do you think you're in danger?'

'Honestly, do you think I am?' Art asked in return.

'Hmm, all I can say is watch your back,' his friend advised, grimly.

Diego's advice got him pensive. He had been too mad to worry about any harm to his person but suddenly, he was seeing things differently.

'Have you filed a report?' he heard Diego ask.

'No, not yet,' he replied thoughtfully.

'Okay, we'll pick up the body and I'll run you over to the station.'

'Thanks,' he stated gratefully, as they both stood up.

At the police station Diego speeded up the process and they were soon ready to go. Ebony's body had to be left behind because it needed to be thoroughly analysed by the forensics department. Art was promised that he would be contacted shortly.

Diego gave him a ride home. Before driving off he promised to call him as soon as he obtained any useful information regarding the dagger.

'I'll appreciate that. Thanks for everything, buddy.'

'Don't take unnecessary risks!' Diego called out as he pulled away.

'I'll try not to!' Art replied sadly, waving at his departing friend.

He was feeling absolutely empty. His eyes were downcast as he slowly walked into his flat. He had lost his long-time companion. The flat felt so terribly empty without the bouncy presence of Ebony. In a daze, he kept gazing at the spot where her lifeless body had been lying. Shortly afterwards, he got out his emergency bottle of Scotch and stared at it for ages. Never did he imagine that he would need it for such an occasion. Eventually he shrugged, broke the seal around the top, snapped the top off the bottle and began gulping the whisky straight from the bottle. He ultimately drank himself into a stupor.

'I'll definitely avenge your death Ebony. It's a promise,' he drawled, before complete darkness took over.

CHAPTER 7

The incessant ringing of the phone began from a long way off, somewhere in his dream. Though he did his best to block it out, it was no use. When he finally opened his eyes he got that sinking feeling, a sure sign that something terrible had happened. However, he could not put his finger on it. To compound his problems the room was spinning like crazy and he was feeling disorientated. He shut his eyes. His head was splitting and the nonstop ringing of the phone was jarring on his nerves.

'What have I done to deserve this?' he moaned, placing a pillow over his head in a futile attempt to block out the persistent jangling sound.

When he could no longer take it he slowly groped his way towards the irritating sound and grabbed the receiver.

'Yeah,' he croaked into it, holding onto his head.

'Oh, you're alive!' he heard.

'Who are you?' he asked, struggling to clear his foggy brain.

'Dude, you sound dead. What have you done to yourself?'

'Oh, it's you buddy.'

'Bingo! The resurrection of the dead,' Diego laughed.

'What time's it?'

'It's time for you to wake up. I've got news for you.'

Diego had barely finished saying that when a clattering sound reached him. He held the receiver away from his ear. Everything around Art had tumbled down with a crash as he was groping for the light switch.

'Hope he hasn't killed himself,' Diego mumbled before calling out louder, 'Are you alright dude?'

'Yeah,' Art groaned, 'I need just a sec to find the light switch.'

'Tell you what, get back to bed.'

'No, no, I'm fine.'

'Listen, forget it; stay put at home.'

Art began making protesting noises but Diego's firm tone halted him. Actually, he could hardly hold himself upright so it was just well. After bidding Diego goodbye he replaced the receiver and crawled back to bed. At least, so he believed.

The next time he opened his eyes it was to the continuous beeping sound of his phone. It was lying next to his head, off the hook.

'What the heck!' he mouthed, looking around.

With a shaky hand, he reached out for the receiver and slowly replaced it on its cradle. With that movement he discovered that he was aching terribly all over. Groaning, he looked around anew and shook his head in disbelief. He had just noticed that he was lying on the floor, in the midst of the clutter he had inadvertently created. He groaned again. His head was splitting, his eyes were smarting, his mouth was awfully dry and his tongue felt like sandpaper. Additionally, his stomach was in turmoil.

As he tried to get to his feet he let out a loud moan. That first attempt failed. Three attempts later, he was swaying on his feet. He held onto his stomach with one hand and with the other, he held onto everything he could find along the way for support and made a slow painful journey to the bathroom. After practically retching out his bowel he spent ages splashing ice-cold water on his burning face.

Although he was dying for a shower, the thought of climbing into the bath was intimidating. As it was walking, which only required putting one foot in front of the other, was too much effort how much more trying to lift one foot after the other in order to get into the bath. He slumped onto the WC cover and held his head between his trembling hands. He was trying to think, another super-human undertaking since his head was thumping away. Suddenly, he turned his head and was facing the corner where Ebony sometimes lolled when it was too hot for comfort everywhere else in the flat. The memory of everything came rushing back and he recognised what that lingering sinking feeling was all about. That realisation brought back his grief. It was accompanied by rage.

Slowly, a vague memory came to him of a telephone call. He wondered if it could be just a figment of his imagination. He was still mulling over that when the phone started ringing. With a loud groan he stood up unhurriedly and began shuffling towards it. For his weary bones, it was a long way to go. Before he could get there the ringing stopped.

'Dammit!' he swore; he was getting more irritable by the second.

Squinting at the Caller ID, he dialled the number with a shaky finger in case he could learn something about the previous call. He got an answer on the first ring and he immediately recognised the voice as Diego's.

'Hey! I was getting worried about you!' Diego's booming voice stated.

'Why?' he croaked.

'You've been out for over a day. Remember me calling you last night?'

'Only vaguely,' he replied dully.

'Vaguely. Anyway, can you meet me in an hour's time?'

'An hour's time,' Art mouthed weakly.

'Yup, can you manage it?'

'Do I have a choice?' he tried to joke, but it came out like a whine.

After hanging up he knew that although he dreaded the idea, he had no other choice but to go for a shower. It was a hot day and he had been feeling awfully sticky since he managed to drag himself up from the floor. Reluctant though he was about the idea initially, he ended up having a long, cold shower — he needed to decongest his befuddled mind. Despite the fact that his head was swimming slightly when he finally emerged from the bathroom, he was feeling relatively fine.

He gulped down a litre of very cold multi-fruit juice — he had been extremely thirsty. As the mere thought of food was unbearable he skipped that routine. Instead, he made himself a cup of extra-strong black coffee and popped a painkiller before beginning the laborious business of getting dressed. He did not care about what he threw on, whether or not he was wearing clashing colours was the least of his worries. He simply wanted to make sure that he left home fully clothed. Indeed, he double-checked himself in the mirror to ascertain that. As he was leaving his phone rang and when he answered it, it went dead. Shrugging and without the least curiosity, he replaced the receiver and put on his sunglasses — his eyes were bleary and burning like crazy — and he shuffled out of his flat.

He could feel eyes boring into his back as he shuffled towards the lift. He knew they belonged to the gossipy bunch, the bearers of the ghastly news about Ebony. They were a gloomy morbid lot so they must have imagined the very worst scenario involving him since they had not seen him for slightly over a day, after the fact.

'Sorry to disappoint you folks; I'm still alive and kicking,' he chuckled — his keen sense of humour was nearly intact, regardless of his foul mood and his sorry state.

For the very first time in the history of their long friendship Diego was waiting for him, although he arrived ahead of schedule himself. He was quite impressed but worried.

'Dude, you look an effing mess!' Diego exclaimed on seeing him.

'Thanks Diego. You're ever so charming and considerate,' he said, forcing a smile.

'What have you done to yourself?' he carried on, while eyeing Art.

'Are you playing cop with me or are you getting interested in me physically?' Art joked. As he began laughing he winced, feeling a stitch.

Diego playfully studied his appearance and told him that he was not his type. They both laughed, Art holding onto his aching sides.

'Seriously dude, what have you been up to?' Diego asked, soberly.

'I wish I knew,' Art replied, equally seriously.

'Want something to drink?' Diego asked, beckoning to a waiter.

'A Coke will do thanks.'

'You; a Coke?' he asked incredulously.

'I'll never ever taste another alcoholic beverage, as long as I live.'

'Are you dying today?' Diego asked, roaring with laughter.

'Oh, come on. Surely, you don't believe I can't do without a drink.'

'Must I answer that?'

'No, only if you want to.'

'Okay, I'm too nice to,' he laughed. 'Well, down to business,' he stated.

Watching his transformed expression, Art was not sure of what he preferred: the bantering that had been going on or what he suspected was going to be grave news. He did not have to wait for long before discovering the startling nature of the news: The dagger used to execute Ebony was identical to the one Diego had referred to in the murder of the African sex-worker. The information almost knocked him off his seat.

'This is serious business, buddy,' he heard himself stating slowly.

'Indeed, it is,' Diego agreed, before continuing.

He said that Ebony's case was being treated with utmost interest due to the dagger link. 'But, not just that link,' he said, studying Art's pale face.

'No? What else then?'

'You forgot to mention the note,' he stated with a frown.

'A note...? Goodness! Oh, yes, the warning,' he croaked.

'I'd say 'the threat'. I wonder how that could've escaped you.'

'Honestly, the past thirty-eight hours are a kind of blur. Is it important?'

'Anything could be important,' Diego replied, reflectively.

Watching Diego's pensive countenance, Art wondered whether to tell him about the first note. However, he changed his mind almost as soon as the thought occurred to him, telling himself that both cases were probably unrelated. He knew though, that that was unlikely; it was too much coincidence that the two incidents were so close in time. He also toyed with the idea of mentioning the troubling sensation that he had — that he was being followed around and that his every movement was being monitored. Also, that his phone had been ringing incessantly in the middle of the night. But for fear of being considered paranoid, he decided not to. Besides, he deemed it better not to distract Diego, better to let him concentrate on the Ebony case now highly important since it had been discovered that the dagger was a key factor. He would do anything — including bearing those inconveniences — to ensure that the perpetrator of that bloody act did not go unpunished.

Towards the end of their meeting he asked Diego how soon he would be able to claim Ebony's body. Diego replied that that depended on the depth and duration of the investigation of the relevant police departments involved. He was disappointed since he had expected to receive her body much sooner, to lay her to rest and get that part of the gruesome painful experience behind him.

Before they stood up to leave Diego confided that although it was not his intention to alarm him as a friend, he must inform him that the "Ebony case" was being taken absolutely seriously. Thereafter, he reminded him of the importance of being vigilant.

'Don't hesitate to call me whenever you feel it's necessary,' he concluded.

'Is there something you're not telling me, buddy?' Art inquired.

'Nope,' he replied rather hastily.

After they said goodbye at the street corner Art remained there for a while, chewing over most of their discussion. He was more worried about Diego's attitude at the end of the meeting than about most of the things he said. He had the feeling that he had not been fully forthright, that he knew much more than he had let on.

'Am I in real danger?' he wondered half aloud.

Paradoxically though, he was excited because as he saw it, if he was in danger then what he was onto was far huger than he had assumed at the outset, which might explain his sensation of being under constant surveillance. Suddenly, every stranger out there became a suspect and he began scrutinising every face that he deemed suspicious. Despite wanting to race back to the relative safety of his home, he believed that fresh air would do him a world of good since he had been cooped up for so long. He walked around for about an hour and then decided to head home. He had become very weak and the heat was getting unbearable.

He was immensely relieved when he arrived; the temperature therein was far better. He stripped down to his underpants and crawled into bed with his notepad. There were so many things he needed to put down on paper. He was scribbling away when his thoughts strayed to Regina. He wondered about her not showing up and if she was okay. It was the first time he had thought about her since he discovered Ebony's bloodied body. He decided that he would try to trace her even though he had no idea of where to start. He finally concluded that Santi's studio premises would be a good starting point, although she had warned him against going there. Shortly afterwards, he dozed off.

He was soon jolted awake by a horrible dream involving Regina. His heart was pounding away and his head was splitting. He became very worried because he had seen her in danger and it seemed so real. He reminded himself that given his concern about her before dozing off having such a dream was natural. That logic consoled him only momentarily; his disquiet continued to grow.

Subsequently, the issue of his safety returned to his mind. For the first time since Ebony's slaying he began wondering how the perpetrator found out where he lived. He was still pondering that matter when his phone started ringing. He slowly reached for the receiver and put it to his ear without saying a word. The caller spoke immediately and the voice was a woman's. Although it sounded frailer than he remembered it, he recognised it. He asked himself if he could still be dreaming since it was practically impossible that she could be calling him. He was absolutely certain that he did not give her his phone number.

'How did you get my number, Regina?' was all he could say.

'You're listed, Art,' she replied feebly.

That resolved his puzzle about how Ebony's executor had obtained his address. That fact had completely slipped his mind.

'Ah, sure, I'm listed,' he said, half to himself.

She then asked him if they could meet right away. His immediate impulse was to ask her if she did not think she owed him an explanation for standing him up but he checked himself reasoning that there had to be a logical reason for her behaviour. So instead, he asked her if their meeting could be the next day. Deep down, however, he was dying to pick her brains right away. Equally, despite his curiosity he was not in the mood to go anywhere; he was still feeling wobbly. She begged him to see her, stating that she was in grave trouble. Never one to turn his back on anyone in need, least of all a lady, he gave in.

She was seated in their usual corner, on the lower floor, in his pet haunt looking desolate, frightened, miserable and even smaller than her petite self. She had bags under her eyes the size of ping-pong balls. She looked every inch a shadow of herself. His heart sank as soon as he saw her. On seeing him she tried to force a smile but it came out all skewed.

'Hey! Are you okay?' he asked, trying to sound upbeat.

She nodded, although her countenance told a different story. She then apologised for not showing up for their appointment. He was so touched by her haggard look that he could no longer be mad at her. He brushed her apology aside telling her not to worry that what mattered was that she was there in one piece.

After settling down he asked her what was going on. She replied that she had been receiving death threats by phone and that on various occasions she had been told to control her tongue otherwise it would be ripped out. The caller warned her that those who talk too much quite often lost their tongue. Art asked her how long it had been going on and she said that the first call was late at night after their meeting. When he asked her if she knew where the calls were coming from she nodded.

Speaking slowly, she revealed that they were from an aggressive gang, members of a very dangerous notorious cult. His eyes popped. Then he shook his head to clear it. To his unvoiced question she replied that she took their threats seriously. Since she knew what they were capable of, she had left home and since then she had been living a kind of nomadic clandestine existence.

'Have you been to the police?'

'Police? Of course not! I can't do that!' she declared, alarmed.

'You can't? Or you don't want to?'

'I can't. My papers are not in order. I'm one of those people vulgarly refer to as "the undocumented". The callers are also threatening me with that, with blowing the whistle on me so that I'll be deported.'

'They are threatening you with that?' Art asked, indignantly.

'Yes. I'm sure they'll do it, too. They've done far worse things.'

'Let's go to the police and try to secure a deal.'

'Come on Art, you know that's out of the question.'

'If they're as dangerous as you claim, don't you think your life is more important than the risk of being deported?' he inquired worriedly.

'Art, I'd rather die than crawl home with my tail between my legs.'

The vehemence with which she made that declaration shocked him greatly. He wondered how anyone could get that desperate.

'It mayn't make sense to you but, I had to give up so much to get here. Everything I had was sacrificed — everything,' she emphasised.

'Could going back to nothing be worse than being taken back dead?'

'Far worse, Art, far worse,' she stated, close to tears.

'So, what exactly do you want me to do?'

'I need shelter for a day or two. Can you help me?'

He needed to consider her request; it was a tough one. Putting her up was complicated since she was not exactly a friend and he was living alone. However, at such short notice he could not call up any of his female friends. But, he was certain that he could not turn his back on her since he was partly responsible for her present woes. The humanitarian side of the issue aside, there also existed the selfish angle: Keeping her safe from any harm was in his interest. In the end, he decided that he would offer her accommodation for the night and make other arrangements later.

His decision brought her great relief. She thanked him profusely.

'I'm so sorry about this inconvenience. I wouldn't come to you if I had any other alternative. You see, I have my back to the wall,' she explained.

'Never mind,' he replied, reassuringly.

Apart from wanting more information about those calls he had many questions he wanted her to answer. However, she was looking awfully frail so he decided that before launching into anything that could vaguely be described as an interview he should offer her something to eat. She shook her head when he did. But unlike during their first meeting this time he insisted on her having a bite; she looked famished. Finally, she agreed to have a snack. He ordered just cola for himself because he was still feeling awfully dehydrated and he was craving something sweet and bubbly.

When their order arrived, she cut her grilled cheese and ham sandwich into tiny bits and she would occasionally pick up a piece with her fork and nibble at it. Clearly, she was not interested in it at all. He sat in silence watching her fiddle with it. Eventually, she pushed the plate aside and gave him an apologetic look, explaining that she had a knot in her stomach and that eating had become a great problem for her since her ordeal began. That information did not surprise him since she presented such an emaciated, miserable, pitiable sight. It was evident that she had not been eating regularly. He told her that given her circumstances, her lack of appetite was only natural. Nodding, she gave him a sad smile and then bowed her head.

'Have you been following the trail of the fires?' she asked suddenly.

Her question surprised him. His surprise was followed by a sense of guilt and then embarrassment. She was having troubles of her own yet she was interested in his concerns whereas, he had placed his journalistic interest before everything else.

'A lot's happened since then,' he stated, avoiding her gaze.

'Really; what have you discovered so far?' she smiled weakly.

He had a strong urge to tell her all about his experience inside the deceased man's flat and about the incredible things he saw there. He was also itching to fire the questions he had prepared for her days earlier. But he was certain that that was not the right thing to do, in view of her present circumstances. She was looking so tired. Instead, he smiled:

'We'll get there. First of all, let's take care of why you're here.'

He was getting really tired too and he figured that since he had decided to let her crash at his place it was unnecessary to continue hanging around. They both needed to rest. Shortly afterwards, they left the tavern at a slow pace. All the way home, he could feel eyes boring into his back. He did not want to alarm her further so he did not mention it. He went on conversing, pretending that nothing was amiss. Although he occasionally stole a backward glance, he could not spot his tail.

'Is everything alright?' she asked on two occasions.

'Oh! Sure, everything's perfect,' he lied.

Her question threw him since he believed that all along, he had been handling the situation with discretion.

By the time they got to his building he had got so uneasy and jumpy that any step further, he would have jumped out of his skin. He was immensely relieved when they walked through the building's front door. She seemed relieved too and even managed a big smile. That smile made him wonder if she had secretly been suffering her own fear of being followed or if his jumpiness had rubbed off on her. Whatever her reason might be, that smile was the best he had ever seen on her face.

CHAPTER 8

No sooner had they stepped out of the lift than he frowned. From that distance he could see something weird in his doorway. Since the tragic Ebony incident he had been making great efforts to be very aware of his surroundings and to watch his every step — literally and figuratively. Given that that awful episode was pretty recent and the wounds were still quite fresh, he was taking his lessons seriously. Regina appeared totally oblivious of what he had sighted until they were almost there. Then her eyes popped and, placing her hand over her mouth, she gasped and scuttled off to what she deemed a safe distance. She was trembling.

Although what was there made him recoil in revulsion, his curiosity would not let him stay away so he drew closer for a better look. There were tiny soft white feathers arranged in a circle on the floor and seated right in the centre was a small earthenware pot. A small white egg was half sticking out of the pool of blood inside the pot. Looking closer, he discovered that the pot also contained a little black pouch and more feathers, as well as various odds and ends which he could not figure out.

'Let's get out of here!' Regina shrieked a step away from hysterics.

'No way,' he declared.

'Did you say 'No way'? Do you know what that is?'

'For all I know it's nothing but an intimidating tactic!' Art asserted.

'No Art, you don't get it. That's *juju,* some kind of black magic.'

'Give me a break, Regina.'

'Agreed, but I'm not going in there,' she stated, indicating his door.

'I wonder how it got here,' he mumbled abstractedly, stepping away.

One by one, he pushed each neighbour's buzzer. But one by one, they shook their heads or shrugged their shoulders — nobody knew anything. At the end of that brief tour he returned, very disappointed since not even the nosiest of his neighbours, *Doña* Pepa, had seen or heard anything unusual. Practically impossible though he believed that was given that they all had a great penchant for minding other people's business, he had to accept what they had said.

The only thing he achieved from his round of inquiries was creating excitement among them. He succeeded in bringing them to their doors and the murmuring and neck-craning began. On seeing what was out there some of them made a hurried sign of the cross and rushed back inside, locking their doors as if that would block out the memory of what they had just seen. None were bold enough to approach for a closer look.

For once, just a glimpse is enough for these busybodies, he reflected.

Nevertheless, he knew them well enough to be certain that in no time twisted versions of what they had glimpsed would be making the rounds, not only of all the floors in the building but also of those on either side of it and probably beyond.

'What have you found out?' Regina asked from afar with anxiety.

'Nothing,' he said, raising his brow in surprise.

'I knew it.'

'How did you know it?'

'Art, when it comes to the occult, never take things at face value.'

'I don't get that.'

'I'll explain it but first of all, let's get out of here, please!'

Before accompanying her he wanted to do just one thing: record the scene, to avoid any tampering. He figured that if whoever that had done that could sneak in and out without being noticed then he or she could also make it all disappear, undetected. So although he was trembling too — but not outwardly like Regina was doing — instead of fleeing he went into his flat for his camera. He took several shots of the scene, put on disposable gloves and dumped everything into a dustbin bag.

He turned around to tell her that he was set and he discovered that she was no longer there. He panicked and dashed off in search of her. To compound matters, he did not know for how long she had been gone. He had been so busy taking the pictures and clearing up the mess that he could not recall when he last saw her. He was so agitated that he initially rushed into the lift without locking his door.

'How could I have let them snatch her right under my nose?'

He was so upset and so convinced that she had been abducted that when he stepped out of the lift and saw her crouching in a corner of the hallway he was quite startled.

'You scared me! I thought they had you!' he gasped.

'You're scaring me more with that,' she uttered, springing to her feet.

When he approached her she retreated. In confusion, he wondered why. Then he noticed that she was pointing at the dustbin bag.

'I'm scaring you with this? Of course I couldn't have left it there.'

'You shouldn't have touched it,' she almost yelled.

'Don't be so superstitious.'

'Very funny, coming from someone who keeps a rabbit's foot and a horseshoe.'

'Of course, you know the cases are unrelated,' he replied defensively.

'Maybe someday you'll tell me how unrelated. But until then let me get one thing clear: Are you really telling me about superstition? I can't believe you, Art!'

She was bristling as she stood arms akimbo, facing him. Though he was seething, he was trying hard to be rational. He understood that she was not living her best moments and he did not want to aggravate her situation. So he stated gently,

'Don't get me wrong. I believe that alternative realities exist. Even if I didn't I've had more than enough reasons in the last few days to do so. Regardless, I'm not going to let anyone browbeat me. See this?" he asked, raising the bag. 'It's absolute trash.'

Having made his point he walked past her, went through the front door, headed straight to the dustbin and dumped the bag and its contents in it with great satisfaction.

When he returned to the hallway he asked her what she was going to do about her situation since she did not want to go into his flat. Close to tears, she admitted that she had no idea. He knew that it would be unfair to leave her to her fate but, he could not think of anywhere to take her. It was getting late and he was exhausted. It had been a turbulent day and he wished he could be by himself for a while, to think. Equally, he felt like talking; he wanted to find out more about what he had just dumped. However, he knew that the time was not right; she was still too shaken by the sight of it. Since he was not disposed to hang around the hallway for an eternity, he eventually suggested that they should take a walk. They both needed some fresh air.

After they had roamed around aimlessly for some time he proposed sitting down for a moment. He was tired and wired up. Since he was dying for a cold bubbly drink, they stepped into a cafe. She would not have anything to eat or drink because she was too strung up to even contemplate either. Conversely, he was so thirsty that he gulped down his first bottle of cola at a go and ordered another.

Quite a few minutes had gone by since they had sat down but they were both silent, each lost in thoughts. While he was trying to come up with a solution for her accommodation problem, she was thinking about how to get out of the mesh she had inadvertently got entangled in. It suddenly occurred to him that he could check her into a boarding house — for the night at least. Nonetheless, no sooner had he come up with that idea than he remembered that it was summer and as usual Madrid was teeming with tourists. The likelihood of finding a vacant room was extremely remote, if not non-existent.

One hour later, though their quest had turned out to be fruitless, something positive came from their effort: in one boarding house they were informed that there would be a vacant room in the morning and that they could have it for one night. He considered that to be better than nothing. He offered to hang around the city centre with her and check her in after breakfast so that she could have some rest and they would meet later to discuss their next step. Seeing her tired face light up and hearing the relief in her voice made the effort worth his every while.

Since they had been together for many hours and she had eaten practically nothing, he suggested that she should have something to eat. To his surprise, he did not need to do any persuading because her relief at having a place to lay down her head was such that she agreed instantly. When she finished snacking he engaged her in small talk until he figured that she was relaxed enough to talk about serious matters.

He started by asking her how she knew that none of his neighbours had seen the individual/individuals who deposited the stuff in his doorway. She shuddered before explaining that she knew that the scene outside his door had been created by no other than the members of that notorious cult.

She paused before adding that they had different magic powers, including the ability to appear and disappear at will.

Although he did not voice his scepticism, his face reflected it and she told him that if he did not believe that information, she would give him the name of the cult so that he could crosscheck it as well as other curiosities related to the practices its members indulged in. Something in her tone gave him the impression that she was slightly offended by his incredulity so he quickly tried to make amends by admitting that for him, it was a totally unfamiliar territory and if in any way he had shown the least sign of doubt it was definitely not because of her account but because of the matter itself. Having tendered his apology, he implored her to continue her story.

She informed him that members of the cult were very close-knit and would do anything to protect one another no matter how far apart they were, geographically. They had a special way of recognising one another and they often communicated through special signs and symbols which also made it possible for them to transmit messages without such messages being intercepted by the uninitiated. Their meetings and rituals usually took place deep in the forest at ungodly hours.

She grabbed his undivided attention when she stated that even overseas, they preserved their customs and rituals. That information took his mind back to the shrine-like room in the deceased man's flat and the eerie experience he had had there. His thoughts strayed momentarily and he began thinking about the weird paraphernalia on display in the shrine-like room. When she stated that what had been deposited in his doorway was a clear proof of such practices he was forced to rein in his straying concentration. He immediately asked her why she interpreted it as a ritual practice and not as a mere coercive tactic. She smiled wryly and told him that she could spend the whole night explaining the reasons to him but clearly, he would not believe her. Therefore, if his assumption made him feel better, it was okay by her.

No amount of assumption was going to make him feel any better about the whole issue particularly after all he had experienced in that flat. However, that was something he was not ready to touch upon yet. His seeming scepticism notwithstanding, he wanted to listen to everything she could tell him about the cult which he knew absolutely nothing about. He was so intrigued by everything he had heard so far that he was not about to let the opportunity of learning more slip past him. Consequently, he tried to make it the focus of the conversation by bombarding her with questions about it.

'Why are you so interested in it?' she asked, anxiously.

'Well, its members got interested in me. So, I'd like to know why.'

'How're you going to do that?'

'I'm thinking of taking the game to their turf and, I need your help.'

'My help?' she uttered, looking around.

'Yes. As things stand right now, you're the only one who can really help me. What's your answer?' he asked, looking at her imploringly.

A gasp escaped her and a worried expression replaced the tired one she had been wearing. She lowered her eyes and was silent for a couple of minutes. Eventually, she raised her head and, looking straight into his eyes, she stated that he was asking for too much from her. He nodded, agreeing with her. When she asked him what exactly he wanted her to do, he replied that he needed to know every tiny detail about the cult. She mumbled that that could bring her lots of problems and he reminded her that she was already in trouble. She nodded slowly.

The first thing she told him was that the name of the cult instilled terror in many people since the members were believed to possess real diabolic powers, apart from the aforementioned ability to appear and disappear at will. She said that in the distant past, the members' rituals included offering human sacrifice in their shrine but that that practice had since given way to animal sacrifice. As he sighed with relief she mentioned that in some circles it was believed that the original practice still lingered, particularly during special ceremonies at certain times of the year. While shivering at that information, he tried to convince himself that it was nothing but an urban myth.

Talking about rituals and sacrifices, he recalled the inscriptions on the hilt of the dagger stuck into Ebony, inscriptions which had got him to conclude that it was no ordinary dagger. Then an idea struck him and he decided to act upon it. He dug into his backpack, brought out the pictures, riffled through them and placed one with a close-up of the dagger face up on the table. He watched her to see how she would react to it. When she gasped and pulled away violently, he smiled to himself. Her reaction was a clear sign that she knew a lot about it. His hypothesis was right.

'The dagger,' she said under her breath.

'Yes, do you recognise it?'

'Yes, I kind of do. It bears the symbol of the cult,' she whispered, looking away.

'What more can you tell me about it?'

'Where did you find that picture?' she asked, hedging his question.

'I took it. The dagger was right outside my door.'

'Outside your door; really?' she asked in awe. 'That's not good. Their leaving it there is like the Mafia leaving their call card.'

'Yes, I've already figured that out.'

She was trembling all over — so violently that she eventually took her hands off the table and placed them on her thighs to hide them.

'I was told that an identical dagger was used to kill an African sex-worker some weeks ago. Did you hear about it?' he inquired gently.

Her face clouded over and her trembling got worse.

'That lady was no sex-worker, Art,' she stated, close to tears.

'How do you know that?'

'She's me!'

'She's you?' he asked, looking at her as though she had gone mad.

'Did I say that? Excuse me. I've been having such a terrible time that I barely know what I'm saying. What I mean is that she was a very close friend of mine.'

'Oh, so you knew her well,' he said, showing great interest.

'I knew her as well as I know myself. We were that close,' she said.

'I'm awfully sorry to hear that,' he stated, earnestly.

'Thanks, Art. But, what she really needs now is justice. Please!'

When he asked her what he could do she implored him to carry on with his investigation to bring the criminals to justice. He assured her that he would but that he would also need her full cooperation. She nodded, looking away. She was trying to hide the tears which were now very close to the surface. She looked so fragile, so helpless and so pained that he truly wished he could help her feel better. At a loss as to how to do that, he decided to concentrate on what he truly knew how to do — conduct a sound interview. That, he hoped, would help him find out how to go about fulfilling her wish.

'So, you knew this woman well enough to know she wasn't a sex-worker. Can you tell me what happened to her and how it came about?'

'Listen Art, it's as simple as this: she was used as an example.'

'As an example?' he asked, puzzled.

'Yes, an example to those who might be considering insubordination.'

'I don't get it,' he said, shaking his foggy head.

'Nobody gets it Art because nobody really cares. Since nobody really cares, nobody makes a true effort to find out the facts!'

'I'm all ears, Regina. Could you enlighten me?' he coaxed.

Reluctantly, she began a complex account through which he learnt that the same bunch responsible for that unfortunate woman's death ran a big-time racket which, among other things, involved the "importation" of girls from Africa — Nigeria, precisely. They were into human trafficking. They sponsored the girls' trips, making all the travel arrangements including obtaining the visas. They made them believe that they were coming to Europe to work in lucrative professions, usually show business. Many of them were young and naive and others were not so young. But, the one thing they all had in common was the dream of a golden future. On arrival, however, they were usually forced into prostitution. They virtually became prisoners in brothels or in flats that were all but brothels. They seldom saw the outside world and if in the remotest of cases they did, it was only in the company of and under the close surveillance of their lords and masters. Art recalled the scene on the commuter train and asked himself if there was a connection.

When he wondered aloud how it was possible to force anyone into that age-old profession, Regina explained that those criminals employed different coercive methods to make their victims become submissive. To start with, the victims were completely isolated so they were at their mercy. The poor girls were sometimes force-fed drugs to create dependency, making them absolutely malleable. Another method was abuse — physical and psychological. Even before bringing the girls to Europe the gang subjected them to psychological warfare in order to safeguard their investments. They made them swear before a shrine that they would pay back every dime invested in them. Before the swearing bit their nails and hair taken from their heads and their private parts were used for another ritual. Since in many parts of Africa there is a strong belief that hair and nails represent the real essence of a person and, could be used to inflict great harm on someone, the hapless victims were made to believe that failure to pay back their debt would mean paying dearly, paying with their lives. In their desperation to escape hardship back home they agreed to such conditions. Frequently, the sum was so inflated that the poor victims were subjected to debt bondage, another insurmountable hurdle.

He was stunned to hear that some of them were even sold to high-bidding European nationals as sex slaves. He was shocked further when he heard that if by chance the girls got knocked up their babies were sometimes sold to desperate couples in Europe in bogus adoption arrangements, another lucrative business. In other words, the poor hapless victims were used to the full.

Another group of victims were young children; children handed over to so-called relatives by trusting parents after being assured that their offspring were coming to Europe to receive a good education, a passport to a brilliant future. Unfortunately, most of them ended up being subjected to domestic servitude.

When he asked her why such victims never took their cases to the relevant authorities in their countries of residence, she explained that it was often due to fear of deportation since with time their visas expired and most of them became illegal aliens. At any rate, many were "undocumented" because they were stripped of their passports on arrival. Lack of freedom; since they lived in virtual prison in their brothels from where escape was difficult and dangerous; was another obstacle. Also, due to such isolation the girls did not speak the language so making their plight known was practically impossible. Regina concluded by stating that the very few who tried to revolt seldom lived to tell their stories, like her friend.

Art asked her to tell him about her friend and she told him that she had been a promising TV actress in Nigeria and that she had been tricked into coming to Spain by one of those con artists. When she met him in Lagos, he posed as a show-biz agent seeking new talent to promote overseas. To make his offer even juicier and to boost her trust in him he told her not to worry about the cost. They signed a supposed agreement in which he undertook to foot the bill for her travel and for everything related to it and she would pay him back after signing her first show-biz contract. On getting to Spain and discovering that the whole thing was a sham, not to mention the deplorable method of payment, she had threatened to go to the police with her story.

'Well, you know the rest of the story,' Regina concluded with a sigh.

When Art pointed out that the area where her body had been found was notorious for sex business, Regina looked straight at him and asked him what could be more credible and natural than a supposed sex worker meeting that kind of horrible end during her normal course of duty. After all, hers was a risky profession given the type of individuals who patronised her and her lot.

'Occupational hazards do exist, you know,' she added, smiling wryly. 'Well, the police are usually not too concerned about investigating such deaths, especially when they involve undocumented aliens. How would they go about it anyway?' she uttered rhetorically, with an ironic smile.

When he expressed his bafflement regarding their leaving their dagger stuck in her, since it could be traced to them, she explained that surely they played on the assumption that the case would not be taken seriously by the police. After all, what was one prostitute's death — an unfortunate prostitute executed with a dagger by a pervert? The group's true intention had been to send a warning to the rest of the girls since on seeing images of the dagger in the news they would surely recognise the symbol.

He took a deep breath. The whole affair sounded weird and much more intricate than he had imagined. Part of his immediate confusion was why Regina had not been subjected to the same raw deal as the rest. He wanted to ask her more questions too as he was yet to find the relevance of everything he had just heard to the fires. But he felt that he had pushed her enough for one day.

His resolution notwithstanding, for some reason he asked her if any members of the cult were involved in art trafficking — if they had art business dealings with Santi. Though it was only a wild guess, he suspected he had hit the bull's-eye when she gave a start. Then he stated that if there was nothing shady around the statuette, he could not understand why he was being persecuted for investigating what to him was a mere paranormal occurrence nor why she was being threatened for talking to him. She was silent. Somehow, he knew that what had started as a paranormal investigation was about to take a totally new direction, an exciting one too.

Suddenly, he declared that he wanted to go to Nigeria. Startled, she asked him what for and he replied that he needed to investigate further.

'Before taking the plunge don't you think you should find out more about this lot?' she urged, after several failed attempts to dissuade him.

'That's exactly what I'm trying to do, Regina.'

'Was that what you meant by 'taking the game to their turf'? It's a rough turf, Art. Really rough turf,' she declared gloomily.

CHAPTER 9

He crashed out as soon as he got home — he was fagged out considering how hellish the last couple of days had been. He intended to spend the whole day sleeping and then meet with Regina in the evening to continue their interview.

However, his plan to have a peaceful rest was soon disrupted by the arrival of an uninvited guest. The first inkling he had that he had company was a fragrance in the air — it was familiar. As he was trying to place it he heard a deep voice that was familiar too. He was wondering where he had heard it when it asked,

'Did you enjoy your tour of the flat, *Oyibo*?'

Of course, the mention of the flat resolved the puzzle. It was the same voice that had addressed him in the deceased man's flat. He immediately understood why both the fragrance and the voice were so familiar.

What are you doing here, he wanted to ask. However, he was suffering from extreme paralysis, typical of such nightmares.

'You're treading an unknown territory, watch your step else you'll end up like her.'

'Who are you and who's the 'her' you mentioned?' he finally managed to croak.

'You'll find out both in due course. But remember, you've been warned. Back off!'

He was still trying to make sense of everything when he saw a man before him. Until then he had only heard his voice and smelt his fragrance. Now he could see his face and his clothes — he was excellently dressed — and many other details.

This must be the weirdest of dreams, or I'm going stark raving mad or — he was analysing the situation when his uninvited guest interjected.

'Once again: you're not mad. You're not dreaming either.'

I must wake up and stop this madness, he went on rationalising.

'I insist, you're not dreaming. Listen, someone's trying to reach you,' he whispered.

The phone started ringing, instantaneously. At first, Art assumed it was just a part of the weird dream so he did not respond to it.

'Come on, react. It could be useful information,' the visitor urged.

He finally forced himself to come awake and certainly, his phone was ringing. The last thing he heard before opening his eyes was,

'This isn't over. Be careful, *Oyibo*.'

He managed to reach the phone just before the answering machine was activated. The caller was Diego. He told him that it was imperative that they met because he had some information related to his investigation. Typically, Art would have jumped for joy at that news but instead, he implored Diego to give him about two hours to get to the venue of the meeting. His priority then was to go back to sleep and hopefully, return to the dream. He was mystified about the close link between his dream where the visitor told him that someone was about to contact him and the real-life ringing of the phone.

As he made his way back to bed he froze and began sniffing the air. He had just discerned, to his greatest astonishment, that the fragrance he had perceived in his dream was hanging in the air, in his bedroom.

'It can't be. I must be imagining things,' he said.

Almost at the same instant it dawned on him that not only did he have a vivid memory of all that had transpired in the dream, but that he also had the image of the subject that featured in it, still very fresh in his mind. He quickly got out a notepad and feverishly made a sketch, including every tiny detail he could recall about the man. He then noted everything he remembered about their conversation. He also jotted down the word "*Oyibo*" by which he had been addressed twice. A casual glance at his timepiece made him aware of how late in the day it was. He could not believe that he had slept for that long.

Be that as it may, he ignored that fact and returned to bed to force himself to go back to sleep and to continue dreaming, hopefully. In the end, however, his effort fruitless, he became rather frustrated and reluctantly got up and got set for his meeting.

Diego was looking serious when he showed up. Even before he took his seat Art knew that something was gravely wrong.

'What's the matter?' he asked, after their exchange of greetings.

'Take a look,' Diego said, pushing a folded sheet of paper which he pulled out from his pocket and placed on the table, towards him.

Art picked it up and slowly unfolded it.

'Tell your friend to back off!' he read.

He noticed that the message was written in the same scrawl and similar ink as the 'Back off, gringo!' message that had been shoved into his pocket.

'How did you get that?' he asked, acutely stunned.

'It's mailed to me at work; can you imagine?' Diego spluttered — he was seething.

'That's puzzling.'

'More puzzling is the fact that the 'ink' is actually blood.'

'What? That's weird!' Art uttered, thoroughly shaken.

'Yes indeed. This is a copy; the original's being analysed in our lab to determine what sort of blood it is.'

'It's clear: I'm beginning to get under people's skin,' Art declared.

He was wondering anew whether to mention the note he had found in his pocket when Diego revealed a more shocking piece of information related to the supposed sex-worker who was brutally murdered. He had gained access to her autopsy report and discovered that not only was she stabbed to death with that ornamental dagger but also that she had had her tongue cut off, among other brutalities inflicted on her.

Art's heart started beating wildly — he remembered the threats Regina told him she received. He told Diego her situation and asked for some sort of protection for her.

'Dude, that's asking for the impossible,' he enunciated.

'Why is it so complicated?'

'As a rule, as long as these people keep their crap to themselves, we don't meddle; we just let them be,' he stated levelly.

'Is that an official stance?' Art asked, aghast.

'Not really,' he replied, looking away.

Art was dumbfounded. Sadly, he began reflecting on Regina's theory regarding the police attitude. He shook his head several times in astonishment because of how close her conjecture was to the attitude Diego had just displayed. From afar, he heard Diego referring to his investigation in a very solemn tone:

'Dude, you don't know what you're delving into. As a friend I believe that you should consider dropping it.'

'You can't suggest that, buddy. Besides, I desperately need your help.'

'And, I desperately need you to stay out of avoidable trouble. This particular crap's huge, far huger than you can ever imagine!'

Once again, Art shook his head incredulously as he observed his friend's serious countenance. He understood that Diego was trying to protect him but at the same time, he could not understand how he could sound so cold and act so nonchalant in the face of somebody's suffering. That was not like the Diego he had known for donkey's years.

Since Art was not prepared to give up he tried another angle.

'Are you telling me to shoo this lady onto the street and pretend that nothing's going on? Come on, you know me much better than that.'

'You're right, I know you. That's exactly why I'm warning you.'

'Please, help me with this lady. She could be in real danger.'

'How's that your business, anyway?'

'It's my business for it's my fault. It all started when she was spotted talking to me.'

'She'd probably have got into trouble with or without you.'

'Who knows? But as things stand, what's happening to her is entirely my fault.'

'I can't promise you anything, dude. But, I'll see what I can do.'

'Thanks a great deal; I owe you one,' Art stated, relieved.

A moment of silence followed during which he thought carefully about the next thing he was going to say. He was hesitant because he was certain about how Diego was going to react to it. Finally, he let it out anyway.

'I'm travelling to Nigeria.'

'Then my suspicion's right; you're completely off your rockers!' Diego roared, glowering at him. 'When did you veer away from your usual line of investigation? Why don't you stick with pursuing your ghosts or whatever?' he raged on.

'Hey! Let's get something clear here: I didn't pursue this lot, they came after me.'

'Dude, just leave the criminals to the police, will you?'

'Diego, you're not listening. I didn't start the hostilities!' Art huffed.

Then there was absolute silence. Diego looked slightly embarrassed. He was analysing his exaggerated reaction.

Art was observing him. He was convinced that his friend knew far more about the case than he was willing to let on. What he did not know was the turmoil Diego was in — he was suffering from divided loyalties. Much as he wanted to help his friend, Diego could not reveal anything or go into details that might compromise an ongoing investigation.

Looking truly remorseful, he eventually spoke. He tendered his apology to Art for what he described as his over-the-top display.

'There's no way I can dissuade you from going, right?' he then concluded calmly and resignedly, forcing a smile.

'You're right.'

'Okay. When'll it be?'

'I haven't worked out the details yet.'

'Goodness! You're crazy, you really are. But, watch your step, dude.'

'I will. I promise,' Art grinned, patting his good friend on the shoulder.

After that get-together Art had some time to while away before meeting with Regina so he decided to take a walk. Though the heat outside was excruciating, he needed to digest the bits of information he had just received. Generally, he processed his thoughts much better when he was on the move. Diego's belief that he could be in danger had really shaken him up, although he had camouflaged that fact. Trying to calm his nerves was another reason for the walk.

After a lengthy walk he sat down for a drink. In want of something worthwhile to do while waiting for Regina, he got out his sketch of the man in his dream. He wanted to include some details, like the scar running diagonally across his chin, which he had recalled while taking his walk. Then he started putting finishing touches to the sketch as a whole.

He was still at it when Regina walked up to his table. She took a look at the sketch and her countenance froze — she was in shock. Surprised by that transformation, he asked her what the matter was. She said nothing. She seemed totally transfixed by the image. When she finally spoke he got staggered because according to her his sketch was the living image of the man who had been struck dead in his flat.

'A living image, huh? What an irony. Do tell me you're kidding'

'That kind of humour's too black for me,' Regina declared, seriously.

Looking as tense as ever, she continued staring at the sketch and shaking her head.

'His name's Friday but he was known as The Prince,' she spluttered.

'Friday; just like the day of the week?'

'Yeah, he was born on a Friday.'

'He died on a Friday too. Weird! What a hell of a coincidence!'

'Yeah, that's life,' she stated, emotionlessly.

He began staring at the wall in front of him, thinking about the spooky Friday coincidence.

'By the way, where did you get that sketch?' her voice reached him.

'I made it,' he replied, turning to face her.

'You made it? How did you do that?' she asked in total disbelief.

'I simply reproduced my dream image.'

'He appeared in your dream? Unbelievable!'

'I share your sentiment but please, believe me.'

At that point he reminded her that she was still on her feet and nodding, she sank into a chair without taking her eyes off the sketch.

'Anyhow, got any idea as to why he chose to seek me out?' Art asked.

'You sought him out first, remember? You were in his flat.'

He was about to tell her about his experience there but changed his mind and asked,

'Do you think his visit is because of mine?'

'Maybe,' she shrugged, before asking, 'Did he speak?'

Nodding, he flipped through his notepad and started reading out their dialogue. When he got to the part where the visitor mentioned a female, she started. But, he was too engrossed in his reading to notice.

'Still the same bully,' she spat out. 'Anyhow, I think he's got something for you.'

'What? He's got something for me? Weird, but interesting,' he said, turning his gaze from the notes. 'Why's he still hanging around anyway?' he asked, facing her.

She explained: 'When people die they don't just disappear. They hang around for a period of time which varies from three months to three years since it takes them a while to assimilate the fact that they're no longer on this plane and that they should proceed onto the next one. The feeling of disorientation is more acute in people who meet a sudden end, as was the case with Friday. Generally, these people, though departed, continue with their normal activities and routines since they're unaware of their new reality. They hang around their usual circles, trying to participate in conversations and in a host of other activities but, they go basically unnoticed. With time, since most humans are completely unaware of their presence, they interpret that as a conscious effort on the part of people to ignore them and they're ultimately forced to "withdraw". Thenceforth, only the gifted would be able to establish any form of communications with them. Some others though, continue hanging around because they need to get things fixed.'

When she paused Art remarked,

'If that's really the case, then people should be bumping into departed loved ones everywhere they go.'

'They often do, both literally and figuratively, but not everybody's capable of sensing the presence of the departed. If you didn't possess special powers, you wouldn't have been aware of Friday's visit, even though there were tell-tale signs such as the trail the fragrance he was wearing left in the air,' she explained.

When Art wondered aloud if that visit could have been a dream, she simply shrugged and smiled. She concluded her lecture by stating,

'Mankind has become so empirical in nature that people are losing other senses, mainly the ability to remain linked to other realms.'

Then there was silence. Art went on chewing on the information he had just been fed, trying to digest it all. He had always prided himself as a true master of the paranormal but after listening to Regina intently it dawned on him that he could do with a refresher or even a beginner course. Suddenly he started feeling weird. The sensation was like the one he had experienced in his last moments in Friday's flat.

'Are you okay?' her voice reached him.

That broke the spell. He described what he had just experienced — gooseflesh and all — to which she replied that someone or something might be trying to reach him.

'Is that a joke?' he asked seriously.

'No, it's absolutely not.'

'Please tell whoever or whatever that I'm not around,' he joked.

She laughed heartily for the very first time. He liked the sound of her laughter. He realised that with each meeting he was getting fonder of her. However, he instantly cautioned himself to concentrate on the great volume of work ahead. Her voice broke into his thoughts at that point. He had not been listening. Since he was too embarrassed to ask her what she had said, he made do with the tail end of it which was,

'Seriously, such sudden gooseflesh usually announces a presence. But don't worry, with time you'll get used to it.'

'Do you receive such visitors?' he asked with interest.

'Yes. They're usually departed relatives. They appear in my sleep to announce important events or to warn me about impending danger.'

'That's creepy!' he observed, shuddering.

'No, not creepy; it's useful and comforting. It gives me the feeling that there are people watching over me.'

He was studying her face to see if she was serious when bits of his conversation with Friday came to him. He asked,

'By the way, what does *Oyibo* mean?'

'It means 'white man'. Why are you interested in it?'

'It's because Friday addressed me as that.'

'Did he? Well, typical.'

'What's that?'

'Never mind; it's unimportant.'

Seeing that she was not ready to go into details he asked her if she had had enough rest. She replied that she had been too worried to sleep. Although he was awfully anxious about her safety, mainly after what he had learnt from Diego, he assured her that everything would work out fine. He was worried about her accommodation problem too but he did not bring it up. His immediate priority was for them to continue the interview.

He needed her help to link the fires, to know how she had escaped the raw deal the rest of the girls had been subjected to and to find out more about the cult. The first question he asked her was the one directly related to her and her answer was quite enlightening. She explained that her arrangement with the crooks was a people smuggling one, which was different from the human trafficking one that most of the other girls had. On asking her the difference she replied that she had paid an exorbitant fee, which had entailed selling everything she had. It had been okay since she had been in need of a fresh start, but she would not explain why. She said that people who were smuggled under her type of arrangement were usually free on arrival at their destination, while those who were trafficked under an all-expense-paid deal were enslaved.

'So people smuggling isn't the same as human trafficking, right?'

'Absolutely right. To start with, the victims of the latter are usually victims of white slave trade, sexual slavery or whatever you choose to call it. That's big business Art; however, no one seems to notice. It's the third biggest revenue generator worldwide, beaten only by drug trafficking and arms smuggling. It's true that in both people smuggling and human trafficking there are innocent victims. But in the former the victims are often luckier — they obtain their freedom, albeit having been bled dry.'

At the end of her explanation he remarked that he could not understand how the perpetrators of both cold-blooded acts managed to make people fall for their scams. Although he had meant that merely as a comment it somehow sounded like a criticism of the victims — even to him. He held his breath, wondering how she would react. To his relief she paid no heed to his tone; she simply went on with her explanation.

'Some believe that they use supernatural powers, thanks to their link to this cult, to convince or influence people to do their bidding.'

'And what do you think?'

'What I think or rather what I believe is that these people are con artists — they are very smooth operators. Furthermore, you can't overlook one important detail: they prey on people's desperation. You know, what the people in both groups have in common is a strong desire to flee their country for various reasons, mainly economic. They just want to better their lot,' she concluded, bowing her head.

He felt guiltier than ever since apparently, before he bumped into her she had simply been struggling to make ends meet. Suddenly, however, all that had changed for her because of him. He knew that he was morally obliged to do all he could to get her out of the mess he had got her submerged in. His acute pang of guilt notwithstanding, he wanted to get to the bottom of his investigation first and make amends afterwards.

No sooner had he made that resolution than he heard himself asking her, 'Tell me; how were you smuggled in?'

'Smuggled in? You make me sound like a kind of contraband goods,' she laughed.

'Okay, excuse me; no offence meant,' he laughed in embarrassment.

'No offence taken; I do feel like contraband sometimes.'

'I'll rephrase that question: How were you brought in?'

'I came in as part of a dance troupe to participate in a music festival in Bilbao.'

Then she looked around. She was wearing a worried expression.

'Is something wrong?' he asked, concerned.

'No,' she replied, still looking around. 'Well, where were we?'

'About the way you came in. It's an original plot; it must've entailed a lot of planning,' he observed, impressed by the intricacy.

'Yes, all sorts of intricate planning are involved in the business.'

'Mm, that's interesting. And, what happened afterwards?'

'I was let loose by the head of the contingent as soon as the whole troupe was through with the immigration formalities at the airport.'

'Fascinating,' he nodded, encouraging her to continue.

She said that from the airport she had called a contact in Madrid who then gave her an address to come to. She had paid an additional fee for that service back in Nigeria and also for a job placement. Allegedly, they had found her something in a museum. They even showed her a professionally written letter on authentic-looking letterhead, supposedly from that museum, confirming the offer. However, on arrival a list of menial jobs, from which she was ordered to choose, was shoved into her face. After protesting, she was told that it was simply a case of Hobson's choice: she could take it or leave it. She later discovered from other victims that that practice was the rule rather than the exception.

He was about to ask her why no one had ever taken any serious action against them when he realised how absurd that would sound. So instead, he asked her to throw more light on the "all sorts of intricate planning" which she had mentioned earlier. She explained that the more one paid, the more sophisticated and elaborate the plans were and the faster, safer and more direct the trip. For instance, the con men often greased the right palms to get their "clients'" names included in the contingent list for international conferences.

'Wow! And do they always pull that off?'

'Uh-huh, without any difficulty. Corruption's endemic in my society.'

'There's corruption even in such high places?'

'Yeah, and sometimes it's much higher in such so-called high places.'

He could not help but acknowledge the ingenuity and the guile, not to mention the networking skills, of the crooks.

Then he asked her about the less-sophisticated deals. She replied that those who paid the cheapest fees got a very rough deal since their trip usually lasted anywhere between nine and thirty-six months. It was a risky round-the-world trip, sort of, which took those poor souls across African deserts, highlands and lowlands and what have you. The last lap was often life-taking — it was usually between Morocco and Spain in crowded rafts or canoes or so-called boats known as *pateras*, in deplorable conditions. The crossing was sometimes made in awful weather.

Some freelance agents in charge of shipping them across from Morocco preferred to do so in terrible weather, when the sea was at its roughest and visibility was at a minimum; that way it was easier for the *pateras* to escape the detection of the Spanish border authorities. A lot of them lost their lives in the process due to drowning since the precarious boats did not stand a chance of surviving under such extreme weather conditions. Generally though, the summer months were favoured since the risk of storms was reduced — the sea itself was treacherous enough. However, dehydration or other unforeseen circumstances became their formidable enemy.

Unfortunately, when those avoidable incidents happened — deaths resulting from drowning, dehydration or sunstroke — the victims were numerous. That was because due to greed on the part of all those involved in that inhuman business, the victims were packed like sardines in their precarious boats with no water or food and poor sanitary conditions.

'Oh, yes. They're frequently featured in the news,' Art observed.

'Sadly, they've become a constant feature of the news,' she intoned.

There was silence again. As he was about to raise the issue of her accommodation she smiled faintly and asked him if he had been able to talk to Santi. He smilingly replied that though reaching him had been tough, he had persisted and finally secured an interview for the next day. Still smiling, she said that he would definitely have fun interviewing him. He needed no crystal ball to know what she meant — he had gathered that from others who knew Santi. He smiled knowingly at her.

Thereafter, he brought up her accommodation problem. He was relieved when she revealed that a friend of hers, a fellow cleaning woman, Amina, from North Africa, had offered her a place for a couple of days. She lived in a shantytown-like settlement with fellow North Africans. Amina had assured her that she would be safe there since it was a close-knit community and any intruder would stick out like a sore thumb. He instantly understood why she had been somewhat calm. Expressing his relief, he offered to accompany her there so she would get some well-deserved rest. Afterwards, he would go home and do the same.

CHAPTER 10

'Gorgeous!' Art gasped as he gawked at the artist's impressive mansion. It was sprawling in a valley, surrounded by elm trees. A mountain range, which was snow covered for many months of the year, formed a backdrop to it. The blend of the mansion and the entire setting was breathtaking. He was transfixed.

After recovering from the impact produced by that magnificent vista, he slowly retraced his steps to the town square — he had arrived way too early for his interview. His excitement over the prospect of finally meeting Santi had reached fever pitch the previous night so he had hardly caught a wink. Consequently, he left home earlier than he had planned. Of course he just had to wait till the appointed time. Santi had laid emphasis on the fact that he should be there at 11 a.m. adding, 'Not earlier and not later.'

He had time to kill so he rambled around the old part of the town for a while, taking in the ancient architecture. He found the low, mostly white buildings with their beautiful slate roofs charming, a great contrast from the tall, massive, intimidating structures he had got used to seeing in big cities.

After sightseeing he stepped into a beckoning cafe for a much needed cup of strong black coffee to clear his increasingly hazy mind. The effects of the previous night's lack of sleep were becoming palpable. The one thing he needed was a clear mind to meet that enigmatic individual, to have what promised to be a challenging interview. And it would be challenging, if all he had heard about Santi so far was anything to go by.

Art wove his way through the packed cafe. As always, he could not help but wonder how the country could progress economically as it was doing then. He believed that the people in the cafe outnumbered those slogging away at their desks in the office. All around him people were chatting away heartily. Everyone seemed to know everyone else — not surprising, as it was such a small town.

He got curious looks as he headed towards the service counter. He supposed that he was sticking out like a sore thumb, what with his foreign looks, quite apart from the fact that he was a stranger there. His assumption was soon confirmed: Keeping a straight face, he looked on as they openly talked about him, wondering aloud what a *guiri* — meaning foreigner or foreign tourist — was doing out there on a weekday. Indeed, they assumed he was a tourist with zero knowledge of the language.

Very much amused, he thought about the usual cliché in Spain: It is believed that the reason why get-togethers, including formal ones, drag on for as long as they do is that no one ever wants to be the first to depart. Doing so would mean exposing oneself to the danger of being ripped apart by the rest, with their tongues. Thus everyone strives to be the last to stand up. While gossiping is unofficially recognised as a national pastime, only a handful of people openly admit taking delight in it. Generally people say that they simply love chatting and knowing what is going on around them, ignoring the fact that most of their so-called chatting is done behind the backs of those concerned.

Art soon began feeling uncomfortable because the air was terribly smoke-filled, a great bother for his smarting eyes. He wondered if Spain would ever contemplate following in the footsteps of his country which five months earlier, had banned smoking in such places. Rubbing his eyes, he ordered his coffee in flawless Spanish, startling most of those standing nearby as well as the waiter. He loved the shocked looks on their faces and although he managed to stop himself from roaring with laughter, he did not suppress his smile of satisfaction.

Serves them right, he chuckled to himself.

He perched on a barstool at the far end of the counter. Sitting at a table would mean getting buried deeper in the smoke-filled atmosphere. The one good thing about being there, apart from his steaming cup of black coffee, was that it was nicely air-conditioned.

He soon forgot all about his surroundings as he got out the notes he had made while interviewing Santi's neighbours and staff. The vague notion he already had of Santi as a person was the sum of the bits and pieces he collected during those interviews. Going through his notes, the highlighted annotation "strange cookie" stood out. He had circled it several times — probably as many times as he had mused about the contents of his notes. Although none of the neighbours and staff he had interviewed used that very term to describe Santi, most of them had inferred it. He was still dwelling on that subject when he absent-mindedly glanced at his timepiece; it dawned on him that he should get moving. Snapping shut his notepad, he paid for his coffee and left.

The heat embraced him right at the door; it was getting unbearable. He set out at a leisurely pace and despite trying his best not to rush he soon got so excited about the interview that maintaining a normal walking pace became a problem as the minutes ticked by. He kept cautioning himself to take it easy, he did not want to get there sweating. As he got closer to the mansion he got rather nervous, which was unlike him.

He barely recalled ringing the bell and when he heard the gentle whirring of the gate as it slid slowly open, he got startled. His attention had been glued to the sign above the bell stating that a video-surveillance camera was in full operation. Reading that notice gave him a mild jolt, it also got him slightly irritated. He was one of those who did not find it the least bit funny that Big Brother was constantly watching. He detested it even more when the surveillance was by individuals. He cursed under his breath. His already mounting discomfort had just risen to a higher level.

Self-consciously, he took a cursory look at his casual outfit, which he had gone to great pains to iron. Ironing it was a great accomplishment since generally he considered ironing an unnecessary hassle and would, as a rule, do his darned best to avoid it. Time permitting he would rather take his clothes to the cleaner's. As a rule, he tried to appear as neat as possible for his interview appointments, even if that meant ironing. He looked downwards. Ever since he once arrived for an important interview in shoes of different colours — one black and one brown — he performed that routine just before interviews. As he looked up he caught a glimpse of his shiny face in the highly polished metal nameplate beside the bell. He fished a handkerchief out of one of his trousers pockets and dabbed at it. Wondering whether he was being watched from within, he ran his fingers nervously through his shoulder-length thick golden locks and told himself that it was show time.

Pushing out his chest he headed down the gravelled tree-lined driveway with determined steps. It was a long walk from the gate to the portico and halfway there, tiny rivulets of sweat started running down his forehead, to his greatest embarrassment and exasperation. Fishing out the handkerchief again, he dabbed furiously at his forehead. At such times he almost questioned his staunch belief that cars were not indispensable. He was convinced though that no sacrifice was too much for the healing of the planet even if that meant undergoing the sort of inconvenience he was experiencing right then. Thus preoccupied, he almost jumped out of his skin when he heard a high-pitched voice. He realised that he had finally arrived at the portico.

He became aware of a red-haired woman in her late 50s. Her freckled face was lit up in a brilliant smile while her greenish brown eyes were studying him with great interest. She was dressed in white, from head to toe in an ankle-length billowing linen skirt, a loose-fitting linen top and a pair of open-toed sandals. For some reason, he found her really interesting; maybe it was the way she was dressed or maybe it was her carefree attitude.

Her clanking colourful bracelets and earrings soon reminded him of his manners — it dawned on him that he was staring at her rather than taking her outstretched hand. Clearing his throat in embarrassment he smiled, acknowledged her greeting and shook her well-manicured hand. Her handshake was warm and firm.

'Hot day, isn't it?' she smiled, speaking in heavily accented English.

'Yes, indeed,' he smiled back, discretely dabbing at his forehead.

'Oh! Excuse my bad manners,' she laughed, introducing herself as Gemma.

'It's okay,' he smiled, referring to her apology, and introduced himself in return.

'Yes, yes, we've been expecting you,' she smiled and asked him to follow her.

As soon as he walked through the sliding door between the marbled portico and the lounge, he had a sharp intake of breath. It was provoked by a couple of factors. The first was the jumble in there in the name of decoration. It was nothing but a glaring clash of cultures: artefacts from all over the globe were lying or standing around, fighting for a position of prominence. It was more like a cluttered gallery than a room in a home.

The second was the sudden change in temperature — the room was extremely air-conditioned.

Fortunately, his reaction went unnoticed by her because she was busy chattering away. He could barely take in half of what she was saying since most of the time, he hardly understood her. She was talking fast, thus compounding his problems with her accent. He was struggling to concentrate. He could not wait to get out of that cluttered room, the dimensions of which seemed endless.

'This way,' she chirped at long last, leading him through an arched doorway.

He was awash with relief as he followed her into a glass-walled enclosure, a sort of roofed patio. It was a more habitable space in terms of temperature than the one he had just left behind. There were plants all over; it was like stepping into a greenhouse. He smiled as he looked around. He liked it there especially since he got a beautiful view of the surrounding mountains and trees through the glass walls. He was still delightfully taking in everything when in the midst of all that foliage he caught sight of the great object of his mission lounging in a black leather chaise-longue.

Two things caught his attention immediately: the black leather eye patch covering Santi's right eye and Santi's bi-coloured hair — half of it was silver-coloured and the other half was blond. Both things were the result of the freak accident. The rays of the sun, penetrating through the glass walls, hit his hair directly, producing a pretty dramatic effect: it was changing colours kaleidoscopically. Though Art had read about the impact of the thunderbolt on Santi in the newspapers, he was still not quite prepared for that sight.

Santi was wearing a sea-blue silk shirt buttoned midway, exposing his grey-haired chest on which an unusual large pendant hanging from a heavy gold chain was resting. He looked like an old rocker. He presented a comic sight, posing in his chaise-longue as if he was getting his portrait painted. Indeed, he was acting like he was some sort of dignitary.

Despite the seriousness of the situation, considering what his host had been through and the fact that he was still convalescing, it took Art all his willpower to stop himself from laughing out loud. He was just a few metres away from Santi and he badly needed to focus his attention elsewhere to suppress the wild laughter threatening to escape him. The first thing that truly diverted his attention was a display of sculptures, human and animal forms, in the garden. The chaos they represented had an immediate sobering effect on him so he was instantly cured of the laughing fit that he had been on the verge of giving in to. Thus sober, he covered the last few steps between him and his host.

His gaze was still glued to that clutter when he heard Santi ask,

'Do you like what you're seeing?' even before introducing himself.

'Oh, well, it's new to me so I've yet to assimilate it,' he lied.

Once again, Art could not help but wonder if there really was a distinctive line between diplomacy and hypocrisy. He was mulling that over when he heard the man speak once again.

'Actually, mine is an original style; it takes a sound knowledge of art to truly appreciate it,' he said, in a voice dripping with smugness.

'Be that as it may, art is highly subjective,' Art replied noncommittally.

'Quite,' the man conceded, turning his seeing sea-blue eye fully on him.

Art could not believe that the man had actually said what he had just heard; he could not believe that he could be so arrogant and vain. He wished that he could tell him the truth about his so-called art but of course that was not his style. Wondering how anyone could refer to that chaotic jumble as art, he smiled to himself.

'Santi,' his host stated unceremoniously, stretching out his hand.

Who else would you be? Art smiled inwardly as he reached out to take the outstretched rough, cold hand.

'Pleased to meet you and thanks for receiving me,' Art said, smiling.

'You're most welcome to my palace,' Santi joked — or did he?

'Do sit down,' Gemma's voice reached him.

'Thanks,' Art said, beaming.

He sank into the super comfortable leather armchair she indicated.

'Something to drink?' she offered.

He was asking for a glass of cold water when Santi interjected,

'You should try her magnificent lemonade. I've asked her over and over to patent the recipe, but she won't listen to me.'

'Okay, I'll try it,' Art replied politely.

'Good,' she smiled, looking pleased.

After Gemma's departure Art got a full view of the pendant. Apart from unusual, the design was fascinating. He thought he was being discrete in his observation until Santi's voice reached him and he realised otherwise.

'Not only is it captivating, but it's also highly potent,' Santi stated.

'What?' he uttered rather embarrassed at being caught out.

'I'm referring to my amulet; I can see you're riveted by it,' he smiled.

'Amulet?' he asked in surprise.

'Absolutely,' Santi replied with pride, fingering it.

Art had assumed that it was just a pendant. Though he was astonished, what came next stunned him further. Santi declared that he was certain that if he had not been wearing it the thunderbolt would have killed him. Art's eyes popped.

'You shouldn't look so surprised; I know very much about you and I know that you believe in stuff like that,' Santi smiled.

'Indeed I do, but —'

'You didn't imagine I did, right?' Santi finished off for him.

He was speechless as Santi went on to explain that he had got his amulet from a friend who was a *meiga*. According to him, he had consulted her after a weird dream he had had and she foresaw that something unpleasant, possibly deadly, was coming his way. Consequently, she gave him the amulet as a protection, warning him to never take it off.

'Besides the amulet, she prepared me a most-potent *queimada*,' he stated proudly.

Meigas are witches, sort of, in Galicia and although the belief in them is very strong there, only a few Galicians openly admit to harbouring it. The *queimada* Santi mentioned is a traditional Galician hot alcoholic drink which is supposed to be a potent potion. It is prepared by mixing liquor and other ingredients which include lemon and sugar. The concoction is then set aflame and as it is burning, it is stirred slowly while an incantation is repeated thus transmitting special magical powers to it and accordingly to those who drink it. This ritual which is usually performed outdoors in the dark goes on until the flame, the only source of light, dies out. It is believed that this drink acts as a powerful protection against curses, besides keeping evil spirits as well as evil beings at bay.

Santi's explanation about the origin of his amulet provided an excellent opening for the interview, saving Art his initial worry about how to get that enigmatic figure talking. He soon discovered that once Santi got going it was almost impossible to stop him. He saw why everyone had warned him that once he warmed to a topic breaking away from his grip was an uphill task. One of the first things Santi told him was that he hailed from Galicia, an autonomous community north-west of the Iberian Peninsula.

Galicia is believed to be one of the most superstitious regions in Spain. Some attribute part of their strong belief in the supernatural to the region's mountainous topography and its weather — the ever-present rain and mist as well as the abundant snow in the winter months — factors which frequently maintain the inhabitants indoors and sometimes isolated for days on end. Therefore, they often get the blues since they usually have very little to do in these icy months. And of course as the saying goes, 'the idle mind is the devil's playground'.

In this region, supernatural powers are attributed to a variety of beings and amulets, charms and rituals are widely available to ward off the evil eye. Prevalent as these beliefs are, funnily enough, like in the rest of Spain, the majority of Galicians deny them. This denial attitude is very much reflected in the popular ironic phrase typical in the region, 'I don't believe in *Meigas*; but they do exist.'

Art and Santi discussed the occult in general until gradually, Art steered the chat to Santi's studio and home incident. As soon as he did Santi warmed to the topic and very excitedly told him that the dream he mentioned earlier was premonitory — it had reflected what he was about to experience. He said that although he could not recall the details on awaking, he recalled that the statuette had featured greatly in it. His feeling of unease about the dream had soon grown to such heights that he chose to consult his *meiga* friend Maite.

'Are you saying that the statuette is linked with all this?'

'Who knows? Since then I've had time to do a lot of thinking.'

'Thinking; about what?'

'It's about everything. Anyway, in the process something which I didn't pay much attention to when it happened came to my mind. It was the strange reaction of a cleaning lady who I showed the statuette to when I had just acquired it. She wouldn't get close to it. In fact, she recoiled violently from it.'

'Did she say why?' Art asked, feigning ignorance.

'Not really,' Santi replied, reflectively.

At that point he paused — he seemed to be giving further thought to that question. Then shaking his head, he added slowly,

'Actually, I don't remember her doing so. The fact is: I was so engrossed in the statuette that I might have missed whatever she said.'

Of course Art knew that he was referring to Regina since she had described that very scene to him. To his surprise and confusion though, Santi had kept referring to her as 'that poor soul who worked for me'. He found it curious that each time he mentioned her he used the past tense. He wondered why. As far as he knew, she was still in his services. He asked himself if it was possible that she had been fired since he last spoke to her. He felt that that would be sad since she had told him that she needed every cent that she made in her multiple cleaning jobs. He then reminded himself that English was not Santi's mother tongue so his could be a grammatical error — an understandable slip-up.

Meanwhile, Santi continued talking and at a juncture he smilingly disclosed that he had psychic powers, which was partly why he survived, unlike his art dealer.

'Oh, so that young man was your art dealer?' Art asked, feigning ignorance again.

'Yes, he was; poor Prince,' Santi replied, showing a bit of emotion.

'What a shame! Could you tell me about him?'

'Not now,' he said, his countenance clouding over. 'It's all still too delicate for me.'

'Okay, never mind; whenever you can,' Art smiled, empathically.

Brightening up shortly afterwards, Santi continued the story about his psychic powers. He said that his powers had been evolving ever since he could remember. Art smiled. He was not at all surprised since he had been warned.

'I do hear voices sometimes.'

'Oh, do you?' Art asked, wondering where that was leading.

'Mind you, that has absolutely nothing to do with schizophrenia,' Santi added, roaring with laughter; clearly enjoying his own joke.

The mere sight of him posing so majestically was funny enough but watching him cracking up at his own joke was hilarious, to say the least, so despite himself, Art joined him. He concluded that even though he had originally thought that those he interviewed had been exaggerating in their overall portrayal of Santi, the fact was that they did fall short.

At the end of the laughter Art asked for more details about the statuette and Santi proudly stated that it was his latest acquisition and that it was unique. He offered to show it to him at the end of the interview — a prospect that Art was not exactly looking forward to. Santi revealed that although he did not feel too comfortable with it from the very first time he set his eyes on it he equally felt an irresistible attraction to it. He explained that his not feeling comfortable with it was something he could not find a logical explanation for. However, the sensation was just there — a kind of nagging feeling of unease at the back of his mind. Then when he had had that weird dream about it, the feeling got compounded. Smilingly, he stated that the more pragmatic could try to explain off his dream about it as a product of his great unease.

At that point he turned his gaze to the window. Soon afterwards, he turned to face Art and emphasised that he was totally sure of what he had experienced that night. When Art asked him why he did not dispose of it considering his great sense of unease, he replied that that was part of the inexplicable attraction he felt for it.

As Art was trying to digest that information Santi revealed that before that unpleasant incident a neighbour at the studio premises told him that he had seen a glow of light in the studio as he was driving into the premises very late one night. He paused before adding that that was on the eve of the incident. When Art asked him what he did thereafter, he replied that he simply made sure that there had been no break-in and that nothing was missing from the studio.

'Do you have an idea of what time that was?' Art asked; just to compare the time with the one that other people had mentioned so many times.

'No, I don't. Why?'

'Pure journalistic interest,' he replied.

He wanted them to stick to the point. He feared that explaining the true reason might get Santi going off at a tangent. Also, it might hurt his overblown ego. Part of the reason he granted him the interview was because he believed that his was an exclusive.

When Gemma came in to announce that it was time for Santi's meds and for lunch, Art realised that they had been talking for almost three hours. Looking slightly disappointed, Santi promised him another meeting soon and tried to make him stay for lunch. Art politely declined the lunch invitation, claiming that he had to keep another appointment. Though he too was disappointed that that weird but extremely interesting interview had come to an end, he was also relieved that it had since it meant that he would leave without being shown the statuette.

But, no sooner had he heaved a sigh of relief than Santi announced proudly that it was time for him to see it. Struggling to hide his momentary bewilderment, he reluctantly stood up and accompanied his host.

Once in its presence Art was so awed that he could hardly blink. He stood there gaping at it, trying to conceal his trembling. Curiously enough, despite his state he had just enough presence of mind to refuse to touch it, albeit Santi's coaxing. He also did manage to take a few snapshots of it. Afterwards, as a consequence of that mixture of reverence and disorientation he would recall very little of what had transpired during that short-lived chapter. Fleeting though the period was, to him time simply froze. He would later describe that moment as an eternity.

CHAPTER 11

The following morning Art set out to pay Regina a visit in her temporary abode to see how she was settling in and to interview her further, if she was willing. He had one great wish all the way there: that she would remember to meet him at the entrance to the settlement since he was clueless regarding where he was headed. Regina's friend Amina, who he had not caught a glimpse of, had met Regina inside the makeshift gate when he had accompanied her to the settlement two nights earlier. Therefore he had not the least idea of where Amina had taken her. He knew that being a shantytown it must be a pretty complicated maze inside so even if he had gone in that night, he would still have had a bit of problem finding Amina's modest home.

Fortunately, Regina appeared almost as soon as he got there. The promptness with which she popped up surprised him. When he voiced his surprise she smilingly explained that she had been watching out for him from a safe spot. Although he observed that she was looking very tired, she said that she was fine.

'At least, I feel relatively safe,' she added with a weary smile.

Right from the entrance he could feel himself being observed, quite apart from the openly curious and sometimes aggressive looks he was receiving. When he mentioned it she told him that the "settlers" were constantly on the lookout since some of them were undocumented aliens. They were very suspicious of strangers in case they were undercover cops. She confessed that even though Amina and her husband had assured her that she could stay with them for as long as she wanted, she could not wait to leave because she suspected that not all the inhabitants were engaged in honest means of earning their livelihood. Thus her main worry was the risk of a raid by law-enforcement officials, rather than being tracked down by those she was hiding from. She was not worried about the latter because the settlement, although littered with ramshackle homes, was like a fortress. That information brought him some relief; it meant that apparently, for the time being he had no cause to worry about Regina's safety. Although she smiled when he expressed his relief, her eyes told a different story. They were sad, sadder than he had ever seen them. He wondered if something was bothering her, apart from the obvious.

Her mention of ramshackle homes got him taking in the surroundings in greater detail. Shanties made from scrap metal, wood, plastic, plastic sheeting, cardboard and what-not littered the whole place. He noticed overhead wires, supported by poles, criss-crossing the settlement in a haphazard manner. Those shoddily done wirings supplied electricity to the community; they were used to tap electricity illegally from the mains. He soon discovered that the water supply was also illegally tapped. He saw outdoor pipes and taps here and there, around which women were doing their laundry manually. As he was studying the scene with interest, Regina mentioned that with ingenious plumbing the homes also had running water, apart from those supplies for public use.

Many hours later, he left feeling pretty upbeat because their interview had been long and rewarding. Regina had also referred him to people who she considered to be important sources. Afraid that she might change her mind regarding her earlier offer, he obtained the information he needed for his trip to Nigeria too. Such information included names and addresses of valuable contacts over there. He was armed with tons of information when he left that fortress. Since he was practically set for his trip information-wise, he stopped over at a travel agent's to make his reservation before heading home.

Though he was feeling most satisfied with how everything had worked out, Regina's behaviour before his departure almost marred the overall outcome of their meeting, particularly the part when she gave him a sad smile and said,

'I just want you to know that I'm truly grateful for everything.'

'I should be thanking you for your immense help,' he replied.

'No Art, someday you'll understand,' she stated, turning away.

By then they were already at the gate and since she could not step outside it, she bade him goodbye. It was a great wrench to leave her in that state. Once outside, he turned round to say something comforting but, she was no longer there. He was puzzled. He could not understand how she always managed to depart so swiftly.

On getting home he dwelt on her circumstances for ages and the more he thought about it, the more worried he got. He was certain that something was terribly wrong with her. Beyond her fear, he sensed something else which he could not put his finger on. Also, when they were together he sometimes got inexplicably uneasy. Finally, he attributed all that to the complexity of her situation. He resolved that before leaving for Nigeria he would try to convince Diego to provide her with some sort of protection.

After a snack he got out the notes he had made during the long productive interview and stretched out on his couch. He was still studying them when he fell asleep — he was that exhausted.

The next thing he knew, his right big toe was being tugged at. It started as a very light sensation but then it became intense. Although he believed that he eventually came awake due to the tugging, with time he would not be so sure. He was certain, however, that it became tremendously cold in there the season notwithstanding. Then he noticed a young black woman standing close to his feet, mute and trembling. She looked terribly scared. He was wondering if he was imagining things when she finally managed to address him in broken Spanish after several failed attempts to speak.

'I know not where I am, please help,' she spluttered in a quivering voice.

'Who are you?' he asked in confusion.

'I'm Mercy, Regina's friend.'

'You're Regina's friend?'

She nodded and he could see that she was making an effort to continue speaking. He was feeling very uncomfortable for her, she seemed to be choking. That persistent effort on her part to speak appeared to be suffocating her.

'I'm sorry, so sorry. It's Regina, I'm so sorry.'

'What's wrong with Regina?'

'She's… she's… she's…' she trailed off.

Her difficulty to speak was deepening. Her image was dimming too.

'I'm very tired, I need rest. Help…help her,' she managed to whisper.

Then her image faded away and he sat up with a jolt. His heart was pounding away. Almost immediately his phone started ringing. Moaning, he reached out for it. The caller was Diego. His voice said it all: something was terribly wrong.

'We must meet straightaway,' he stated without preambles.

'What's up, buddy?'

'I'll pick you up in about a quarter of an hour,' Diego stated crisply and hung up.

Art stood up shakily and stumbled towards the bathroom. After splashing water on his face he started getting dressed. That was when he realised that it was past 3 a.m. He could not believe that he had slept for that long, on the couch too! Of course it stood to reason: he had been getting too little sleep and doing lots of running around. Still slightly groggy, he asked himself what could be so urgent that Diego could not put off till morning.

Diego pulled up almost as soon as he shuffled out of the lift.

'Hey! What's up buddy?' he asked while getting into Diego's car.

'We've just found a body,' Diego replied, even before Art could settle into his seat. 'It's a black woman's and I'm hoping it's not your friend's.'

'Come on buddy, of all the black women in Madrid!'

'Yeah, I agree with you. But, remember the ceremonial dagger?'

At that point Art's heart started beating wildly. He recalled the death threats Regina had been receiving. His heartbeat got so loud and wild that it drowned out Diego's voice for a moment. He did not know for how long Diego went on talking before he heard him anew.

'The doctors aren't too optimistic but they're doing their darned best.'

'So she's still alive,' he said, heaving a sigh of relief, at the same time wondering why his friend had used the word, "body".

'Yes, but barely so. They say it could be a question of hours. She's badly battered and repeatedly stabbed, among other unmentionable tortures.'

'Oh, please don't go on.'

They were soon at the hospital and after Diego flashed his badge and identified himself, they were allowed into a private ward by the officer on guard at the door. Like a somnambulist Art stumbled towards the bedside of the almost completely swathed figure. The patient had so many tubes running in and out of her and all sorts of machines beeping and bleeping that she looked more like some sort of electronic device than a human being. On getting to the bedside he peered at the visible part of her face and, but for Diego's swift reaction he would have hit the floor. He was trembling and moving his head from side to side. He was clutching his chest because he could barely breathe.

'So sorry dude,' Diego whispered, hugging him tightly.

'That's… that's… that's not Regina,' he stuttered with difficulty.

'If that's not her what's your problem then?'

'That's the woman who appeared in my dream before your call.'

'She appeared in your dream, huh? Dude, you've been under a great deal of pressure lately. I'll take you home and hopefully you'll get some well-deserved rest.'

'Listen, I know what I'm talking about,' he said, controlling his urge to explode.

'Come on let's go, we'll talk about this later in the day.'

'Will you listen to me!' he eventually thundered, after mustering up enough strength.

He had always been tolerant and understanding of Diego's scepticism towards the paranormal. His tolerant and understanding nature notwithstanding, he was just not in the mood to be taken for a joker right then. His nerves were on end — too little sleep and too much coffee were both gnawing away at his nerves. Not to mention the stress he had undergone all the way there until he was able to ascertain that the woman on the verge of death was not Regina. Regardless of those mitigating circumstances right after his explosion he wished that he had stopped himself from reacting that way.

His outburst startled both Diego and the officer outside the door who came rushing in to inquire if all was fine. After assuring the officer that everything was okay, Diego told him he could return to his post. He then turned to face his friend. In their many years of friendship he had never ever seen Art so ruffled. Raising his hands in mock surrender he smiled and said soothingly,

'Okay, okay, okay.'

'Excuse me,' Art murmured his apology, cheeks flaming. 'Like you said, I've been under a great deal of pressure but believe me I know what I experienced,' he stated calmly, controlling his breathing.

'It's okay, I understand. Shall we go somewhere to talk?'

Nodding his agreement Art inched closer to the bed and took a long look at the individual lying therein. Sadly, he wondered if she was going to pull through.

As he left the ward for the car park in the company of Diego the beeping sound of the life support machine and the bleeping sounds of one or two other machines accompanied him. They were stuck in his head; there was no way to make them go away. He was deep in thoughts and so was Diego. In that preoccupied state they both got into the car.

When they were leaving the hospital premises Diego mumbled that apart from the visible evidence of the brutalities the victim had suffered, her tongue had been cut off too.

'Oh, crap! How can people be so vile?' Art asked rhetorically.

A moment later Diego said that the fact that the victim's tongue had been cut off, apart from the presence of the ornamental dagger at the scene where her battered body had been recovered, heightened their suspicion that the perpetrators of that inhuman act of atrocity were the very ones who killed the sex-worker. Art was too numb to speak.

'In other words if she survives she mayn't be able to provide much information,' he managed to contribute, finally finding his tongue.

'Well, if she could use her hands she'd probably do so in writing.'

'Are her hands affected too?'

'Her limbs were beaten into a pulp,' Diego stated, tightening his grip on the steering.

This new info made Art shudder and wince. He was speechless.

The first thing he said when they got to their destination and sat down was that since the victim was Regina's friend he could be the reason why she was in hospital. Diego remarked that there was no logic behind that assumption since he had no direct relationship with her. But he insisted on his hypothesis and Diego stated that his fear for Regina's safety might be beclouding his judgement. Art shrugged off his observation.

Out of the blue Diego asked him how his investigation was going. He looked at Diego in disbelief, astonished that he was showing interest in his investigation. Then he replied that he was making some progress. Diego startled him further by declaring that he would consider obtaining inside help for him if he chose to carry on with it. He could not believe that Diego was beginning to see things his way, i.e. that there was more to the fires than met the eye. He could not help wondering why.

A pause followed during which he kept studying Diego's face. He knew him well enough to know that he was worried; a fact which he was trying hard to conceal. Eventually looking straight into his eyes, he asked him in all seriousness,

'Buddy, am I in danger?'

'They aren't that stupid,' he replied with a forced smile.

'But if they cold-heartedly bumped off one woman and were about to—'

'One, as far as we know; there could be more,' Diego interjected.

'Yeah, as far as we know. So, back to my question: am I?'

Diego explained why he believed that he was not likely to come to any harm: The gang felt safer operating so callously within their own territory with the assumption that no one would be interested enough to poke their nose into their affairs. As an aside he conceded that unfortunately the gang was often right in that assumption since frequently, its members committed such horrendous crimes with impunity. He then revealed that things were about to change thanks to on-going investigations and to Art's tiny contributions. Diego's recognition of his contributions surprised him and though he felt like smiling, he could not get himself to.

'And, back to your question: I'm almost certain that they won't be bold enough to venture outside their circle,' he concluded.

Even though Diego's optimistic conclusion should tranquillise him, it did not and deliberately, he reminded Diego that they had dared to send him a threatening note despite knowing that he was a law-enforcement officer. Diego nodded, noting his point. After a reflective pause he reluctantly admitted,

'Indeed, it's difficult to know for sure what a desperate mind is capable of coming up with and the way things are, the gang members seem to be getting pretty desperate.'

'Meanwhile though, I don't think they'd get erratic enough to inflict any physical harm on you,' he added after a slight pause.

'Are you categorically stating that I needn't worry about my safety?'

'For the reasons I've put forward, I believe so,' he asserted.

Again, though Art should feel relieved he could not for he sensed that Diego was not telling him everything. His new attempt to study his face to see if he could extract any hidden information failed because no sooner had he begun the exercise than Diego said,

'We've got to go, dude. I'll keep you posted on our progress.'

'Thanks buddy,' he stated, earnestly.

'It is okay; what are friends for?' Diego smiled wearily.

Seeing how tired he was looking Art wondered whether to give voice to something that had been gnawing away at him all night: The desperation in Mercy's voice; Mercy, the young woman in his dream who curiously, was the same person in the hospital; when she talked about Regina needing help. The more he thought about it the more worried he got so in the end he braced the issue, albeit Diego's tiredness.

'Hey, buddy. Do you remember my request regarding Regina?'

'Regina?' he asked stifling another yawn.

'My friend slash informant.'

'Hmm, we're still looking into your request.'

Art tried to persuade him to take the matter seriously, revealing that his worry about her intensified after the woman in his dream told him that she needed help. True to his expectation Diego looked heavenwards and groaned,

'Oh, come on dude, that's just a dream. Considering how worried you've been about her it's normal that you have such dreams.'

'Listen buddy let's not go over this whole thing again. Like I told you earlier I'm perfectly sure of what I experienced,' he stated levelly.

'Okay, okay, I'll see what I can do. Right now, I'm whacked. It's already dawn; let's go get some sleep, alright?' he said, imploringly.

Just before Diego dropped him off Art mentioned that he would go and check on Regina straightaway if she lived elsewhere. Diego asked him where she lived and when Art told him he laughed out loud, nodded his head vigorously and stated resignedly,

'You do love complications, don't you? All I can say is, while you're out there, watch out for the glue-sniffing layabout youths. All they do is fart around all day instead of being at school. Seriously, wait till full light before venturing there and remember to watch your back,' he advised, before zooming off.

Art could barely wait till full light but he just had to. He then set out in search of Regina in a feverish rush. On dashing into the shantytown he realised that he had underestimated the complexity of the mission ahead. The shacks were more similar to one another than he had assumed and the landmark he had chosen the previous day, in case of such an emergency, turned out to be absolutely unreliable.

Going round in circles, he came across wide-eyed wild-haired very young kids running around merrily. He got an occasional shy smile as he walked towards or past them. He also stumbled past wild-eyed angry-looking teenage boys hanging around aimlessly in small groups. He received aggressive looks and challenging stares from these ones. He wondered if they were the glue-sniffing ones Diego had warned him against.

To a large extent he understood the look of anger and aggression on their faces. Misery was abundant everywhere he looked: The overflowing garbage bins, abandoned old furniture and household appliances; most of them collected from all over the city; littering the winding dirt tracks that criss-crossed the settlement, lean hungry-looking dogs wandering around, the clothes — probably hand-me-downs — flapping desolately on the clotheslines, shacks that were barely more than tents and lots of other items, all told different stories of misery and abject poverty.

He could not recall seeing so many kids when he had been there with Regina. He reasoned that it was probably because he had been so engrossed in their conversation that he did not notice their presence or because that visit had been at a very different time of the day or maybe because Regina had taken him through a distinct route.

Everywhere he went, he could feel eyes piercing into him though he could not always see those the eyes belonged to. The few attempts he made at trying to ask for directions were met with absolute silence. He was not sure if that was because the individuals he asked did not understand the language or because they were simply shunning him. It did not take long for him to admit that he was treading dangerous waters; that he could be in great danger wandering about that weird settlement all alone. Regardless, he resolved that there was no turning back. He must find Amina's shack.

Eventually, despite the suspicious glances, occasional aggressive looks and challenging stares he received all through his quest, he managed to stumble across the shack Regina had taken him to the previous day. Well, actually they had hung around the vicinity of the shack; she had simply pointed it out. The finding was so unexpected. Heaving a huge sigh of relief he rapped on the rickety wood and zinc door and was surprised when a woman who identified herself as Amina opened it. He had expected to see Regina not her — he had expected her to be at work. She was looking really worried, with huge bags under her eyes.

After they had exchanged greetings he introduced himself to her, adding that he was Regina's friend. She gave him the ghost of a smile before stating that she was relieved to see him because she did not know who to turn to. Looking around in confusion, he asked her what she was talking about and she said,

'Oh, thought you're here for that. My friend Regina's missing.'

'What do you mean? She's safe here. That's why she's here; right?'

'Yes, yes. I thought she's safe too *Señor* Art.'

He was so agitated that he began talking awfully fast. So fast that the poor woman who was barely muddling through the language got totally lost at a stage. Her child-like gaze said it all. He cleared his throat in embarrassment and very slowly, he asked her what had happened. She said that she had received a call on her mobile phone from a woman who identified herself as Mercy.

'Wait a moment. Did you say Mercy?'

'Yes, yes, Mercy. You know Mercy?'

'Well, kind of. And …?' he prompted.

She explained that following the call Regina went to see Mercy who needed to talk to her. She sighed heavily before adding that Regina had said that she would be gone for just a moment but that moment became an eternity and there was still no sign of her.

Amina suddenly realised that they were still on her makeshift stoop.

'Oh, *Señor*, come in please,' she stated effusively, making way for him.

'Thanks,' he said, squeezing past her and stepping into her cramped lodgings which Regina had told him she shared with her husband and their three young kids.

A couple of toys were lying around the floor and she hurriedly grabbed them and some items of clothing, apologising for the state of the room. Self-consciously, she added that she had not had time to tidy up. Brushing aside her apology, he acknowledged that he knew his visit was rather early, unscheduled and inconvenient but that given the nature of the matter in question, he had been unable to put it off till a more opportune moment. They were still on their feet and she was observing him through weary eyes.

He noticed how hellishly hot it was in there, despite how early it was. Not surprising, given the flimsy construction of the shack. He wondered how the household managed to put up with extreme weather conditions. Amina seemed to notice his discomfort because she walked to the only window in the room and parted the faded curtains.

'Tea?' she offered.

'No thanks, just had breakfast,' he replied.

Although he was dying of thirst, he did not want to bother her further. As it were, he was feeling like a great nuisance popping up at her doorstep so early.

She offered him the only comfortable chair in the room, cleared the pile of clothes from a not-too-comfortable-looking one and perched on the edge of it, crossing her arms and legs. She then asked him what they were going to do about Regina. Being a stickler for details and thinking that she had probably given him inaccurate information because of her problem with the language, he decided to first of all take her back to something she had said almost at the beginning of their conversation, lest they wandered too far from that point.

He asked her if she had actually said that she received Mercy's call. She confirmed that information, adding that Regina had been forced to switch off her own phone since she had been receiving death threats on it. She offered her the use of hers so that her close ones could call her. She explained that she did not want Regina to remain incommunicado because apart from being her guest she was her friend too. Moreover, she felt great solidarity for her as a foreigner, 'Like me,' she added needlessly before concluding,

'Personally, I wouldn't like to be in a situation in which the family I left behind in my homeland wouldn't be able to reach me, for whatever reason.'

By the time she got to the end of that drawn-out explanation he had sunk very deep into analytical thinking. He reached the conclusion that it was too much of a coincidence that the woman who appeared in his dream had identified herself as Mercy, just like the person whose call Amina had answered. He remembered Mercy saying that she was sorry and wondered if that was because she had been used as a bait to lure Regina out of hiding or if she had collaborated willingly. It was also possible that she had blown Regina's cover quite unwittingly. The more he analysed the situation the more worried he got by the second, especially since Mercy had told him that Regina needed help.

He spent the next half an hour or so trying to find out if Amina could remember anything that could be useful to him but it was no use. Finally, he gave her his phone number asking her to get in touch in case of any development. He also asked her for hers. But she gave him her husband's number since Regina still had her phone. He obtained her number anyway. He intended to give it to Diego hoping that somehow, for example through tracking, the Police might be able to establish Regina's whereabouts.

Just before he made his hasty departure she stated,

'Ah! Another thing: Why you come now to look for Regina?'

Assuming the word 'now' was a subtle hint at how early it was he replied contritely,

'I needed to discuss something really urgent with her.'

'Really urgent?' she asked, showing incomprehension.

'Yeah, yeah, very important; know what I mean?'

'Ah, yes!' she nodded with an uncertain smile.

After reassuring her that Regina would be fine, he headed for the rickety door with her trailing behind him. He walked through it and waved at her. She raised her hand slowly and waved back.

Giving way to the tears she had been holding back while he was around, she sadly watched him as he walked away. She was praying and hoping that he would take some action. She was also relieved that at last, apart from her husband, she had been able to talk to someone about her friend's sudden disappearance. She had been too scared, given her status as an undocumented alien, to approach anyone. She had been afraid of deportation, for herself and her family.

As he made his way out of her presence he knew that he had to get moving, literally and figuratively, and the faster the better. He was certain that wherever Regina was, she was being held against her will so he had to get immediate help for her. Logically, the first person he tried to get in touch with was Diego. Unfortunately, his frantic efforts yielded no fruit. He finally left a message begging him to call him once he listened to it.

Then he decided to go ahead and keep an important appointment Regina had fixed for him days earlier. His meeting was with a young man who was profitably engaged in the human trafficking business. Regina had informed him that the man would let anyone have any number of girls for keeps if they offered the right price. She had warned him to be extra careful with him because he was known to be extremely ruthless.

When he arrived at the venue, a fast food restaurant; armed with a video camera to secretly record the interview; the man was already there, ahead of schedule.

What the heck, he thought, freezing momentarily, on seeing the man.

'Have we met?' the man asked, glaring, even before saying hello.

'I don't think so,' Art replied, unblinking.

His apparent calm notwithstanding, deep down Art was quaking since the man was no other but the bully who had glowered at him on the commuter train. His gaze was chilling. He was flanked by two young African females whom he claimed were twenty years old. Art could see, however, that neither of them was over sixteen.

CHAPTER 12

The days following Art's awareness of Regina's disappearance were hectic. His frantic fruitless efforts to find her thoroughly wore him out. He was so desperate that he seriously considered cancelling his trip. Eventually he chose not to since Diego was handling the matter as professionally as ever. Thanks to him a structured search was going on. Without Diego he would not have known where to begin.

Very late at night on the eve of his departure he received a telephone call. The caller's voice was so distorted that at first he could not make out what s/he was saying. In the end he got the main message being put across:

'If you go on this trip you'll be brought back in a box.'

Just having been roused from sleep, he was too numb to react initially. When he finally gathered his wits and was trying to tell the caller to go to hell s/he hung up.

Needless to say, he could not sleep anymore. He thought of calling Diego to tell him about the incident but he gave up the idea almost immediately because till the very last moment Diego had tried to talk him out of making the trip which he labelled as 'suicidal'. Diego had also warned him that he was playing with fire. So calling him would only serve to buttress his argument and invite more sermonising.

He kept replaying the threat in his head and each time he did so he got crosser and even more determined to go. At the same time there were so many questions going round in his head the most important being,

'How did the caller know about my travel plans?'

He wondered if s/he could have some sort of connection with the Nigerian Embassy. Suddenly his biggest concern became the safety of his friend Adrian Collins with whom he was going to put up in Lagos. As

Adrian was his sponsor he had had to furnish his personal details including his home and office addresses — standard visa requirements.

His flight was scheduled for 06.55hrs and he had planned to be at the airport at 05.00hrs. But since he could not go back to sleep he decided that he might as well head for the airport. After a quick shower he gulped down a mug of his typical syrup-like black coffee. When he was set to leave he took a wistful look around his flat. He wanted to remember everything as it was in case he did not make it back. Although he had been telling himself that the weird call had been just a bluff, he was also worried that it might not be.

As he got out of the lift and was heading towards the front door he noticed that his mailbox was overflowing with advertising leaflets and junk mail; not surprising because he seldom bothered to clear it out. Since he was going to be away for some time he decided to empty it since burglaries increased significantly in summer and too many of those leaflets spilling out could give undesirables a clear hint that nobody was at home.

While he was at it an envelope addressed to him in an untidy scrawl caught his attention. Eyeing it suspiciously, he opened it and got out an equally untidy piece of paper.

'Get on that flight and you're a dead man!' the message read.

It was written in that same brownish-red ink which incidentally had been confirmed to be human blood. He dropped the paper as if it was red-hot. However, he immediately braced himself and picked it up. He was about to dump it in the wastepaper basket when he changed his mind. He shoved it into one of his trousers pockets.

He found the message both eerie and ominous. Once again he considered calling Diego but he changed his mind and walked defiantly towards the door instead. However, before stalking through it head high and stepping onto the sleepy street to wait for a taxi, he looked cautiously around. His outward stance of bravery and defiance notwithstanding until a cab eventually appeared he was pretty jumpy. All sorts of things startled him — lurking stray cats were at the top of the list.

Barajas Airport was bustling with activity when he got there. It was August, the popular holiday month, so logically the place was swarming with people. Long queues formed by travellers of every race, creed and gender were snaking around the place. Some travellers were looking so dishevelled that they gave the impression of having spent days there. Many seemed to be in transit. The scene was like a marketplace. There was an incredible hubbub from all over — wailing babies, restless kids and yelling harassed mothers. Curiously, in the midst of all that bedlam some travellers were fast asleep, using their luggage as bed and others were stretched out on the floor in corners or wherever.

The suspension of direct flights to Nigeria by the national carrier Iberia was still on so Art had to fly Lufthansa to Frankfurt first. When he ultimately got to the check-in counter he concluded that it was just as well that he arrived so early since he would probably have missed his flight if he had stuck to his original plan. After checking in he managed to grab a quick coffee before boarding. Even so he had barely strapped on his seat belt before he dropped into deep slumber.

He soon felt himself being prodded and on opening his eyes he noticed that breakfast was being served. He had had little to eat in the last few days so breakfast would have been most welcome but he was so exhausted that he preferred to skip it. The next thing he knew, there was movement all around and he realised that they were in Frankfurt.

After going through passport control and all that he considered going into the city to do a bit of sightseeing since he had a three-hour wait before his connection. But he discarded of that idea almost at once. It would be too much hassle for his weary bones. As an alternative he explored the airport briefly before sitting down in a snack bar for coffee.

About an hour to boarding time he moved closer to the gate. The panorama transformed dramatically. Everywhere he looked there were Africans. That was logical considering his flight destination: Lagos and then Accra. He started getting apprehensive — that weird call had come to his mind. In the Frankfurt bound flight most of the passengers had been Europeans so he had managed to get his mind off it.

Despite his apprehension he soon got engaged in the study of that compelling scene. He observed that curiously enough, the majority of the Africans were bearing foreign passports. Bearing is probably not the word; flaunting is more like it. They seemed to be showing off their achievement; naturalisation in the supposed developed world. There was a representation of so many countries in the world — every continent was represented. The very few bearing African passports seemed to have gone overseas on a business or shopping trip. The great majority of the children had foreign passports. Certainly they were overseas-born and were probably just visiting Africa; some, for the first time.

Watching them was a great delight. Some were strutting about like peacocks, flaunting their acquisitions. Bling, bling was everywhere — chains, pendants, rings, studs, gold watches, you name it — the larger the better. Most of them were dressed to kill. Some were decked out in impeccable 3-piece Italian suits, regardless of the summer heat. Those who decided to go casual were sporting all the best names in sportswear. Whether they were dressed casually or otherwise the one thing everyone had in common was the bling, bling they complemented their outfit with.

Of course in this day and age technology products and electronic gadgets are part of the modern man's acquisitions so they are worth displaying too. Thus the travellers were also showing off their latest in MP3 players, PDAs, laptops, mobile phones, digital cameras and other gadgets from hi-tech to low-tech. The kids were not left out of the great display. They were happily exhibiting their electronic toys.

Something else caught Art's attention: the amount of luggage each traveller was carrying. He wondered what they had checked in if what he could see all around was hand luggage. It was not just the number but also the weight that he was dazed by. Many of the travellers were struggling under the sheer weight of the numerous bundles, plastic bags, paper bags, duty-free shop bags and whatnot.

Art looked on as they chattered away in different English accents. Nobody seemed to be a stranger to the other or at a loss as to what to say. He found that familiarity and their loose use of the words 'brother' and 'sister' totally amazing. Everyone was being addressed as either. They were competing in loudness too — literally and figuratively. Though their chattering was interesting at first he soon found it slightly tiresome since it simply went on and on in raised voices. It dawned on him that it was not going to be a quiet flight. Bored with the scene, he eventually moved to a relatively quiet corner closer to the gate.

He had barely settled down when another situation he considered curious caught his attention. At the very front of the gate there were a couple of white men and an African and though they were all seated pretty close physically, there was not much interaction among all three. Rather the two whites were chatting while the African was totally disconnected. He appeared quite uninterested in them and their natter — he was looking longingly towards the other side as if he would rather be among his "brothers". Yet he seemed attached to the duo by some invisible string.

Not long after Art noticed them boarding began. They were the first to board. As fate would have it they were on the same row as him so he had a clear view of them to his right. They were occupying seats 53-H-J-K — the African was sandwiched between the whites. The centre row with seats D-E-F-G stood between Art and them. His was the aisle-seat 53-C with seats 53-A and B occupied by an Accra bound couple.

There was a frenzy of activity all around him as passengers kept boarding noisily. It was just as well that he had got on the aircraft as soon as he did because in no time all the overhead luggage compartments were jam-packed; getting them closed required several tries. Then people started stuffing things under seats, some jutting out onto the aisles, between seats and wherever their imagination led them. In some cases the flight attendants had to put down their foot to make sure that some of the luggage was moved to the back of the aircraft for safety reasons. It took ages to get the multiple pieces of luggage stuffed away. Thereafter getting some passengers to sit down and fasten their seat belts became yet another story. It was almost like a scene in a kindergarten. Although the flight attendants were wearing their professional plastic smile it was easy to see that they were exasperated.

Finally it was time to go. While some passengers totally ignored the safety demonstration, some others found it hilarious for whatever reason and as it was going on they mimicked it, making parallel comments in their language. The flight attendants running the demonstration ignored their disruptiveness and stoically went on with their routine. When they finished they practically dashed to the back of the aircraft making what might have passed for harmless comments in German. Even though Art was no expert in German he could pass for one when it came to identifying the expletives. He smiled to himself mainly because the flight attendants tried to camouflage the series of expletives they dropped with the best of their professional plastic smiles.

No sooner had the 'fasten your seat belt' sign gone off than some passengers sprang to their feet and continued with their socialising. Art stood up and walked to the toilet where a queue had already built up. He saw some flight attendants huddled together at the back of the aircraft, looking worried. Surely, they were wondering if they were going to be able to put up with the rowdiness during the almost six-hour flight.

Nearly one hour into the flight pandemonium erupted. Incidentally Art had just returned his attention to the trio wondering what kind of relationship theirs was when the African sprang up and punched the man sitting on his left on the face, around the nose. The attack was so swift that the victim could not duck so he received the full impact of the blow. Blood began spurting from his face as if from a fountain. In no time there was blood everywhere. Then in slow-motion his companion reacted and a scuffle ensued between him and the aggressor. The latter broke away from his restraining grip, jumped over the dazed bleeding victim and was at the back of the aircraft within the twinkling of an eye. He began yelling his head off. Unknown to everyone a nightmarish scene was about to unfold.

It turned out that the African was a deportee and the white duo were plain-clothes policemen escorting him to Nigeria after his release from prison for innumerable offences. He was threatening that rather than be deported he was going to make sure that the aircraft crashed. He soon roused the ire and sympathy of many of his "brothers" by claiming that he had been tortured and abused in unmentionable ways by cruel white men while in detention. Many of his "brothers" got to their feet and started chanting threats at the cops.

Meanwhile the victim continued bleeding profusely. His companion was standing some distance from the aggressor at the back of the aircraft still trying to apprehend him. Both of them, escort and ward, were breathing heavily, facing each other like two wrestlers in a ring, each waiting for the chance to make the right move. They were covered in blood, the assailed officer's blood. The aisle was full of people, angry clamouring people. The flight attendants were running around in total confusion, apparently at a loss as to how to handle the escalating tense situation. A couple of them rushed to the cockpit.

The pilot Captain Aksel Schwartz, a clean-cut man in his late 50s, soon appeared, flanked by those two. In terms of appearance and demeanour he fitted perfectly into the frame of the stereotype of a German — big, strong, contained and all that. His no-nonsense steel mask was very much in place as he took in the situation briefly before issuing orders in a cool, crisp manner in German to the flight attendants. One of them scuttled off, in search of the first-aid kit while the other asked if there was any doctor aboard. Luckily there was: a young man in his mid 30s proudly stood up and strutted over to attend to the injured officer.

Captain Schwartz had not moved a facial muscle since he came out of the cockpit. Outwardly he was cool and composed and his steely blue eyes did not blink as they took in the situation. However, his was just an act because hiding behind that steel mask was an individual gravely worried about the possible outbreak of serious trouble. But many years of experience had taught him that no matter how bad the situation he should never let it be known that he was worried or frightened. Above all, he should never give in to intimidation.

After assessing the situation he tried to calm down the passengers in English, in a heavy German accent. He also asked those on their feet to please return to their seats. Next he announced that given the prevailing circumstances the aircraft might have to return to Frankfurt or make an emergency landing at the nearest airport. Either way, he was awaiting instructions from Frankfurt.

'What? No way!' many passengers bellowed in indignation.

The idea of going anywhere other than their original destination was not funny and those who believed their "brother" had been wrongly treated were getting ever more furious.

A story about a mutiny by sailors aboard a ship at sea came to Art's mind. The situation did not end too well, at least not for the captain. Art was feeling seriously uneasy at the same time thinking: *If the on-going situation were on firm land one could wait for the right opportunity to scram but being on an aircraft, so many metres above sea level, short of a miracle bolting is definitely not an option.* Then slowly, he began seething. He was indignant about what he deemed an act of flagrant irresponsibility on the part of the German authorities: placing a deportee on a full commercial flight without handcuffs.

Meanwhile the agitation continued gathering momentum alarmingly. He wondered if those backing the deportee were aware that their own lives were in danger too.

As if the ongoing situation was not dangerous enough, the aircraft got into the roughest turbulence Art had ever experienced in his flying life. The positive side of it was that it got those clamouring for justice to rush back to their seats and strap themselves in. He thought, *Divine intervention, maybe?* He was praying and fiercely clutching the arm-rest of his seat with both hands. He became almost sure that he was destined to perish on that flight. *First, someone was menacing to bring it down and then the force of nature's taken over, threatening to do the same,* he mused on. He wondered if the note he had received was not a threat after all but simply a harsh recommendation and if he should have heeded it.

His mind dashed to his daughter, his parents, his good friends like Diego. He recalled how much Diego had tried to discourage him from making the trip. He wondered if he would see his loved ones again. He realised that though he had written so much about death, he had never truly dwelt upon it. Although he had always held the belief that death was not the end he was certain then that he did not want to experience it; regardless of if it was the beginning or the end. He felt that there were still so many things left for him to do here on Earth, so many things he ought to have said to those he truly cared about. He prayed to be given the chance to at least do that, if nothing else. His eyes were tightly closed, his hands; released from clutching the armrest; were clutched in prayer. For some reason Regina came to his mind and strangely, the thought of her brought him some peace.

He was so engrossed in his own situation that he got fully detached from the drama evolving around him. When he reconnected, he noticed that he was surrounded by all kinds of noise like the clinking of glasses and bottles, probably from the galley, and screams. As some passengers were screaming in fear others were praying aloud in their mother tongue or in English while a handful were clowning around. Many over-stuffed overhead luggage compartments had sprung open, disgorging their contents.

When the proverbial calm that comes after a storm ultimately descended the silence was so profound that at first it felt slightly eerie. Then it was broken by a round of spattered applause and gradually the applause became heartier.

As is usually the case after devastating storms, the cleaning up exercise began and so did the return to reality. The flight attendants had a lot of cleaning up and tidying up to do since it was not only the luggage compartments that had spilt their contents — some humans had done so too. The sight was disgusting. But things were getting back to normal after that disruption and confusion that had raged for an eternity.

Art got up on wobbly legs and made his way to the toilet. He needed to wash his face, to calm himself down. His feet felt like jelly and he was aching all over. He had been rattled so badly by that turbulence that he felt like he had spent ages working out in the gym. Not really one for physical exercise, he was convinced that he was going to suffer from stiffness for the next couple of days, at least.

Not far from the toilet he observed something which he deemed the height of irony: The deportee was sitting strapped in a jump-seat at the back. He smiled inwardly as he wondered if the man had not announced that he preferred to die rather than be deported. *Why did he bother to adopt that safety measure?* he mused, avoiding eye contact with him.

The Captain's voice reached Art then: he was apologising for the incident, over the loudspeaker. He also called for calm just like he had done at the onset of the turbulence.

The deportee seemed to have been waiting for that cue because he sprang up and began making his racket anew, yelling out fresh threats. In the midst of all that chaos, during the nightmarish pandemonium of screaming, praying, cursing and crying, he had got hold of a screwdriver-like object and still covered in blood, he was wielding it like a crazed man.

One thing was hollering that he did not want to be deported but another was repeating his threat to bring down the aircraft. After what everyone had just survived most passengers were not exactly in the mood for further nervous tension. Hence although he had lots of sympathisers there were also others who were level-headed enough to recognise that their lives were on the line. Consequently they reached a decision and one of them approached him and began trying to calm him down. However, the more the peacemaker tried to reason with him, the more agitated he got. Meanwhile a couple of hefty guys were inching towards him from the other side of the aisle. Since the pacifier had his attention he did not notice their manoeuvre until in a synchronised move they pounced on him and pinned him down. He began howling, issuing empty threats while struggling on the floor.

In that instant the uninjured officer, who had washed his face and hands clean of his partner's blood though his shirt was still bloodied, approached. He was holding a transparent resilient-looking plastic strap provided by one of the flight attendants. Kneeling across the back of his squealing pinned-down ward, the officer quickly transformed the strap into a flex-cuff and restrained him. That action was greeted with a hearty round of applause.

Art shook his head in wonder as he observed his fellow travellers. He was amused too. Their attitude to life was like nothing he had ever known. He looked on as the deportee was led back to his original place between his two escorts. The injured one was sitting in a reclined position — his face had become very red and swollen, doubling its original size. There was a cold compress on his forehead and he was definitely having a rough time.

Shortly after the deportee was returned to his seat the captain was on the speaker again. He announced that since the situation aboard was back to normal he had received clearance to proceed. His message was greeted with another round of applause. Thereafter everything could have been described as business as usual but for one fact: From nowhere, a couple of men whipped out a cloth cap and began passing it around after a moving short speech by one of them in which he implored the passengers to donate to the cause of their "poor brother" who was being deported with no possessions other than the shirt on his back, alleging that all the wealth he amassed in Germany had been confiscated by the cruel racist authorities. Therefore he would need to start from somewhere on getting home.

As they went down the aisles from row to row, the cap began filling out with euro and dollar notes and of course pounds sterling, no matter how small the denomination. Those who had run out of foreign currency put in naira, the Nigerian local currency.

Art took in the scene in amazement. He was impressed by how seriously most of them seemed to be taking the concept of brotherhood — through thick and thin there they were standing by their "brother".

Is this an opportunistic move or genuine empathy? he kept wondering as he watched them continue on their rounds.

Since his research on scams began, particularly the "*419*" scam, he had learnt so much that he could not help but wonder if indeed the deportee was going to receive every cent being collected in his name.

After lunch which was not exempt of drama by a handful who wanted to be served more wine than they were entitled to, relative calm reigned. Most of the passengers went to sleep while the few who were awake were absorbed in the in-flight entertainment. The silence was occasionally punctuated by a crying baby or raucous laughter or the beeps emitted now and then when passengers required a flight attendant's attention.

Art welcomed the relative calm. He tried to take a nap but he was still too wound up to. Then he tried to just relax and free his mind of all worries. Again, that was difficult. Subsequently his mind strayed to his friend Adrian. They had been inseparable as kids. They had been quite a handful too; pretty mischievous and a bundle of trouble both at school and out of it. As adolescents they had not been too different. He smiled inwardly as he remembered some of the practical jokes they used to play on people. Adrian was working for the UNDP and had been living overseas so they had not seen each other in ages. He wondered if Adrian had changed much since the last time they met in Ireland while visiting their respective families at Christmas. Although Adrian had, on numerous occasions, invited him to his different stations, he had never been able to give him that pleasure. Thus when he called to inform him that he was planning a trip to Lagos, Adrian was overjoyed. He immediately invited him to put up with him. He smiled, wondering if Adrian would have been so eager to play host if he had known the true motive for his visit.

His reminiscence was interrupted by the voice of the pilot announcing their proximity to their destination: The Murtala Muhammed International Airport. As the pilot went on with details such as temperature, humidity and so on Art's mind became occupied with other things. He was thinking about all he had heard about the airport. He had been warned that safe and secure were not exactly adjectives that could be used to describe it and that he needed to have eyes everywhere particularly at the back of his head to get out of there with his belongings intact. He had also been advised not to trust anyone there not even the uniformed officials or officers. He wondered if things were really that bad or if that depiction had been embroidered in any way. He was jolted by a round of applause and hearty cheers. The pilot had just landed safely.

The aircraft had barely stopped taxiing and the 'fasten your seat belt' sign was yet to go off when most of the passengers began scrambling to grab their luggage. The aisles soon became congested — those still struggling to get their stuff out of the over-stuffed overhead luggage compartments were blocking the way of others who had equally impatiently rushed onto the aisles. As Art looked around, still strapped in his seat, he noticed that just like him the trio were still strapped in theirs. In fact they would be the last to disembark.

When he stepped from the aircraft into the concourse he felt the big change in temperature. It was uncomfortably warm there since the air-conditioning system was not effective. Neither was it in the terminal, he soon discovered. As he was waiting to go through passport control he spotted the deportee being handed over to two Nigerian police officers. The two German plain clothes policemen were met by a German who was probably from the German embassy since as a non-traveller he would need some sort of diplomatic pass to get that far into the airport. However, one of the lessons Art would learn later was that in Nigeria just about anything is possible with the almighty naira.

Anyway, immediately after the Germans left he observed that the deportee's attitude changed. He began behaving quite familiarly towards the officers he had just been handed over to. Later on, on telling people the story Art would laughingly be told that the possibility of the deportee having been released right there, with palm greasing of course, could not be ruled out. His shocked reaction would be met with more laughter. He would be indignant on two counts. The first was that the man could have made everyone lose their lives on the aircraft and the second was that the assaulted officer could have lost his life; but for sure he had obtained a scar for the rest of it; maybe for nothing.

Art was still paying close attention to the three men to know their next move when the baggage carousel started rolling. Dusty suitcases, boxes, bundles and stuff began tumbling out. As luck would have it his suitcase, by now really dust-coated, was among the first. It was a relief since the heat was becoming agonising. Conversely, he would have loved to hang around to know if the young man left there in a squad car on his way to prison or on his own, after spending all or part of the collection made on his behalf to grease palms.

'Welcome *Oga*,' a customs officer addressed him with a toothy grin.

'Thank you,' he replied with a smile, impressed by his seeming warmth.

'What have you brought us?' the officer asked, his grin broadening.

'Sorry?' he asked, completely at sea.

'Good evening, officer,' a voice Art recognised instantly said beside him. 'Are you having problems with my friend?' its owner continued, stretching out his hand for a handshake at the same time flashing his ID with his left hand.

'Oh, no *Oga* just welcoming him,' the officer stated, laughing self-consciously as he took the outstretched hand.

Still laughing awkwardly, the officer told Art that he was free to go and wished him a pleasant stay in Nigeria. With a sigh of relief Art swung sideways and was embraced by Adrian. It was just as well that Adrian's diplomatic pass had permitted him to get that far. Bidding the officer goodbye, Adrian picked up Art's dust-coated suitcase with a boyish grin.

'Shameless rogue,' he muttered, still grinning as he waved at the officer.

Art burst into laughter, telling him that he had not changed one bit.

'That corrupt officer was asking you for money back there; can you believe that?'

'Really, was he?' Art uttered in shock. 'So what I've been told is true!'

'Whatever you've been told, multiply it by a million and you'll still be right.'

After that he smilingly asked Art about his flight.

'Nightmarish, action-packed and ...'

'Meaning what?' Adrian interjected with an expectant smile.

'Let's talk about it later, okay? Right now I'd like to hear about your life here.'

'Okay then,' Adrian smiled, opening his car door.

As soon as they got into the car he locked all the doors before fastening his seat belt, stating that he was glad that the flight had arrived on schedule because being in Lagos Mainland after dark was not too safe. He then announced that they were going to race all the way to the Island although it was not dark yet. Smiling at Art, he added,

'Armed robberies occur in broad daylight so imagine at night-time.'

'Wow! How do people cope with that?'

'By avoiding some places altogether or knowing certain facts like areas to avoid after dark or that by stopping at traffic lights after dark you could become a sitting duck.'

'Goodness! Sounds like the Wild, Wild West,' Art laughed.

'Well, once you know what's what, it's not that bad. Anyhow, the Island's pretty different from the Mainland in terms of safety and all that.'

'Same city different rules; pretty interesting,' Art observed.

'Actually, not too different from what obtains all over the globe. I guess there are places in Madrid you'll think twice about visiting.'

'Sure, but not in order to avoid stickups,' he laughed.

'Oh, yeah; guess you're right there.'

As soon as Adrian had made that concession he cursed and swerved to avoid being hit by a car that had recklessly invaded his lane.

'Boy! That's close,' Art exclaimed, readjusting his sitting position.

'Sorry. Yeah, you haven't seen anything yet. After driving in Lagos you can drive anywhere else under the sun,' Adrian laughed.

After that the ride was quite smooth apart from the occasional traffic jam. Along the way they did a lot of reminiscing as well as filling each other in on what they had been up to in the years they had not been in touch. Occasionally Art commented on some of the sights they drove past. He was impressed, particularly by those on the Island. Though through the years he had concluded that cityscapes were not too different from one another, irrespective of what part of the planet one was on, he was still quite pleasantly surprised.

It was getting dark by the time they got to Adrian's home; a huge fenced one storey white house in an exclusive part of the Island known as Ikoyi. The vast compound had lots of grounds, both green and paved. The hedges were well-manicured and the shady trees well-trimmed. There were brightly coloured flowers in the front garden and a vegetable garden in the backyard. Somewhere at the back of the impressive building, shielded by huge trees, were the servants' quarters. Nevertheless, Art would not discover the additional beauty beyond the extraordinary floodlit front yard till the following day.

At the sound of the car horn the tiny window of the guard post came open and a head popped out. It belonged to Adamu, the gatekeeper.

'Although he recognises the sound of my horn, the routine's always the same,' Adrian observed in amusement.

'From all you've said I guess one can never be too careful,' Art smiled.

'Guess you're right but sometimes this ritual of his gets exasperating.'

'Welcome *Oga!*' Adamu called out as he threw the gate open with a broad smile.

'Thanks Adamu,' Adrian smiled. 'How're things?'

'No problem, *Oga*,' he beamed.

'Good, Adamu,' Adrian called out while driving in.

'He looks a cheerful sort,' Art observed.

'Indeed. He takes his work very seriously too. He won't let anyone in without due clearance even if he's seen them a million times. My pals often get miffed,' he laughed.

After Art had taken a much deserved shower Adrian announced that he was taking him to another area of the Island called Victoria Island to give him a taste of the good life.

They went to the favourite hangouts of diplomats, expatriates and the well-offs in the society. Their last drink was at an Irish Pub — a replica of their favourite joint back home.

'Wow! How did you discover it?' Art enthused, looking around delightfully. 'It's incredible! Complete with our team's colours too!'

'That was exactly my reaction the first time I came here. I was so delighted that I told Patrick about you and about the love we have for the one back home.'

'Who's Patrick?' he asked in confusion.

'I'm Patrick,' a cheerful voice spoke up behind him.

Turning round Art saw a huge curly haired blond bloke with blue smiling eyes stretching out his hand. He took it and his was almost crushed in a most enthusiastic handshake.

Patrick was the proprietor of the joint. He was Irish too. After the handshake Art asked him what he was doing in that neck of the woods and he replied that it was a long story. But the abridged version was: he was married to a Nigerian so meanwhile that was home. He then declared that their first drink was on the house.

Many more drinks would follow. It turned out to be a memorable evening in every positive sense of the word. Indeed Art had the time of his life. Come morning, he would not recall how he arrived home.

CHAPTER 13

An annoying sound which was somewhere between a buzz and a whirr was going on non-stop. It began after Art fiddled with a child's toy motorcycle. He wound it and placed it on the floor and it started going round and round. He gave it tiny pushes to make it move forward but it was no use the toy simply went on spinning and emitting that irritating sound. The sound soon got so infuriating that he got terribly desperate to stop it. He began asking himself why he had fiddled with the toy.

'At my age, what do I need a toy for?' he asked repeatedly.

He tried to ignore the sound but it was deeply embedded in his head.

At a stage he began wondering if he could be dreaming and when he finally pried his eyes open he discovered that the sound was coming from his newly acquired mobile phone. It was spinning on the bedside table and emitting the sound he had associated with the toy motorcycle. He noticed that its screen was blinking. After peering at it for a while he made out the word '*Oluwole*'. Slowly, it dawned on him that it was a reminder; he could not recall setting it though. His problem became how to make that irritating sound stop.

He had bought the phone just a day before his departure from Spain, on Diego's insistence. After failing to dissuade him from making the trip Diego advised him to get himself a mobile phone, reasoning that in case of an emergency not only would he be able to reach out for help but, he would also be easily located. At first he had put up strong resistance since he was not really a fan of such devices. Exasperated in his futile effort to persuade him, Diego offered to buy him one. Then just to get Diego off his back he had gone off in a huff and got himself a really good phone.

As he sat there trying to figure out how to shut the phone up, he regretted having bought it. His unfamiliarity with its workings was made worse by the fact that he was feeling so woozy from the previous night's excesses that he could not recall the little he had read about such functions in the manual that came with it. He kept fumbling until in the end, in utter exasperation, he simply turned it over and yanked out the battery.

'Peace at last!' he uttered.

Relieved, he stretched out on the bed again and shut his eyes. His head was throbbing away. He was suffering from that infirmity known as hangover. At such times he usually vowed never to allow anything with alcohol into his system as long as he lived. He desperately wanted to go back to sleep though he knew that that was practically impossible considering how terribly his head was aching. Suddenly the full meaning of the word on the phone screen sank in.

'Of course Oluwole!' he exclaimed, springing out of bed.

He lost his balance and crashed against some furniture before hitting the floor, creating a great racket. Shortly after that commotion there was an almost inaudible tap on his door. At the same time he heard Adrian calling out sleepily:

'Are you okay?'

'Yeah, sure; excuse the disturbance, I only lost my balance.'

He had sprung out of bed because Oluwole was uppermost on his 'must-visit' list. That list included the places he considered of utmost interest as far as his investigation was concerned. Oluwole was a very notorious area in Lagos where all sorts of shady deals took place. It was the den of master forgers, perhaps the most adept in the world, reputed for their creative talent and their extreme skill. The artistry employed by those incredibly talented artists in their forgeries helped the swindlers who patronised them carry off their schemes easily, worldwide. All kinds of tools used by scam artists to pull off their tricks were forged there. Such tools included an assortment of stamps and seals of banks, courts, ministries and even the President's.

Oluwole was also well-known for the trading in foreign currencies that took place in and around it. Those currencies were not always genuine. Documents of all sorts were sold there too — some of them were forged while others were stolen. They included foreign bank cheques, postal orders, international passports, bank statements, international driving licences and a variety of certificates like certificates of incorporation of companies, birth certificates, marriage certificates, death certificates and certificates from universities and other institutions. Some of those documents were employed by crooks interested in identity theft. They were also useful for acquiring false identities and for financial frauds.

Before his trip to Lagos Art had learnt from the section of the FBI website dealing with organised crime that such financial frauds perpetuated by, what the website described as the Nigerian Criminal Enterprises, cost the US alone up to $2 billion each year. Individuals as well as businesses and government offices were targeted in those frauds that included fake cheque scams, credit card scams and of course the great-grandmother of them all, the intricate advance fee fraud known as "419".

The first time Art heard about "419" from Regina he had not the least idea of what she was talking about. But by the time he had concluded his research which included thoroughly interviewing her and those she had referred him to, in addition to devouring all he could lay his hands on, plus almost everything he could find online including in Wikipedia, he got pretty close to becoming an expert on the matter.

He learnt that the term was derived from the relevant article of the Nigerian Criminal Code dealing with fraud, which this criminal practice infringed. He wanted so much to be educated on the subject that apart from consulting the aforementioned FBI website he also consulted most of the information provided by many law enforcement agencies around Europe and other parts of the world. He obtained information through a valuable source too: Diego. He put him through to some of the victims that the police had on record. Diego was convinced that there were far more cases but that people often felt too embarrassed about having fallen for such scams that they did not report them. Many were ashamed of being considered either greedy or gullible or even both.

One of the cases on record was that of a victim of the Spanish lottery scam. Since he was residing in the Netherlands Art had a telephone interview with him. The man confided that he received an e-mail informing him that he had won a huge sum of money in the Spanish state lottery and was required to pay the sum of 500 dollars which was supposed to be the processing fee, tax and stuff; ignoring the fact that such wins were free of tax in Spain, at least in those days. Interestingly enough that e-mail was supposed to have been from the Ministry of Finance. Asked how he fell for the trick, he replied that it was easy because the presentation of the e-mail — the information contained therein, complete with phone numbers and e-mail addresses — looked so genuine that he just did. He concluded that he was fortunate to have lost only 500 dollars because since then he had come across people who had lost far more.

What truly perplexed Art was that when he asked the man if he had played the lottery at any point prior to that his answer was no. Several times that day he would wonder: *how can anyone believe they won the lottery if they didn't buy a ticket?* He was not sure if people fall prey to such con artists because they are outright dumb or greedy.

Actually that guy's story was far better than that of an investor in the crude oil business — Bunkering — who Diego put him on to. Although the guy had agreed to meet him because it was Diego who fixed the appointment, the meeting lasted barely ten minutes. That was as long as it took them to introduce each other, exchange pleasantries, order their drinks and take the first couple of sips. As soon as Art stated his reason for being there the meeting came to an abrupt end. It turned out that the word 'Nigeria' was anathema to him. In fact on hearing it pronounced he rushed out of there as if the devil was hot on his trails. That was how scathed he got in his attempt to invest in some so-called lucrative deal. He lost practically everything he had, including his marriage.

Taken rather unawares and feeling pretty shocked at the man's lightning exit, Art could not go after him. Indeed he needed a while to assimilate what had just happened. After that he numbly finished his drink, settled both bills and left.

Since the victims he interviewed or whose case he heard of were contacted via e-mail by the scammers, he wondered if those tricksters would have been so successful in pulling off their scams worldwide if the internet had not existed. Anyway, those victims were completely taken in by the ingenious ways the scams had been presented to them. The tools for those scams, he discovered, had been obtained in the Oluwole area.

Most of those he told about his intention to travel to Nigeria including Regina, after she realised that she could not stop him, encouraged him to go to this infamous area to talk to some of those "artists" since the clues to resolving many of the riddles he was dying to get to the bottom of lay there. He had heard so much about it that he became convinced that visiting it was a must in his quest for answers. Hence he had it at the top of his 'must-visit' list. Little wonder then that although getting out of bed initially had required every bit of his willpower, when he finally did he got ready for his visit in a crazy whirl.

When he was set he could hardly sit still while awaiting the arrival of Wole, his Lagos guide. Curiosity was eating him up; he was dying for more info and for knowledge. Though he was excited at the prospect of that first visit he was also slightly apprehensive because he could not help thinking about the warning Diego had issued him. He had emphatically told him to steer clear of that area and to keep away from the con artists. Evidently he had inside info about the area and its prowlers.

Part of Art's unease, apart from Diego's serious warning, stemmed from the fact that other sources had told him all sorts of weird things about the goings-on in the area and the individuals who ran those affairs. The eeriest thing he heard was that in some parts one could easily obtain or place orders for human body parts; fresh or dried up; for powerful rituals. Such rituals were usually performed by a *Babalawo* on behalf of those who wanted to achieve instant wealth or to obtain overwhelming success in the realm of politics or any other. They were useful too when it came to unleashing serious harm on adversaries, political or business opponents, and on rivals as far as the affairs of the heart went.

He was so shocked on hearing that human parts could be acquired like any other commodity that he almost fell off his seat. The person who gave him that information roared with laughter on seeing his reaction. At the end of his laughter he stated that body parts were also available for purchase in the professed developed world, in the name of organ transplant. When he replied that those cases were for medical reasons the guy retorted that in both cases they were for healing purposes. Astounded, he asked the man whether he was pulling his leg or just trying to shock him and the man looked straight into his eyes as he replied,

'In your so-called civilised world not all organs for transplants are obtained in the way they're nicely claimed to be. Sometimes people are maimed or even killed to obtain them. Food for thought Mr Art: Do you know how many mutilated bodies are sometimes left behind in some developing countries so that those in your developed ones can have those transplants? You're an investigative journalist check that out. Why don't you make it your next project!" he concluded with derisive laughter.

Although that guy was a most valuable source of information; Art obtained important facts from him about the human-trafficking and human-smuggling networks; he gave Art the shivers all through the interview, making him resolve that under no circumstances would he want to be alone with him, except in public. He was the chap Regina had strongly warned him against and he did discover why. He was a very intense fellow who believed that the end always justified the means.

'Be very careful about where you go when you get to Nigeria because the body parts of whites; every tiny bit from hair to toe nails; like those of albinos are deemed extremely valuable ingredients in the concoction of highly potent potions!' he declared at a stage, making Art even more convinced about his earlier resolve.

'Do you know how much a lock of your hair will fetch?' he smiled.

'What?' Art uttered in consternation.

'Big bucks,' the bully sniggered.

Seeing the disconcerted look on Art's face he asked,

'Are you scared, Mr Art?'

Art was so dumbfounded by everything he had just heard that he could only gawk at that unpleasant individual who then took his silence to mean yes and roared with laughter.

'Good, you should be. That way you'll be extra careful when you get there. You're not going on a safari, you know,' he declared with a snigger, stood up and strutted off.

Although that brash annoying character really scared the wits out of him in addition to making him feel super uncomfortable, Art believed every piece of information he provided him. Paradoxically he admired his candidness, his brashness notwithstanding. That was precisely why he decided to take his warning seriously.

During his first meeting with his guide Wole that guy's claims about the availability and easy acquisition of body parts in Oluwole and some other areas of Lagos would be one of the initial questions he would ask him. To his consternation all he would receive in the form of an answer would be a noncommittal:

'Everything's possible in *Naija*, Art. There are many areas in Lagos that personally I wouldn't step into during the day how much more after dark.'

'That's comforting,' he would state, rather dryly.

Anyhow, that would be much later in the day. In that instant he was restlessly awaiting Wole's arrival. Regina had recommended him, explaining that her choice was mainly because apart from holding a degree in the History of Art, he was streetwise too. So he would explain many art-related matters to Art and help him get in touch with people with relevant knowledge of the goings-on in the art world as well as the underworld. She had stressed that he was highly trustworthy and discreet hence the perfect candidate, apart from his other qualities. He asked her why discretion was such a great issue and she replied that the mission he was embarking on called for that since it was extremely dangerous.

'I'd stop you from travelling if I could,' she had added, matter-of-factly.

That morning apart from being excited about his first adventure in Oluwole he was also looking forward to meeting Wole. His only contact with him had been on the phone the previous evening, before his night on the town with Adrian. So he only knew that Wole had a booming voice and a hearty laugh. He had also come across as cheerful. During their conversation Art somehow knew that they were going to hit it off.

Since he had been told that there was something known as "African time", in other words people hardly ever turn up at the appointed time, he was surprised when the buzzer at the gate rang at nine on the dot. Soon afterwards Adamu, the gate-keeper, rang the doorbell to announce that there was somebody asking for him at the gate and requested his permission to let him drive in. He told Adamu that he would meet the visitor outside.

Art found Wole seated in a flashy luxury sports car. The emphasis Lagosians placed on flashy cars and 4WDs was something that grabbed Art's attention all the way from the airport to Lagos Island.

Wole appeared relaxed listening to rhythmic music which Art later learnt was called Afro-beat. He got out of his car to greet Art. His physical appearance was close to how Art had imagined it: tall and well-built. He was ebony-skinned with well-set sparkling white teeth. He was decked out in a 3-piece embroidered traditional outfit made of tie-and-dye brocade material, which he complemented with a matching cap. He was sporting very expensive-looking watch, gold chains, bracelets and rings.

Everything about him seems expensive, Art observed.

He was wondering how there could be such disparity between people in the same society since he saw quite a bit of misery in some neighbourhoods on his way from the airport, when Wole's voice reached him. He wanted to know his impression of the city. He replied that although he was yet to see most of it, he was impressed by the little he had seen. Wole then promised to introduce him to the swinging Lagos nightlife and he smilingly thanked him before saying:

'I had a tiny taste of it last night and wouldn't mind another bite.'

They both laughed.

He soon discovered that Wole was a passionate speaker who gesticulated a great deal while trying to make his point. He also had the mannerism of punctuating almost every sentence with the phrase, 'You know'. He was quick to laughter and told so many jokes. Most of those jokes went over Art's head, however. Wole was great company apart from a good source of useful information.

Shortly after they set out they were caught up in traffic jam also known as 'go-slow' — a constant in Lagos. When Art commented on it Wole told him that at that time of the day it was even worse on the Mainland. He asked himself if anything could be worse than what they were experiencing. As they got closer to central Lagos the traffic became absolutely chaotic.

Okadas — commercial motorcycles — were crazily weaving their way through that rush-hour traffic. The operators flagrantly beat traffic lights and infringed every traffic regulation in total disregard of the safety of their passengers and other road users. Though *Okadas* should carry one passenger in some cases there were not just two passengers but three! At times the third was a child, sometimes an infant strapped to his/her mother's back. Art stared incredulously at the scene, occasionally shaking his head. Every so often he held his breath due to some crazy manoeuvre. Regardless of the enormous risk which all that frenetic zigzagging of the *Okadas* in and out of traffic entailed many of the passengers were not wearing a crash-helmet.

When he made that observation Wole said that by law they should but in some circles it was believed that people were known to have vanished on putting on the helmet they were offered by operators. Those people later appeared in places where criminals who trafficked in human parts did whatever they desired with them and then with the bits that were left of them. The goriness of the last part of the story notwithstanding, Art could not help bursting into laughter —the vanishing part was particularly amusing. He asked if those stories were ever verified and, between laughter, Wole replied that all he knew was that they were published and reported on TV and that people attested to having witnessed them.

'That's beyond amazing!' Art exclaimed, laughing louder.

When he stopped laughing Wole told him something that got him rocking anew with laughter. He said that he had watched a report on TV in which some motorcycle operators, considering the mandatory crash-helmets too expensive, resorted to manufacturing theirs by painting calabash, to which they attached rubber straps. He said that they looked quite convincing in some cases although the safety aspect was another story. When asked if they managed to fool the law-enforcement agents that way, Wole laughed, making a gesture the meaning of which he explained as: Once money exchanged hands most law-enforcement agents did not give a hoot. He then asked Art to look carefully at the crash-helmets and see if he could detect funny looking ones. To Art's greatest surprise he did find a couple or so.

'But that's a great risk,' he observed between incredulous laughter.

'Such safety issues don't matter much to people; this is *Naija*!'

Okadas were not the only menace out there. There were also huge ugly yellow commercial buses called *Molues*. Art observed that their rust-coated bodywork was plagued with multiple dents. He watched the buses in awe as they waddled along, straddling lanes menacingly, audaciously leaving clouds of black smoke — billowing out of their belching silencers — behind as they fought for dominance of the asphalt. Despite how unsafe they appeared, they were overflowing with passengers clinging to every available space. Some were even hanging from the rickety doors! He wondered aloud how any right thinking person could have certified the roadworthiness of such death-traps and Wole laughed aloud and asked,

'Road worthy what? Art, do you think people really care about such stuff in *Naija?*'

Shaking his head in absolute wonder Art turned his attention to the traffic once again. He noticed that not to be left out of that madness were *Danfos*. Those were minibuses and many of the ones he saw were yellow in colour, like the *Molues*. Regardless of their size inferiority they were out there competing for dominance of the asphalt with the *Molues* as they recklessly invaded the lanes of oncoming vehicles, overtaking vehicles from every possible side. Wole explained that such races were to get to the next bus stop before the rest to pick up waiting passengers.

The infernal traffic jam notwithstanding that ride was anything but boring — there were amusing anecdotes and shocking ones too. Finally Wole announced that they were within a short distance of Oluwole area and they began discussing their plans for the day in detail. Wole seized that moment to point out that things could turn really ugly if the Oluwole crowd discovered that they were there merely to snoop around so they would have to pretend that they were truly interested in contracting some services. He hoped that since he was well-connected and had lots of acquaintances there their inquiries would not cause anyone to raise their eyebrows. Shortly afterwards he declared that they had arrived and that their next feat would be finding a parking spot. In the end, however, they did so pretty fast as a security guard let them park in a company's private parking lot after being bribed.

The first thing that stunned Art in Oluwole was the audacity with which those brazen "businessmen" touted their services and their wares. It was as though they were going about normal business activities. During his research apart from the warnings he received he also learnt a lot about the criminality in and around the area. So much that he had expected to find rough-looking, tough-talking, intimidating thugs and not the smooth-talking, well-dressed smiling folks everywhere he looked. Also, he was extremely surprised that the atmosphere was that relaxed considering all those weird stories.

When he voiced his thoughts Wole burst into laughter. Wondering what was so funny, he gave him a questioning look. Still amused Wole explained that practically every one of them held a university degree or a diploma and that given their "profession", most of them were required to use their brains not their physical strength — the roughing up part was often outsourced. Shocked, Art asked if indeed it was sometimes necessary to resort to brute force and Wole's matter-of-fact reply was,

'Like in many businesses anywhere in the world, don't you think?'

Since he was wearing a poker face Art was not sure if he was joking. Anyhow, he asked him why, if those folks were graduates, they had resorted to earning a living that way instead of practising their profession. He replied that although every one of them was there for a varying number of reasons ranging from greed to absolute necessity, many of them had taken to that way of earning a living because of the socioeconomic situation in the country. He explained that the scam business began in the 1980s when the oil-based economy of the country suffered a crisis due to the slump in the price of crude oil exports. That led to massive unemployment which in turn led to the beginning of the country's brain-drain. Young professionals started trooping out to countries like the US and the UK. Since then there had not been much if any hopes of a turn-around; what with the greedy leaders who had always been in the helm of the affairs of the nation.

'How tragic; hopelessness often leads to desperate acts,' Art observed.

'You know, you can say that again,' Wole stated pensively.

After that he said that the great increase in criminality in the country stemmed from that dramatic slump and that most of those committing such crimes explained off their activities as a question of survival, full-stop. He paused again before stating that some of them saw themselves as victims of a corrupt system. He said that the situation was so complex that he often had the feeling that there was no light at the end of that particular tunnel. Asked if that was not a pessimistic viewpoint he shook his head before saying,

'When the head is bad the whole body is affected.'

He blamed most of the problem on the mismanagement of public funds by those whose obligation it was to manage them wisely. According to him, as long as the leaders selfishly continued enriching themselves at the expense of the masses very little was going to change. As he saw it the most annoying and hypocritical aspect of the matter was that those so-called developed countries that criticised the system were the same ones that were doing absolutely nothing to stop the stolen money from being stashed away in banks in their countries or from being invested either in big companies or in real estate over there, as a way of laundering it.

They had been walking around engrossed in that discussion when they were approached by somebody offering them cheap flight tickets. At first Art was tempted to go along and have a chat with him about that angle of Oluwole business but he restrained himself. He wanted to focus on his real reason for being there. Among the series of curiosities he wanted to satisfy was to get to the bottom of how the Madrid con team operated; basically, how they managed to smuggle works of art out of the country. During one of his conversations with Regina she informed him that the Federal Government had passed a law in 1963 which controlled the export of antiquities. Consequently all forms of antiquities, including all ritual art objects, could not be exported except with the express permission of the Department of Antiquities or the Curator of one of the National Museums. If it was so how could Santi pile up such a huge collection of Nigerian Art?

The first person he asked about that law was Wole and his reply was a staccato of laughter. Utterly surprised he asked him what was funny about his question and he replied,

'Man, this is *Naija* you know, and with special arrangements Satan can see God. That is: anything's possible in this country if you're ready to grease the right palms.'

'Are you talking about bribery?'

'You can call it bribery but most people simply see it as an incentive.' Art gazed at Wole for a bit, trying to digest that information.

'I see,' he mouthed finally though he did not quite see the point.

With time he would determine that so many people in Nigeria needed "incentives", irrespective of their position, to perform even the job they were paid for! He would also learn that adopting that modus operandi was indeed a catalyst; business got done very fast that way. It accelerated matters, making it possible for one to circumvent bureaucracy.

'And the *Naija* bit — what's it? I've heard it repeated so many times.'

'What about it?' Wole asked.

'I mean, what does it mean?'

'Oh, it's just a fond way we refer to our nation, instead of Nigeria.'

'Interesting,' Art smiled.

Another motive for his firm decision to visit Oluwole was to test the theory Regina put forward as to how the self-styled art dealers carted their loot out of the country: They got a bogus certificate, supposedly from the Department of Antiquities, which attested that the works of art in their possession were merely commercial art. To further back up their story they obtained fake invoices, from so-called souvenir shops, for such works of art which showed their price as way below their real worth. The certificate rendered them worthless as far as national treasures went thus taking care of the section of the law prohibiting the export of valuable works of art while the invoices allowed them to pay next to nothing in terms of export duties because the prices printed in them were so low that if duties were necessary, they were insignificant. He learnt that such duties were hardly ever paid; what with many corrupt customs officers who would usually look the other way no matter what was being smuggled in or out after getting their palms greased by smugglers of every kind. The certificate also cleared the supposed dealers of illegal art trafficking or any such offence at their port of entry overseas.

In Oluwole Art not only confirmed all that but he also got a free course on how to go about it. After all he had posed as someone interested in going into the art dealership business. When he saw a copy of the bogus certificate for the first time he was forced to admit that it looked highly authentic in every way — coat of arms, seal, relevant signature and so on. It was one of the many extremely impressive "creations" he was shown. He was so impressed that he eventually requested a copy.

Luckily the man did not seem to find his request odd which made him believe that he had swallowed his story hook, line and sinker. Both he and Wole experienced a brief moment of panic, however, when out of the blue he asked them for a description of the pieces of art and the quantity. Then Wole quickly spun him a tall yarn: the exact quantity was yet to be established as the source had not confirmed it. The artist seemed to buy that too. Regardless, he said that it would have been better if he entered the items artistically in the certificate. Apart from acquiring that certificate to cover up his true reason for being there Art also did it because he considered it a beautiful work of art worth acquiring and conserving. He needed a souvenir of that incredible setting and that artful forgery.

As a matter of curiosity he asked one "artist" if he had Irish passports. Since the man did not deal in passports he obtained a copy from a "brother" of his. It was complete with visas, supposedly obtained from different foreign embassies, and immigration stamps at different airports around the world. On comparing it with his he was surprised that as far as his eyes could see there was hardly any difference between them. Of course he did not know if any differences would be detected if it was subjected to hi-tech scrutiny. Since he did not need it he managed to wriggle out of paying for it by stating that he had not enough money on him then.

At the end of the day although the two visits he paid to Oluwole area left him more confused than ever in some respects they did provide answers to most of his questions apart from confirming that the imagination of those con artists had no limits. Many of those he talked to showed him an assortment of certificates and other documents that looked a hundred percent authentic. So much so that to an extent he understood how the scam victims mentioned earlier had fallen so easily for them. Indeed he reluctantly admired the craftsmanship of those "artists".

He also had moments of perplexity there: When he was offered a death certificate, for example. At first he assumed that they were kidding. But that was not the case. He was shown a sample and told that it could be made to meet the standards of any country in the world. Astounded, he asked them why he would want a death certificate. Their reply was,

'*Oga* you can never tell; you could want it for insurance claims.'

'Also, you could want to escape from it all — from your wife, your lover, your creditors or business partners, from your—' one artist explained enthusiastically.

'Okay, okay, I get the picture,' he interjected in awe amid an explosion of laughter at his expense.

When he asked if people actually paid for death certificates he was told that without demand there is never supply. He found the matter-of-fact way the answer was delivered revealing. They said that the law of demand and supply applied to every "product" and service available there. He secretly admitted that that was totally right. Indeed apart from the demand and supply bit the chicken-or-egg scenario was all around him.

He found the Oluwole experience unique. He obtained answers to most of the endless questions he had been asking himself since his investigation began. Sadly, although he still had a few unanswered questions their visit came to an abrupt end. Wole received a call and after getting off his super sophisticated phone he grabbed him by the shoulder and told him they were getting out of there in a flash.

They departed in a near-run, keeping that pace all the way to the car park. Art was panting and puffing. The fact that he was being made to race without being told why was not at all funny. As soon as they were safely inside the car he turned to Wole and breathlessly demanded an explanation. Wole panted that the call had been from an informant operating nearby. He warned him that word had begun spreading that Wole's mate was not who he claimed to be.

'What?' Art uttered, absolutely horror-struck.

CHAPTER 14

Next on Art's must-visit list was the National Museum at Onikan, to check out a really macabre piece of information related to the statuette and to learn more about that 1963 law through official sources. Although his appointment with the curator was at 12.30 p.m., he got there much earlier because Regina had advised him to have a tour of the museum. Actually she had insisted that he should, to see the artefacts which dated from 500 BC to 200 AD. When he asked her why the tour was so important, she replied that no amount of words she came up with would be enough to portray the picture to him.

He was struck by the beauty everywhere as soon as he stepped into the exhibition hall; it was simply breath-taking. He saw her point immediately. As he walked through the hall he had the sensation that he was journeying back in history, witnessing the evolution of various cultures of the country through centuries. Mouth agape he went around like one in a trance, gawking at the artefacts. They were like nothing he had ever seen. The lighting and the fact that the hall was deserted made him sink deeper into his bizarre state.

Breaking free from the spell of his surroundings and everything therein was tough but eventually he managed to. A tentative look at his timepiece confirmed his suspicion: it was time for his appointment. He got fully jolted out of that peculiar state he had been in. Wondering where all the time had gone, he reluctantly interrupted that unique tour.

He was still so marvelled at all he had seen that on walking into the curator's office the first thing he told the curator was how mesmerised he had got during his tour of the museum. The curator smilingly acknowledged the compliment and stretched out his hand for a handshake at the same time introducing himself as Bode Cole. Realising that he had not introduced himself, Art did so after an apology. Bode waved off his apology, confiding that he was not the first to be thus impacted. After the handshake he offered Art a seat.

He settled into the comfortable leather armchair and asked for a glass of cold water; he was dehydrated from his pub-crawling with Wole who had taken him to "explore" some select nightclubs on Victoria Island, the previous evening. He could not help but recall what a mixed evening it had been. Images of what had transpired, of how what had been a wonderful evening had almost been marred by a close-shave with tragedy, flashed through his mind. He began having recollections of how he had almost got robbed, as he had thought, or far worse as Adrian informed him when he narrated the incident to him on getting home. Those memories gave him palpitations and reflexively he clutched his chest; a gesture that did not go unnoticed by Bode. He asked him if he was okay and he smiled.

His mind was on how it all began: Sam, a friend of Wole's, had offered him a ride home because when he decided that it was time for him to call it a day Wole was still very much engrossed in an interesting business discussion. He decided to leave so as to be rested enough for his appointment at the museum. Also, he had got to his limit, that point beyond which holding down more alcohol would be virtually impossible.

The last nightclub he had been at with Wole's crowd overlooked the lagoon and the other side of the Island. The view through the glass walls or the deck, if one preferred the outdoors, was spectacular. The play of lights, from tall buildings and from boats moored on the other side of the lagoon, on the water surface was picture-perfect. It was like a scene taken out of a travel magazine. Given the whole setting and the great atmosphere around the table it was with great regret that he announced his intention to leave.

As he shook hands with everyone in the group they tried to persuade him to stay on, saying that the night was still young. He replied that he wished he could but that he had a busy day ahead. When he told them how much fun he had had they chorused that they would be expecting him the following night and he laughingly stated that it would depend on if he survived that night's excesses. They burst into laughter.

On the way out he asked Sam how the guys could knock back so much booze and remain so sober. Laughing, he replied that practically every one of them was a bottle. Noticing his puzzled expression Sam asked him if he had ever seen a bottle drunk.

'It doesn't matter how much alcohol a bottle holds it never staggers, it never sways; it simply sits or stands wherever as steadily as ever.'

Maybe due to the amount of alcohol Art himself was holding or because he really found that explanation hilarious but the fact was, he roared with laughter.

'That's a good one,' he said. 'I can't wait to tell it to my friends.'

'Go on, do so; I'll demand no royalties,' Sam laughed.

The amount of alcohol consumed at those tables was not Art's only source of surprise. He was also amazed at the number of business transactions. He had never heard so many dollars or pounds sterling mentioned at any single sitting. Of course naira was mentioned too but to a lesser extent because most of those conversations had to do with overseas business dealings and money transfers. There had been a lot of name-dropping too; he heard the names of top-ranking politicians, royalties and the rest of the crème de la crème of the society. Funnily enough each time a name was mentioned someone was kind enough to explain to him, the role that person played in the society or the position s/he occupied. Lots of wheeling and dealing took place too. All in all those gentlemen had not just been drinking.

After they got into Sam's car Sam announced that first he needed to make a quick run to an area called Apapa to deliver some blueprints. Art nodded. He then voiced something he had been mulling over: he had noticed how young some of the girls in the different nightclubs he had been at looked and that they had been hanging around foreigners — expatriates and tourists. Looking at him, Sam smiled impishly and said,

'They're around them because that's what many of your brothers come looking for.'

'What's that supposed to mean?'

'You said it yourself; you observed who the girls were hanging around.'

'Oh! Are you saying what I think? What's the legal age for access into nightclubs?'

Sam was silent for a while, his whole attention seemingly on the road and on his driving. Just when Art began wondering if he had heard his question he cleared his throat and turning to Art he stated clearly,

'Art, being minors; just like what obtains in Europe and elsewhere in the developed world; they're accompanied by their guardians. Sadly, they're pimps posing as such.'

'But the girls are so young,' Art pointed out, aghast.

'Indeed they are and highly malleable too. Some of them are brought from their villages under some pretext; for example, the prospect of being given a sound education.'

'Just like that; how do their parents buy such stories?'

'Unfortunately the perpetrators of such deplorable acts are often relatives of the poor gullible folks. The parents fall for such a ruse because of that. What's more, they're very grateful that their children are being offered the chance of a lifetime: the opportunity to acquire a good education. Ironical, isn't it?'

'How can people take so much advantage of others' desperation?'

'That's what most of the world's all about right now Art: Money. Most people don't seem to care how you make it — just flash it.'

Art nodded while thinking: *Undeniably big money has become a worldwide phenomenon.*

After a slight digression the conversation wound back to the foreigners and the young girls hanging around them. That in turn led them somewhere else: a drawn-out debate about double standards. Sam, who was no longer smiling, was of the opinion that most of the foreigners who came to the country and hung out with young girls protected their own children in their countries and were sometimes the most vocal when it came to condemning such practices yet they did just that as soon as they stepped onto foreign soil.

'Indeed they look for the tiniest opportunity to sneak into bed with girls, who are sometimes younger than their own children or even grandchildren,' he concluded, sadly.

After processing the information he had just received Art asked,

'Are you trying to say that in this society no man hires their services?'

'Hires whose services?' Sam asked abstractedly.

'I'm referring to the young girls we've been talking about.'

'Ah, yes of course, the girls! Definitely I can't make such bloated claims. But you're there and you made your observation. The percentage is pretty low in comparison.'

'What's the explanation for that?'

'It's easy: Apart from some foreigners' predilection for young girls they're also more willing to dole out gifts and cash; FX for that matter. Consequently many of the girls consider them more generous than some Nigerian men or sillier. Also, since they're suckers for the tales of woe they're told by the girls, they meet their every financial demand.'

'That's interesting!'

'Uh-huh. Furthermore, in many cases these guys are here without their families so they're freer too. Thus they dedicate more time and affection to the poor young girls.'

'That's so kind-hearted of them!' Art stated with sarcasm.

'Yeah, and tender too!' Sam smiled, matching Art's cynicism. 'Well seriously, it's glaringly obvious that their motives are not altruistic.'

They went on to discuss human trafficking and human smuggling. As Sam saw it, part of the reason human trafficking was so rampant was because overseas, there was great demand for practices linked with it. He was referring to sex trade particularly with very young girls — minors in many cases. As Sam was talking Art was analysing a similar conversation with Regina. Then Sam grabbed his complete attention when he said that he could put him through to people who were one way or another involved in or affected by either human trafficking or human smuggling.

He could not believe his luck! That was exactly what he needed: talking to insiders. He told himself that in the end Wole's inability to give him a ride did turn out to be a blessing in disguise. He was a firm believer that things happen for a reason. Smiling to himself, he tried to act cool although he felt like leaping with joy.

'Thanks Sam, you're truly a goldmine of valuable info,' he said.

Sam had barely got to the end of 'My pleasure' when his car started stalling. He was taken aback since he had just had it serviced. He implored it not to fail him, at least not anywhere around that spot, but it simply sputtered and died. Looking around in consternation, he cursed out loud. They were on one of the many flyovers in Lagos. Telling Art to wait in the car, he got out to take a look inside the bonnet. Art decided to join him anyway, not that he knew a thing about the workings of cars. He staggered out and stood swaying on jelly-like legs beside Sam who was still cursing.

Sam had barely opened the bonnet when a yellow taxi, whose interior was dark, appeared. As it was drawing close he called out: 'Run!' Wondering what the matter was, Art looked around. On seeing that Sam had taken off like lightning he began moving his jelly-like legs one after the other, like an automaton. Still confused he managed a backward glance and understood that indeed there was cause for alarm: Four heavily armed men had alighted from the taxi. From then the sprint for dear life began.

Seeing them got him quite sober and he would later aver that he felt an almost supernatural surge of energy course through his body and that he ran like he had never ever done in his entire life; considering his lifestyle of zero exercise, maybe. Anyway, embellishment or not, the fact was that he managed to keep on running and to maintain Sam's back within sight. His effort must be commended since Sam was a seasoned sportsman. He jogged regularly too. Although Art had always claimed that he detested exercising, the importance of it dawned on him as he panted and puffed way behind Sam, determined not to lose sight of him on that dark bridge. His zero knowledge of his surroundings strengthened his resolve to puff along — the staccato sound of gunfire too.

It turned out that they were close to the foot of the flyover and they raced down it with that petrifying sound accompanying them. Art was convinced that the men meant business. Just as he became almost certain that he would not leave Lagos alive a police checkpoint popped out from nowhere. It was in the dark, under another flyover. A weapon brandishing policeman ordered them to halt. They were trembling like leaves. Art could barely stand upright as he spluttered, 'Good evening, officer,' in reply to the officer's barked 'Evening, gentlemen!'

Then tongue hanging out he doubled over, clutching his chest. His breath was coming out in huge gasps. It took him ages to realise that Sam was being grilled. It also took him that long to notice that there were six armed policemen there. Between gasps he managed to contribute to Sam's report. The officer in charge listened to them with very little interest. In fact he was acting bored and they had barely got to the end of their report when he impatiently waved them through the barrier.

Art could not believe that that was all and he asked Sam if their report was not supposed to be taken down. Sam stated resignedly,

'This is *Naija*, man."

Once again that same worn out phrase, he was thinking and rolling his eyes at it when Sam told him that they should thank God they were alive. He shook his head in disbelief as a feeling of frustration laced with rage surged through him. Then he looked around, wondering how they were going to get home. Personally after the scare he had just experienced he was prepared to spend the night right there as he was feeling kind of safe.

He turned to Sam to know his view and discovered that he was gone. He panicked. But mercifully he spotted him some distance away, engrossed in conversation with the officer. Then he observed a swift movement of hands as money passed from one to the other. He gawked in disbelief. After that the officer moved over to his men. Sam signalled him to approach. When he got close enough Sam whispered that two officers were going to escort them to the car. Disgust flashed across his face and he began expressing his indignation over Sam's greasing the officer's palm for him to perform his duty.

'Shh!' Sam let out sharply before he could finish.

After that in tow of arms brandishing officers, he and Sam headed for the car. Miraculously it had not been tampered with — even the officers were surprised. One of them observed that they were extremely lucky since the time they spent at the checkpoint had been more than enough for the robbers to clean out their car — they usually operated at lightning speed. The assumption became that they spotted the checkpoint during the pursuit and then split the scene to avoid an armed confrontation. So it was just as well that he and Sam had headed in that direction. He would later learn that quite often armed robbers knew where the checkpoints were although the police tried to set them up arbitrarily so as to make their illicit activities practically impossible.

Anyway, one of the officers who had a knowledge of mechanics tinkered with the bowels of the bonnet briefly and certified the car ready to go. As he and Sam got in he realised how lucky he was that the car had not been tampered with in any way because his backpack, containing lots of information related to his investigation, was lying under his seat. Sighing with relief, he pulled it out and hugged it close to him.

Though he was still trembling slightly from the nightmarish experience he had just undergone, he was also dying to brace the issue of corruption, a practice he had seen so much in the course of his short stay. However, that would not be because after what they had just been through Sam was not in the mood for conversation. Except for an occasional monosyllabic answer to his questions Sam was in dead silence. He was visibly shaken by that dreadful ordeal. As a result Art did not raise the issue. Nor did he ask Sam how he had known that the appearance of that taxi spelt danger.

He wondered, *was it due to the dark interior?*

He was so submerged in those unpleasant thoughts that the sound of Bode's voice jolted him back to the present. He smiled, embarrassed. Bode asked him how he was coping with the heat. He replied that coping with it was easy since temperatures in Madrid were no different in summer. Looking surprised, Bode remarked that it was funny that somewhere in Europe could compete with Lagos in that regard before adding smilingly that his memory of Madrid was of an extremely cold city since his visit had been in winter.

'Madrid's a city of extremes, weather-wise,' Art smiled.

At that point they were interrupted by the ringing of Bode's phone. While Bode was on the phone Art seized the chance to browse through his questions for the interview. He had had the intention of waking up early to revise them but waking up at all had required every bit of his willpower considering the truly crazy night he had had. Then there was also the issue of the massive hang-over he had had to wrestle with.

Well, he had barely gone midway through them when Bode got off the phone and invited him out for lunch, explaining that their lunch venue would provide a better atmosphere for the interview. The invitation was so unexpected that at first he was at a loss for words. Then he considered turning it down because he had promised Adrian he would have lunch with him. Since his arrival apart from that first night they had on the town, they had hardly had time to be together because of Art's hectic social cum professional life. He saw so little of Adrian that he occasionally felt guilty. Nevertheless, the hospitality of everyone he had come across so far had been overwhelming. He had always had to give in to invitations because he did not want to offend his new friends or acquaintances. The case in question was one of such situations. It was even more complicated because besides not wanting to appear discourteous by saying no, he did not want to do so since he had the feeling that he was about to obtain a big scoop. As he did not want to miss the opportunity he would just have to disappoint Adrian once again, despite himself.

The short walk to their lunch venue took them past a bus terminus called Race Course and he saw those monster *Molues*. Seeing them menacing and harassing other road users; with their sheer bulk and recklessness; was intimidating but seeing so many of them at such close quarters went way beyond that. Fierce-looking touts known as *Area Boys* were all over the place menacing the *Molue* and *Danfo* drivers and brazenly collecting "commissions" from them — i.e. extorting them. Many of them had bloodshot eyes — evidence of their drug and alcohol use.

Area Boys were a rowdy lot who engaged in criminal activities that ranged from petty crimes to really violent ones including murder for a fee, for a living. Their other crooked activities included extortion and drug peddling. Many people were terrified of them. When Art learnt that they often supplied *Molue* and *Danfo* drivers as well as their conductors with drugs — marijuana in the main — he understood clearly how those drivers could put up the sort of crazy displays he had witnessed on the road.

Hawkers peddling all sorts of wares like fruit, vegetables, cooked food and stuff were part of the chaos out there. And so were blind, lame and maimed beggars singing for alms at the top of their voices. The din was unbearable. It included the ear-splitting horns of the *Molues* and the honking from cars caught up in the fast building up lunchtime traffic jam. All that noise was made more intolerable by the intensity of the overhead sun.

Apart from the din the air pollution caused by the dust raised by the buses and the individuals milling around; most of the surface around was not paved; the plumes of black smoke belched out by the *Molues* and the *Danfos* and the exhaust pipes of badly beaten-up bangers was another matter. Art needed no measuring apparatus to determine that the level of fumes in the air was much higher than what any human lungs should be made to endure. However, while he was struggling to breathe, the people around him were smilingly going about their business as if they were breathing pristine early morning air in the country.

The abundance of smiling faces everywhere he went — sometimes in really harsh settings — was the one absolutely remarkable thing he had noticed since his arrival.

His uneasiness had been worsening not only due to his respiratory discomfort, but also because of the presence of those touts and the hustle-bustle all around him. Thus he was extremely thankful when he and Bode finally crossed the road that lay between the bus terminus and their destination. That few-minutes' walk seemed to have lasted forever.

The restaurant was part of a Tennis Club. Walking through the door, Art noticed that the atmosphere therein was such a sharp contrast to the hell he had just survived. Furthermore, the pace of activities there was totally different from the one he had just witnessed. Everything inside was so civilised, orderly and peaceful. He found it amazing that a road's breadth was all it took to separate those worlds — worlds which were so entirely dissimilar. In a way, he found it ironical as well as saddening.

Right from the club entrance there was a lot of boisterous joviality between Bode and his friends. Bode introduced Art to them and they all hung around the downstairs bar. Art turned down several invitations to a beer; he was still suffering acutely from the previous night's indulgence. Moments later Bode took him upstairs to the restaurant and recommended the outdoor seating area. Art welcomed the idea because of his state — he needed lots of fresh air. He discovered that the wide terrace not only guaranteed fresh air, it also commanded an impressive view apart from overlooking the centre court.

Bode excused himself soon after they got seated. Once alone Art relished the peace and calm up there. He soon made out the sound of racquet against ball and he got to his feet. He discovered that it was coming from the centre court, from club members who were using their lunch hour to keep fit despite the scorching weather. Leaning against the handrail, he watched them whacking away at the ball. He admired their great courage since to him exercising under such heat entailed nothing but that. Then he let his eyes wander. He got a generous marvellous view of most of the club and beyond. At the same time he could feel light breeze blowing gently against his face and gently ruffling his golden curls. He loved the feel of it. He closed his eyes for a moment, relishing all those sensations. It took him some time to realise that Bode was standing beside him.

'You seem to be in a different world,' Bode observed, startling him.

Lunch was hot and spicy — literally and otherwise. Before the main meal Bode coaxed him into having a taste of the club's *suya* — spiced skewered barbequed meat. Though it was not his first go at *suya* that one was special, he found it even tastier than Bode had sworn it was. He thoroughly enjoyed it. Although his stomach was yet to recover from the excesses it had suffered, he dared order a bottle of *Odeku* with the *suya*.

Odeku is the nickname for Guinness stout, the large bottle. The first time he tasted it, following Adrian's recommendation, he had to admit that it was way different from what he had been used to back in Ireland or Spain. He found it kind of thicker and with such a kick, the like of which until then he had never experienced though he claimed to have put away many bottles of that dark liquid.

Even spicier than the delicious meal was the information he gathered from the relaxed interview that went with it. Right from the beginning he knew that it was going to be memorable because when he mentioned the statuette Bode flinched. Then when he showed him the pics he had taken of it at Santi's he recoiled. He asked him if he had heard about the incident in Madrid and he nodded thoughtfully before stating that he read about it online. Till then neither he nor anyone else in the museum had had any news of it since its mysterious disappearance from there. Smiling wryly, he stated that it was possible that no one really missed it in view of the havoc it had wreaked there. Seriously, he added that its disappearance was still being treated as theft and was still under investigation.

'It's still under investigation?'

'Oh, yes. The authenticity of the statuette in Madrid can't be established until it's been subjected to some tests,' he explained.

'In other words, you're assuming it's not the original?'

'Art, the facts are there and so are the acts therefore one can assume that it is. Officially though, the procedures are like I've just explained them to you.'

'Does that mean you're going to try to get it repatriated?'

'It's usually a lengthy process but of course we'll have to do just that.'

When Art asked about the bizarre incidents attributed to it Bode lowered his voice to a conspiratorial whisper as he explained that it was believed that a curse had been cast on it by its rightful owners. That was because it had either been wrongfully taken away from them or stolen from their ancestral shrine.

The word shrine reminded Art of what Regina had told him about ancestral shrines and the idols they held and how families held strongly unto those idols because they represented their ancestral spirits. Such shrines were very sacred places and the idols were jealously guarded. That was why she believed that the statuette must have been stolen.

He switched his mind back to what Bode was saying: He was not too sure of how the statuette made its way to the museum since he had not joined the museum then but he later learnt from some sources that it had been a legal acquisition. Unfortunately nobody who could confirm that version was alive and strangely, there did not seem to be any documents around to back or refute that version of events; a fact which he found pretty odd because the provenance of every artefact was usually documented. He concluded his explanation by saying that though there were still discrepancies as to how it got there, everybody agreed on one fact: Its stay there had, without doubt, been unforgettable.

Bode confirmed Regina's story about the inexplicable deaths involving those in top management. In a period of less than six months three consecutive Directors met bizarre accidental ends. Weirdly enough, they had all been struck down by thunderbolt and in each and every one of those cases there had been no storm just sudden thunder and lightning in apparently fair weather. Also, eerie happenings and sightings had been reported mainly late at night in the museum while it was there. After the third death it got virtually impossible to fill that position — nobody seemed prepared to die that sort of dramatic mysterious death.

The words thunder and lightning made Art think about the Madrid incident. He found it uncanny that in those mysterious deaths Bode had just mentioned both had featured although the prevailing weather conditions had not called for them — exactly like in the Madrid case. He deemed that to be one hell of a coincidence.

Bode revealed that rumours had it that all those deaths bore the signature of *Shango*. On hearing *Shango* Art's face lit up because though Regina had mentioned him, they had not dwelt on the subject since they had had so many issues to discuss. So he seized that golden opportunity to ask Bode for details. Bode joked that he was dazed that someone as interested in the occult as him did not know much about *Shango*.

'Clearly I don't,' he admitted, matter-of-factly.

'*Shango*'s the god of thunder and lightning,' Bode stated slowly, as though he was teaching a slow child his lessons.

'That much I already know,' he smiled expectantly, eager for more.

Bode went on to inform him that although *Shango* was originally a Yoruba god he is also worshipped in different cultures around the globe presently, particularly in Latin America and the Caribbean. He is usually portrayed bearing a double-headed axe which represents rapid and equitable justice. He is believed to have an explosive temper and during his outbursts he creates peals of thunder by thumping and banging violently with the axe. He produces lightning by hurling thunderstones down to earth against his targets, those who have provoked his rage. The flaming stones set everything they strike ablaze and raze them, killing those who offended him and setting their houses on fire.

Art was getting seriously intrigued as Bode went on about *Shango*'s modus operandi. He recalled that part of Santi's studio had been razed and so had a wing of his mansion as well as the room in which the African young man had got struck dead. He wondered if indeed Santi's survival had been due to supernatural mediation initiated by his *meiga* friend, like Santi had claimed, or a mere coincidence or even an exaggeration of his.

He was deep in thoughts so when Bode spoke he almost jumped out of his skin.

'Did I scare you?' Bode laughed.

'No,' he smiled, 'I was just trying to digest your valuable info.'

He then asked Bode if there was any possibility of *Shango* venting his rage twice over the same provocation. He wanted to know if there was any chance of a repeat of the Madrid incident. Although that question caught Bode unawares, judging from the look on his face, he did not lose sight of the allusion because after a brief pause he explained that according to traditional belief as long as *Shango* is not appeased he rages on until he is. He explained that in the case in question the answer was absolutely affirmative. And, appeasing him would entail first of all returning the statuette to its rightful owners who would then coax *Shango* into calling off his offensive by performing the necessary rites.

Art knew that the interview had come to an end when Bode told him that he had a meeting scheduled for 4 o'clock and that unfortunately it was already 3.30 p.m. Art expressed his surprise at how time had raced by and thanked him for his generosity time-wise, for the information and for the lunch. Bode replied that he was glad to have been of help since he considered any friend of Regina's as a friend.

'By the way, I've not heard from her in ages,' he stated contemplatively.

'Oh, is that right?' Art uttered, forcing a smile; simultaneously praying that she would be found so that he could tell her about Bode's kindness.

Bode walked him to the taxi rank opposite the club. It was empty. He explained that most of the taxis were probably caught up in post-lunchtime traffic. Assuring Art that he would not have to wait for long, he apologised for his inability to keep him company. As Art was waving off the apology, his phone started ringing. Bode begged to be excused, bade him goodbye and rushed off.

Art's caller was Wole. Without preambles Wole asked him where he was. Art noticed an uncharacteristic tension in his voice and asked him what the matter was. Wole immediately asked him about the previous night's incident making his mind return, for the millionth time, to that unpleasant episode. He started feeling anxious anew.

'Oh, that; I can see that Sam's filled you in,' he mumbled.

'No, not Sam; I received an anonymous call.'

'You received what?' Art asked, his tone rising. 'How's that possible?'

'I've asked myself just that. I was told to tell you: pack up and go!'

He then repeated his earlier question regarding Art's whereabouts. Art replied that he was outside the Tennis Club and he asked him to go back in and wait for him. Art started telling him not to put himself out for him that he would make it home safely. But Wole interjected, insisting that he should wait. He finally gave in, they were supposed to meet later in the evening anyway, to discuss his next move.

Wole appeared sooner than Art had expected and they drove straight to a lagoon-side bar, part of a five-star hotel chain. After listening to the details of Wole's news Art ordered some spirit despite his earlier vow to avoid the stuff. His mission there was no longer a secret; Wole had been asked to tell him that if he did not back off, he was going to meet the befitting fate reserved for snoops. He was badly shaken. Regina came to his mind again and he mused: *Could they be responsible for her disappearance?*

Startlingly, at that very instant Wole asked after her, just like he had done when they met for the first time. Again, he considered telling him about her disappearance but for some strange reason he could not get himself to do so.

'Curiously enough I had a dream about her last night,' Wole disclosed.

'Really?' he asked, rather fast.

'Yes. It's really weird.'

Just as Wole was about to explain how weird, his phone started ringing. On getting off the phone Wole announced that he had to run along, business as usual. He offered to run Art home but he thanked him and politely turned down the offer. He was still dazed and he just wanted to hang around, gazing at the view beyond the lagoon and feeling the soothing effect of the sea breeze against his burning face. He wanted to be alone, to further assimilate Wole's nerve-racking news.

Wole informed him that everything was set for his trip to Benin City and gave him all the necessary data, explaining,

'Just in case you decide to cancel tonight's get-together.'

He welcomed Wole's idea since he had started feeling extremely weary. Part of the information Wole gave him was the name of his escort for the trip and that the man would contact him later in the evening for them to finalise the fine details such as their departure time. Also, he had contacted a well-connected individual in Benin City to act as Art's guide there. Assuring him that the fellow would take good care of him, Wole apologised anew for not being able to accompany him personally due to his numerous commitments in Lagos.

Waving aside his apologies, Art thanked him for his immense help. They then exchanged a firm handshake after which Wole patted him on the back, wished him luck and bade him farewell. Returning the pat, Art assured him that he would be okay.

CHAPTER 15

Come the following morning Art was headed for Benin City despite Adrian's effort to dissuade him. Adrian warned him that he was playing with fire especially if those he was investigating had links with cults. He replied that he was not going to yield to intimidation of any sort. Adrian tried to make him see that when it came to cults in those parts, there was no such thing as intimidating tactics; those individuals simply resorted to action. He went on to inform him that people had been known to disappear for doing far less than he was doing. Eventually, it did not matter how much dissuasive argument Adrian presented, he simply refused to listen. His mind was totally made up.

What Adrian did not tell him initially was that when he got home the previous evening Adamu informed him that a couple of sinister individuals had been hovering suspiciously outside the gate. One of them eventually approached him and asked if a visitor had arrived there in the last few days. Since he had been observing their suspicious movements, he had deduced that they were up to no good so he pretended that he did not understand their question, that he spoke no English.

Desperate to dissuade Art from leaving, Adrian ultimately threw in that information.

'Sorry buddy, I know you mean the very best but I'm here on a mission,' Art stated.

'You're a stubborn goat!' Adrian uttered in frustration.

'Yeah, I know,' he smiled, picking up his bag and getting into the waiting hired car.

His original plan had been to travel by air in order to save time. However, Omo, his escort, had classified the local planes as *flying coffins* and stated unequivocally that there was no way he was going to board one.

He chose that qualification to make a salient point: most of them had very poor safety record. As a result of his vehement objection they were in for a four-hour journey, though it was a distance of just 210kms. Omo warned, however, that it could take even longer since they could stumble into lots of unforeseen circumstances as the road was plagued with armed robbers, both those acting supposedly within the law and those operating outside of it. Catching Art's questioning look, he explained that sometimes even the police used their position of authority to rob people. He was referring to the unappeasable appetite many corrupt officers had for bribe.

He also declared that there would be other problems like potholed roads, endless police checkpoints and all kinds of surprises. Too many things had been happening lately so Art was not exactly in the mood for surprises, at least not unpleasant ones. He preferred to have that point clarified so he asked,

'What do you mean by all kinds of surprises?'

'That means that anything can happen. This is *Naija*, *Oga*,' Omo smilingly affirmed.

'Oh, no; if I hear that expression one more time, I'm going to throttle somebody,' Art mumbled — he was grumpy from lack of sleep, a result of the previous day's worries.

'What did you say, *Oga*?' Omo asked.

'Why does everything boil down to: 'This is *Naija*'?'

'The rules are different here and sometimes, anything goes. *Naija's* unique,' he said.

'Yeah, I've observed that too,' Art acknowledged grumpily.

'You have? And what do you make of it?'

'Hmm, it depends,' he replied noncommittally.

He was dying for another cup of coffee. Apart from the sleepless night he had had, another source of that uncharacteristic grumpiness was that too many changes had been made to his original travel plans. The departure time was another relevant change he had had to accommodate to. He had wanted to set out very early in the morning so as to arrive at noon latest and dedicate most of the day to his investigation. However, the driver had insisted that he would not set out that early for safety reasons — safety from armed robbers of all sorts. He preferred to leave Lagos when it was fully light and drop them off early enough to be able to return in broad daylight too. That had been his explicit condition.

Indeed, in the end the journey lasted far longer than had been projected due to a number of incidents which even the most comprehensive of planning could not have detected or taken care of. First, they had two flat tyres because of the sorry state of the road. Afterwards they had one mechanical problem after the other and then the car started overheating. Consequently, they were forced to stop every so often to give the engine time to cool off. To crown it all, when they were less than 50kms from their destination they got wilfully delayed at a police checkpoint since the driver, by now sick of bribing officers at several checkpoints along the way not to mention all the car problems, refused to play ball.

After a long time of them trying to sit it out Omo raised a significant point: being there when it got dark could turn out far more expensive in terms of their lives. He went on to tell them stories of people who had got shot at checkpoints by the police and were later branded as armed robbers resisting arrest. In most of such cases just the police version of the incident ever got published. Only in very few cases was the truth made public because somebody managed to get away or happened to witness the incident, undetected. He told them of a personal experience: He had been accompanying a cousin of his, who had come on a visit from the US, to their hometown when they were stopped at a checkpoint on that same highway. The police tried to extort them, claiming that his cousin had brought some banned items into the country and if he did not "cooperate", they were going to confiscate all his belongings. His cousin, as vociferous as ever, began yelling about his rights and stuff and the officer in charge bellowed that if he did not stop that 'imported stupid attitude about his rubbish rights', he was going to shoot him right there.

'You'd then have all the time in the world to talk about your stupid rights before your maker,' the officer had concluded menacingly.

Art was getting weary of it all by the second and he was quite shaken up by everything he had witnessed; particularly seeing the muzzle of a gun shoved forcefully under the defiant driver's chin. Listening to Omo's story did not make his frame of mind any better. He began questioning his sanity anew. He could not understand why the heck he was keeping at that investigation when everyone had been warning him to back off.

However, as soon as that doubt reared its head he told himself that he had single-mindedly come that far so there would be no turning back.

With this new resolution to fight on he decided to forgo his principles regarding bribery and his resolve not to interfere so he offered the defiant driver some money to grease the palms of the greedy officers. At first the man stubbornly refused to accept it, claiming that he had had just enough and that he was prepared for the worst. An exasperated Omo whispered harshly into his ears, asking him if he had gone crazy and if he wanted to get them all killed. The scariest part was that one of the officers who was clearly drunk, had threatened that he would not hesitate to do just that, stating categorically that no witness would be left standing.

Ultimately, the driver reluctantly accepted the money and took it to the officers. The gratitude he received was, being pushed around a bit and in the end being shoved in the direction of his car after being told that he had just narrowly escaped joining his ancestors. That experience was an ordeal that Art was certain he would not forget in a hurry. At long last when they were ordered to leave, he did not look back. He wanted to leave that horrible experience behind him, literally and figuratively.

On their arrival in Benin City he was warned against venturing out alone after dark due to the endless stream of armed robberies and kidnappings in the city. He did not care too much for the city on that first day anyway; after that nightmarish journey he was too tired for anything except sleep. It was just as well that they had had something to eat in a *buka*; a make-shift roadside restaurant; just before they got held up at that checkpoint. Consequently, he was not at all hungry since he had really stuffed himself in the *buka* picked out by Omo, out of the trillions lining that stretch of the road.

Omo had persuaded him to taste the house speciality, a popular dish known as *bush meat. Bush meat* is smoked dried game, such as antelope. That area was claimed to be one of the best in the nation as far as bush meat went. Indeed they stopped there so that he could add something new to his gastronomic experiences — quite apart from the fact that they had all been ravenous. Although Art found the sauce extremely hot, he admitted that the meat tasted pleasantly different from any other he had had till then. Omo also tried to make him taste a dish of fried snails which he ordered with some beers after the *bush meat*. Those were the largest snails

Art had ever seen — as large as a giant's hands, he claimed. Though they looked quite appetising in the tomato sauce they were served in, he had decided to pass since he was so full from the bush meat and the couple of *Odekus* he had had.

As his culinary affairs had already been taken care of all he needed on arrival at his comfortable hotel was a very long shower and another bottle of chilled *Odeku*. The shower was a must because after so many hours on that rough road in baking temperatures, he was feeling all dusty, sweaty and sticky. He was so exhausted that he barely got to the bottom of his last glass of that dark liquid before he crashed out.

When the jangling of the phone awoke him he could not believe that it was already morning. He moaned as he reluctantly got out of bed. He had a long hectic day ahead. Additionally, the night would be a sleepless one due to a most risky yet exciting mission he would have to embark upon. Bearing those facts in mind, he planned on starting the day by plying himself with strong black coffee after a long shower.

When he got downstairs he found Omo in the hotel lounge chatting away amicably in Edo language with a middle-aged man. As he approached they switched to English. Omo introduced his companion as Efosa. Efosa was a British trained local journalist who was an expert in secret societies and the occult. He was the guide and mentor recruited by Wole because he was very knowledgeable in the matter under investigation. He was also well-connected in the society since he was a descendant of the royal family — a detail which Wole deemed of vital importance. Apart from the fact that they shared the same profession and the same interest in the occult, Art took to him instantly because of his wittiness.

The trio were soon on their way to their first destination: a sleepy little village on the outskirts of Benin City. It took them about two hours to get there because the roads were not in the best of states; they were mostly dirt roads. As soon as the party stepped out of the car Art became something of a sensation in that small village where the closest most of the inhabitants had come to a white man was on their TV screens. Round-eyed carefree children; most of them naked from the waist up exposing their round, seemingly well-fed bellies; trailed behind them smiling shyly at them especially at Art, calling out '*Oyibo!*' He recognised the word and recalled learning its meaning from Regina.

They looked quite happy as they followed the visiting party around. As the minutes ticked by a couple of the more daring ones overcame their awe of him and broke away from the pack. They inched forward towards him and tentatively reached out their tiny fingers and touched him. They did so fleetingly at first. Then they became bolder and let their fingers rest on his skin for longer. Turning to their friends, they gave them a toothy grin with an expression on their faces that seemed to say,

Hmm, he's human too!

Then just as hesitantly as they had approached him they withdrew to join their friends, continuing the procession.

The amazing world of kids, he reflected, smiling.

While some of those inquisitive children tagged along still calling out after him, the elderly men and women craned their necks, scrutinising the visiting party from their doorsteps with caution or interest or both. They were not used to such visits and most of them were either wondering what was going on or calling out that question to neighbours. Many parents were busy hollering their children's names to ascertain that they were okay. But their voices got drowned in the depth of the ongoing excitement.

The party was there mainly because a young woman named Grace who narrowly escaped from the claws of those human traffickers only because she was deported from Italy had directed them there. She was living in hiding and in fear because the gang were trying to track her down in order to send her back under a new identity, to work her way out of the huge debt imposed on her. Meanwhile her humble family was being hounded and menaced. She was desperately seeking a solution.

It was such a coincidence that Efosa had heard about her roughly a week earlier. Somebody linked to an NGO working with ex-victims of human trafficking; and sometimes harbouring them; had contacted him, hoping that he could use his connections and his clout to do something for her. So when Wole phoned him, telling him about the purpose of Art's visit, he imagined that Art could be interested in her story. Given her precarious circumstances they had promised her absolute discretion when they spoke to her on the phone. However, their present situation in which practically every child in the village was following them around as though they were the Pied Piper could not exactly be defined as discreet. In the end they agreed that a telephone interview would be the ideal solution.

Nevertheless, they would keep their appointment with her mother who did not seem to care about who saw her talking to whom.

The first thing she told them most candidly was that in granting them that interview she expected that they would help her daughter out of her predicament since apart from that NGO; whose pace she insinuated was rather slow maybe due to the volume of cases they were handling; nobody else had been willing to assist her. She was hoping that they would help her get the word out there and save her daughter. She said that as a mother she was suffering greatly since the life her daughter had been living was no life at all; it was like being buried alive. She implored them to find a solution to her daughter's predicament.

The first question Art asked her through Efosa, who was interpreting, was how her daughter had got mixed up with that lot. She replied that her daughter had been tricked, not to mention her very self. She explained that the individuals were no strangers to her so it was not as if she had handed her daughter over to complete strangers. They were from the same village; indeed, their parents lived nearby. She had been sold the idea that her daughter was going to be engaged in show business overseas. But, only when her daughter was deported did she learn that the show in the business had been her body. She confessed that initially that discovery repulsed her seriously. But, all that mattered to her then was that her daughter was back and she would sacrifice her own life to save her a repeat of that terrible experience. She then got too distraught to go on and thus ended that emotive interview.

They left there feeling awfully shaken. They had learnt a great deal about her circumstances and those of her children. She had also informed them that lots of girls were being recruited from that village and from nearby ones and encouraged them to add a couple of those villages to their itinerary since they would certainly come across interesting accounts. She believed that some villagers would gladly talk to them if approached because unfortunately, until then nobody had bothered to listen to them.

The team would soon discover though, that those villagers' purported willingness to talk was not quite so. Most people were living in fear of reprisal. The individuals operating the trafficking networks happened to wield a lot of power and influence in that village and in neighbouring ones. They were known to belong to that powerful cult and were dreaded.

Shortly after they stepped out of Grace's mother's humble home another desperate mother ran after them screaming that she wanted to tell them her daughter's story. On catching up with them she wailed that she had not heard from her since she was promised a pie in the sky and lured away five years earlier. As she began proclaiming from the rooftops that her daughter had been stolen from her by a gang of shameless delinquents, she was implored by a couple of relatives to keep down her voice since she could be endangering her life. However, she could not care less — she raised the volume even higher. She was desperate, she wanted her daughter back. She thrust an old picture of her into Efosa's hand and flung herself to the ground. She was wailing, pulling at her hair, calling out her daughter's name and pleading with them to find her.

The picture showed an innocent face smiling shyly into the camera. She must have been in her early teens when it was taken and for all they knew her face had possibly undergone great changes — if she was still alive. Though that mother's story was not at all different from that of the others, she told it in such a way that every member of the party was terribly affected by it. Just the sight of her was heart-wrenching particularly as she lay writhing on the dusty ground.

Art would be haunted by all he heard during that visit, for a very long time. From one destination to the next, he kept thinking about those poor women. As he saw it, entrusting one's child to a stranger must be the height of desperation — desperation for survival. A mere glance at the surroundings was enough to see that a huge number of them were living in dire straits. He fully understood how those heartless opportunists could easily prey on their unsuspecting, ignorant victims; ignorant in the sense that over and over again, they were sold the idea that the streets in the West were paved with gold.

Due to time constraints the party was able to visit only three villages. In the third one something struck Art as way out weird: on three occasions he was approached by mothers who were willing to let their very young children go to Europe with him. They begged him to take them with him and offer them a bright future, the kind they would never be able to achieve in the village or even in the country. The mothers stated that he could have their children as houseboys or maids if he so desired and/or obtain apprenticeship for them in any field of handicraft he deemed fit.

The first time he got that proposal he thought it was a joke. But when he asked Efosa to inquire if that mother was serious, she reiterated her offer. On the other occasions, he was equally stunned. There he was a complete stranger and he was being offered those poor children. He could be the devil himself straight from hell to where he would disappear in a flash with their children in tow. The word desperation came to his mind anew and he asked himself if things could ever get worse than that.

Those incidents took his mind back to Lagos, to those young girls in the nightclubs hovering around men who were in some cases old enough to be their grandfathers. He recalled his conversation with Sam about their circumstances and the betrayal of the trust vested in relatives by parents who had entrusted their children to them. Nevertheless neither he nor Sam had considered the possibility of the girls' parents having approached those ruthless crooks. Anyhow, regardless of who approached who, those desperate parents must have believed that they were simply seeking the very best opportunities for their children.

It suddenly struck him that practically all the girls whose ordeals they had heard about had been minors at the time they were lured away. He asked Efosa how come they were able to obtain passports and visas and leave the country without documented parental consent. Efosa replied that none of those issues were a problem. As to the passport he said that to obtain a Nigerian passport you did not necessarily need to present a birth certificate — usually a sworn affidavit would suffice. And affidavits could be fraudulently obtained in Oluwole. In an aside he smilingly mentioned,

'I learnt that you paid a couple of visits to the area. You saw the quality of the work done there so you can understand how easily people get fooled by it.'

'Indeed it's more than anything I've ever seen,' he admitted.

'Probably more than anything you'll ever see. If only such talents were channelled to legit activities. Can you imagine what impact that could generate for everyone?'

'I guess they're thinking about themselves, not about everyone.'

Thereafter Wole continued his explanation: 'The date of birth is usually falsified in the Statutory Declaration of Age. Not that the dates are thoroughly scrutinised in most Passport Offices anyway, because of bribery; the cankerworm gnawing at the society.'

'What about the visas; how are they obtained?' Art inquired.

'Corruption isn't exclusive to the Nigerian society, Art.'

'Are you saying that in the embassies there could be corrupt staff?'

'What do you think?'

Anyhow, of all the cases they heard Grace's first person telephone account of her own ordeal was probably the most traumatising. It was on the one hand a tale of abject poverty, deprivation of all kinds, cruelty and desperation and a tale of opportunism on the other hand. All told it was a tragic story. She had believed that by going overseas she would be able to help her widowed mother educate and take care of her seven younger siblings whose ages ranged from 14 to 2. She herself had been barely a child then. She had just turned 16 when she was offered that fantastic life overseas. Accepting the offer had been a huge sacrifice on her part because until then she had never been away from home. Regardless, since she had believed that it was for a good cause she had gone ahead.

She ended up living in captivity for two years. In that period she was not only subjected to white slavery but also to abuses of all kinds. On her arrival, after her captors had savagely raped her they set her to turning tricks though she had no idea of what to do initially. She received lots of beatings from them and clients alike for her fumbling. She also got badly beaten for the heck of it by the often drunken rowdies she was forced to sleep with or by her captors who knocked her about for whatever alleged reason such as her not smiling enough to attract customers; even when she was ill or in pain due to overwork. She never stopped working, not even during that wrong period of the month. She hardly ever had time to herself; not at night, not during the day; so though she contemplated taking her own life so many times, putting those thoughts into practice had been impossible. That was the general pattern of her miserable life until mercifully she was ultimately busted one freezing night for prostitution in the streets of Rome and for residing in Italy illegally.

She recalled actually smiling as she was being shoved into the squad car. Taking a deep breath she stated that although she felt greatly relieved the moment she got arrested, as the minutes ticked by she began feeling highly disappointed and devastated. That was because she had always believed that she would be free from her captors some day and then find a decent, legit means of livelihood in order to accomplish the dreams that had lured her there in the first place: giving her mother a better life and helping her provide for her younger siblings. That belief had always been the driving force behind her survival in the darkest moments of her captivity. She lamented that her every sacrifice had been in vain.

During most of that interview Art could visualise a poor scared child though she occasionally sounded defiant. The bitterness embedded somewhere within her was sometimes discernible. At such times her voice acquired a steely quality and Art perceived that her age of innocence was long over — snatched away from her. The question was if she would ever recover fully, if her wounds would ever heal.

He kept thinking that it was just as well that in the end they had not been able to see her in person. Though a professional to the core and despite having put in many years in the profession, he sometimes could not help letting the human side of him take precedence over the professional one while on the job. Being the father of a teenage girl himself, he was especially touched by Grace's story and the suffering she had undergone. But her remarkable resilience, despite her age, impressed him greatly.

Her interview left the whole team dumbfounded. Their protracted silence was eventually broken by the word: 'Unbelievable!' It came out as a gasp from Omo. The other two acknowledged it with nods; they could not bring themselves to discuss that interview.

Not until the following day would they brace themselves to tackle that most unpleasant issue. When they finally did, they would not agree on how to go about helping her. Art would propose going to the police and his companions would simply laugh out loud. They claimed that that move would be akin to smoking a rat out of its hole to get it killed. When he said that he did not get it they informed him that there was no witness protection programme in Nigeria — at least not like it was known in the UK or the US. So for the time being she was far safer in hiding. They confessed that sadly enough, trusting the police could sometimes be complicated especially regarding cult related matters. He asked them if that meant that some of the cops were cult members and they replied that when it came to such matters one could not trust even judges. That, coupled with the issue of corruption among many officers could make turning to them a rather sticky issue. Therefore, it was best to let sleeping dogs lie. He was disappointed by their stance. He then asked them what the point was in Grace telling them her story.

Afterwards he would have a serious talk with Efosa, reminding him that his contact that got them acquainted with Grace's case certainly did so because he expected much more from them than merely listening to her story. He implored Efosa to use his position as a journalist and as somebody with connections to obtain some sort of justice for Grace and for her suffering family. After much deliberation Efosa would agree to pull a few strings adding though, that there was no quick-fix for Grace's situation. Satisfied with that promise, Art would make a mental note to follow up the matter.

Curiously enough in the midst of all the prevailing want and desperation they observed during their tour of the villages there were also rare signs of opulence in the form of a couple or so huge monstrosities called buildings sprawling at one end of the villages, far removed from the modest homes. They had huge grounds and were fenced all round, guard post included. They belonged to traffickers. Those extravagant ugly buildings were a clear testimony of the traffickers' affluence and influence. They stuck out like a sore thumb considering all those modest homes.

One of those buildings had a history with a particularly ironic twist. It belonged to a woman, a woman who had been a victim but later became a victimiser. Art found her story utterly mind-blowing and mind-boggling. It was a confirmation of the belief that the human mind-set is pretty complex. If not, how could somebody who had suffered deprivation and oppression in her own skin be involved in meting out the same mean treatment to others?

The woman was taken to The Netherlands many years earlier. In fact she was one of the first victims from her village. Years later she appeared from nowhere with a Baby Benz and soon after that her mansion was built. Initially people believed that she had been engaged in lucrative legit business during her years away. Bit by bit, however, the story about her true occupation leaked out, to the astonishment and repulsion of many. With time though, she started throwing money around and the more money she threw around the more blurred most people's memory got. She even managed to acquire something akin to respect in some circles, up to the point that she was awarded a chieftaincy title! Rumours had it that she was still throwing money around despite having managed to provoke amnesia in many people because she was aspiring for a political career in her Local Government Area.

Regarding her freedom, the initial story flying around was that after years of white slavery during which she endured countless abuses and humiliations that go with such occupations she eventually worked her way out of her debt. But the ultimate version was that she became the mistress of a Mafia boss from Eastern Europe who she met in the line of services. He then coerced her former owners into letting him pay off all her supposed debt.

Nonetheless, somebody linked with an association fighting for the release of victims of human trafficking told Art that he was more inclined to believe the latter version since single-handedly working one's way out of the human traffickers' web was highly improbable. He explained that as a rule those criminals kept on inflating the amount supposedly owed them. So much so that to be able to pay it off their victims would need several lifetimes of working as sex traders or a miracle which could come in the form of raids by law enforcement authorities. Sometimes some lucky girls were rescued that way.

Another possibility which was fast catching on in many countries in Western Europe was that victims were guaranteed residence permit and protection if they went forward to testify against their exploiters and incarcerators. But of course to be able to enjoy such privileges one had to be able to escape first and doing that was pretty complicated. Successful escapes had been accomplished by very few and sometimes the girls were still reached, regardless of their protection programme. If not directly they were often reached in the form of reprisal against their relatives in their country of origin.

Well, back to the woman. Although the stories surrounding her freedom were a million and one, the plain fact was: she got free. Since becoming a Madam herself she had established a string of thriving illegal businesses among which the prostitution network was relatively, the "lightest". She co-ran those businesses with her Eastern European lover. Concerning the prostitution network, she supplied and controlled the girls while her lover provided the pimps and the bullies. He ran the drug end of the business and the young girls were often made to peddle small quantities of drugs, supplying their clients with them.

By the time that phase of their mission was accomplished the team was feeling exhausted. Art was feeling absolutely drained, physically and emotionally. He had heard and seen things which until then he had considered most improbable or even impossible. The stories about the girls' sufferings in different parts of Europe had been no different from the ones Regina had told him about the nightmare the girls in Spain usually underwent. So obviously, the members of the gang applied the same modus operandi everywhere.

As the team headed back to Benin City Art had just one desire: to get drunk enough to drown his sorrows or at least blur his mind. Nevertheless he knew that getting drunk was definitely out of the equation since another mission lay ahead. They were going to be taken to witness a ritual during which a group of unsuspecting victims would be prepared for their overseas adventure. So the team would be venturing into the cult's territory with the aid of an insider. Since it was a very dangerous venture Art needed to keep his wits about him.

When he got to his hotel he went straight for a shower. He was covered from head to toe in red dust, product of the red soil that is typical of Benin. He found the colour utterly curious since he had never seen any soil that red. He learnt that the colour was because the soil was rich in iron oxide. But mythology had an entirely different, fascinating version.

After his long cold shower he got into fresh trousers and a clean shirt. He took a light jacket with him, like he had been advised to, since the temperature could get quite low where they were headed — the only information he had been offered about their destination. Having made sure that he had everything he needed in his backpack he wearily made his way downstairs, to the hotel lounge. He was so worn-out that he did not feel like eating — chewing would require too much effort. As he was feeling pretty dehydrated, he had been sweating all day, he ordered a bottle of chilled *Odeku* which he drank, staring into space.

Efosa arrived on schedule at 10 p.m., in the company of the insider Ogbe. Without him that mission would be practically impossible since trying to get anywhere close to the venue of that ceremony would be nothing short of suicide — if at all they would be able to locate it. The cult's circle was hermetic so the help of an insider was absolutely necessary. Of course Ogbe was not being a Good Samaritan. They had had to "persuade" him with a great deal of irresistible "incentive".

Ogbe was just a pseudonym for obvious reasons. He was a very serious huge man who spoke very little and who from the very beginning made Art nervous. His gaze was piercing, chilly and often quizzical. From the start Art got the sensation that Ogbe was looking right into his soul.

There was a perfunctory introduction and before they set out Ogbe warned them that theirs was a highly dangerous mission so they could not afford to make the slightest slip. As a result they would have to listen carefully to his instructions every step of the way because failure to do so could be dreadfully costly. Looking straight at Art he emphasised that if the team was discovered they could be made to disappear forever, without leaving any trace. That revelation made Art quake. After ascertaining that his instructions had been understood, Ogbe said that it was time to go.

As they all filed into Efosa's car Art noticed that Efosa and Omo were as shaken as he was. They were downcast and pensive, avoiding his gaze. The mood in the car was beyond apprehensive. It was like they were headed for an execution: theirs.

CHAPTER 16

As they found themselves in the middle of the forest — they left the nearest village behind them ages ago — Art fully understood that indeed anything could happen to them out there. There were eerie forest sounds all around. He got the occasional goose bumps as they progressed and sometimes a strange chill which began at the nape of his neck spread down his spine and all over his body. Being told that getting either sensation meant that a wandering spirit had just gone by did not make him in the least more relaxed. When he asked if such spirits were harmful or if they were simply going about their own business the answer he got was: depends. He found that totally unsettling. He got a few scares like the sudden hoot of owls and other animal sounds. When he heard the rustling sound of dry leaves and was told that that was a giant snake gliding away after sliding over Ogbe's bare feet, he almost freaked out.

Then came the moment when he was shoved viciously. He lost his balance as a result and as he was trying to scramble back to his feet he felt somebody or something breathing down his neck. Ogbe rushed to his side and helped him to his feet, reciting some incantations and patting him all over with a broom-like object made of raffia which he had whipped out from nowhere. When he finished he told Art that he had just cleansed him of any hex the spirit might have cast on him.

'What, a spirit?' Art screeched, forgetting that they were only supposed to whisper.

'Shh!' Ogbe whispered sharply at the same time gesturing that they should continue.

Art was frozen on the spot. He could not understand why that spirit had chosen him out of the four that made up the party. He did not know that he had actually voiced his thought till Ogbe stated that the spirit had not chosen him, it was just that he had crossed its path. He proceeded to explain that just like humans some spirits are more impatient or ill-tempered than others. Maybe a more even-tempered one would have simply stepped aside, like lots of the ones they came across earlier on had done. He concluded his explanation by saying that even in the city we walk past or into them time after time.

Shuddering, Art decided to stick to Ogbe's side, Ogbe's inexplicable subtle hostility towards him notwithstanding. As he hurried to keep up with the pace of the rest the true depth of their precarious situation sank in; certainly, they were in the middle of nowhere and were progressively advancing into the bowels of that thick forest. They could be attacked, if not by humans or spirits then by the animals whose territory and privacy they were invading. Worse still they were not armed and as far as he knew, they would have no way of defending themselves if attacked. His heart; which had been beating faster than normal since they got into the forest and even more after his attack; started pounding almost out of control. He broke out in sweat despite the cool night air.

After almost an hour's walk in near darkness to avoid detection, they discerned drumbeats. They were by now bare-footed because they were close to the sacred ground, their destination. Their setting out at the time they did had been calculated by Ogbe so that they would approach the venue of the ceremony when the preliminaries were already under way. That way the drumbeats would disguise any accidental noise they might make, like tripping on twigs or simply stepping on and snapping them. They must not be heard at all.

The rhythmic sound of the drums was subdued at first but as they drew closer and closer Art could feel it thumping within him. He was in a cold sweat and still in awe of everything that had happened on the way especially the fierce encounter Ogbe had with another spirit, a really mean one, just before they made out the drumbeats. It was only when the battle was raging that he noticed that Ogbe had lots of charms around his neck. He wondered when he had donned them. He also realised that the stick in Ogbe's left hand was in fact a potent wand. His dread of Ogbe surged while he was having that encounter with the spirit. He later learnt that as well as a senior cult member Ogbe was a great medicine man.

After witnessing that fierce clash Art had stood unmoving, gawking skywards, mouth agape. He was gaping at an immense black smoke billowing into the night sky. Still glued to the spot, he could actually feel the electricity in the air. When he was told that he had just witnessed the exit of the defeated malevolent spirit he could not believe his ears. He was so submerged in thoughts of those horrific tense moments that when he felt a light tap on his shoulder he was so startled that he almost passed out.

Slowly he understood that he was being signalled that it was time for them to "take cover". Following Ogbe's instruction and indication, they all crouched behind some tall bushes. From that point Ogbe left them on their own and continued alone, to join his fellow cult members. In a way Ogbe's departure caused him some relief since his presence had been making him feel truly uncomfortable. What with that look he kept giving him through those piercing bloodshot eyes of his. Conversely, Ogbe's absence brought him a feeling of defencelessness because all along his presence had guaranteed some sort of protection — psychologically at least.

From their hiding spot, which was some distance from the "sacred ground", a large clearing in the middle of that luxuriant forest where the ceremony was taking place, they commanded a good view of the arena. They were facing an enormous red earth shrine with a raised altar bordered by lush vegetation and massive trees. The vegetation behind it was so thick that it was impossible to see beyond it. Sitting majestically at the altar was an imposing life-sized idol presiding over smaller ones.

Art could make out blood-stained feathers and down and caked blood on the idols. Since he had been told that human sacrifice had long given way to animal ones he told himself that all that was nothing but animal blood. Then he recalled that when he asked his informant if there was any guarantee that human sacrifices were extinct the man had said,

'Nothing is guaranteed when it comes to cults and the occult.'

That recollection made him shiver. He got really perturbed and tried to distract himself by concentrating on the scene. The life-sized idol looked the scariest of everything up there. There was something truly chilling about its look and its elevated position gave him the impression that the idol was overseeing the affairs below. He noticed that there were also black earthenware pots and an assortment of bric-a-brac including skulls and huge bones of animals there. He found everything in that setting eerie.

Still gawking, he heard himself speaking before realising that the words were actually from his own mouth:

'Doesn't this setting ever get disturbed by outsiders?'

'Do you know how deep into the forest we are?' Efosa asked him.

'Thanks for calming me down,' he replied with heavy irony.

'Not at all; thought you'd like to know,' Efosa smiled.

Although Art became really apprehensive he told himself that there was no need to worry as more than once, the exact way he was going to die had been foretold and a forest in Africa was certainly not the setting for that event. Momentarily, he drew some consolation from that thought. But that consolation was short-lived. Since such predictions had not been put to test he reckoned that they were not infallible.

When he managed to tear his eyes away from that enormous altar and its captivating as well as intimidating occupants, he moved them to the centre of the sacred ground. In wonder, he took in the figures of bare-footed half-naked men and women. They were clad in skirts made from palm fronds, with amulets hanging around their necks. They were also wearing bracelets and armbands made of cowries. Their faces and the rest of their bodies were painted with a white chalky substance known as native chalk. He was told that native chalk and cowries were crucial ingredients in most ritual practices and ceremonies related to traditional religion.

Like one in a trance he watched the men and women, some with their eyes closed, gyrating and contorting their bodies in tune with the drumbeats. They were singing aloud. Occasionally one of them would jump incredibly high into the air or perform some complicated acrobatic movements, letting out an unnatural howl at the same time. Apart from the moonlight additional lighting came from a burning pile of wood in the centre of the sacred ground. The not-so-bright lighting, the drumbeats, the movements of their bodies as they performed their ghastly dance routine and something else which he could not put his finger on gave him the shivers. It was as if most of them were only physically present. He shuddered again; from terror not from cold.

'They look possessed,' he whispered hoarsely.

'Of course they're possessed,' Efosa whispered back.

'They're ...?' he asked incredulously.

'Uh-huh,' was the grunted answer he received.

Suddenly the tempo of the drumbeats increased and the dancers got into frenzy, shouting in ecstasy. He felt Efosa's nudge and heard him whisper: 'Attention!' Before he could ask why, he saw a sight that froze him: A female figure clad in a skirt made of wide strips of red and white cloth strung together with a string around her waist popped out of the bushes behind the altar. She was swirling round and round. With every movement she made, the strips flew here and there, revealing a pair of red shorts. She was covered in native chalk from head to toe. Her face was all white and in that dim lighting her bright eyes and gleaming teeth; she seemed to be wearing a permanent smile; created an eerie effect. He could not look directly at it for long periods of time as it was doing weird things to his mind.

Shaking his head, he looked away briefly and then back again, this time avoiding her face. He noticed that she was carrying an earthenware pot on her head. Though Efosa told him that there were all sorts of mysterious ceremonial ingredients in it, he could only see the palm fronds hanging out at close intervals around its circumference. He also saw thick smoke billowing from it. Since it is believed that there is no smoke without fire he wondered if indeed she was carrying fire on her head. He found both her appearance and her movements extremely astounding. She was swirling frenetically, her eyes now tightly closed. Yet another source of astonishment was that although she was not holding onto the pot, it was sitting firmly on her head despite those frenzied movements.

Another possessed one, he said to himself.
Her hands were occupied; she was brandishing a gleaming machete with one and holding a bottle of schnapps in the other. She swirled along, reciting incantations and pouring libation.

Efosa whispered that she was the high priestess of the shrine. She was performing a vital ritual: cleansing the ground before the ceremony. Though Art could not figure out her age — what with all that "make-up" completely covering her face — as far as he could see she was definitely at the peak of physical fitness. There was not a milligram of fat in any part of her body. As he watched that lithe individual who seemed incapable of keeping still racing around he kept on wondering how she managed to maintain the balance of that pot.

Then for some reason he got transfixed by the sight of that gleaming machete of hers — it looked hellishly sharp. He was still staring at it when something really bizarre happened: The priestess' face took on a monster-like appearance. Her tongue became serpent-like and dark, almost black. She flipped it out occasionally, raising it to her nose and each time she did that it emitted dark sparks.

Thinking that he was losing his mind and that all that transformation was going on in his head, he turned sideways. He noticed that Efosa was staring unblinkingly — he was obviously in shock. Omo did not appear to be faring any better. Relieved that he was not the only one witnessing that transmutation, he turned his attention back to her.

In that instant she came to an abrupt halt. She seemed tense, like a predator sensing the presence of a prey. Her eyes, which had been firmly shut, flew wide open. They were blood-red and wild. He cringed as her wild look settled on him — at least that was the strong sensation he got. Then it was no longer a notion. Indeed, she was staring right into his eyes. He felt gooseflesh start from the nape of his neck and spread all over his body. His head ballooned to twice its original size and he went numb all over. It was as if he was outside his body, watching a scene from a horror film in slow motion. His greatest desire then was to be able to move his hand. He wanted to clutch at his amulet, to feel it between his fingers, but he could not move any muscle in his body. Thus in total paralysis, he gaped in stupefaction as with a blood-curdling ear-splitting cry she headed in their direction, wild-eyed like a crazed one, with a diabolic smile pasted on her terrifying face.

Somehow, he ultimately managed to break free from the grip of numbness. He had been holding his breath for so long that he had turned red. He let out a gasp. He was nudged for gasping. That nudge was so unexpected that he gasped again. He heard her shouting out something at the top of her voice. He turned to Omo to ask him what was going on and noticed that he was so rigid with fear that he could have passed for a wax figure. He seemed resigned to his fate as he crouched there staring unblinkingly at the high priestess' approaching figure. His mouth was moving but at first Art could not make out what he was saying. Gradually, he made out the words as: *'Jesus, Mary and Joseph, I give you my heart and my soul.'* Omo kept babbling those words over and over again, his fists tightly clenched. He soon shut his eyes firmly. He presented such a comic sight that although Art himself was under the firm grip of fear he almost burst into nervous laughter.

He looked in Efosa's direction, hoping that he would be able to answer his question. He observed, however, that Efosa was gasping and that his brow was covered in sweat, tiny rivulets of which were draining into his unblinking eyes. Efosa was petrified. Though he seemed to be in no condition to answer his question, Art realised that he himself could not formulate the question. As the high priestess drew closer he got desperate enough to finally splutter, 'What is she saying, what's going on?'

Surprisingly, Efosa managed to respond. He croaked that she was in a trance and speaking in tongues, that most of what she was saying could only be translated by a few priests well-versed in that sort of matter. Although he appeared to have more to say, he stopped suddenly. He was having a bit of problem breathing. After pausing to catch his breath he stated that he could make out something she had just said in plain language: 'She could sniff outsiders, intruders.' Art asked Efosa how that was possible and he replied that she was renowned to have extraordinary powers of perception.

Partly because of the alarm in Efosa's voice and the way he was trembling, quite apart from the ominous information he had just conveyed, Art's own fear level rocketed. His heart started thumping away more wildly.

'Now, what?' he inquired in a shaky voice.

'Await our fate,' was Efosa's resigned reply.

Efosa had barely got to the end of it when they heard the jingling of a tiny bell. At the same time the drumbeat got even more frenzied. He whispered in a trembling voice that it was midnight and that the ceremony was about to begin.

The high priestess that had been within a few steps of where they were crouching and cowering began swirling even faster and faster but this time, away from them. She was swirling so fast that it was hard to make out her form.

Art sighed with relief — they had just been saved by the bell. Rubbing his shirt sleeve against his brow to wipe the dripping sweat from it, he heard his heart beating away crazily. He placed his hand against it as if by so doing he could steady it. Simultaneously, his nose twitched. For the first time he noticed the foul air around him. He did not know whose fault it was but despite his circumstances he reflected on how powerful the grip of fear could get — firm enough to squeeze the worst stench out of people. It was just as well that they were in the open because indoors, that pong would have been deadly.

Then he heard a rustling sound. Momentarily, his heart went totally still. He believed the end had surely come. Luckily, it turned out to be only a lone animal on its nightly prowl. Seemingly oblivious of all the commotion going on around it, it simply went its own way. His head was spinning wildly and he was feeling seriously dizzy. He heaved a weak sigh of relief as he realised that they were out of harm's way.

Art shook himself out of his stupor and noticed that the priestess had continued her frenzied swirling towards the altar where a goat on a leash was being held by an acolyte, another sturdy bleary-eyed individual with a mean look. The goat was new to the scene. It must have appeared while he was undergoing his private hell. Still in her trance-like state, the priestess approached the goat and with a deft movement of her machete-bearing hand she hacked off the defenceless animal's head. He gazed in open-mouthed astonishment as, as if by an act of magic she caught the head with the same hand with which she was clutching the schnapps bottle. Watching her gulping down the blood gushing out of it, he retched. He started fighting an almost uncontrollable desire to throw up. Despite his agony he forced himself to keep his eyes glued on her in order not to miss any detail; morbid curiosity, perhaps. He observed in disgust as she flung the head away and it was caught by the same man who had been holding the goat. Their actions were so synchronised that Art reckoned that they had enacted that scene over and over in the past. No sooner had she discarded of the head than she took a swig from the schnapps bottle. Strangely enough, during the course of all that, she never missed a step from her frenzied dancing.

'Is she human?' he whispered, his eyes popping.

'I'm no longer sure,' Efosa mumbled, equally astonished.

What she did to the goat with that machete made Art unconsciously rub his hand against his neck; he could not believe that that machete was that sharp. He wondered if she would have done the same to the team. He was glad that her attention had got drawn away from them due to the call of duty, her priestly duties. Those rites had to begin at the stroke of midnight. Midnight was a sacred hour and it was strictly observed. Thank goodness for such precision otherwise, who knew what would have become of them. He never imagined that his mission could get that complicated. It was getting more and more complex too.

He observed that with blood splashed all over her, she presented an even eerier sight. Her native-chalk-painted face now splattered in red was like nothing he had ever seen. Her blood-red eyes were looking around wildly and for another weird instant he thought she was staring into his eyes again. As gooseflesh spread rapidly all over his body he felt his head balloon again. By now the tempo was at a crescendo and everyone was gyrating wildly, some were screaming. The ambience was really electric.

Then a dozen or so young girls were led in, in blindfold and lined out before the altar. Unlike the rest of those present, they were stark naked except for the coat of native chalk covering them. He was about to witness in person, the reason why he had made that highly risky trip. Those poor hapless girls were about to be prepared for their journey to Europe — to "greener pastures". Their oath-taking ceremony was about to unfold, a ceremony which unknown to them, would bind them practically forever.

They remained blindfolded as the high priestess began sprinkling some sort of liquid from a gourd all over them. Thereafter she blew a powder-like substance at each of them. She was sanctifying as well as granting them protection from any evil spirits that might be lurking nearby because since they were not initiates, they were not strong enough spiritually to fend off any such attacks. When she was done with all that preparatory paraphernalia, the real business began: The girls' fingernails and toenails were hurriedly cut with a gleaming ceremonial dagger by an acolyte.

Despite the distance from which he was taking in the scene Art recognised the dagger immediately. It was the very same type that had been stuck into Ebony. He underwent a series of emotions in a split second: sadness, rage, dread and curiously, elation. The latter was brought on by the sudden realisation that he was not simply groping in the dark. The dagger was a tangible proof that he was on the right track.

Switching his mind back to the moment, he asked Efosa why their nails had been cut and he replied that he should pay attention because that was not all. Fully alert, he watched wide-eyed as some hair was cut from their head and genitals. From the swift way the action was performed he concluded that the dagger was seriously sharp. Efosa explained that the nails and hair were going to be used as vital ingredients in the formulation of a potent *juju* that would be left there at the shrine under the watchful eyes of the huge idol and if the girls reneged on their promise to pay back every cent that had been spent on them, the idol would be invoked to do serious harm not only to them but also to members of their family.

He asked Efosa if he knew of anyone who had ever paid off those debts. Efosa's answer came in the form of the question, 'How good is your mythology?' When he replied that it was fairly good Efosa likened the debts to the mythical Hydra heads: 'They keep multiplying, no matter how much you try to cut them off.' He looked a bit sad when he finished. Then nudging Art, he motioned towards the altar with his head.

In amazement Art watched as an incision was made in the thumb of each girl. The blood from their thumbs went directly into a small mortar held by one of those officiating at the altar. Efosa explained that apart from the blood there were some mysterious ingredients in the mortar, known only by the high priestess and a few of those at the higher echelons of the cult. Art looked on as everything therein was crushed by the acolyte, with the aid of a tiny pestle. Then in alarm he watched the high priestess grab another ceremonial dagger. After what she had done to the goat he had become terrified and wary of her every move.

When she positioned herself before the girls he held his breath. With that weird look on her face she approached the first girl and, with a clean stroke of the dagger she made an incision on her forehead. She went from one to another doing exactly the same thing. Next the mortar was brought to her. Standing in front of each girl, she called out what sounded like the same phrase and one by one, they murmured something in return.

Art asked Efosa what was happening. He explained that while the potent concoction in the mortar was being applied to their cuts, the girls were being reminded that there was no way they could escape without bringing harm upon themselves and their families since the deity before whose altar they were standing would track them down and wreak destruction upon them. They in turn were murmuring their well-rehearsed oath.

Despite the much touted potency of that concoction there were sceptics who believed that the cuts on such girls' foreheads, which were generally inflicted in a particular way, were what made it very easy for them to be identified wherever they went and not any supernatural tracking device. Very vulgarly and very simply put: they were usually branded like cattle. Art, who was more inclined to the latter viewpoint, asked himself how anyone could fall for such mumbo-jumbo — no puns intended. Someone once told him he would make remarkable progress in the realm of the occult if the wiring of his mind were not so analytical. He disagreed. As he saw it, though he believed in the occult he was also able to question cases he deemed to be sheer opportunism, like that ceremony.

He inquired reflectively if what those innocent girls were being made to undergo was not simply a mind game, a kind of psychological warfare.

'Psychological warfare or not, it works and that's what matters,' Efosa said. 'If it's worked for so many years, people believe in it. Since they do, it's an effective tactic.'

Art listened, nodding thoughtfully before thinking aloud for the umpteenth time:

'How can people be so desperate?'

'Umm, it's the economic situation of the country,' Omo remarked.

It was the first time he had spoken since the horrific experience they had undergone, since they had come so close to losing their heads, literally.

Thank goodness, he's regained the use of his tongue, Art smiled to himself.

Just then Art saw the high priestess grabbing hold of a bottle of schnapps. As she approached each girl she took a swig from it and blasted the spirit into the fresh cut on her forehead. 'Ouch!' he uttered in a low tone, squirming at the same time because he imagined that that must really sting. From that distance, however, he did not notice any outward reaction from the girls. They were standing as still as they had been doing all along. He would have given anything to know what was going on in their innocent minds then.

Immediately after the last spray of schnapps was let off a ceremonial bowl; a large calabash stained on the outside; containing some concoction was brought in. Judging from its appearance that calabash must have been around for aeons and it must have been passed around innumerable times during numerous such ceremonies. Each congregant took a gulp from it and passed it on. Whatever concoction it contained had to be blood based, going by the smear it left around the mouths of some or the stains on their hitherto gleaming teeth.

The sight of all those people with terrifying painted faces displaying bloody lips and/or bloody teeth, making blood-curdling sounds as they contorted their bodies was like a scene only possible in the bloodiest of nightmares. The dim lighting made the whole scene even more outlandish. Art found it difficult to believe that any of it was truly happening. He almost pinched himself sore because he kept telling himself that he had to be living one of those rare horrible nights of endless nightmares.

Whatever that concoction was, it seemed to energise them more. The frenzied dancing which had been going on for what seemed like an eternity simply went on and on. He was wondering how they could go on dancing so frenetically for so long without a single break when he heard the tinkling of the bell. He checked his timepiece. It was exactly 3 a.m. It was uncanny; the same hour many people had mentioned in Madrid during his interviews. Curiously, it had also been associated by some with drumbeats. Also, it was the hour he had awoken each night after his recurring dream. *What a weird coincidence,* he thought.

At the sound of the bell the drumbeats became slower, the dancesteps too. He watched as a circular pad made from palm fronds was placed on each girl's head and a small earthenware pot from which palm fronds were sticking out was placed on it. All through that long ceremony the girls had been facing the altar but at that point, following indications, they turned sideways, forming a single file. The high priestess took up the front position and the devotees, singing and dancing at a much slower pace, fell in behind the girls. The drummers assumed the rear position and the long procession out of the sacred ground began.

He asked if that was the end of the ceremony and Efosa shook his head. He said that they were headed to a river where there would be another ceremony that would not be as long as the one they had witnessed. He explained that the contents of the earthenware pots were offerings for the river goddess. After making the offerings the girls would be given a special ritual bath in the river by the high priestess. Next, they would put on their clothes and that would be it.

As the thumping of the drums receded the party knew it was time to get moving. Ogbe had warned them that trailing along would be tantamount to suicide. He had told them to wait until the din had died down and then hotfoot it out of there without a backward glance at the sacred ground. He had harped on the latter, cautioning them that not heeding his warning could lead to fatal consequences for each of them.

As they abandoned the area the temptation to look back became almost insurmountable for Art. Human nature being what it is the mere fact that they had been told not to do so made it so tempting. As he waged that battle within himself, he easily understood Lot's wife's dilemma in the Bible and how come she finally gave in to the temptation. However, unlike her, he managed to control himself. He placed the well-being of Efosa and Omo way above his curiosity.

Leaving the forest turned out to be a daunting undertaking. The path was riddled with obstacles and dangers, literally and otherwise. Being in that thick unfamiliar forest was a complicated matter but being there without torchlight or any other form of light was an additional complication. They were simply groping in the dark. All around the foliage of the trees was so dense, not to mention the huge towering trees themselves, that seeing the full moon was difficult. Bumping into those giant trees particularly the palm trees with their rough bark was a torture. To aggravate matters at a stage thunder and lightning, the strength of which Art had never experienced before, were suddenly unleashed by the heavens. The thunder was deafening and the lightning was occasionally blinding. Not for the first time that night, the trio got gripped by terror.

During one of those flashes of lightning Efosa observed that it was likely that they had been going round in circles because he had just recognised a gourd attached to a palm tree that he had seen earlier on. He noticed it the first time around because it had a distinctive shape — a very unusual shape for a gourd. His observation dampened their already low spirits further. At a point Omo hushed them, whispering that he could hear the drumbeats faintly. They all listened carefully and it turned out that he was right. Following that discovery Efosa voiced his worries about them stumbling across the cult members and their procession. All three of them exchanged alarmed looks. They knew what the consequences would be.

Art wished that Efosa had kept his worries to himself because till then he had tried hard to shake off such worries each time they reared their head.

Suddenly the heavens opened up and it began pouring down. It was a fierce thunderstorm. Although they were protected in most parts due to the thickness of the foliage, they still got drenched. Their worst problem, however, was the fear of being struck by thunderbolt; lightning kept zipping here and there. Though the storm did not last long, it lasted long enough to set loose all kinds of crawly creatures. It became cold, really cold, especially since their feet were exposed. They were feeling terribly disgusted and miserable.

They were still trembling with cold and crawlies-induced repulsion and frantically looking for a way out of the jungle when they discerned a human figure approaching them. They soon made it out as a man's. Efosa said that he could be a hunter or a trapper out so early to hunt or to check his traps. They watched him with mixed feelings. Even though they were relieved because they figured that he could be of great help — he could provide directions to enable them get out of the immense maze — they were also worried in case he was a member of the cult.

Although Art found the presence of a lone individual in that environment at that hour somewhat unsettling, he chose not to voice his thoughts. He did not want to worsen his companions' anxiety.

When the individual got closer they all noticed that he was an unusually tall man. He was a mountain of a man! They exchanged surprised looks as they took in his extraordinary size. He had not appeared nearly as large earlier. Shockingly though, when he was a short distance from them they observed that he had become barely taller than a seven-year-old. Then when he was a few centimetres away he disappeared, just as suddenly as he had appeared. Could it have been collective vision or hallucination? Whatever...

As if on cue they took to their heels. They ran and ran, stumbling, tripping, falling down and getting back on their feet. They never looked back, they never uttered a word, they just continued running. Efosa and Omo kept alternating the front position. Art was always the last. They kept running even after they got out of the forest since it took them a long time to realise that they were out. Eventually, it dawned on them that they were free, that their feet were no longer getting entangled in undergrowth or anything. The way they got out was quite mysterious and accomplishing that feat took them ages since in addition to all the hurdles they had had to scale, the number of times they had got lost and gone round in circles had been innumerable. Regardless of the fact that they were all scratched and bruised and their clothes were in tatters, they ultimately made it. That was all that counted.

They were a good distance from where their car was parked but that did not matter in the least to them. When they found it they did not get in immediately. They could not. They needed to regain their breath first. When they finally got in the car would not move. It was stuck in mud. The storm had converted the ground all around into a muddy plain. After three failed attempts to get it moving, Efosa got out and let out an ear-splitting scream. Then he began kicking it and cursing — that was how he chose to vent his pent-up frustration. Meanwhile the other two, extremely exhausted, could only look on in silence.

When Efosa had let off enough steam he got back into the car without uttering a word. Art got out and got hold of some branches and leaves ripped off nearby trees by that fierce storm and started placing them around the tyres. Reluctantly Omo and then Efosa joined him and when they were through Efosa got behind the wheel while Art and Omo started pushing the car. After several attempts, during which they both got splattered with mud from head to toe, Efosa eventually got it in motion.

The drive into town was in silence. Nobody was in the mood nor had enough strength to talk about their bizarre experience. It had been a gruelling, awfully long night and an outlandish one too. Not even when Efosa dropped Art and Omo off at their hotel did any of them say anything. They nodded at him and he nodded back at them before zooming off. It was almost 7 a.m.

Art and Omo limped through the hotel door in silence. As they parted to go to their separate rooms they merely exchanged grunts. Art had that sinking feeling at the pit of his stomach, the feeling that something was acutely wrong. He was feeling extremely unsafe.

CHAPTER 17

A rt was a sorry sight as he limped into his room all bedraggled in tattered clothes. He could barely use his numb hands as he bent over to take off his mud-caked shoes. His back was killing him but, much as he wanted to sit down to perform that action, he was too muddy all over to consider placing his backside on any surface. His arms were feeling terribly sore too. As he gently peeled off his muddied ripped clothes he discovered that his body was covered with scratches and cuts sustained during that wild blind dash through the forest. There were insect bites and red weals of every shape and size all over his skin. Luckily his face was not as bad as the rest of his body — he had done his best to shield it with his arms all through. He was glad that he had taken anti-malarial and anti-tetanus shots before leaving Spain.

Regardless of how black-and-blue and dead-beat he was, he knew that a long hot shower was a must. The first blast of hot water against his skin made him yelp in pain. He almost crawled out of the bath. It was real torture. He was smarting all over due to his bruises and wounds. With the aid of a face-flannel he painstakingly managed to get rid of all the mud without making his bruises and wounds worse. Washing the caked mud out of his hair was no mean feat. When he felt clean enough he gently towelled himself down and applied some aftershave lotion to some of the nasty looking bites and scratches. The pain was beyond excruciating. Mercifully, the stinging sensation soon subsided and so did the itching from the bites. He then popped a painkiller and crawled into bed.

Initially sleep would not come despite his exhaustion mainly because he could not find the right position for his aching body. Besides, his mind was racing, going over most of what he had experienced. The excitement, the tension, the panic and every other emotion he had undergone were still too fresh to be swept aside easily. Tossing in bed was a very tricky and painful affair; it was an ordeal. Each time he unconsciously did so he cried out in pain.

When he finally dozed off he had a dream in which Regina featured. He asked her where she had been, stating that everybody was worried sick about her. Instead of answering his question she smiled sadly and told him to watch out that he could be in grave danger. He asked her what sort of danger and she simply stated, 'Stay under the bed!' Then his phone started ringing. Just before he woke up she said, 'Remember...' She then waved and gave him another sad smile.

The call was from the reception desk, to inform him that he had a visitor downstairs. He looked at his timepiece and cursed. So much time had gone by since he crawled into bed yet he had had such little sleep. He was feeling pretty woozy. Slowly, it dawned on him that his visitor had to be Efosa — they had agreed to meet at noon for their next mission. He admired Efosa's professionalism and tenacity. After all that had happened, his showing up so promptly for that mission was praiseworthy. Very few people would do that. He replaced the handset and forgetting how bad his physical condition was, he tried to spring out of bed. He yelped in pain and stood up really slowly. After popping a painkiller he began getting set for the mission ahead, preoccupied with his strange dream.

Omo was already downstairs with Efosa when he got there. They were engaged in what seemed to be a really serious conversation. He disguised his limp as he approached them. After exchanging greetings with them he apologised for not being there on time, explaining that he had had a hard time falling asleep. They waved his apology aside, admitting they had had the same problem. Omo jokingly added that the adrenaline rush they experienced during the risk sport they engaged in had got them too excited to go to sleep.

After getting seated he proposed breakfast and they laughed, asking if he knew what time it was. 'Lunchtime's round the corner,' they chorused. Since they were all feeling tired and sluggish, they ordered strong black coffee. As they were waiting to be served he observed his mates and marvelled in silence at the healing effect just a few hours of sleep had had on both of them. They were almost back to their normal selves, at least mood-wise. He took a furtive look at their visible war wounds, so to speak, and discovered that despite the fact that they were as many as his, they did not look quite as nasty.

Over coffee Efosa informed Art that when he joined them he had been telling Omo that he got word from Ogbe soon after he arrived home. Ogbe notified him that right after the final ceremony the high priestess held a rather impromptu meeting with the elders of the cult. She was hopping mad as she opened the meeting by declaring that she was convinced that the sacred ground area and thus their privacy was violated during the ceremony. She lamented not having had enough time to check out the area thoroughly like she had set out to do before the tinkling of the bell announced the beginning of the ceremony.

That information got Omo sitting bolt upright and his eyes popped. It startled Art. He swallowed and started coughing nervously. Efosa gave him a knowing look and stated,

'You can't imagine how lucky we were that the bell tinkled when it did.'

'Oh, yes; I can,' Art replied, recalling the look on the high priestess' face as she raced towards their hiding spot.

He also remembered how she hacked off the goat's head. How could he forget any of that? He heard Efosa saying that Ogbe also informed him that she had asserted that the matter was not over, that she was going to investigate it. Art asked Efosa if that should be taken seriously. Nodding, he lowered his voice and disclosed that he was feeling slightly uneasy. Then he confided that his sole consolation was that he had Ogbe on the inside so he would be informed about any moves she might make and take necessary precautions.

Omo who had not uttered a single word till then because he had been dazed suddenly spluttered that after all he had witnessed the previous night he would not go back there, not even for a million dollars. Art looked his way, wondering where he got the crazy idea that any of them would want to go back there from.

'Well, just saying that in case that idea ever occurs to you,' he told Art.

Art studied his face for a while and smiling benevolently, told him not to worry that that chapter of their adventure was over and done with. Looking reassured, Omo nodded.

They were soon on their way to a tiny town on the outskirts of Benin City to interview the owners of the infamous statuette. During the journey they finally broached the topic they had been avoiding: their experience during that weird ceremony. They also talked about the strange incidents that occurred during their frantic attempt to get out of the forest, particularly the very last episode. None of them could furnish any explanation for *the diminishing man*, as they dubbed him.

Talking about him even in broad daylight made them feel uneasy because the incident was very fresh on their minds and still as spooky as it had been when it occurred. Art felt his head swell exactly like it had done when they chanced upon that outlandish creature. As they were discussing that terrifying experience he recalled Ogbe's parting shot after instructing them on how and when to abandon their hiding place. He had warned:

'Beware! The forest's quite mysterious, especially at these hours!'

When he voiced that recollection Efosa and Omo nodded thoughtfully as they concurred, 'That's quite true, he said just that!'

With a contemplative expression on his countenance, Art asked them if they had noticed what the creature's face looked like — it had just occurred to him that he had no recollection of that detail. It turned out that neither had they. They had been far more absorbed in the metamorphosis taking place than in anything else. Additionally, none of them remembered if he had been clothed or not.

Efosa told them that that forest held lots of mysteries and was avoided by many people because of the bizarre stories tied to it. Some believed that in the dark past lots of human sacrifices took place therein thus so many strange things were happening there. While others believed that the possibility that such sacrifices were still taking place could not be totally ruled out. Either way, it was believed that the large number of strange sightings reported was due to its dark past or present or both. He said that some of those sightings were in broad daylight.

'Wait a minute; did you say in broad daylight?' Omo asked, alarmed.

'Oh, yes. Certain hours of the day are as dangerous and as mysterious as the night.'

'Hmm, that's interesting!' Art observed.

'Why do you think that certain places give you gooseflesh irrespective of what time of the day it is?' Efosa asked.

'Till now, I believed such things only happen late at night,' Omo said.

'Well, now you know it's not so,' Efosa smiled.

He stated that the forest covered hundreds of kilometres and it was said that at one of its limits the living shared boundaries with the dead.

'Come on, stop that!' Art laughed out loud, thinking he was just pulling their leg.

'No, I'm not kidding, Art. There've been testimonies of people who've seen their departed relatives there and such stories. There are also cases where people claim to have overheard conversations taking place there. It's been reported that things sometimes mysteriously disappear from homes, mainly from the kitchen, because they're borrowed and are later returned with apologies. At first, centuries ago, there's a lot of fear on the part of the living. But with time people learnt that their neighbours were harmless. Consequently over the years, they adapted to the situation and let them be. Children are the ones who see them the most and the ones who accepted the situation as "normal", from the beginning. They've always shared games with 'the kids from the other side', as they're referred to.'

'Has anyone who's not from the village ever borne witness to this peaceful cohabitation or do these stories emanate only from the villagers?' Art inquired, smilingly.

'There've been independent reports too. Know what? If you're really interested in the occult you should consider spending some time in these parts. There're cases that are by far stranger than fiction, especially regarding the issue of life and death. Often times you don't really know where one stops and the other takes over, or even if one stops at all.'

Right after that brief lecture Efosa announced that they were at their destination. As Efosa was parking Art noticed a shrine made of red earth at the entrance of the large compound. He was staring at it when Efosa told him that it was where the statuette had been extracted from. He noticed that apart from being a red earth shrine like the one he had seen the previous night, it was also similar to that one in many more ways: the presence of blood, bloody feathers and down, bronze figures covered with blood, cowries, mirrors, strange objects hanging here and there and more things. Though it was far smaller, it was equally intimidating. Standing so close to it soon made him feel so nervous that he moved away.

He turned his attention to a more relaxing view — the huge front yard. It was quite interesting for a number of reasons. It was completely hedged with small trees and lush vegetation. Inside, there were lots of vegetation and fruit trees. Banana, plantain, cacao and cola nut trees were everywhere. The greenness was impressive. He also saw chickens and goats wandering around or simply lazing about. Outside the TV screen he had never seen such a beautiful sight; that of chickens and goats roaming about in such a carefree manner. Everything seemed so peaceful and quiet.

He also noticed that the outside walls of the building, a bungalow, were coated with red dust in most parts — consequence of the red earth. The initial fascination he felt for that unusual colour was steadily dwindling since getting rid of it from his clothes, his body and his thick golden locks was never easy. It simply clung, reluctant to let go.

The party was received at the entrance to the compound by a young man who led them to the veranda of the bungalow. He motioned them to one of the two long wooden benches there and asked them to sit down. He then excused himself and went indoors. Shortly afterwards he emerged, bearing a tray laden with glasses and ice-cold bottles of beer and placed it on a stool. Art was not in the mood for any alcoholic beverage but when Efosa and Omo accepted the drinks with thanks, he reluctantly did the same.

In that instant an elderly, bent-over, white-haired man emerged from the house and shuffled towards them with the aid of a walking-stick. When Efosa and Omo stood up as a sign of respect and greeted him with a slight bow, Art followed suit. The old man's small watery eyes went from one face to the other as with a nod, he acknowledged their greeting. The young man introduced him as his grandpa, Pa Eghosa. Pa Eghosa was in his early 90s. They all remained on their feet, respectfully waiting for him to take his seat. When he finally did they all did the same, except the grandson who seemed to be awaiting orders.

As soon as he was comfortably seated on the bench facing theirs, Pa Eghosa gestured to his grandson who bent over and listened attentively to him. Nodding, he hurried into the house. When he reappeared it was with another tray in which there were: a white saucer bearing a cola nut, a bottle of gin and tiny glasses — the type used for serving shots. He placed the tray before his grandfather who first of all poured a libation to his ancestors and then offered prayers for the protection of his visitors and his family. After that he split the cola nut, the lobes of which he tossed onto the saucer. He studied them and fixed his watery eyes on Art briefly before speaking to his grandson who listened carefully to him. He then told Art that his grandpa had a message for him. It was:

'Welcome home, son.'

Baffled, Art asked him what that meant. He replied that according to his grandpa, Art had hailed from those parts in one of his past lives and had been a great medicine man. Art's jaw dropped in surprise. After recovering from that initial impact he started laughing. He could not imagine himself as a medicine man, the idea alone was inconceivable.

Pa Eghosa calmly waited till he stopped and then gave him a brief description of his past lives. Some of the details coincided in every way with the vision Art had had during his past life regression. He was dumbfounded! Pa Eghosa added that he had died violently in all those lives and warned him to be very careful so that history would not repeat itself. As he voiced his confusion Pa Eghosa stated that he was dabbling into something dangerous and he was in imminent peril. Looking slightly worried, Pa Eghosa gathered the lobes of the cola nut in his hand and tossed them again. Studying them briefly, he looked into Art's eyes and emphasised that he should not let his guard down if he wanted to stay alive. Thereafter he turned his attention to the lobes again and a smile played on his lips. He revealed that he could see that Art had a lot of protection from the world beyond, particularly from a female who did not wish to be identified. Puzzled, he told the young man to ask his grandfather why the woman did not want to be identified. The grandfather shrugged, stating that he was just a messenger and was acting on cue. After that he told Art things about his present life.

'Good luck, son! Always follow your instinct!' he concluded.

Art was awfully flabbergasted. Everything he had just been told about his present life was so true that it was as if a background check had been run on him. But, from whom, from where and to what end? Bearing in mind that Pa Eghosa had not asked him for even a dime, so it was not as if he had been out to rip him off, the whole situation was even more baffling. Moreover, most of those revelations could not have been known by anyone else so the theory of a background check would not hold water anywhere. Equally amazing was the fact that he had completely forgotten some of the events mentioned.

In a trance-like state he followed Pa Eghosa's every move as his focus shifted to Efosa and then to Omo. Since they spoke the language there was no need for the grandson to interpret what he told each of them so he could not listen in. Nonetheless, their facial expressions and their overall body-language reflected what was happening to them. They got increasingly shocked or perplexed as the visions and predictions progressed.

When Pa Eghosa was through with both of them he poured a shot of gin into each of the tiny glasses for everyone. Then taking a lobe of cola nut from the saucer, he asked his grandson to pass the saucer around. Wondering what he was supposed to do with his lobe Art looked around and noticed that the rest were chewing theirs so he took a bite of it. It was his first taste of cola nut and he did not find it particularly pleasant. Of course he could not spit it out so to get rid of the not-so-nice taste he downed his gin in one gulp. The young man mistook that action for an eagerness for more spirit and rushed over to pour him some more. Forcing a smile, he gestured to him not to worry. He could not speak as his chest was on fire; he had gulped the spirit too fast. Clutching at his chest, he dabbed at his teary eyes.

There was general laughter at his expense as tongue hanging out, he went on gasping. After his mouth, throat and chest stopped burning, he laughed too. Then he was told that he had just had *Ogogoro,* a locally brewed gin. *Ogogoro* is far stronger than the gin he was used to and for which he had mistaken it. It is also known as *Agbakara,* among its millions of names. The name varies, according to what part of Nigeria one is in.

When he heard Pa Eghosa clearing his throat, it dawned on him that the interview was about to begin. The young man resumed his role. In a shaky voice Pa Eghosa stated that the person who had extracted the statuette from the shrine had not been just a member of the family but, one of his own grandsons. Initially though, the family had ascribed its disappearance to a stranger since none of them could remotely have imagined that it had been otherwise. Lowering his head in sorrow, he lamented not having consulted his ancestors first before calling upon *Shango* to do his usual summary justice.

'But, who could have expected such treachery from one's own blood?' he moaned before bowing his head again.

Shortly afterwards he raised his shaky voice and continued his narration: It was only after his grandson had got struck following his invocation of *Shango* that the truth about his involvement in that mysterious disappearance dawned on the family.

'How can anyone be so sure it's *Shango*'s act?' Art inquired tentatively.

'Nobody can mistake the fierceness and swiftness with which *Shango* acts,' Pa Eghosa explained patiently. 'Besides, it's not just that my grandson got struck it's also the way that it happened that made us become fully aware of that fact.'

When Efosa expressed his surprise that a member of the family had actually done that Pa Eghosa sadly explained that too late, the family discovered that he had had a secret drug habit which was why he had done the unthinkable: mess with something so sacred and valuable. The statuette had been in the family for a very long time, long before the Benin Expedition — the British punitive expedition to Benin in the nineteenth century — which it survived. Art's eyes popped at that information. Pa Eghosa revealed that by the time his grandson's secret was known it was far too late because he was gone forever.

Till that moment neither he nor any member of his family had had any idea of the statuette's various sojourns within and outside the country. They had also been totally oblivious of the havocs it was believed to have wreaked in those places, in the period of time it had been away from the shrine. Nor had they been aware that it was overseas and that it was news there. He was shocked and saddened by all that info.

Through the grandson Art asked him whether there was any way *Shango* could be appeased and thus stopped from wreaking further havoc. The answer he got was similar to the one he had already received: until the statuette was returned to the shrine, nothing could be done. When he asked if the family nursed any hopes of recovering it some day Pa Eghosa replied that since its disappearance the family had never given up hopes of that happening. He gave Art a toothless grin as his grandson interpreted the last part of his reply which was,

'You're going to be the agent of that recovery.'

'Why does he think so?' Art asked the grandson, startled.

'I don't think so son, I know it,' Pa Eghosa stated in English.

Hearing him almost knocked Art off the bench; he had been thinking that he was dealing with a stark illiterate. Subsequently it was revealed to him that Pa Eghosa was a retired civil servant. In the colonial days he had worked as a court clerk.

Still stunned about his background, Art haltingly asked him how he was going to be the agent of the recovery.

'Everything happens for a reason son. You're here because you're destined to return it to us, your people. I know you've been in contact with it,' Pa Eghosa grinned.

'You know I've been in contact with the statuette?' Art asked, perplexed.

He got genuinely worried. He wondered who else knew he had been in contact with it. When he asked if having been in contact with it exposed him to any sort of reprisal from *Shango*, Pa Eghosa replied that unless he intended to keep it, he had no reason to worry.

'The gods have eyes you know; they're not at all blind,' he concluded.

I do hope so, Art said to himself.

'Indeed, they see,' Pa Eghosa reaffirmed, reading his mind.

When they were ready to leave Pa Eghosa led them to the family shrine where he jingled a tiny bell and poured another libation to his ancestors before offering prayers to them, begging them to grant his visitors a safe journey and to protect them. Reaching into the shrine, he brought out a small pouch from where he gave them a piece of native chalk and a cowry each, to guarantee their safety. He told Art to make sure that he preserved his, making him ask himself if he really needed protection that badly.

Tongue-tied, the trio drifted absent-mindedly towards their car and so they remained for some time. They were still dazed; a state brought about by what they had been told about themselves and about the events surrounding them. Finally, when they broached the topic they could not stop talking about it. All the way to their next destination they talked in amazement about how exact the revelations concerning each of them were.

'What do you guys make of the reincarnation bit? Art asked, at a point.

'What do we make of it as in: 'do we believe in it' or 'do we believe that you've been around so many times'?' Efosa inquired.

'Both ways,' Art replied.

'In that case my answer is: I believe absolutely in it,' Efosa stated.

'You do?'

'Yes, of course. What's more, I've seen so many cases with a huge pile of astounding evidence. For instance there's the case of a little boy in my hometown. He's supposed to have been around so many times, leaving his parents heartbroken each time he died. The last time around though, they had got so tired of suffering that they decided to teach him a lesson: they chopped off several toes and fingers before burying him. I'm sure you'll never guess what happened afterwards so I'll just go ahead and tell you. This child returned without those fingers and toes and he's still living. He's no longer accepted on the other side since he's mutilated.'

'Couldn't his condition be some form of congenital malformation?'

'Hello! Art. Have you been listening to me?'

'Yes, but—' he began but Efosa was eager to conclude his point:

'Yours is an interesting theory but, the congenital whatever had to appear exactly in the digits that had been amputated, right? Typical Western attitude: Seek some sort of scientific explanation for things you don't understand when none's easily available, try to manufacture it. This time around it's congenital what-you-may-call-it," he ended, laughing.

Art began analysing the point Efosa had just made and at the same time thinking about the "birthmark" on his own chest — the product of that war he had fought in, in his other life. Considering his personal story and everything he knew, he wondered why he had sounded so sceptical about Efosa's story; could it be exhaustion.

Their next destination was any good restaurant. They were all starving since breakfast had been just black coffee. But, that was not the only problem; they had also had that fiery spirit called *Ogogoro*. They all claimed they could eat a horse each. Laughingly asserting that the spirit had eroded his stomach lining, Art described his stomach as having a huge hole in it, so large that an elephant could fit into it. He was feeling that voracious!

They took their time over their substantial tasty lunch since they had more than enough time before their next appointment: an interview at a cybercafé with a con artist who called himself Guyman. When Art expressed surprise at the name Efosa explained that "*419*" con artists were usually referred to as that. He was surprised though, that that one had chosen to adopt it. They suspected that it could be his own way of ensuring anonymity since he knew that he was dealing with journalists.

Though they arrived ahead of schedule, Guyman was already there since according to him: 'Time's money.' The place was quite busy even though he informed them that that was not the normal "business hour". It was usually night-time for several reasons. Importantly, it allowed them to operate within the same timeframe as their overseas victims particularly those in the US and to run other businesses during the day. Such cybercafés were where lots of internet scams were planned and hatched including The Nigerian Dating Scam, The Nigerian E-mail Scam and others. The place, like others like it, was so ordinary-looking yet it was used to unleash massive financial harm world-wide.

Well, Guyman held a degree in Business Management and had been "operating" successfully for years. He was a boisterous fellow who also seemed pretty friendly and charming; like most conmen. He was a smooth-talker too and in no time he began trying to convince them that his business was not different from most businesses since they were all out to make money at people's expense. When Art pointed out that most businesses gave something in return; irrespective of the quality; for the money they were paid, he laughed aloud and stated that most of them ripped people off, period. He believed that nobody held a knife to the neck of the *Mugus*; victims of "*419*" scam; they became preys mainly because they were greedy. Though Art was seething at the man's lame justification of his criminal acts, he outwardly remained cool; he did not want to make a botch of the interview. When it ended he felt pretty satisfied because he had obtained quite a scoop despite not having taken notes. One of Guyman's conditions for the interview was: 'No note-taking, no recordings.'

On arrival at their hotel he and Omo were surprised that there was nobody at the reception desk. After a short wait they went behind the desk for their keys. They then rode the lift to their floor and as they were about to go to their separate rooms they agreed on what time to meet for dinner.

As Art made his way to his room he was thankful that at last he could nap to make up for the previous night. He was about to insert his key into the lock when he noticed that the door was a crack open. Cautiously, he pushed it wide open and stood transfixed. Mouth agape he took in his room in disbelief. It had been completely trashed in his absence. There was no doubt in his mind that robbery had not been the aim of the break-in — the degree of violence unleashed therein was excessive for a mere robbery.

Though he was not sure of what whoever had been looking for, he was glad his research material had not been lying around. Dazed though he was at the total disarray, he decided to take a few shots of it before backing out of there.

Just then he heard movements in the bathroom and was considering going there to find out what was happening when he heard some scuffling in the corridor. He instinctively squeezed under the bed, believing that since the room had been trashed it would be overlooked by those out there so he would be relatively safe. Meanwhile, the movements in the bathroom had become serious banging around.

Then two pairs of legs appeared in the room. He immediately recognised a pair as Omo's. His knees were rattling against each other. Next, another pair of legs appeared at the bathroom door and the owner barked out something in Edo and Omo babbled whatever. The trembling of his legs intensified. Art began quaking under the bed. He was confused. To aggravate matters, he did not understand the ongoing exchange. He got terrified. His eyes began smarting; sweat from his forehead was draining into them. The legs at the bathroom door moved close to him; the shoes were right in his face. He could smell them. He could not turn his face away because he was trapped between the floor and the bed.

The shoes in his face moved towards Omo who began babbling anew. He was being screamed at and then the shoving around began. Art took advantage of that distraction to pull the bedspread lower, leaving just enough slit to allow him follow the action. Then in horror he clamped his hands over his ears as Omo let out an ear-splitting scream. At the same time, Art saw the first drop of blood hit the floor. It was followed in quick succession by three larger drops. Omo's next piercing scream blended with the wailing of sirens, followed by the sound of heavy footfalls. The footfalls belonged to the fleeing assailants.

When the police, accompanied by a seriously breathless Efosa; who fortunately got word of the attack and implored a high-ranking friend for a speedy response; stormed the room Omo was so disorientated that he was totally unaware of their presence. He was glued to the spot, holding onto his neck and screaming,

'I'm dead! I'm dead!'

Each time Efosa asked him about Art he simply went on repeating the same thing.

'Can't you hear yourself screaming; how can you be dead?' Efosa asked, patiently trying to convince him that he was alive.

Eventually an exasperated officer grabbed him by the shoulders and gave him a sound shake, bringing him back to reality. Then he began screaming that he wanted to return to Lagos, to his family. He bawled that he did not want to stick around a second longer since before departing his assailants had declared him a dead man.

'If they'd wanted to kill you they'd have done so from the word go,' Efosa explained, in a bid to calm him down but it was no use.

Fortunately, on inspection, it turned out that his cut was superficial so it was not really an emergency. Relieved that he was okay, Efosa's main problem became Art's fate.

Meanwhile, Art was still too petrified to move. In the end, he crawled out from hiding and Efosa wrapped his arms around him telling him how pleased he was. Still trembling, he told Efosa that he was glad to see him. Turning to Omo, he apologised for all he had undergone before shakily asking Efosa how he had known about the assault. Efosa replied that he had received reliable info that he was in extreme danger.

'In danger?' he asked dazedly, though that fact was more than obvious.

'Yes, very much so,' Efosa replied grimly.

'Before rushing out they also told me to tell my *Oyibo* friend to pack up and leave town otherwise his body would end up in the forest,' gibbered a slightly disorientated Omo.

'How's that possible? What have I done?' Art asked needlessly, an incredulous look flashing across his countenance as he looked from one face to the other.

'Well, that's not the question right now. The question's how to get you out of here immediately and in one piece,' Efosa said, soothingly.

At that point the officer in charge of the operation declared that he was taking Art and Omo to the police station since he deemed it the safest place then. Efosa nodded.

When they got there Omo's wound was treated. Afterwards, Efosa revealed that going by the information he had received, the idea of them travelling by road was out of the question so he could help them get on a flight that same day. Quite apart from pressing safety reasons, Art was totally in favour of the air travel as the unpleasant details of his trip to Benin City were still vivid in his mind. However, recalling the strong objection Omo had raised about air travel, he asked him what he intended to do since his own mind was made up. Not surprisingly, Omo replied that he was totally willing to hop onto the first available flight — flying coffin or not. He simply wanted to abandon Benin City, to leave all those awful experiences behind him.

As soon as he got the green light Efosa made oodles of calls, pulled every string, called in every favour and finally obtained a couple of seats. However, it was at almost triple the normal price — it included the cost of palm-greasing. Paying that exorbitant fare did not bother Art; he would have paid any amount.

While at the police station Efosa kept receiving updates — things were that bad. Close to departure time he rode with Art and Omo to the airport in a squad car.

Just before boarding Art asked Efosa how the gang had known that Omo and he were at that hotel and also discovered their room numbers.

'It's not so complicated, Art. Anyway, after all you've learnt about them I'm surprised you're asking me such questions,' Efosa replied.

'Yeah, you're right; but I still find it bizarre.'

Then he told Efosa how much he appreciated his having put himself out for him. He also apologised for all the trouble his visit had caused him. Efosa waved his apology aside, affirming that it was a pleasure. Next, he asked Art to do all in his power to help Pa Eghosa recover the statuette. He promised he would. In turn he implored Efosa to help Grace.

Fortunately the flight was without any incident. However, as the plane hit the tarmac in Lagos Art's immediate worry became how to get to Adrian's in one piece.

As it turned out, his worries were unnecessary since a grim-faced Wole was at the airport waiting for him. Wole explained that Efosa had called to notify him of his arrival. He had also told him to warn Art that an all-out manhunt was on for him. Before Art could react to that stunning piece of news, Wole informed him that Efosa had emphasised that he should convince him to leave the country immediately.

Hence though Wole's being there took care of his transport worries, it also gave rise to a totally unexpected source of worry.

CHAPTER 18

All the way to Adrian's Wole's attempt to persuade Art to take the warning seriously fell on deaf ears. He kept insisting that he was not going to let a pack of criminals run him out of town. As they got close to Adrian's gate he noticed that the place was teeming with policemen. The sight of them everywhere made him fear the very worst. He got terribly worried about Adrian. Right away, he made a solemn vow that if Adrian was safe and sound he would save him further troubles by packing up and leaving the country.

Such was his agitation that he could barely wait for the car to stop before jumping out. However, when he got to the gate the officers there refused to let him into the premises. Since neither Adamu nor Adrian was there to identify him, his frustration got compounded. His frame of mind had got so muddled that he totally forgot about Wole until he heard him asking for the officer in charge. When the officer finally approached the gate Wole did a bit of name-dropping and smooth-talking and that did the trick. Unhurriedly, the gate was opened and they were ordered to step in — they could not drive in. Very fearful of what he would find beyond the gate, Art took a deep breath before crossing it.

As he looked past the officers in the front yard the first thing he saw was the lifeless bloodied body of Bruno, Adrian's Doberman Shepherd. He had been brutally slain, exactly in the same way as Ebony. Art's knees almost buckled under him. The sight of that body brought back memories of Ebony's and the intense pain and sorrow he had felt then resurged. Those terrible feelings were aggravated by the fact that he was yet to see Adrian. Since he had been informed that there was a price on his own head, not seeing Adrian got him worrying that he might have got mistaken for him and been disposed of. His heart began palpitating so much that he felt faint. He had been so confounded and dumbfounded since he entered the compound that he was yet to ask any question. He simply kept running his fingers through his hair.

Knowing that an earthenware pot; the contents of which from experience he could imagine; was lying in the front yard drove his panic level higher. He knew that all that had happened was because of him; no two ways about it. He was still standing around in utter bewilderment when he saw Adamu being shoved into a squad car. He heard him screaming at the top of his voice in an unfamiliar language, as he was whisked away, sirens blaring.

Siren sounds had become quite familiar to Art and so had the indiscriminate use of sirens by uniformed men — be they soldiers, policemen or what have you — especially with their superior officers in the car. In lots of cases the use was highly unnecessary. He learnt that that practice went beyond the presence of officers in squad cars or unmarked cars: that "honour" also extended to their wives or even mistresses.

Anyway, he switched his mind back to the whisking away of Adamu. He would later be told that the language he had been screaming in was Hausa and that Adamu had been screaming that he was innocent and swearing that he had seen nothing amiss while on duty. Obviously, the officers did not believe him, if their handling of him was anything to go by. Art, however, believed him — what with all what he had gathered about the cult members and his own experiences since his investigation began. Thus he would testify in his favour if given the chance. Not then anyway since he was yet to find his tongue.

When he eventually found his tongue he voiced the question that had been going round in his head: the whereabouts of his friend. The officer closest to him gestured in the direction of the porch. Dreading the most horrific of sights, he turned that way very, very slowly. Looking past the officers standing there, he made out the still figure of Adrian. He noticed that Adrian was as white and as rigid as a statue. He was relieved though that Adrian was not in a prostrate position. He was seated and staring into space. He was still in suit — the way he had left home for work. He looked utterly desolate.

Seeing Adrian alive brought him so much joy but though he kept willing his legs to take him to Adrian's side, they refused to respond.

Finally he managed to wobble there and, obviously in shock, Adrian kept staring at him as if he did not recognise him.

'Hey, buddy,' he whispered, placing his hand on Adrian's shoulder.

'Who could've done a horrible thing like this, Art?' he whispered tearfully at length.

Robot-like, he asked that same question over and over. Art wished he could give him an answer, no matter how irrelevant, but he could not find the words to express himself. Never before had he seen his friend like that.

That awkward situation persisted until the officer in charge approached them. He announced that the team's work was done and they were leaving. Adrian looked on zombie-like as the officer told him that Bruno's body would be taken along for further investigation and that he would personally ensure that it was returned afterwards. He then insisted that Adrian should get indoors before the team departed. Adrian had the status of a diplomat so his safety was the nation's responsibility.

Art had to help him to his feet and steer him towards the door — he was that dazed. Wole offered to remain with them till morning. Art made half-hearted attempts to convince him to leave but, he was adamant. Satisfied that Adrian was safely indoors, the officer detailed two of his men to guard the house. Thereafter the rest of them departed, sirens blaring regardless of how late it was. As that jarring sound receded the two officers locked the gate and took up their position. Their watch began.

Adrian broke down once he was indoors — the anaesthetising effect of shock had worn off. Sobbing, he told Art how surprised he got when Bruno did not meet him at the gate when he returned from work. He asked Adamu about him but he could not recall the last time he had seen him. After locking the gate Adamu went around, calling out Bruno's name while he drove towards the carport. And almost simultaneously, they discovered his body. Once again Adrian's body was rocked violently by a fresh bout of sobs. His grief was logical: Bruno had been part of his family for a bit over nine years. The fact that he had been without his family in the two years he had been in Lagos had made their bond even stronger.

Art was feeling terribly guilty. If he had not put up with him, none of that would have happened. He was feeling totally impotent as he watched Adrian grieving. He wished he could do something to relieve his pain. At a stage, at his wits' end, he stood up and poured him a generous shot of whisky. Adrian shook his head but he insisted so much that finally he reluctantly accepted it. Art then poured Wole a shot and one for himself.

At first they all sat there drinking in silence, like people in mourning. They would occasionally either stare into their glasses or into space. However, by the time Adrian had knocked back his second stiff drink he appeared to be emerging from his zombie-like state. Art's desperate action seemed to have turned out to be a brilliant one.

Soon it became increasingly obvious that they were all getting drunk — to different degrees, but the tell-tale signs were there. After the last generous shot Adrian poured himself, the next time he picked up the bottle he did not seem to understand that it was empty. He kept staring at it as if trying to will it to refill itself. He gave up that attempt at magic or miracle when it slowly dawned on him that it was no good. They had downed its contents in record time. Subsequently he stood up unsteadily and staggered out of the room.

When he returned, it was with a fresh bottle and with something akin to a smile pasted on his hitherto blank face. He had got rid of his jacket and tie. As he plunked down in the sofa, he broke the prevailing silence by telling Art that he bore him no grudge for what had happened to Bruno. His words were so slurred that at first Art had trouble making them out; what with the whisky haze he was in. When the words finally sank in he felt deeply touched. Taking a deep breath to control his emotions, he thanked Adrian for his grand gesture and apologised for the trouble and sorrow he had caused through his foolhardiness.

'Well, as you jolly well know, a friend in need's a bloody nuisance,' Adrian joked.

They all broke into drunken laughter. Following the laughter, Adrian drawled that given the circumstances Art should leave town for his safety. Wole, who was yet to utter a word, seconded that motion by nodding vigorously. Art asked Adrian what he was going to do about his own safety and, looking straight at him through glazed eyes, Adrian made an effort to appear his usual confident self as he assured him that he was not worried about himself since he was highly protected.

Talking about protection Art remembered Adamu and asked Adrian what he thought about his arrest. Adrian's glazed eyes became fixed on his glass — he seemed to be weighing his answer. Then he spluttered that he believed in Adamu's innocence because Adamu had been in his service for as long as he had been in Lagos. After acknowledging that he understood that the police had to do their work, he drawled that come morning he would go to the police station to bail him. Those words brought Art relief — he believed that the mess Adamu was in was his fault.

They continued drinking and their by now booze-loosened tongues continued wagging. They started telling one drunken joke after another. They seemed to have pushed aside or even forgotten the tense moments they had been through. The more booze they quaffed the more jokes they told and the more raucous their laughter got. Suddenly they all fell silent as if on cue. Art felt goose bumps all over his body. The chill running down his spine made him shiver. Although the silence did not last long, it lasted long enough to make them all feel terribly uncomfortable. It was broken by Adrian who laughing nervously, stated that an angel had just gone by. Wole drawled that he would say a ghost. They began laughing uncontrollably again. They were clearly beyond drunk. At a stage Adrian turned to face Wole and still laughing, he drawled,

'Did you say ghost? Do you really believe in such stuff?'

Confused, Wole looked around. Obviously, he could not recall using that word. Well, how many people keep track of everything they say when they are awfully drunk?

'Shh, did you hear that?' Art whispered before Wole could think of what to say.

'Hear what?' Adrian laughingly whispered, imitating Art's tone.

'I think I heard something like, 'Get down!''

'We're getting too dr-u-u-nk,' Adrian tittered. 'We're now hearing things soon we'll start seeing things.'

'Maybe we should get down anyway,' Wole laughed, crouching.

'Yes, maybe we should; it's probably a divine message,' Art laughed, crouching too.

'Well, the heck with getting too drunk the heck with hearing things,' Adrian slurred.

Then lurching towards the whisky bottle, he drawled,

'Let the party go on!'

'Yeah, let the party go on!' the other two echoed, rolling with laughter on the floor.

Just as Adrian reached for the bottle they all heard what sounded like a car engine backfiring. Startled, they looked at one another. Then before any of them could say a word the sound got more distinct: unmistakeably, it was the sound of gunfire. In a flash, they all took cover behind the sofa.

It goes without saying that that sound shook them out of their whisky haze immediately. It is amazing how close to sober most people become — no matter how drunk or distraught — when subjected to a sudden extreme condition. Well, there they were crouching behind the sofa wide-eyed and trembling like three cornered mice.

'What the hell's that?" Art mumbled.

'Those were gunshots,' Wole replied, needlessly.

'Of course I know they're gunshots. But, what's going on?'

'Probably armed robbers,' Wole responded.

'There's never been armed robbery in this area,' Adrian whispered.

'There's always a first time,' Wole whispered.

Deep down, however, Wole was worried that the warning he had been given regarding an imminent attempt on Art's life could be materialising. His going to the airport to meet him had been to ensure his safe arrival at Adrian's because Efosa's tip-off had been from a reliable source. Of course he did not voice his fears; he did not want to worry them unnecessarily in case his fears were unfounded. But he knew that Adrian's observation was absolutely correct because given the status of that neighbourhood — it housed diplomats, expatriates and the really well-offs in the society — there was constant police patrol. Thus incidents of armed robbery, albeit endemic in most parts of the city and the country as a whole, were unheard of there. That buttressed his suspicions but he kept mum.

They soon noticed that the sound of gunshots was getting closer and closer. Art was dying of curiosity so he decided to go and peep through a window. As he got to his feet Adrian whispered harshly that he should get down, instead of jeopardising his life. However, he was too consumed by curiosity to heed Adrian's advice fully so although he did get down, he headed for the window on all fours. On parting the blinds, what he saw froze him. At first thinking that he was imagining things, he let go of the blinds. Nevertheless that was only momentarily, he parted them again.

'Oh no, this can't be happening,' he mumbled. 'I'm seeing things, no doubt; serves me right for guzzling so much booze.'

Then robbing his eyes, he peeped again at what was going on outside.

'What's happening; what can you see?' Adrian whispered from behind the sofa.

'They're at the gate,' he whispered back.

'Who's at the gate?' Wole asked.

'Must be armed robbers; there's a dark Humvee out there.'

'What? Where are the policemen?' Adrian asked in consternation.

'No sign of them anywhere,' Art reported back.

'Oh, crap!' Wole uttered.

Not knowing which he preferred, the cult members or armed robbers, Wole went on to explain in a shaky voice that in that society armed robbers were often better armed than policemen and frequently, rather coordinated and organised. Some people believed that many of them were former members of ECOMOG who never turned in their arms after being discharged, on returning from their overseas missions. Then for want of a means of livelihood they took up armed robbery. While others alleged that some of such troops sold their arms to delinquents and robbers. Either way the salient points were: most armed robbers in the city were well-armed and they operated with absolute professionalism in the way they manipulated their weapons and in the way they carried out their operations.

Wole told them that things could get really ugly since apparently, the men at the gate were in a far superior position than the policemen — both in number and fire power. The officers were just two with mere handguns, facing dangerous unscrupulous well-armed —going by the booming sound of the gunfire reaching them — thugs packed in the Humvee. He figured that the officers were probably dead or taking cover while awaiting back-up or just hiding and hoping that the trouble would blow over.

Adrian and Art found his information disheartening and worrying. Who ever said that knowledge is power? In their case they would have preferred the bliss that goes with ignorance because being blasted with so much information i.e. receiving knowledge, had not given them any advantage. It was all to the contrary.

As Art continued taking in the scene outside from his position, he suddenly realised that the men were trying to bring down the gate with the aid of the heavy vehicle. Drawing a deep breath, he turned round and told his mates what was going on. They were all panicky. But, Art and Adrian were particularly so. Wole telling them that armed robbers in Lagos were sometimes so vicious that they did not simply cart away their booty but stuck around to inflict tremendous pain and suffering on their victims, escalated their state of alarm.

Art's mind flashed back to the not too different situations he had lived in Benin, particularly the one at the sacred ground. Though he had felt sheer terror when his party's hiding place was being approached by the high priestess, somehow that was nothing compared to what he was experiencing then as he numbly watched the gate yielding bit by bit. He believed a brutal end was imminent.

A banging on the back door startled them. Nobody responded to it. It was not that they were ignoring it — they simply could not respond. They were paralysed with terror. Without exception they were sweating profusely, despite the air-conditioner. Suddenly they heard a voice filled with urgency calling out Adrian's surname. They gawked at one another when the speaker identified himself as Constable Bamgbose, one of the officers. Wole warned that it could be a trick. Although he was suspicious too, Adrian headed for the door on all fours.

'Be careful!' Wole cautioned nervously.

'Identify yourself better!' Adrian whispered on reaching the door.

By now Art was right behind him. The officer identified himself convincingly enough for Adrian to open the door a crack. The officer shoved it open and staggered in, partially bearing the weight of his wounded sergeant — he had been shot. Panting as a result of the weight he had been lugging, he stated that reinforcement would arrive soon.

'When's soon? After those animals must've come in to finish us all?' Wole snapped.

'Easy; we're just two and we've done our best!' the constable bridled.

'Look at my sergeant, he needs help!' he added, applying pressure on the wound.

Right then they heard a great crash. They exchanged horrified looks — the gate had just given way. The constable asked if any of them knew how to use a firearm. Before they could respond his wounded sergeant assured him that he would be able to cope. Their guns looked like toys, compared to what the ones booming outside must look like. No one said anything but they were all thinking: *These toys are no match for the real things out there.*

As the Humvee made it into the front yard a shot rang out, shattering a window — the one Art had been at. Luckily, the bullet found no human target inside. They were all paralysed fleetingly. Then Adrian reacted. He suggested they should head for his servants' quarters through the back door since hiding out there until help arrived would be far safer than hoping to fend off the imminent attack with those toys. They all nodded eagerly and crouching, they set out scurrying. The officers brought up the rear because the wounded one was being supported by his subordinate who was virtually bearing his full weight. The duo barely made progress as they trailed along, leaving a worrying trace of blood along the way.

They had just got to their destination when the heavy front door yielded. They heard somebody, presumably the leader of the gang, screaming out orders which they could not make out from their hiding-place. They were sweating and trembling, praying and hoping that the intruders would not trace them before help arrived.

Fortunately, that classic pessimist in most groups undergoing such a dreadful ordeal — that one who usually squeals hysterically that everyone is going to die — was not among them. So they were not more terrified than they already were.

Meanwhile the banging around in the main house had become such that despite the long distance separating it from their hiding-place, they could hear everything distinctly. To make matters worse they did not know how many people they were hiding from. But, if the racket they were creating was anything to go by, they must be at least an army.

They soon heard a huge crash and shortly afterwards they heard the men's voices clearly. The back door had just collapsed and it would not be long before those thugs got to them. In absolute horror, they looked at one another. There was ominous silence.

'Where in hell are they?' the leader of the pack bellowed impatiently.

'Just a moment, I think I can see something,' one of them announced.

'I'm asking about them not about what you think you can see!' the leader barked.

'Easy, easy... Yes, it's blood so they must've gone that way.'

'Let's go get them!' another voice declared gruffly.

As the cowering party heard heavy footfalls headed in their direction, they believed that each of those steps was bringing doomsday closer. Their panic level hit the roof.

'So when's this frigging back-up you're supposed to have called for going to arrive?' Adrian asked indignantly, facing the officers.

'I wonder what's holding them up,' the wounded one mumbled feebly.

'Let's be calm, we should think of something before they get here,' Art whispered.

He was trying hard to conceal the fact that he was so scared that he could pee in his pants if that situation did not come to an end, one way or another, soon.

'Think of something ... like what, Art? Like what?' Wole growled.

'Relax buddy, you're going to give our position away if you continue like this,' Art whispered. 'Something's bound to happen,' he added, more to himself than to anyone.

Then the heavy footfalls stopped outside their door. They all froze, listening attentively.

'Shh-h-h-h!' someone outside whispered.

Absolute silence followed. Art imagined that the men outside were either listening for any tell-tale sound that could give away their preys' position or were trying to decide which of the many doors to bring down first in their bid to find them. Or simply, they were playing a sadistic mind game: they already knew where they were, but were just trying to get them to the very limit of fear before attacking them. Indeed inside, they were all paralysed with fear.

However, the paralysing effect of that scare tactic was short-lived — it wore off sooner than any of them could have imagined and in a most unexpected way. The wounded officer suddenly grabbed his gun from his partner, uttering in a harsh whisper,

'If I'm going to die, it won't be without a fight!'

Wincing with pain, he managed to crawl close to the door and took up position. Seeing that act of bravery on the part of his wounded superior, the constable crawled over to take his place beside him. The sergeant's attitude spurred the rest of them into action. Since they were in the gardener's storage room the other three armed themselves with shovels and whatever tools they could grab. Although they were not really convinced that they stood much chance of effectively defending themselves or of defeating the thugs, they were not prepared to take what was coming their way lying down. They were prepared to fight and to go out defending themselves to the last man. That outward act of bravery notwithstanding deep down, each of them was praying for a miracle.

After what seemed like an eternity to them, the waiting game came to a startling end. The ringing of Wole's mobile phone jolted them.

'Damn the cursed phone!' Adrian growled, facing Wole.

Right after that the door gave way under the impact of synchronised heavy kicks. At the same time, the long-awaited answer to their prayers ultimately came in the form of blaring sirens and the deafening sound of gunfire. The police had arrived, in full force too. The first volley of their shots made the gang turn around to return fire — a heaven-sent distraction. The staccato sound of the ensuing gunfire was immensely frightening. Art and co were so enveloped by the noise that they were worried about becoming victims of stray bullets so they burrowed deeper into every available nook.

When the din eventually died down they continued in hiding since they did not know what side had won the battle. Ages later, they were dug out. Through his haze Art observed that the place was swarming afresh with policemen. Although most of what happened in the first few moments would become hazy in his mind with time, certain details would always stand out in his memory. The first was the sight of a couple or so bodies lying outside, not far from the door of their hideout. The second was a most uncharacteristic scene: Adrian flying into full rage — rage directed at the officer in charge of the operation. He could not believe that the officer had provided him with such flimsy protection. The third detail was seeing a disorientated trembling Wole who could barely sustain himself on his feet reel towards his car screaming that he had had enough and that he was leaving. Fortunately, he was stopped by an officer who rightly considered him unfit to drive.

As soon as the police were sure that they had secured the premises, the officer in charge instructed Adrian and Art to pack an overnight bag since the place was unsafe and unfit for the time being. Neither of them had thought of staying anyway.

Anyhow, in they went and no sooner had they stepped in than they noticed two bodies lying in the living room. Adrian vowed that he was never returning there. The place was pretty well trashed. They had to watch where they placed their feet, to avoid stepping on sharp objects or blood. Among the handcuffed men sitting around, waiting to be transferred to the police station, Art thought he recognised one. There was such hatred and hostility in the man's stare that Art was grateful that he was securely cuffed. He shuddered and scurried away, wondering what he could have done to arouse such degree of antagonism in a total stranger. Of course he packed all his stuff. He had had his fair share of adventure; enough to last him this lifetime and the next, he claimed.

It was already dawn when he and Adrian were whisked away in a squad car, sandwiched between armoured vehicles — sirens blaring, of course. They were taken to a five-star hotel on the Island and lodged there, courtesy of the government. Regardless of the luxury and comfort all around and despite not having slept a wink all night, neither of them could sleep. They had experienced too much adrenaline rush.

Their exhaustion notwithstanding, they had to spend much of the day answering all sorts of questions from the police. The entire experience was tedious and tiresome since they repeated the same story over and over again as the questions were always the same. In the end Art was urged to leave the country for his safety — as if he needed any convincing.

Top-level string-pulling eventually got him a seat on a Frankfurt-bound flight the night after that nightmare. Although he was relieved, he was immensely sorry that he had to leave Adrian at such a crucial moment. He felt like he was leaving him holding the baby, irrespective of how much Adrian tried to reassure him that his leaving was for the common good, so to speak. After joking that he felt much safer with him far away, Adrian got serious as he confessed that he had been extremely worried about Art's safety since his arrival. So, he was glad and relieved that he was departing in one piece.

All through the day Art felt like a caged bird — his movements were restricted. Every step he took was monitored by the police. Actually he could not step outside his hotel room, how much more beyond the hotel premises. When night mercifully came it was a badly shaken up him that was smuggled from the hotel, bundled into an unmarked squad car and off to the airport to board that Frankfurt-bound flight amidst top security. Indeed he was led right up to the aircraft door by two armed officers.

The Lagos-Frankfurt leg of the trip was terrible for him since it was full of Africans. He was jumpy. He was suspicious of everyone and everything, even his own shadow — experience had taught him that those thugs were virtually everywhere. He did not switch off his overhead light all through the flight since he felt far safer that way and less inclined to fall asleep. Luckily unlike that Lagos-bound flight there was no serious incident. There was a mild turbulence just before dinner — the closest they got to an incident. He turned down dinner since he was still too distressed to eat anything. He asked for just a beer.

They arrived at Frankfurt Airport before 5 a.m. and he stumbled across a scene, the like of which he had never witnessed throughout his travelling life: As he was about to alight from the aircraft he almost bumped into immigration officials. They were at both doors. He found their presence enormously odd and surprising. Though apparently they were asking everyone for their passport, the fact was: they were targeting the Africans.

Later he found out that the measure had been implemented to combat illegal immigration since due to corruption people without the proper visa often slipped through the controls in Lagos. Thus that measure was to ensure that such people did not disappear into the airport— before getting to Immigration control — and lurk around till the right chance presented itself for them to sneak out and melt into the city. He was told that illegal immigrants adopted such ploys in many European countries.

Once he stepped onto European soil he started feeling slightly relaxed because in a way he was feeling safe. After clearing Immigration he went to confirm his reservation for his Madrid flight though in Lagos, he had been assured that it had been taken care of. He also requested to be assigned a seat towards the front of the aircraft.

Afterwards, he decided to freshen up before going in search of coffee — all those sleepless nights were getting him awfully woozy. As he bent over the washbasin and made to wash his hands the door into the gents burst open and an African man entered.

'Hey! Did you enjoy the flight?' the man asked, hostilely.

'Do I know you?' Art retorted.

He was surprised at himself. Affable and outgoing by nature, he would have ignored the man's brash behaviour. He might even have struck up conversation with him. He was still analysing his reaction to the annoying man's attitude when another African stormed in.

Before he knew what was happening he had been hemmed in between the two men. Although he towered over both of them, they still managed to work up enough menacing attitude to intimidate him.

'I asked you a question,' his antagonist smiled menacingly before saying something in some African language, making his newly-arrived mate laugh.

Art could not believe that yet again he had got into a situation in which he was terribly helpless. Just when he could move no further because his back was literally against the wall, the door burst open anew.

This time two stern-faced Spanish-looking middle-aged men stormed in. They took in the situation and one of them addressed him in heavily accented English.

'Is everything okay?' he asked.

His accent confirmed Art's suspicion — indeed they were Spaniards. As to the question Art was asked, he could only blink and swallow.

'We're only asking about his flight,' the Africans chorused.

'Hmm, interesting,' the other Spaniard said, studying Art's pale face.

'Okay, we're leaving,' the Africans said, scuttling towards the door.

'No, no, no, not so fast!' the first Spaniard declared.

'Let them go,' Art finally managed to splutter because he had had enough of filing police reports and stuff like that.

After the two individuals had scurried out he slowly washed his hands and face under the watchful eyes of his newly-acquired guardian angels. Then he shook hands with them and introduced himself. When they introduced themselves, he realised how extremely lucky he had been once again. They were plainclothes policemen who belonged to the Special Crimes Unit, just like Diego. Of course he did not tell them about Diego since he occasionally passed him sensitive information for his investigation. They were headed to the US for a conference involving the EU and the US on Special Crimes. They had been having coffee while awaiting their connecting flight when they observed that the Africans were trailing him. Seeing that he had not the least inkling of what was going on, they had decided to discreetly tag along. He thanked them profusely and asked them to join him for coffee.

Over coffee he told them where he was coming from and why he had travelled there.

'You must be out of your frigging mind, going off to Nigeria just like that on such a mission! Do you know what could've happened to your damn arse?' Carlos, the more vocal of the two bellowed.

'Yeah, you're not the first person to say that. As to your question, believe me I did come pretty close to having so many things happen to me and my arse,' he laughed, before giving them an abbreviated version of some of his worst experiences in Nigeria.

'Goodness! You're a lucky devil,' Roberto, the other officer, said.

'Nobody gets so lucky so many times in a row for too long so watch your steps and your back,' Carlos advised.

'So many weird things happened to people I know who went to that land, even in the line of duty,' Roberto told him and turning to Carlos, he asked: 'Do you recall the case of those colleagues involved in that deportation operation, two years ago?'

'Oh, yeah I surely do! Pepito's cousin's one of them, right?'

They told Art the story of several officers who had been detailed to escort some deportees to Nigeria. Once there, the deportees alleged they had maltreated them on the flight so they hexed them. Shrugging it off, the officers returned to Spain and weeks later, one by one, they started falling mysteriously ill. The symptoms they presented were not consistent with any known disease on record. The myriads of tests they were subjected to, revealed absolutely nothing known to the various specialists they were referred to. Ultimately their illness was diagnosed as psychological. Later it was classed as some tropical disease, yet to be catalogued. The tall and short of the story was: none of them became fit enough to report for duty.

'Wow! That's certainly weird!' Art observed, astounded.

'What lesson have you learnt from this story?' Carlos asked.

They all laughed out loud as he replied,

'Never stick your arse or nose into unknown territories; for instance?'

They were still laughing when his flight was announced. They exchanged telephone numbers promising to meet in Madrid. Before he departed they informed him that in the force, issues related to Nigeria were handled with extreme care and seriousness and advised him to do the same. He thanked them and headed for his gate, very much on the alert.

CHAPTER 19

Sleep was the only thing on Art's mind when the aircraft touched down at Barajas Airport, bringing his nightmarish adventure to an end. He was feeling extremely drowsy despite the multiple coffees he had consumed. Due to the numerous hectic sleepless nights he had had, coupled with many hours of flight, he was not exactly lucid. Consequently, when she popped out of nowhere he could not believe it at first. He saw her right after clearing both Immigration and Customs. He thought he was imagining her being there — she had been on his mind since Diego's call three days earlier. He blinked and looked again thinking that she would disappear but, she was right there. He remained on the same spot, gawking at her. She walked up to him and beamed,

'Why are you staring at me instead of saying hello?'

He did not know that he had been showing his incredulity so openly.

'How did you know I'm coming back today, Regina?' he uttered.

'Your friend Diego told me,' she smiled.

'My friend Diego?' he asked, puzzled.

Her saying that Diego told her he was returning on that day got him even more stunned than seeing her there. To start with, he had not told Diego his original arrival date since before leaving Spain he had not been sure of it. He had simply wanted events in Nigeria to determine that. But still more than impossible was him telling Diego his present arrival date since it simply happened due to unforeseen circumstances.

'You do remember having a friend called Diego, don't you?'

He was speechless; he could only gape at her smiling face. The more he tried to get himself to think, the more confused his mind seemed to get. In addition to his mind, his body was beginning to reflect the effects of the abuses it had endured. It was getting more sluggish by the second. Acute sleep deprivation was affecting him seriously. His wooziness notwithstanding, he had a nagging funny feeling at the back of his mind that apart from the arrival date enigma, something else was not quite in place. He shook his head, frantically trying to clear it. Eventually he told himself that what mattered was that despite his past few weeks' nagging worries she was safe and sound so he said,

'Thank Goodness! You're back, Regina! Have you seen Am…?'

'Ah! Amina; sure, I've seen her. She's a great friend.'

'Indeed. She's terribly worried. What happened to you?'

'We'll come to me soon; I'm dying to hear all about your trip first. Look at you, you look pretty worked over. Don't tell me you were rough-handled over there!'

Until she mentioned it he had almost forgotten about what a sight he must look. Apart from the signs of fatigue written all over his face, he still bore marks of all the banging around he had undergone in his attempt to get out of that terrifying forest. Her observation got him slightly self-conscious. He wondered what everyone else must have been thinking. When she realised that her playful banter had upset him, she smiled sweetly at him and said gently,

'Excuse my silly joke. Seriously, hope you didn't suffer an accident.'

'Something similar,' he replied, trying to smile.

'Please, tell me about your experience.'

As much as he preferred to hear her own story, he agreed to do it her way. After all she had played a great role towards making his trip possible. Regardless, he just could not get her sudden disappearance and her unexpected reappearance out of his mind. Diego's call came to his mind again. He asked himself if her reappearance had been the reason for it. He could not tell since all Diego had managed to say was,

'Dude, it's about your friend …' and they lost the connection.

Later, try as much as he did, he could not get back to him — a fact he attributed to network problems. Finally, he had given up trying.

He was still dwelling on that matter when they walked through a sliding door and joined the short queue at the taxi rank. He shuddered. It was somewhat chilly — a sharp contrast to what the weather had been before his departure, less than two weeks earlier. As she cleared her throat he turned to face her. Smiling, she asked him how much his thoughts were worth. Smiling back, he apologised for his distraction. For the first time, he noticed that she looked far better than she had in the days leading up to her disappearance. She appeared quite relaxed too. Indeed she looked really beautiful.

He asked her to repeat her question and smiling broadly, she asked him about his experiences in Nigeria and his impression. He pondered her question briefly and replied that though most of his experiences had been weird on the whole, the trip had been worth his every while. He acknowledged that it was all thanks to her since the leads and contacts she had provided unearthed goldmines, information-wise. Shrugging off his thanks, she stated that he had been of immense help to her too. When he asked her how she replied that he would find out soon enough.

She's so full of riddles, he said to himself.

As they settled into a taxi she observed him closely, asking how he had sustained his bruises and what he meant when he said that most of his experiences had been weird. He took a deep breath before mentioning where he had sustained his injuries but would not go into details. He said that though he did not know how to explain all he had undergone, he was certain that he obtained most of the answers to the mysteries surrounding the fires and related matters. She said that she was pleased it turned out to be a productive trip.

'Oh, absolutely; you can't imagine how much!' he enthused.

He then turned his gaze to the midmorning traffic and his mind wandered off again. A moment later he felt her nudge. Turning sideways, he met her questioning look.

'Can we talk about your weird experiences?' she smiled.

He replied that although they were several, three really stood out in his mind as the weirdest of the weird and that ranking them in order of weirdness was virtually impossible. She laughingly stated that curiosity was gnawing away at her and smiling broadly, he declared that he was about to end her suffering.

'Wole took me to visit a *Babalawo*,' he revealed.

She laughed aloud, assuming that he was joking. But he told her it was no laughing matter considering the information he obtained.

'Seriously...? What sort of information?'

'Regarding my past lives.'

'Lives; so you've been around more than the one time you told me!'

'So it turned out,' he replied seriously.

He looked out of the window briefly before disclosing that funnily enough, he received the same revelation twice. He went on to tell her about Pa Eghosa's divination.

'Do you believe everything they both told you?'

'That's not the question. The fact is: I experienced some of it first-hand since the old crank of a *Babalawo* made me go into a trance.'

'He put you in a trance?' she asked in amazement.

'Uh-huh,' he nodded.

'I've heard about all sorts of divinations but not this one. It must've been a one-of-a-kind experience. I know you're tired but can you tell me a bit about it?" she pleaded.

The way she said it, he could not refuse so pushing his fatigue aside, he plunged into his tale. He told her everything about his visit to the weird-looking wild-eyed shaggy-haired *Babalawo*. She appeared completely spell-bound as he described the ceremonies preceding the trance and most of the images he had seen while in it. She got so impressed by some details that she gasped. When he finished she went on looking at him as if expecting more and then slowly, she uttered just one word: 'Wow!'

After a pause he started talking about Pa Eghosa and when he mentioned his revelation about the young woman watching over him from the great beyond, she sat bolt upright. Mildly surprised by her reaction, he asked her why she had reacted that way and she laughed nervously, stuttering that she found that information spine-chilling. He admitted having had the same sensation. Thereafter, he continued with his story about the elderly gentleman's revelations. Lastly, he mentioned the native chalk and the cowry.

Then there was silence during which his mind flashed back to the events that had precipitated his exit from Lagos. Noticing the gloomy expression on his face she asked him what the matter was. Since he was not willing to go into such unpleasant details yet, he told her that he preferred to talk about the third of his weirdest experiences: The oath-taking ceremony and the related rituals he witnessed in the forest. He said that top on the list of all the weird things that happened that night were: the metamorphosis of the high priestess and their encounter with *the diminishing man*.

Speechless, she studied him briefly before stating that she could not believe that he had risked going into the cult's territory.

'You must know that going that deep into that forest without being a member of the cult's like visiting the land of the dead. You should be grateful you came out in one piece.'

'Actually, in several pieces; I came out with scratches, bites and bruises,' he joked.

'It's no laughing matter, Art. I can see that you don't get it,' she stated sternly, looking straight into his eyes.

That look that he glimpsed in her eyes got him somewhat uneasy. He did not know what to make of it. When he asked her why she was giving him that look, she replied that she was simply worried about him and his impulsiveness.

In that instant the cabbie asked for his exact address. It dawned on him that they were in his street and, very close to his building. He had been so engrossed in that conversation that he had not only completely lost his bearings but also track of time. He gazed at his familiar surroundings fondly, really glad to be home. After getting his stuff out of the cab he asked her if she would like to come upstairs for coffee or if she would rather they went to the cafeteria across the street. She opted for the former and offered to help him with a piece of luggage. He gladly accepted her offer since he was laden with souvenirs.

However, no sooner had he thrown his door open than he regretted inviting her upstairs. He had totally forgotten the state he had left his flat in, in the flurry of his preparation for his trip. He turned to apologise for the chaos and he discovered that she was totally oblivious of the disarray. Her whole attention was focused on the iron horseshoe above his entrance door. Sensing that he was looking at her she faced him, smiling.

'Your horseshoe!' she uttered excitedly, pointing at it.

'Yes, my horseshoe,' he replied slowly while processing a thought.

The thought was the argument they had had outside his door weeks earlier, when they discovered the stuff deposited there. He recalled how miffed she had got when he scoffed at her claim that the stuff should be taken seriously as it could bring him grave consequences. Also, how she had angrily thrown it in his face that he kept a rabbit foot and a horseshoe yet he would not accept that what was on his doorstep was *juju*; despite not having gone close to his door, how much more crossing the threshold.

'Remember the argument we had outside my door some weeks ago?'

'Yes, sure,' she replied with a brilliant smile.

'How did you know I keep a horseshoe if you'd never been in here?'

'It stands to reason, doesn't it? You believe in the supernatural, the paranormal and all that so a horseshoe in your house isn't exactly out of place. Pure logic, Art,' she smiled.

'Come on, a horseshoe? I know many people who dabble in the occult but none of them, I repeat, none of them have a horseshoe in their homes,' he stated with a squint.

'Well, call me a good guesser,' she grinned.

A good guesser indeed, he said to himself, scratching his head.

'You don't believe me, do you?' she smiled.

Looking at her for a moment, he tried to smile but it did not come out right. He then shrugged, excused himself and headed for the bathroom to wash his hands and face.

After that he made his way to his cluttered kitchen. He was lost in thoughts as he started banging around, engaged in the task of getting coffee ready. He could not concentrate fully on that task because his mind was on many things — the horseshoe conversation they had just had for instance. That nagging feeling that something was not quite what it should be was getting him pretty uneasy.

When he returned from the kitchen bearing two mugs of steaming coffee Regina was comfortably seated. She had made some room for herself at one end of his chaotic sofa. Handing her one of the mugs, he smiled, 'Hope it's to your liking,' before walking over to an armchair. Unceremoniously, he dumped its jumbled contents on the floor with his free hand and plunked himself down in it. He was distracted. She thanked him with a sweet smile, took a sip and told him it was perfect.

She watched him out of the corner of her eye briefly. She could sense his unease. She looked around and then focused her attention on a picture on the bookcase.

'What a lovely girl!' she uttered, smiling.

The picture was of a cute blonde little girl, frolicking on a sandy beach with a much younger, athletic-looking Art. They both appeared awfully happy. Her remark was so sudden that since he was lost in thoughts, he started. When he realised what she was referring to a warm smile spread across his weary face. He walked over to take a close look at the picture.

'Ah, yes,' he smiled all reminiscent, 'that's Abby, my little sunshine.'

'How sweet!' she smiled. 'I didn't know you're a family guy.'

'A family guy,' he laughed. 'I'm everything but that. I think I'm just too free for my own good; too independent for any lasting relationship.'

'That picture must've been taken donkey's years ago,' she observed.

'Are you calling me Methuselah?' he laughed.

'Oh, no, excuse me, just a harmless observation,' she replied, amused.

He told her that his daughter was in Ireland, beginning her second year at university. She moved there with her mother after their marriage broke up and since then he usually saw her during family celebrations and some holidays. He joked that he often wished he could freeze her in the period reflected in the picture because she had grown up to become a little monster; given to answering back, too headstrong and opinionated for her own good. Then seriously, he declared that he was very proud of her and her way of being, adding tenderly that she was a beautiful blend of his ex's and his best qualities and features.

'A far better blend, than you can ever imagine,' he smiled.

He then picked up another picture, of a cheery-faced teenager, from the bookcase and passed it to her. She studied it and admitted that she had striking looks.

'So she's an undergrad! But you referred to her as your little sunshine,' she teased.

'She'll always be my little sunshine. She's so cute!' he enthused.

'Typical dad; can you see how you're drooling?' she teased him again.

'I can't help it,' he laughed.

She soon pried it out of him that Abby was a product of a passionate, albeit turbulent, short-lived marriage. He met his ex in Madrid, at university. They were both so young and so madly in love. She was Irish too. He said that although they were pretty much the same kind of people — intensely idealistic — their idealism was channelled towards different ends so the frictions were constant. He reflected that perhaps things would have worked out differently if they had been a bit older and learnt how to temper that trait which was so beautiful yet destructive.

He revealed that the break-up was raw and bitter at first. It was pretty hard on both of them. Eventually, however, they had to work out a way of putting up with each other for their daughter's sake. Curiously, with time they ended up becoming the best of friends.

'Yes, time heals most wounds,' she remarked reflectively.

'I thought it healed all wounds,' he smiled.

'I doubt it; some wounds run too deep to heal.'

Wondering what she meant by that he looked at her, hoping she would volunteer some explanation. But she seemed oblivious of his expectation. She was deep in thoughts. She was gazing at the pictures on the bookcase and her expression was totally blank. Then all of a sudden her face lit up and she turned to him and asked about Wole.

She's done it again, he told himself.

He had observed that she had the knack for artfully and successfully steering clear of any personal question tossed in her direction. At the same time, however, she would skilfully squeeze really personal information out of him. At such times he could not help but wonder who the journalist was. Until he met her nobody had ever beaten him at that game. Regardless he held a secret admiration for her, for that quality.

The mention of Wole's name brought a huge smile to Art's face. He had such fond memories of him and of the great times they had had together. Wole had stuck out his neck for him till the very end.

He told Regina that Wole was the coolest guy he had come across in ages and she smiled, saying that she was not surprised that they had got along so well. When he told her that Wole had expressed a strong desire to hear from her, adding that he had sounded worried about her silence, her face clouded over. He asked her if she was okay.

'Everything's fine now Art,' she replied.

'What do you mean by that?' he asked slowly.

He was grappling with self-control. Fatigue and sleep deprivation were increasingly tightening their hold on him and he was not exactly in the mood for a game of fencing or for her riddles.

Seemingly unconscious of his internal struggle, she smiled and gave him a look he interpreted as a sign that she was about to open up.

Consequently, he became all ears. But before she could start talking his phone began ringing.

'Damn!' he uttered under his breath.

At first he tried to ignore it because he reckoned it was just telemarketing. He found those calls irritating mainly because politely getting the callers off the line was never easy. Although folks usually said that it was as easy as simply replacing the handset, being that rude to people, even if they were tiresome call centre employees, was not his style.

The caller became so persistent — the phone rang several times in a row — that he figured it was not the usual telemarketing stuff. Wondering who could be calling so insistently since no one knew he was back, he excused himself, told Regina to feel at home and went into his bedroom to take the call.

As he heard Diego's voice he thought: *How come everyone knows I'm back even before I've landed?*

'How did you know I'm back?' was the first thing he told Diego.

'Your friend informed me,' Diego replied.

'My friend?" he asked in surprise, remembering Regina's same answer.

'Yes. I called Lagos last night and he told me you're arriving today.'

'Oh, you mean Adrian! Anyway, it's good to hear from you, buddy.'

'Glad you're back in one piece, dude."

'Me back in one piece? Well, barely,' he laughed. 'You can't imagine how close I came to being brought back in several pieces.'

'Oh yes, I can. Told you, what you're dealing with is frigging huge.'

'Hmm, so how's the going?'

'Pretty rough; I've been working my arse off,' he replied, yawning. 'Listen, um—'

'The other day you said you're calling about my friend,' Art interjected.

'Oh, yes. We found something that could be of great significance.'

Thereafter, he acknowledged that most of the information Art gave him before leaving town turned out to be of great help to him and the team handling the investigation and that Art had been of absolute help to everyone involved in the case. Trying to curb his excitement, he affirmed that the team was headed in the right direction towards cracking the case. Infected by his excitement, Art tried to pry out more information but he cautioned that certain things should never be discussed on the phone.

'Yes of course,' Art agreed.

'Well dude, we'll talk more about your friend when we see.'

'Okay. Till we see then, buddy. But, isn't it great that she finally resurfaced, just like that? Though she's yet to tell me her story, she seems fine,' he announced excitedly.

There was deep silence at Diego's end. When Art asked if he was still there he cleared his throat before answering hesitantly,

'Sure, I'm here. What do you mean by her resurfacing?'

'I mean just that. She's right here.'

'There with you? I'd like to show you something. Can you come?'

'You want me to come over straightaway?' Art asked.

'I'm sure this will interest you.'

He became silent for so long that Diego asked if he had heard him.

'Sure, I did. Okay, I'll be there as soon as she leaves.'

'You mean you can't get here sooner?' Diego asked, impatiently. 'Well don't take forever; you know how hectic it gets around here,' he added brusquely before hanging up.

Art replaced the receiver, wondering if apart from the impatience in Diego's tone he had also detected incredulity, judging from the way he had sounded when he asked the question, 'Right there with you?' Scratching his head in bemusement, he returned to the living room hoping that Regina would still be willing to answer his question.

He discovered, however, that she was no longer there. He assumed that she was in the bathroom until he noticed that the bathroom door was wide open. He checked the kitchen and every other room in the flat. After confirming that she was nowhere he sat down briefly and asked himself why she had left in such a hurry, without saying a word to him. Then he got up and checked every surface in the living room in case she had left a note but he came up with nothing.

'Curious lady,' he mumbled, his perplexity deepening.

Shortly afterwards he started getting ready to go and see Diego though what he really wanted was a decent rest. Equally, he was dying of curiosity — not only because Diego had sounded like what he had to show him was extremely important but also because their brief conversation had got him truly intrigued. All set to leave, he grabbed his camera; he had a lot in it to show Diego, time permitting.

On his arrival at the huge maximum-security premises he was signing the visitors' book at the reception when no other but Diego himself appeared, to his greatest surprise. The usual practice was that he was escorted to Diego's office. After expressing his shock at Art's appearance Diego practically bundled him into the lift. Art was thoroughly perplexed by the way he was behaving and during the lift ride he kept trying to read his face but his expression gave nothing away.

As soon as Diego closed the door to his office he looked straight into Art's eyes and lowering his voice, he asked him if he remembered their conversation weeks earlier about the African sex-worker who had been brutally slain. Art replied that he remembered every detail of it. Of course he would not forget that conversation in a hurry since the slaying of Ebony was what had led to it.

He was about to ask Diego if he had made him come all that way just to discuss that issue yet again when he heard him saying that the lady could be related to Regina, according to the findings of the investigation triggered by Regina's disappearance. That caught Art's full attention. He told Diego that he was aware that Regina knew her. But Diego said that he did not mean that kind of relationship, that it was more complex.

'It's more complex? What kind of relationship is it then?'

Diego's general demeanour was getting Art more baffled. What he did not know was that Diego was struggling to find the exact words to explain the complex information he had for him. Finally, he plunged into his story.

He disclosed that in the course of the investigation those directly in charge of the case interviewed a Moroccan woman living in a shanty town. They traced her because the phone found in the dead woman's handbag had the same number as the one Art had given him before his departure.

Art found that information familiar. Telling himself it was too much of a coincidence, he asked if the Moroccan's name was Amina.

'How come you know her name?' Diego asked, astonished.

'Because I visited her; without her I couldn't have known that Regina was missing. Furthermore, I got that number from her.'

'That's impossible. Something isn't quite right here,' Diego declared, scratching his head. 'Something's acutely wrong with everything, particularly with our timelines. We're talking about the same case yet we seem to be on different frequencies.'

Art agreed with him. Indeed, something was not right at all. He recalled Amina telling him she had given her phone number to Regina so she could be called on it, and that Mercy had called her — the last call she received — after which she left home with the phone. He told himself that he was going crazy because the slain woman had met her terrible fate weeks before he met Regina and Regina's disappearance had been weeks after that. In other words, there was just no way to reconcile those two unfortunate incidents.

'Buddy, you said something isn't quite right and I agree with. But do I need to know anything else?' he finally addressed Diego, who was staring into space.

'Never mind, I'll explain that to you soon enough,' Diego replied slowly and deliberately. 'But I need to run you over to the morgue so you can take a look at the body.'

'What body?' Art asked in confusion.

'The body of the slain African woman we talked about.'

'Are you kidding me? I didn't know her body's still lying around — excuse the pun,' he uttered in shock, lowering his voice to match Diego's.

'I didn't know that either,' Diego confessed. 'That fact was revealed to me when I got involved in the investigation of your friend's disappearance. Curious, isn't it?'

'I'd say, way beyond curious.'

'Anyway, let's go,' Diego said, grabbing his car keys from his desktop.

All the way to the car neither of them uttered a word. When they were driving out of the maximum-security premises Art told Diego about his encounter with the two Africans in the gents in Frankfurt Airport.

'What?' he uttered in surprise.

'Yeah ... I wasn't expecting anything like that at all.'

'And, what happened?'

Art told him about the timely intervention of the two members of his unit. When he mentioned their names Diego smiled and said that he was not surprised since they were really sharp and extremely good at their job.

'If you got that treatment here in Europe I hate to think of what they'd have done to you if you'd been in Nigeria.'

The remark made Art talk about the incident that led to his hasty exit from Nigeria.

'I hate to say so but, I warned you!' Diego stated emphatically.

'Indeed and I thought of you a million times over during that ordeal.'

'Goodness! How can people be so lawless? I wonder what would've happened if the police hadn't shown up when they did.'

'I probably wouldn't be here and you would probably have spent the rest of your days saying: 'I told him not to go' or 'I should have stopped him',' Art laughed.

'That's not at all funny, dude,' Diego stated, seriously.

'Yeah, it wasn't funny and it still isn't but, I can't exactly cry over it now; can I?'

'You can't but you definitely need to be extremely careful!'

Thereafter they both lapsed into silence. Art was thinking of how many times he had come awfully close to losing his life, starting from the strange incidents on the flight to Lagos. He was amazed that he had emerged from all those hair-raising encounters unscathed, so to speak. It got him thinking whether indeed, there was a Divine or supernatural protection around him, shielding him from all sorts of danger. He was so submerged in those reflections that when Diego cleared his throat, he started.

He asked Diego if he had said something and he replied that he had said some things. He apologised and asked if he could repeat them. Without taking his eyes off the road Diego replied that he would repeat just one: Mercy was still hanging on though the doctors were sceptical about her pulling through in the end. Art was not only surprised by that information but also by the fact that he had forgotten all about her; what with Regina's disappearance, his trip to Nigeria and all that. When he asked Diego if his team was getting any closer to finding the perpetrators of that horrible crime he shrugged before declaring:

'It's only a question of time.'

Right then Diego's phone began ringing. At first he ignored it but it just went on ringing and in the end, letting off a staccato of unprintable expletives, he grabbed it. Scowling, he grunted a hello into it without bothering to check the caller ID. After listening for a second or so, he came to full attention, wrinkling his brow. Wondering what was going on, Art observed the transformation in his mien with interest.

When he got off the phone he announced that there was an immediate change of plans. The call was from his boss: they were about to embark on a top-priority top-secret operation. Cursing, he made a u-turn right in the middle of the road, drawing a rain of insults from other road users. He totally ignored them all. Noticing Art's disappointed expression he shrugged and gave him a look that meant: *Duty comes first.* He then expressed his regret and offered to run him home.

Diego dropped him off in front of his block of flats and apologised once again before zooming off, clearly preoccupied. Art was feeling rather dejected as he opened his door and tottered into his flat.

When he rushed off to keep that appointment, lured by the prospect of learning about the important discovery Diego had mentioned, he had somewhat overlooked his tiredness. However, coming home empty-handed, he became fully aware of his exhaustion. Actually he could barely sustain himself on his feet. He staggered towards his bed and slumped onto it.

It turned out that sleep was a long way off. He had too much on his mind — apprehensions, worries and puzzles. To begin with, memories of the incident at Adrian's were causing him a lot of distress. Then his thoughts veered to Regina. He wondered about her — what had happened to her, why she had taken off that way and if she was still in danger of being harmed physically by those after her. He did not know that he eventually dozed off until he was jolted by the jangling of the phone.

The caller was a friend. He wanted them to meet for a drink and a talk. Despite his initial resistance, the friend got so persistent that he finally yielded. At the end of the day, he would reluctantly admit that the night out had been a pleasant distraction. He arrived home late, barely able to keep his eyes open and he went out like a light as soon as his head hit the pillow.

On awaking, he tried to take his mind off another unpleasant dream he had had about Regina by plunging into the business of the day. Top on his to-do list were two phone calls. The first was to Diego, to find out when they would be able to meet to accomplish what they had failed to do the previous day. The other was to Santi, to arrange a meeting with him.

CHAPTER 20

Based on his promise to Pa Eghosa, Art was determined to do everything in his power to convince Santi to return the statuette to its rightful owners. Besides, since he had learnt that *Shango*'s fury had no limits he wanted to let Santi know that he could be exposing his family to the same degree of danger he himself could be facing. Indeed, he was bent on doing his utmost to make him give up the statuette willingly to save himself and his family any form of unpleasantness. Those were his main reasons for visiting Santi.

Santi, who was still recovering from his freak accident, was quite pleased to see him. He had lots of stories to tell him too. The afterlife had become his latest passion. After their exchange of pleasantries he excitedly plunged into the details of why he had taken up that interest. Basically: he had been having weird dreams related to life in the great beyond. He disclosed that most of them involved him directly and one of them, which he found rather unsettling, was recurring. Shuddering visibly, he revealed that it prompted him to start researching the realm of the afterlife. He paused and began staring into space.

Art got absolutely curious about the dream because Santi was looking extremely ill-at-ease — the smile he was wearing notwithstanding. He observed Santi without barging into his thoughts. He waited patiently until Santi's reflection came to an end, as abruptly as it had begun. He simply gave a short laugh and continued:

'Since time's been no constraint I seized the chance to amass tons of material on the afterlife and I've viewed the subject from the point of view of several cultures around the globe. The amount and diversity of the material I've come across is amazing.'

That disclosure got Art very interested and he began firing questions related to the subject at Santi and that got him going. They dwelt on it for ages, during which Santi talked about some of the curiosities he stumbled across while researching. Art could not help but smile as he observed him jabbering on enthusiastically, in a child-like manner. When he was through with sharing most of his information they compared and contrasted points of view regarding the topic.

After that Santi wanted to know what Art had been up to and about his investigation. Hearing that Art had been to Nigeria to investigate further grabbed his undivided attention. He expressed his desire to hear all about Art's adventures there. Somewhere along the line, while telling him about his experiences in Benin, Art seized the chance to squeeze in the reason for his visit.

Although Santi's facial expression changed more than once as he listened to the story concerning the statuette, he patiently heard Art out without the least interruption. He also listened attentively as Art made his point about the need to return it. When it was obvious that Art had come to the end of his presentation, so to speak, he smiled. Then looking straight into Art's eyes, with his seeing eye, he stated emphatically that he was sorry that the statuette had been extracted from its lawful owners. Be that as it may, since he paid for it, it was lawfully his so he had not the least intention of letting go of it.

Later, he stated that the recurring dream was related to it and Art asked haltingly:

'May I ask how related?'

'Maybe some other day; definitely not today,' he intoned, staring into space again.

Although Art found that faraway look in his eye troubling, he did not pry. He simply went back to his attempt to make him reconsider his decision to hold onto it. However, try as much as he did, Santi remained adamant. He soon changed the subject by inviting Art to see the addition he had made to his collection after Art's last visit. Wondering how many so-called art dealers he possessed, Art accompanied him.

Santi proudly showed him a couple of ceremonial masks from Africa. Art found them quite intimidating, particularly given his recent experiences. When Santi told him that he could take them in his hands for a closer observation and better appreciation he smiled, shook his head and told him an outright no. Laughingly, Santi stated that he was losing his grand sense of adventure and he replied that he had had enough adventure for a good while.

'Thank goodness that it isn't forever!' Santi smiled.

On their way out they walked past the statuette. Art noticed that it had been given a place of honour in the living room. It was prominently displayed on a beautiful antique piece of furniture made of oak. The first time he was around it had been in a room, with the rest of the acquisitions from Africa. As he observed it in awe from a respectable distance, its eyes glowed. He recalled the glow people attested to having seen emanating from Santi's studio for three nights before it got razed, the same glow that had been associated with the statuette's presence in the museum in Lagos.

How strange, he said to himself, scratching his head, before turning to Santi and asking him in awe, 'Did you see that glow?'

'What glow?' Santi asked, showing genuine surprise.

'The glow emitted by the statuette's eyes,' he responded, pop-eyed.

'Now, you're kidding me, right?' Santi asked, with a tentative smile.

'Of course not; I swear!'

'I can see you'd do or say anything to try to convince me but, the answer is still no,' he stated, roaring with laughter. Clearly, he was convinced that his leg was being pulled.

Following Santi's reaction Art doubted briefly if indeed he had seen that glow. Finally he chose to believe that it had been a figment of his imagination. So shrugging it off, he turned his full attention to Santi's tales about his latest acquisitions. He was still listening when thankfully Gemma appeared to announce that lunch was ready. Although she tried to convince him to stay for lunch he politely declined the invitation, claiming that he was running late for another appointment. He simply wanted to be gone since the mere thought of that glow was becoming nerve-racking. He thanked her anyway.

Even though he was glad about the chance to leave, he was greatly disappointed that he had not been able to make Santi change his mind. Regardless, just before leaving he gave it a final shot. He reminded Santi of the imminent danger he could be facing. However, Santi refused to take him seriously. He laughed, pointed at his amulet and stated,

'Can't you see that I'm fully insured?'

'I'm not so sure, Santi. I'm not so sure,' he replied, shaking his head.

His trip to Nigeria had taught him so many things. He was genuinely apprehensive and he fervently wished that he could convince Santi to hand the statuette over.

'Hey! Art,' Santi uttered suddenly.

By then Art had known him well enough to discern what that tone of voice meant: he had some exciting information to share.

'Yes, Santi; what's the juicy info?' he smiled.

'You know me so well now, Art,' he laughed. 'Anyway, do you believe in portents?'

'I've seen so much recently that I believe almost everything. Why that question?'

'No reason; just another fascinating topic for our next meeting. Goodbye, Art!'

'Sure, looking forward to it. See you soon, Santi,' Art smiled.

They shook hands and on that note Art's ineffective visit came to an end. All the way home he could not get that look in Santi's eye out of his mind. He tried to attribute it to boredom caused by so many weeks of sitting around, convalescing. Yet, as much as he tried to push it away, he could not. He had this persistent uneasy feeling: Santi had been far more troubled by those dreams of his than he had been willing to admit.

Three days after that visit he was going past a newsstand when a headline splashed across the front-page of a newspaper caught his attention.

'Well-known artist dies under strange circumstances!' it screamed.

Art had the sensation that he knew the rest of that story even before paying for the newspaper mainly because the previous night he had had a dream in which Santi featured. He had seen him looking bedraggled. He had been limping too. When he asked him what the matter was he replied,

'You'll find out soon enough, Art.'

On hearing that he became frozen and speechless and in that state he watched Santi limping away. And, just before turning a corner he paused in his track, turned around and smiled,

'It's not so bad over here, Art.'

He waved and was gone. Art then woke up with a jolt. He had been grappling with a terrible feeling of foreboding since then.

Grabbing the newspaper, he started skimming frantically through the article — he could not wait to get to the part where the victim's name was mentioned. It turned out that his suspicion was right — the victim was none other than Santi.

'Oddly enough, it's the second time he's been struck by lightning in less than three months,' the article highlighted.

It then went on to explain how it was not unusual that people became a sort of magnet to lightning once they had been struck once. Of course Art knew better than all that blah, blah, and blah in the paper about lightning, magnet and stuff. His eyes clouded over as he folded the paper with trembling hands. He was totally devastated.

He headed home. He wanted to be alone, to grieve in private. He regretted not having insisted a bit more to make Santi change his mind although he knew that Santi being who he was, that would have been unattainable. He also knew that insisting more than he had would have verged on rudeness. But that knowledge did not comfort him at all.

Suddenly, he felt a desperate need to pay Gemma a visit. Apart from the need to offer his condolences in person, he also felt a greater one: To warn her about the danger which having the statuette in her possession spelt for her and her family.

It took him about one week to finally get her to receive him. Preparing for that visit was difficult for him. The thought that Santi would not be around was so agonising. To make matters worse, it was only slightly over a week earlier that he had been sitting with him, listening to his whacky stories about the afterlife. He remembered the laughter too.

As soon as Gemma came out to receive him, like she had done on previous occasions, he noticed that she was just a shadow of her old bubbly cheery self. It was so obvious that she was making a great effort to be strong. She listened with apparent serenity as he said all the niceties people are expected to say at such times, and thanked him. Then fighting back tears, she revealed that but for a split-second absence she would have met the same fate as her husband. When he asked her why, she explained that for some strange reason the chain around her husband's neck came off. He panicked, inspected it and discovered that curiously enough, a link had come apart. He asked her to fetch him a pair of tiny pliers so that he could fix it and she rushed into the house immediately since she knew how much faith he had in his amulet and its protective power.

However, she had barely dashed indoors when she heard a roar of thunder — the sky had suddenly darkened. As she was wondering about the dramatic turn the weather had taken, a blinding lightning descended and she heard a piercing scream. She came running and what she saw was unbelievable, totally numbing. Wringing her hands, with tears streaming down her cheeks she spluttered that all that was left of her husband was a charred barely recognisable body. The sight rendered her completely paralysed; she simply stood there staring at the carbonised smoking body with incredulity. Then very slowly, she regained the use of her limbs. After running in and out of the house several times in confusion, she gathered her wits and called the emergency services, hoping against hope, that they would be able to do something to save him. At that point she could not continue her narrative. She was crying her eyes out.

Art was so confused and embarrassed. He did not know whether to try to console her or just let her get on with it. Eventually he decided that a bit of weeping might do her some good so he passed her a box of tissues and in embarrassment, waited for her to have her fill. When she had cried to her heart's content she apologised for having broken down. He responded that her doing so was only natural, that he should apologise for being there so soon. She assured him that she appreciated his visit. A moment of awkward silence ensued. She broke it shortly afterwards by whispering that she would be right back.

Once alone, Art started analysing her story. He very much doubted her presumption that she would have met the same fate as her husband. Santi had been *Shango*'s target — its rage had been directed at him, exclusively. As Art's mind wandered to the broken link he wondered if that could have been by design, if *Shango* had been behind it. He recalled Santi telling him that his *meiga* friend had expressly warned him never to take it off, guaranteeing him that as long as he had it around his neck he would never come to any harm. He remembered the enthusiasm in Santi's voice and how his eyes lit up as he gave him those details. It had been so clear that he had absolute faith in the *meiga*.

In that instant a freshened-up Gemma returned, bearing a silver tray in which there was a jug and two glasses. As he realised that the jug contained lemonade his mind went back to his very first visit and how Santi had encouraged him to try it, bragging that she made it excellently. That memory almost made him choke up. He wished he could turn the drink down but he did not want to hurt her feelings. Luckily it was a warm day, unlike the ones preceding it, so he told himself that that was a good enough reason to try to relish it.

As she placed the tray on the glass coffee table she mumbled that her husband loved her lemonade so much. After filling their glasses she began talking about him. She talked about his fervour for life and his dedication — to his family and to his favourite pursuits. She went on and on. Just as he adopted a very comfortable sitting position convinced she would go on forever, she stopped abruptly. The memories had overpowered her.

The ensuing silence dragged on — it got truly uncomfortable. Then suddenly, she said something that jolted him: On the day Santi met his tragic end he had told her at breakfast that he had dreamt about the statuette. When she asked him about the dream, he had merely shrugged and said,

'Maybe it appeared in my dream because three days ago, I discussed it with Art.'

Since she had just concluded a course in dream interpretation, every opportunity to put it into practice was exciting so she expressed a fresh interest in the dream. But, assuring her that he would tell her about it later in the day, Santi had changed the topic by mentioning something he had read the previous night on the Internet about the afterlife. Consequently, they talked extensively about the article. She said that talking about that subject got him so excited and happy that she loved listening to him each time he was at it. She disclosed, however, that towards the end he often got so immersed in it that it was like an obsession.

Suddenly, she asked him what exactly they discussed about the statuette. Though the question caught him off-guard since she sprung it on him, he was glad about it because he had been wondering how to steer the talk towards his quest without sounding abrupt.

'I don't want to sound like the prying wife but it's just that following your visit he got quite pensive and several times, I caught him staring at the statuette,' she explained.

Unwilling to miss that great opportunity that had just presented itself, he plunged into his story and, like her husband, Gemma heard him out patiently and like him, though she made all the right noises about understanding the rightful owners' rights and stuff, she refused to surrender the statuette.

'My husband loved it too much for me to give it away just like that,' she stated, snapping her fingers to emphasise the '… just like that' part.

No persuasive tactic he employed would make her change her mind. The set expression on her face made it more than clear: she simply would not budge. He wondered if she understood what he was trying to tell her, if she really understood the gravity of it all.

As he departed he was frustrated that yet again, his trip had been in vain. His homeward journey seemed much shorter. He was thoroughly lost in thoughts that revolved around her safety. He badly wanted to protect her and her children. He even considered turning to Diego for help. He figured that if the statuette could be confiscated as a smuggled, stolen piece of artefact they could probably save her from looming tragedy since she would be far from it. On second thoughts, he shelved that idea since it could get her into another kind of trouble: illegal possession. He was still mulling over all the options at his disposition when he noticed that the rest of the passengers were on their feet. Only then did he notice that the train had arrived at its final destination. Time had simply whizzed by.

Three days later, he was still weighing up his options when he received a totally unexpected call, early in the morning. The caller sounded so agitated that if she had not identified herself as Gemma he would not have recognised her voice. Just as he was asking what was wrong, she practically ordered him to come and get the statuette out of her home. After recovering from his initial shock at her completely unexpected turnaround, he asked her what was happening. She simply repeated her request, fully ignoring his question. Since she seemed unwilling to go on talking, he assumed that that was it and was about to thank her for calling when she took him unawares again by spluttering,

'I had a dream involving it and my husband. He wanted me to call you. I won't go into details — they're too complicated and painful.'

'Oh, really?' he managed to utter.

Their peculiar conversation came to an end shortly after that. The oddness of it notwithstanding, he was awash with relief as he replaced the receiver. At least, he no longer had to worry about her safety.

His newest dilemma became how to treat the matter: make it official or not. Given that the statuette's last recognised place of abode was a Nigerian museum, his promise to Pa Eghosa and Efosa notwithstanding, he debated whether to get the Nigerian government involved by going to the Embassy to report its recovery after getting it from Gemma. However, since during his investigation he had discovered how much interest it aroused in many quarters, he was worried that involving the embassy could mean the statuette disappearing yet again and reappearing later to provoke strange deaths all over again. That concern coupled with his promise, made him more inclined to favour returning it to the place from where it had been extracted: the family shrine.

His deliberation was interrupted by the ringing of the phone. Wondering whether it was Gemma again, he approached the phone slowly. He hesitated before answering it.

'Hey! Dude, did I catch you in the middle of something?' Diego asked.

'If musing could be described as something, then the answer is yes,' he laughed.

He was pleased that it was Diego and that he could take a break from his complex musing.

'Well, you're always musing anyway,' Diego laughed, before adding: 'Listen; I'm picking you up right away. I've got something for you.'

'Wow! Do you really mean that? Great! Where're we going?'

'We're going to grab a scoop!' Diego stated briskly and hung up.

Art was set in a flash and was downstairs when Diego arrived. Itching to learn more about their mission, he began badgering Diego with questions but he would not offer any details. As Art excitedly kept up his hail of questions in a bid to prise information out of him, he only stated that the scoop would be worth his while. Eventually though, he volunteered a clue: they were going to a university campus.

'A university campus; is that really where the scoop is?' Art asked, his curiosity deepening and his excitement rising.

'Uh-huh,' Diego beamed.

Obviously, he was enjoying the game of suspense and its effect on Art. It was clear too that he was going to maintain the suspense. Finally, seeing that he was not going to get more out of him, Art decided to wait. There was just one university campus in the direction they were headed anyway, and they were getting close to it. Despite the initial calming effect of his resolution, he began getting fidgety shortly afterwards.

About a block from their destination he saw Regina. She was smiling sadly. She held his gaze momentarily before waving at him. The wave was so fleeting that it was almost imperceptible. He wound down the car window and stuck his head out but before he could call out anything she was gone, swallowed up in the crowd. He shook his head, asking himself if she could have been the product of his mind, of his deep longing to see her, to talk to her. However, as much as he tried to dismiss her fleeting presence as a figment of his imagination, he could not — she had been there.

His actions and the look of bewilderment on his face did not go unnoticed by Diego who asked him what was wrong. He briefly considered telling him but changed his mind.

'Never mind, it's nothing,' he replied.

'Yup,' Diego uttered.

Diego's tone of voice said it all: he did not believe him one bit. He did not push the matter further though. He simply concentrated on his driving.

'Yup; what's that supposed to mean? You sound like you don't believe me one bit.'

'I wonder why you think so,' Diego said, still focusing on the traffic.

'Come on, buddy; we've known each other for ages.'

'That's exactly my point, dude.'

'Okay, okay. I think I saw Regina back there.'

Diego mulled over that declaration briefly before asking,

'Talking about Regina, when's the last time you saw her?'

'About three weeks ago, the day I got back from Nigeria. I told you she simply split as I was on the phone with you and since then, no contact from her; except in my dreams.'

'In your dreams?' he asked, laughing.

'Why's that so funny?' Art asked, confused. 'Oh, come on buddy! I didn't mean that sort of dream. Your mind is warped, go straighten it out,' he laughed, after catching on.

'There's nothing wrong with my mind. Do you know how you get when you talk about her?' Diego said, still laughing.

Suddenly, he stopped laughing.

'Seriously, now that we're talking about her...' he broke off.

He began scratching his head. He seemed to be at a loss for words. Looking concerned, Art asked him what the matter was. He reflectively replied that when he called he had intended to ask him if he could get hold of her.

'Get hold of her; what for?' Art asked, interestedly.

'Well, we're practically at our destination so I might as well tell you: remember the body we set out to see weeks ago?'

'Yes. What about it?'

'We're headed there so you can see it. I'd hoped that if we brought her along she'd probably help us identify the victim. As for you, since you're so engrossed in this investigation I want you to see the state the body's left in so you can appreciate what the thugs you're running after are capable of,' he explained, occasionally glancing at Art.

Learning about their destination got Art so excited that he completely ignored the underlying warning in Diego's explanation. His thrill was such that he could not sit still and he could hardly string words together. He began speaking mainly in monosyllables.

'Oh, okay! Wow! Great!' he grinned at Diego.

'I'd also figured that even if she couldn't identify the victim, she might at least come up with clues to help us do so. But when I called you, I somehow forgot to ask if you could get hold of her. What a blunder!' Diego added, shooting Art a sideways glance.

'Indeed, she would've been of help. She knows oodles about them crooks.'

Shortly afterwards they were at their destination: The university campus where the Forensic Institute was located. The building housing it was old and although it had a lot to offer architecture-wise, it bore glaring signs of utter neglect: walls from which the paint was flaking off, as well as walls and ceilings exhibiting assorted outlines of stains — some in overlapping layers — caused by damp.

Inside and outside the building, there were medical students — some looking rather bored — waiting to participate passively in autopsies. Being present for a stipulated minimum number of autopsies was a prerequisite for them to pass their exam in the subject: Forensic and Legal Medicine. So they had absolutely no choice but to be there.

On their way in Art commented on how busy the whole place was because inside and around, the premises was crawling with people. Diego explained to him that victims of every death considered unnatural had to go through the Institute. Unnatural death did not only refer to murder but also to industrial and automobile accidents. Cases involving people who just happened to drop dead in the street, for whatever reasons, were also included. So given that broad classification of unnatural death, the number of bodies brought in each day was unbelievably high thus the personnel was seriously overwhelmed by work. To aggravate matters, they often had to work with limited resources.

'You civil servants always complain, anyway,' Art smiled.

'Maybe; this time though, it's not quite the case,' Diego laughed.

While waiting for clearance they could hear the service lift creaking and heaving as it went from floor to floor, bearing its heavy burden. After due clearance, they were led to the office of the Chief Forensic Pathologist, Dr Rodrigo Pinto. His shining bald head was the very little they could see of him from the door — he was almost completely hidden by the mountain of paperwork on his desk. As they walked in a pair of bespectacled bloodshot dark eyes — eyes which spoke clearly of many hours spent poring over paperwork — peered at them briefly before recognition set in. A ghost of a smile appeared on his face immediately. He seemed genuinely pleased to see Diego, although his attempt at a smile had not gone too well, perhaps due to lack of practice.

He rose to his full height, which was not much; he barely rose above that mountain on his desk. A quiet sort, he was in his late 50s and his furrowed forehead gave the impression of him being a constant thinker or frowner or both. He appeared quite reserved; he could even be described as shy. After shaking hands with them he explained that he had an impromptu important meeting coming up so he would not be spending much time with them. Diego said it was okay, that his receiving them at such short notice was sufficient.

As he was leading them to the autopsy room he warned them that the African woman's case was still sub judice so nothing they saw there could be used publicly, yet. Of course that warning was not meant for Diego; being familiar with the system and the proceedings, he knew the rules of the game perfectly. As a result, when they were approaching their destination he had warned Art that theirs was a top-secret mission.

The room told a tale of neglect: it was screaming for maintenance, like most things in the premises. It had an autopsy table, with the usual contraptions that go with such tables, a tier of seats around the room, surely for the medical students, and little else. Dr Pinto caught Art's incredulous stare. He gave Art his trademark ghost of a smile and stated,

'At least the freezers here are working perfectly; can't say that for all.'

Walking briskly over to one of the freezers with four drawer-like compartments, he reached for the handle of the one marked: 'UNKNOWN'.

'Art, Diego told me you have a friend who could help us identify this poor "Jane Doe" we've had here for weeks. I sincerely hope so,' he said, pulling slowly.

With the pulling action the body gave the impression of giving a slight start. That movement startled Art greatly. Additionally, unlike Diego and Dr Pinto, he had never seen a body in such an environment so he was truly impressed. His heart was pounding wildly.

When the body came into full view he froze. The battered figure was lying still, as if in deep peaceful slumber. The face looked so familiar yet so very unfamiliar without that smile he had got used to seeing on it. Unmoving, he stared unbelievingly at the frozen face. He felt an indescribable cold sensation in his bones, his spine and all over his body. He began trembling. His trembling soon got so violent that Diego, fearing that he would hit the floor, led him to a chair and helped him sink into it. As if from a long way off he could hear a voice that sounded very similar to his, but which he did not recognise as his, repeating,

'It's impossible, it's impossible ...'

Meanwhile, a totally confused Diego, who was still standing beside him, kept on repeating like an automaton, 'What's the matter, dude?'

'That's Regina,' he finally mumbled through clattering teeth.

'That can't be Regina. That's the woman we talked about weeks ago, the one who got tortured to death by the gang. Remember?' Diego explained gently as if to a toddler.

Though he was saying that, he was not sure — part of the evidence he stumbled across when he got involved in the investigation made him suspect that the body could be Regina's. But he sometimes got confused after listening to Art's stories about her.

'But dude, this lady was killed before you met Regina,' he said, despite his doubt.

'Do you think I don't know that?' Art whimpered.

'Calm down, please, calm down.'

'Calm down? How do you expect me to calm down?'

Thereafter, most of what transpired, within and outside the room, became a complete blur to Art. He would not recall Diego apologising to a confused Dr Pinto who, equally apologetic, told Diego that he had to lock up since he was running late for his meeting. Nor would he remember how they got out of that drab room. Also, he would not recall how a totally embarrassed Diego practically carried him out of that beehive of a place, amidst curious stares. Only later would he learn that Diego took him straight to a bar and got him thoroughly drunk before driving him home.

Diego's most embarrassing moments were: Getting him into the lift in his building, practically bearing his full weight, and then struggling to get him out of it. Meanwhile, they were under the close scrutiny of Art's notoriously nosy neighbours' prying gaze.

Later Art chose not to imagine what must have been going through his busybody neighbours' minds as they took in the drama.

Diego finally managed to get him into his flat, undress him as much as he could and tuck him in. He passed out as soon as his head hit the pillow and Diego pulled a chair to his bedside, sank into it and watched over him all through the night.

'That's Regina,' he would mumble every now and then, throughout the night, in his restless sleep.

CHAPTER 21

Three weeks had gone by since that traumatic incident and Art was still in a haze. After that stunning blow that knocked him out, the only way he gradually managed to get back on his feet was by throwing himself furiously into his investigation. Not surprisingly, he made admirable progress due to the single-minded approach he adopted in his pursuit of it. He frequently took his phone off the hook because it had been ringing non-stop due to his friends' concern about him and his self-imposed state of incommunicado. The only calls he occasionally took were Diego's.

On the day in question, apart from his state of haze, he was feeling awfully petrified because he was about to embark on a trip which if he could, he would avoid. Diego had tried to talk him out of it but he was hell-bent on going ahead with his plans — typical. He was convinced that dangerous or not, he was duty-bound to make the trip — Regina's body was being repatriated. He had been up practically all night getting things done and his morning had not been easy either. He had had to put his affairs in order, paperwork included. Consequently, he was feeling exhausted so he lay down for a nap.

He was in that phase between sleep and consciousness — he was fully aware of his surroundings yet he was not in full control of his reflexes. As a result initially, he did not know whether to classify the ensuing episode as a dream or an encounter.

It all began when he felt a current of really cold air. It sent an intense chill up his spine and he felt the hairs all over his body stand on end, starting with those on the nape of his neck. Trembling violently, he wondered where the draught was coming from and wished he could reach for a blanket. But he could not move at all, he was in total paralysis.

Then he realised that he was not alone. There was a figure in the room. It was hovering all over the place. He panicked because he could not identify it. Due to his paralysis he could do little else but follow it with his eyes — the only part of his body that he could move at will. After what seemed like an eternity the mystery surrounding his visitor was unravelled. The visitor was Regina.

'Hello! Art,' she chirped.

'Hello! Art; just like that? Where have you been?' he managed to utter, between rattling teeth, after several attempts.

'Away. Felt you needed time to reconcile yourself to the fact that I'm no longer here,' she explained, sounding apologetic.

'And, how do you figure I have?'

'I'm hoping you have. It's so good to see you,' she stated gently.

Smiling, she asked him how he was faring. Blinking and wishing he could do more than that, he slowly replied that he was trying to get his life back to normal. She whispered that she was sorry about everything. Meanwhile he was musing about all that had occurred. One day she was there and the next it turned out that she probably never was. He was confused. He was asking himself if she was really there when she said,

'Thanks a trillion times, Art.'

'I'm still in a daze; how's this whole thing possible?'

'Remember what I told you in the very beginning?'

'Follow the trail of the fires?'

'No. Before that I told you things aren't always what they appear to be.'

'Things aren't always what they appear to be; did that include you?'

'What do you think?' she smiled, observing his countenance.

He recalled their first meeting at the language school and the weird conversation they had then — all the riddles and whatnot. He also remembered her strange behaviour. He was recalling so many things.

'Well, actually, I was referring to the case,' her voice reached him.

Another conversation they had in one of their subsequent meetings came to his mind: The afterlife. He asked her if she remembered it and she smiled before replying that she remembered everything. When he asked her why she had not revealed her true ID to him then, she mouthed the words 'true ID' and laughed a bit sadly before stating,

'I once let it slip. Think. Anyway, I didn't want to scare you out of your skin, Art.'

'Yeah we're talking about Mercy then!' he recalled. 'This requires getting used to.'

She started moving around the room once again. She seemed nervous. She stopped when he asked her if she had ever been around physically in any of those meetings they had had or if her presence had simply been in his mind. Laughing, she inquired if he recalled ever touching her on any of those occasions. He thought briefly and replied that he could not recall ever doing that. When she said that he could do so then, he wondered how, given his paralysis. Then tentatively, he reached out and surprisingly, his hand obeyed him.

'Phew! Indeed you're here, thank Goodness!'

'Of all the questions you could ask me, why that particular one?'

'Just to know if on those occasions I sat all alone talking to myself.'

She told him not to worry that she had been there on every occasion they met, as real as life. She then laughed at the irony of her simile.

'At least I still have a bit of credibility left,' he sighed with relief. 'Can you imagine people watching me having those often animated conversations all alone? Surely, that would've gone a long way towards enhancing my loco reputation.'

She laughed again — that tinkling laughter of hers he had come to love so much.

'Seriously, why did you fool me for that long Regina?'

'I simply wanted to take you through my last days as a mortal.'

'Do you know how terrible you made me feel when you disappeared? I felt awfully guilty about having got you into trouble. I couldn't stop blaming myself. It's so hard!'

'Sorry, but that got you much more focused on the story,' she stated sadly. 'If you hadn't got your friend Diego involved do you think this matter would've been taken this seriously by anybody? I mean the authorities.'

Art recalled her comment, the very first time they talked about the slain supposed sex-worker who incidentally turned out to be her. He also recalled how Diego had waved off the matter the first time he raised it and then warned him not to get involved. Once again, he admitted to himself that she had been right about the point she made in the past and which she had just reaffirmed, regarding the authorities' attitude.

He was still mulling over that when something that he had been musing about for days occurred to him and he said,

'I need you to straighten something out.'

'What's it?'

'Are you the person you initially claimed to be?'

Looking extremely sad, she told him that indeed, she had been that person. It was heart-wringing hearing her refer to herself in the past tense. He braced himself and asked her what led to her meeting that kind of brutal end. She was silent for so long that he thought she was ignoring the question. Then she started speaking.

She asked if he recalled her saying that when she got to Spain she found herself saddled with a cleaning job instead of the specialised one she had been promised. He nodded. When she protested, the gang told her it was only temporary. With time, she got more impatient and her protests got more vehement. Then the statuette arrived and she got desperate. Since she was familiar with the macabre story associated with that cursed piece of sculpture, she had not wanted to be under the same roof with it.

She had also tried to warn the "art dealers" about what they were about to bring upon themselves. However, instead of taking her warning as a well-intentioned gesture they somehow interpreted it as a threat and concluded that she was a source of serious complication. Thenceforth, they made her life hell: the threats over the phone began. Later, everything else that happened was exactly as it had been re-enacted to him.

'Everything else?' he asked.

'Yes, about Amina, Mercy and all that.'

When he asked if Mercy had been used to lure her out, she confirmed his suspicion.

'As you've seen, despite her cooperation they ultimately made her pay for her initial resistance. Art, I bear her no grudge. This lot threatened to harm members of her family in Nigeria and she did what she had to. Survival instinct; you know? However, little did she know: Never make deals with the devil! These people are the devil's incarnate. You can't imagine the atrocities they've committed,' she explained.

Her mentioning her feelings towards Mercy reminded him of that vision he had had of a very weak highly apologetic disorientated Mercy. Naturally, then he did not know that she was so remorseful because of her role in luring Regina out of hiding. Till that moment he had never had the opportunity to mention that apparition to Regina and when he did, he laid particular emphasis on how sorry Mercy had sounded. Regina reiterated her lack of resentment for Mercy's actions, repeating that she had done what she had to.

'I see. Talking about Mercy; do you think she'll pull through?'

'Poor Mercy, you'll receive news about her today.'

'That sounds bad.'

'Yes,' she whispered.

Then she began staring into space with a very unhappy look in her eyes. Clearly, she was suffering greatly. Seeing her that way was heartbreaking. Telling him about her harrowing experience seemed to have brought the whole hell back. He did not want to prompt her to continue her story — the decision had to be hers.

When she started speaking he was sad since that would mean her reliving her pains. Conversely, he was glad. Close to tears, she said that it would be practically impossible for anyone with a normal mindset to fathom out the degree of cruelty and pain — both physical and psychological — the heartless brutes were capable of meting out and how much pleasure they derived from it. They tortured her so much that she passed out several times. But each time, they revived her and continued their sadistic pleasure. She got extremely frustrated every time she came to because she simply wanted to die. However, they were not ready to give her that pleasure, so to speak. She begged and begged them to put an end to her suffering but they only intensified it.

Shaking her head pensively, she stated with an ironic smile that in those tortuous moments she totally agreed with those who consider death a great coward: A coward for it often shies away from those who challenge it, who fervently wish for it, those who seek it out in all sorts of ways like leading reckless lifestyles. It does not dare rear its ugly head around them. Paradoxically though, it creeps upon those who appreciate and treasure life, those who feel a sense of panic at the mere thought of its visit.

After that aside, which he found most thought-provoking, she continued with her horror story. She said that to make matters worse they filmed it all, telling her that her experience would be used to send a message to the rest of the know-it-alls like her. Her eyes clouded over as with a shudder, she asked in a near-whisper,

'Can you imagine them making those poor young girls, who they lure into their net with fantastic promises, watch such gory images and scenes?'

The mere thought of it made his skin crawl. He winced. Although he was utterly shocked when she stated that it was just as well that they filmed it all, he fully understood her when she proceeded to indicate where the tapes were. They would be collected when the police raided the different premises of those criminals. The tapes and other such incriminating evidence would ultimately become their undoing.

After a pause to regain her composure she continued her narrative: The worst part of her agony was when they yanked off her tongue — she described the pain as way beyond excruciating. Shakily, she related that while they were at it they kept howling,

'This is the treatment snitches get!'

He winced again. He wanted her to stop but at the same time his curious nature and the professional side of him wanted to hear the full story so he just had to bear it.

She told him that she instantaneously lost consciousness. Her heart simply halted. What with the multiple stab wounds inflicted on her with the ceremonial dagger and the yanking off of her tongue. She realised it was over when thankfully, absolute peace took over. She began floating above her body, taking in the bloody scene from there. She sorrowfully concluded her account by reflecting,

'They made me go through all that torment just because I warned them about that stolen statuette for their own good. Ironic, isn't it?'

He inquired how come nobody heard anything while everything was going on and she explained that it happened in an abandoned farmhouse on the outskirts of town — the perfect setting for such horrendous acts. She disclosed that hers was not the first nightmare that took place there, nor was it the last. Whispering, she said that Mercy was "taught her lesson" there too. Thereafter, there was dead silence during which she shivered a couple of times. He was tremendously ill-at-ease.

'Don't worry, Art. Nobody can do you any harm; not when you undertake this trip and not at any other time,' she uttered suddenly.

'How do you know that?'

'I have a crystal ball,' she laughed.

'Funny ghost,' he said, trying to sound good-humoured.

'Ghost, hmm... Sounds strange, nobody's ever referred to me as such.'

'Excuse me,' he apologised self-consciously. 'That's pretty inconsiderate.'

'Let's call a spade a spade,' she smiled sadly.

He was not sure if to take everything as light-heartedly as she was doing. He was confused. He had had weird experiences but none could compare with that one. Could he be dreaming? He was thinking of pinching himself to ascertain that when he heard her say,

'Thanks Art, for not letting me end up in an unmarked mass grave or as another "Jane Doe" in the Anatomy Department of some Med School.'

'At least you'd have been of great help to humanity in the latter case,' he smiled, imitating her apparent light-heartedness.

'Maybe; but I know how some med students handle those poor nameless cadavers.'

'I should thank you for saving my reputation. Initially many people believed I was chasing a shadow or even that I was stark raving mad.'

'People like your friend, Diego,' she smiled.

'Among a host of others,' he laughed.

'I still believe I owe you more thanks. I'll never forget you, Art.'

He looked away. He was feeling very sad. It had just dawned on him that she was saying goodbye. Strangely, he was beginning to miss something he had never really had. During her first disappearance he had attributed his worries and sadness purely to guilt — guilt about having got her into trouble for helping him with his investigation. He had also assumed that his sadness had in part been because she had been a great source of useful information. With time though, he discovered that he had developed enormous fondness for her. She had a way of making him laugh without making the least effort. Hers was a peculiar kind of humour.

He turned in her direction. He wanted to tell her how much he was going to miss her. He noticed that her image was wavering. He implored her not to go, at least not yet. She was looking at him in a special way: with great affection. She seemed to be reading his thoughts, to be reciprocating his feelings for her. She was not uttering any word yet she was saying volumes. Under her fond gaze, he blushed.

'Never mind, this isn't goodbye,' she finally chirped, trying to loosen the tension.

'If it isn't goodbye, what's it?'

'It's we'll see soon.'

'Are you sure about that?'

'Yes — as sure as death.'

'That's rather morbid!'

After smiling at his remark, she asked him if he could do her a favour and he replied that he would do whatever she wanted. She stated that she would be grateful if he could help with Mercy's identification. He responded that he would if he knew how to go about it. She then furnished him with the necessary information. After assuring her that he would act on it, he asked her who Mercy really was.

'Remember the friend I told you about; the newscaster who got killed?'

'Oh; was that Mercy? But you told me she'd been killed weeks before I met you.'

'Well, did you expect me to reveal that that victim was me?'

'Not really,' he mumbled before stating, 'Regina, this is all so mind-boggling.'

Looking at his sad, confused countenance she smiled sweetly, saying,

'Cheer up! Don't forget that behind every cloud, there's a silver lining. In this case that lining lies in the fact that I've given you enough exclusive material to write the book that'll surpass your other book.'

'How come you know about that book?'

'Art, I know everything,' she smiled impishly. 'Want to know something else?'

'Now what?' he asked, feigning alarm.

'You're truly gifted and you'd be of great help to many. When you came to the language school and finally saw me — the only person that had really seen me till then — I knew immediately that I could count on you to help me obtain justice.'

'Was that why you thanked me?'

'The justice aspect aside, I thanked you for seeing me; remember? Generally people acknowledge my presence by saying stuff like: 'Ooh, how cold it's got suddenly'. That hurts. But, you went from hearing me in that recurring dream to actually seeing me. Do you remember our conversation about how spirits communicate from the other realm?'

'How can I forget it?'

Indeed, how could he? It was the very first earnest and informative conversation he had ever had, regarding that realm.

'Art, you can help make lots of people truly glad by getting their messages across.'

'I'd rather take it that you're pulling my leg once again,' he replied.

'Seriously, I'm not. At any rate, when the time comes you'll know. One more thing, Art: Pay attention to your dreams; not all dreams are just dreams,' she said, smiling wryly.

She broke the brief silence which followed by saying,

'I must go, Art. But I'll keep in touch, like I promised.'

'No, please not yet. I have one more question.'

'We could spend an eternity doing this. Though I have an eternity, I must go now.'

Sadly and helplessly, he watched as her glowing image began wavering anew. All of a sudden, she reminded him of Pa Eghosa's revelation about a young lady watching over him. She revealed that she had never left his side since they met, as she had wanted him to solve the case without coming to any harm, and that she never ever would. Slowly, he understood why she had sat bolt upright in the cab when he disclosed that revelation.

'Can I reveal something else to you?' she asked just as he thought she was leaving.

'Sure, why not?'

'Do you promise not to blow your top?'

'Actually, I seldom do that.'

'That's true,' she acknowledged with a smile.

'Okay, here it goes: I was never there,' she said, hesitantly.

'You're never where?' he asked, searching her face.

'I was never anywhere.'

'Please tell me you're joking,' he implored, earnestly.

His mind drifted back to all those times they had supposedly been together, particularly in his favourite haunt, and his heart sank. He ran his fingers through his hair as he said to himself: *I'm truly screwed!* He tried to draw consolation from the fact that their meetings there had been at the lower level, in a corner. But, he did not feel much relief.

'Do you mean that I was the only one who could see you? What about in the cab?' he asked, anxiously.

'Uh-huh. In the cab too,' she replied to his two questions, with an imploring look.

'Oh, my God!' he said, again and again.

He had just understood the strange looks he kept getting from the cabbie. He also understood why the man could hardly wait for him to get his last piece of luggage out of the cab before zooming off as if the devil was after him.

Clutching his head with both hands, he turned to face her.

'Please don't hate me,' she pleaded.

'I don't think I could, even if I tried,' he replied, slowly and sadly.

'Thanks again Art. Thanks for everything,' she whispered.

Then she blew him a kiss. She was feeling utterly sad and he was faring far worse. He raised his hand to wave at her as he realised that her image was fast fading. He wanted to tell her that he was not mad at her but she was gone before he could put that into words.

After her disappearance he came fully conscious with a jolt. He was telling himself that surely, he had dreamt it all when he sniffed her perfume. It was very much around. His mood acquired a sudden boost after he inhaled it; the solid proof that she had been there. When he recalled what she had said: '...this isn't goodbye,' he began feeling happier than he had felt in ages.

Whistling, he got up and headed for his wardrobe to see if he had enough clean clothes for the hitherto much dreaded trip; a trip he had always known there was no wriggling out of. He had been dreading it partly due to the emotional burden involved. Anyway, as he dug into his wardrobe and began to tackle the task at hand, his phone rang. Somehow he knew that Diego was the caller.

'Hey! Buddy,' he uttered cheerily.

'Wow! What a dramatic change!' Diego observed, referring to his mood. 'And, how did you know it's me?'

'An educated guess,' he laughed.

'An educated guess,' Diego repeated before declaring, 'I have news for you, dude.'

'It's about the African lady, isn't it?'

'And, how did you know that?' he asked in wonder. 'Don't tell me it's through her.'

'Then I won't!' he laughed; he knew that Diego had been referring to Regina.

He became serious when Diego informed him that the lady had given up the ghost. He then inquired if Art could get in touch with anyone who could identify her. When Art informed him that her name was Mercy and that he would give him the relevant data for her identification, Diego heaved a sigh of relief and thanked him. Having settled that, they agreed to meet for a drink later, as Art was departing the next day.

Several weeks had gone by since that phone call and the get-together. Art had returned from that important mission: successfully overseeing the repatriation of Regina's body. He had attended the funeral as well as the protracted related ceremonies.

Being there had been an eye-opener: he never knew that a funeral could last one whole week! He also discovered that in Nigeria music and dancing, eating and drinking were present in every occasion ranging from birth to death. He learnt that traditionally, in the area Regina hailed from parents were not supposed to attend the funeral of their children since children were expected to outlive their parents, not the other way round. He discovered that fact during Regina's burial ceremony when he overheard some people expressing their shock at the presence of her parents there. Obviously, her parents did not care for that aspect of their tradition: they chose to be present at that befitting funeral which they gave her.

Watching her parents go through the rites was heartrending. He admired their courage, bearing in mind that he had almost backed out. Regina's mainly serene demeanour during their memorable "meeting" gave him the strength to endure it and to assume the not-too-pleasant task of talking to them. He told them that she was where she deserved to be: home. He was glad that they did not have the least inkling of how she almost never made it.

Taking him aside, Regina's mother confided between sobs that she had had a premonition of what was going to happen to her daughter, prior to her departure. As a result she warned her not to leave. But of course she could not stop her. She said that when she did not hear from her for three weeks, she knew for sure that something horrible had happened since it was unlike her to go for that long without getting in touch with her family. Her conviction was based on an uncanny episode she underwent one day which she interpreted as a sign from her daughter. The date she mentioned coincided with the one on which Regina met her gruesome end. Art was astounded.

Honouring Regina's wish he handed her mother the gold chain and crucifix she had been wearing when she met her violent end. Clutching the crucifix close to her heart, she burst into fresh bouts of weeping as she told him that she had given it to Regina for protection after her vision. Art consoled her. He hoped that with time having it would bring her comfort.

Art also had to face a devastated Wole who wanted to know everything about his dear friend's passing. He chose to spare Wole the gory details. He only divulged that the gang had been directly involved. He informed Wole that the ones in Spain were already being rounded up due to the overwhelming evidence he unearthed, stopping short of adding: 'with Regina's help'. He was in no mood for complex explanations. He vowed to keep fighting despite warnings and threats, to make sure that every one of them in Spain paid for their crime. Wole swore vengeance. He was going to pull every string available to make sure that those of them in Nigeria involved in that gruesome act faced justice.

Following the amazing weeklong ceremonies Art left Nigeria with a bitter-sweet taste in his mouth. He was sure that he would not go back there, at least for aeons. Apart from the danger that such a trip might entail, the emotional burden was still too heavy.

He was absolutely relieved when his aircraft hit the tarmac at Barajas Airport and even more so when he got home. He was exhausted due to the marathon funeral rites and his carousing with Wole and co, in a bid to drown their sorrows.

The first thing he did was take a long nap. Thereafter, he took a very long shower. Next, he got on the phone to inform Diego that he was back, to calm his fears since he had been fretful about him going. He also wanted to invite him out for a drink — they both had a lot to celebrate.

Diego had been decorated, while Art was away in Nigeria, for helping bring down that terrible gang that had eluded the different law enforcement agencies for a very long time, though they had been shadowing them for ages. His superiors and colleagues kept asking themselves how he had been able to penetrate the network to obtain so much information. Of course, his secret lay deeply buried.

While Diego received what his Chief described as a well-deserved decoration, Art received recognition for his exhaustive investigation in addition to an enormous advance payment for a book. A book detailing the intriguing story about how that which began as an apparently natural phenomenon became tagged supernatural and ultimately led to a huge international police operation — a book that would be seen by many as a product of pure exhaustive journalistic investigation. If only they knew!

The huge joint operation ultimately revealed that the gang's crooked business network comprised not only human trafficking, people smuggling, prostitution, sex trafficking of minors, domestic servitude, sexual slavery and art smuggling but also phishing, racketeering, credit card cloning, drug smuggling and intimidation, among a host of others. The Europol was involved in that extensive coordinated operation and lots of girls were released across the continent. The operation was the biggest ever of its kind.

The operation also exposed certain facts related to the day this whole story began. More about the affairs of the African who got struck dead by thunderbolt in his flat came to light, giving Art an explanation for why there had been so many brand new expensive stuff stacked in the room he tagged "the diamond mine". Those goods had been acquired through credit card cloning and credit card scam, i.e. at others' expense, and were periodically shipped to Nigeria where they were sold quite expensively. Till then Art had been unable to fathom out how anyone could so compulsively indulge in so much luxury.

His visits to Nigeria had exposed the people's insatiable appetite for name brands to him, his friends and acquaintances were no exception. The business of looking good was very profitable over there because to many, appearance was everything. Therefore it stood to reason that such businesses were continually booming. So in addition to smuggling works of art and people, the lightning victim had also been into that lucrative shady business, among a legion of other shady businesses.

Another mystery was unravelled. It had to do with a charred, hitherto unidentifiable body found near an abandoned farmhouse. Even though it was later established that the death had occurred on the day of the phenomenon in the sky, nobody ever related it to that event. The body had been lying in the morgue, constituting an immense headache for the authorities. With time something about the circumstances surrounding it made Diego see the overwhelming resemblance it bore to the case of the African lightning victim — quite apart from the fact that both incidents had occurred in the same locality.

Ultimately, he prompted Art to ask Regina about it. When he did she smiled and asked him if he remembered that during their first meeting she had told him about Santi's two so-called art dealers. He nodded vigorously. She asked if he recalled her saying that one of them was the guy that got struck in his home. Before she could continue he excitedly interjected, asking if she thought that those charred remains were the other art dealer's. She replied that she did not think, she was affirming that they were.

'Do you figure that it's *Shango*'s work too?' he asked, excitedly.

'What do you think?' she smiled wryly.

'Yet another victim of greed, of Shango's wrath,' he reflected.

'I'd say: Another example of *Shango*'s dispatch.'

To the police though, that charred body was nothing but a message from one gang to another: The settling of old scores. So they believed, and so was it certified.

Whatever the circumstances might have been, Art believed that what mattered was that the deceased was identified, he ceased being simply a "John Doe". Art figured that that should count for something, for the family at least. Additionally, he saw the situation as Divine justice on Regina's behalf. Be it through *Shango* or not, in the end the man had paid a fair price for his multiple barbaric acts.

Art wanted to know Regina's view about it so he asked her if she felt that justice had been done.

'Art, as I see it, justice would've been me living long enough to realise my dreams,' she stated and then paused, staring into space.

'But of course you can't win them all, can you?' she finally reflected, smiling sadly.

Though her reflection made him feel terribly rotten for asking her that question and opening old wounds, instead of dropping the matter altogether he heard himself asking,

'Just one curiosity: Why were all the bodies charred except Prince's?'

'That'll be another chapter of another story,' she smilingly responded.

Art had been lost in reflection. He was taking time off his writing — his recollection of all that had transpired since that fateful Friday the thirteenth. It was a beautiful spring day, another Friday the thirteenth and he was in *El Retiro* taking a leisurely walk as he had taken to doing whenever he needed to reflect or relax. Being there brought memories of Ebony and the good times they had shared there, closer.

Suddenly, his mind flashed to Regina and her humorous reference to his book and he immediately felt his right cheek caressed by a gentle breeze. He had a strong sensation that he was not alone — he sensed a presence beside him, on his right. It was such a welcome presence, so comforting. Since her visit he had never felt that peaceful.

'Hey! Are you here?' he smiled, 'in case you are and you're listening to me, thanks for everything!'

He felt accompanied for a good while before that gentle breeze caressed his cheek once again. Then it was gone. He recalled her promise that she would always be there. Could what he had just experienced be a manifestation of that promise?

His stomach growled. He had been too busy all day to have a proper meal. As he wondered what time it was, he heard the chiming of a clock. He counted the chimes.

'3.00 p.m.! All's well that ends well,' he smiled, recalling when and how it all began exactly nine months earlier.

Printed in the United States
By Bookmasters